Outsiders

The Collection

Lynn Ames, Georgia Beers,
JD Glass, Susan X Meagher and
Susan Smith

Books By These Authors

Lynn Ames

Heartsong
The Flip Side of Desire
The Value of Valor
The Cost of Commitment
The Price of Fame

Georgia Beers

Finding Home
Mine
Fresh Tracks
Too Close to Touch
Thy Neighbor's Wife
Turning the Page

JD Glass

Punk Like Me
Punk and Zen
Red Light
American Goth
X
Yuri Monogatari 6 (Sakura Gun [London])

Books By These Authors

Susan X Meagher

Arbor Vitae
All That Matters
Cherry Grove
Girl Meets Girl
The Lies That Bind
The Legacy

Contributing Author to:
Undercover Tales

I Found My Heart In San Francisco series
Awakenings
Beginnings:
Coalescence
Disclosures
Entwined
Fidelity
Getaway
Honesty
Intentions

Susan Smith

Burning Dreams
Of Drag Kings and the Wheel of Fate
Put Away Wet

Outsiders

© 2009 by Lynn Ames, Georgia Beers, JD Glass, Susan X Meagher and Susan Smith

ISBN (10) 0-979-92545-2
ISBN (13) 978-0-979-92545-0

This trade paperback original is published by Brisk Press, New York, NY 10023
Edited by Linda Lorenzo
Cover design and layout by Carolyn Norman

First printing: October 2009

The Collection

In a Flash

By

Lynn Ames

Yazhi Begay stood under the blistering hot August Arizona sun and stared hard toward the distant southeastern sky. As she watched, a bolt of lightning streaked downward out of a cluster of dark clouds. The sight propelled her into motion.

"Ben!" she shouted into a walkie-talkie. "Ben, do you read me?" Even as she listened for an answer, Yazhi rummaged in the storage shed and grabbed a heavy climbing rope, a construction helmet with a headlamp, and a flashlight.

She jumped into her beat-up Jeep, threw the equipment in the back, and keyed the radio again. "Ben, do you read me? You have to get out. Now. Ben?"

She swore and punched the gas pedal, spinning out on the gravel and dirt. Within minutes she spied her older brother's pickup truck in the parking area near the entrance to Lower Antelope Canyon. According to her watch, Ben and the photographer he was escorting had been in the slot canyon for nearly forty-five minutes.

"Ben?"

Again, there was no response. That was when she noticed the walkie-talkie lying on the seat in Ben's truck. Yazhi watched another lightning bolt light up the southeastern sky and her heart jumped into her throat. She was out of time, and her options were dwindling.

***

Renée Maupin considered herself a patient woman. After all, her profession required that she sometimes spend hours standing in one spot, watching, waiting, for just the right moment. But the presence of this man who insisted on shadowing her through the canyon set her teeth on edge.

She lowered the camera and glowered at the guide. At another time, she might have liked to photograph him. With that flawless, reddish-brown skin and those deep, dark eyes and dramatic black hair, he was…beautiful. She sighed. "Please, for the last time, just go. I'll pay you extra. It's not like I can't find my way out. What could be so hard? You either go forward or backward. I tell you what, you can even wait for me at the end if it makes you feel better."

Ben Begay simply blinked and continued to lean against the side of the canyon, his limbs loose, his attitude indifferent. That he was clearly unaffected by her entreaty enraged Renée.

"Give me some space here. You're in my light." He didn't budge. "Look, I'm sure I'm not the most pleasant person you've ever dealt with. This would go a lot quicker if you'd just humor me and move on down the road." Still nothing. "I'll make you a deal. If you disappear, I promise I'll finish up within a half hour and you can come back for me. I won't move from this spot without you. Whaddaya say? Pretty please?"

Finally, the guide shoved off the wall with a grunt and sauntered around the next curve of rock and out of Renée's line of sight. She tipped her head back and surveyed the narrow gap between the rock walls some one hundred feet above, tilted the camera on the tripod, spread her feet shoulder-width apart, and looked through the viewfinder. The light was almost perfect. Just another couple of minutes and she'd have the shot she'd come all the way to Page for.

She sucked in a deep, long breath and let it out slowly and evenly as she depressed the button and listened to the familiar and comforting "click, click, click" of the high-speed shutter. Satisfied, she unscrewed the camera from the tripod and replaced it in its hard-sided case.

As she closed the clasp, her mind registered a roaring sound. Idly, she thought it sounded akin to the running of the bulls in Pamplona that she'd shot the previous summer.

Renée turned in the direction of the sound, and her eyes opened wide at the sight of a massive wall of water hurtling down upon her. Instinctively, she thrust the hand holding the camera case high up in the air just as the tsunami-strength wave lifted her and smashed her other shoulder against the rocks. She screamed in horror as she caught a glimpse of tree trunks and boulders hurtling past. Her body was tossed about like a rag doll. *Stay afloat.* She kicked off the wall and desperately scissored her legs to keep her head above water. She was losing the battle and she knew it. *I'm going to drown—in the desert.*

A huge section of pine tree glanced off the rocks and barreled straight for her head. Renée closed her eyes. Spots dotted the inside of her eyelids, and she tasted blood. She felt a strong tug under her arms. *So God is coming for me, after all.* She thought to complain that she had much more she intended to achieve on earth, but ran out of time. Her world ceased to exist.

***

"Hello?"

"It's me, Yaz. How's she doing?"

Yazhi glanced at the various machines as multi-colored squiggly lines marched across the screens in tandem with beeps and whirring sounds. The figure in the bed was very still. Too still.

"Hey, Ben. No change. She hasn't woken up at all."

"Have the doctors been in?"

"A while ago. She's got a fractured skull, a dislocated shoulder, a couple of broken ribs and a lungful of water."

"It's my fault. If I'd had the walkie-talkie on me…if I hadn't left her in there by herself…"

Yazhi rubbed her tired eyes. "Ben, sweetie. What's done is done. Beating yourself up will not change the outcome. She is alive, and it appears that she will stay that way. All things considered, she's a very lucky lady." Yazhi could tell from the silence on the other end of the connection that her big brother didn't share her assessment. In truth, it wasn't what she was thinking, either, but Ben had already suffered enough for his carelessness. She didn't want to add to his misery.

Eventually, Ben broke the silence. "Are you going to stay in Phoenix?"

Yazhi regarded the woman under the thin sheet. Her pallor was pasty, her head was swathed in gauze, tubes protruded from her left hand and right arm, and her eyes twitched underneath bruised lids. They hadn't been able to find any emergency contact information for her. She would be all alone and scared when she awoke.

"Yaz?"

"Yeah. I'm going to hang around for a while. I'll call you if there's any change." She clicked the End button on her Blackberry and rose to look out the window at the mountains, now framed in shadows by the setting sun. The scene was so peaceful, so benign. Yazhi was struck again by the contrast from the tumult of just a few hours earlier.

It had all happened so quickly, in the end. There was no time to process. Now, as her mind quieted and her heart rate finally returned to normal, Yazhi could no longer keep the images at bay.

When she saw Ben casually walk out of the canyon several seconds after finding his walkie-talkie in his truck, she was elated. He was fine, after all.

Her joy was short-lived. "Where's the photographer?"

Ben shrugged. "Wanted to 'be alone.' Chased me out. Told me to come back in half an hour."

"No! Ben, quick, help me get the rope." Yazhi made a beeline for her Jeep.

"Where's the fire? What's going on?"

Yazhi tried to keep the panic out of her voice. "Where is she in the canyon? Can you pinpoint it from up top?" She could hear Ben breathing heavily behind her, trying to keep up.

"Yeah. She hasn't moved in twenty minutes."

Yazhi flung the rope across her shoulder and threw the hardhat to Ben. "Show me!"

Ben led the way, stopping at a point roughly three hundred yards from the parking area. "She should be right below here."

Yazhi knelt and put her ear to the ground before springing to her feet once again. "Come on!" She ran another hundred yards, stopped abruptly near a narrow fissure in the earth, and uncoiled the end of the rope.

"What're you doing?"

Yazhi's hands were sure as she tied the rope with a double knot around her waist. She handed the other end to Ben and motioned to him to follow suit. "Flash flood coming." She visually measured the opening and nodded. "Anchor yourself around that"—she pointed to an outcropping of rocks a short distance away—"and give me slack until I yank on the rope."

"Yaz, you can't—"

"It's her only chance, Ben."

"Then let me be the one to go down."

"Can't. You won't fit. One tug to give me slack, two to hold position, three to haul me up."

As Ben started to object, Yazhi snapped, "Stop arguing and get going. We're out of time." She ignored the fear in her brother's eyes and strapped on the hardhat.

Ben looped the rope around the rocks and positioned himself for maximum leverage. When he signaled that he was ready, Yazhi threw herself into the opening and rappelled down the rocks.

She could hear the roar of the water. She waited, her legs braced against the side of the canyon and her hands gripping the rope. By her calculation, she was just above the waterline.

A flash of something silver to her left caught her attention. She yanked once on the rope, then twice when she judged herself to be at the right height. Part of a tree trunk flew by and Yazhi pressed her body against the rock wall.

As she looked back, she saw the glint of light reflect off silver again and readied herself. She would only get one chance, she knew. Yazhi slowed her breathing, said a quick prayer, and pushed off the wall.

The power of the water was almost too much to overcome. Yazhi threw out her right arm and grabbed a handful of cloth. The pressure of the deluge as it beat against her was almost unbearable, but she refused to let go.

She realized she would need to reposition herself if she was to have any chance of holding on. Yazhi took a deep breath, ducked below the water, and wrapped her left arm under the woman's armpits. As she yanked upward, something sharp sliced into her back. Yazhi ignored the pain, threw her legs around the woman's waist, released her grip on the handful of shirt she still held, and tugged hard three times on the rope.

It wasn't until she was lying prone on the ground that Yazhi released her hold. She rolled onto her side and sucked in fresh air. Her back felt like it was on fire, and her heart pounded against her ribcage.

"Yaz?…Yaz, say something."

"Untie me."

Ben's shaking fingers picked at the knot ineffectually.

"Never mind," Yazhi said as she pushed his hands away. She finished undoing the knot herself and sat up. "Call 911. Tell them we've got an airlift for them. Then call Amà. We need a healer. Quickly."

"But you could—"

"Mother is the healer in this tribe. Get her. Now."

Yazhi gently turned the unconscious woman and cradled her head, which was bleeding profusely. She pried the woman's fingers from the handle of a silver case and shook her head. How had the woman held on to it?

Ben returned, his anxious face peering over Yazhi's shoulder. Without looking up, Yazhi said, "Give me your shirt."

"My—"

"Just do it."

Ben stripped off his T-shirt and Yazhi tore it into strips.

"Hey!"

"Get over it." Yazhi wrapped a wide swath of material around the woman's head. "Get her information out of the Jeep. We're going to need to know who she is."

Ben disappeared and reappeared several minutes later. "Her name is Renée Maupin. New York City address."

"Is the helicopter on the way?" The woman's skin was cold and clammy and, apart from the blood that ran in a line from above her left temple, her face was devoid of color. Her breathing was shallow and Yazhi could hear a gurgle that she assumed was water in the woman's lungs.

"Yes. Amà too. I raised her on the walkie-talkie." As Ben said it, another Jeep drove up and a woman jumped out. She was dressed in traditional Navajo garb.

"Move," the healer commanded Ben as she approached. She knelt alongside Yazhi and, with expert hands, examined the unconscious woman. After several moments, she began to chant, moving her hands in a path parallel and slightly above the woman's torso and head.

"Will she be all right?" Yazhi asked, when her mother sat back on her haunches.

"I think she might make it, thanks to you."

Yazhi ducked her head self-consciously. "I am not you, Amà. I do not have your skill."

"Nonsense. Let me have a look at you."

"I-I'm fine."

"Then why are you favoring that arm?" The healer pointed to Yazhi's right arm, which she held tightly against her chest. "And what about the blood on the back of your shirt?"

"It's nothing." The sound of a helicopter interrupted Yazhi's protest.

Paramedics were on the ground in seconds. They consulted the healer, then readied the patient for transport. As they prepared to load her onto the helicopter, Yazhi said, "I'm going with her."

Before anyone could argue, Yazhi grabbed the clipboard from Ben and stood up. As she was about to get on board, she noticed the silver case and scooped it up.

"Ben, keep this for me until I get back, will you?" Yazhi shoved the case into his hands and climbed into the chopper.

***

Renée cracked open one eye. The fluorescent brightness made her eye water and she closed it again. If she was on the other side, why would her head still hurt this much?

"You're awake."

So much for the death theory. Renée opened her mouth to speak, but the throbbing in her skull rendered her speechless. She tried to lift a hand to her head and let out a strangled cry.

"Shh. Don't. Stay still."

The voice was smooth and silky. Like honey. "Hurts."

"I know. I'll ask the nurse if you can have anything more for pain."

"Where am I?"

"You're in the hospital."

"Hurts like a bitch."

"I'm sure it does. Let me get the nurse."

Renée wanted to protest—wanted the voice to stay—but she couldn't formulate the words fast enough.

"Let's see, dear."

Different voice. Efficient and starchy. "Hurts."

"I'll have to call the doctor and ask if we can increase your pain meds. I'll be right back."

"H-hello?"

"I am here."

Ah, the melodic voice. "What's wrong with me?"

"You have some pretty serious injuries."

9

"Hurts."

"I know. Hang tight. The nurse will be back soon."

Renée felt a warm hand on her arm and resisted the urge to pull away. "So?"

"I'm sorry?"

"What are my injuries?"

"Oh. You have a fractured skull, dislocated shoulder, broken ribs, and a lungful of water."

"That all?"

The melodic voice laughed. The sound was like wind chimes on a warm summer breeze. Cautiously, Renée opened her eyes.

"Ouch. Can you turn the lights down?"

"Sure."

Renée watched as the petite woman crossed the room to the light switch and clicked it off, leaving only the dim glow from the bedside lamp. The relief was immediate. "Better. Thanks."

As the woman approached the bed again, Renée noticed for the first time that she wore a sling on her right arm. "What happened to you?"

The woman averted her gaze.

"It's nothing."

Before Renée could pursue the matter, the nurse returned.

"Doctor Billet says you can have one of these now."

Renée opened her mouth to receive the pill and drank from the cup the nurse held for her.

"When can I get out of here?"

"Not for a few days, I'm afraid. Doctor Billet will make rounds in the morning and he'll explain everything to you."

"Terrific." If she'd been in any less pain, Renée would've found a way to get up and walk out on her own.

The nurse bustled out, and Renée realized her mysterious visitor was standing unobtrusively in the corner.

"Who are you, and why are you here?"

Yazhi shrugged self-consciously. "Is there someone I can call for you? You didn't have any emergency contact information with you."

Renée grunted and closed her eyes. She'd alienated anyone who had ever cared about her. She bit her lip. "You can try my sister Elaine, but I can't guarantee that she won't hang up on you."

"She is your sister and you're injured. I'm sure she wouldn't do that."

Renée snorted. "Don't bet on it." She recited the number and watched as the woman left the room. Briefly it occurred to her that the stranger hadn't introduced herself, and then Renée's eyelids began to droop.

***

"What the hell did you do to yourself this time?"

Renée opened her eyes grudgingly as her sister swept into the room. "Good to see you too, sis."

"God damn it, Renée. I have to read for a part tomorrow and I haven't finished memorizing my lines. Then I get a call from some woman I don't know, with a name I can't pronounce, telling me you're in rough shape in a hospital in friggin' Phoenix. Phoenix in the summertime? What're you, nuts?"

Renée looked around for the first time. "Where is she?"

"She who?"

"The woman who called you."

"I told her to take off." Elaine waved her hand dismissively, then paused. "Let me guess, you wanted to get out of bed and shoot her. What is she, a model? A bedmate?"

"Huh?"

"Well, she was hot. So it stands to reason—"

Renée's ears flushed red. "Believe it or not, I don't jump into bed with every attractive woman I meet." *Why didn't I notice how pretty she was?*

11

"Sure, sure. Anyway, she's gone."

A pang of regret pulled at Renée's heart. "What was her name?"

"I don't know. Sounded like a board game."

Renée ignored her sister's obvious irritation. "A board game?"

"Yeah. When's the doctor going to get here so I can get the skinny and get back to LA?"

As always, where Elaine was involved, Renée's temper flared. "Your concern is touching."

"Listen, I'm here, aren't I? What have you done for me lately? Or my kids, for that matter? When's the last time we saw you? When's the last time you called? I haven't heard from you in more than a year. The kids barely remember who you are. Now this."

Renée closed her eyes against the truth of that. Over the years she'd perfected the art of disappearing for long stretches at a time. It was just easier.

"Sorry to have put you out. You can go now. I'm alive, as you can see. I'm sure I'll be out of here in a few days. Break a leg on your audition."

***

Yazhi watched from around the corner as the sister stormed self-importantly out of Renée's room. Her lips formed a thin line of dissatisfaction. "Bad energy, that one," Yazhi mumbled.

Although technically she wasn't eavesdropping, Yazhi heard every word of the conversation between the sisters. She had been on her way to the elevator, happy to get out of the presence of the injured woman. She was drawn to her in a way she'd never been to anyone before, and it was disquieting.

Just as the elevator arrived, Yazhi hesitated and turned back. She stopped just outside the room. Renée's energy was so powerful it was very nearly overwhelming, but there was a disconnect in her field that Yazhi couldn't explain. She thought about stepping inside to make sure Renée was all right, then changed her mind. With a resolute nod, she strode away and caught the elevator just as the doors were about to close.

CHAPTER TWO

Renée stepped back and stared critically at the photograph pinned to the wall of her studio. She moved to the left, then to the right, eyeing angles and the effects of the room's lighting on the image. Absently, she rubbed her sore shoulder. Although she'd been out of the hospital and back in New York for two weeks, Renée still wasn't sufficiently healed to lift a camera, carry a tripod, or develop her own film. Instead, she worked with digital images and tinkered with various exposures and effects.

When the intercom buzzed, she put her hand to her racing heart, the unexpected sound loud in the cavernous space.

"Yes?" Renée said, depressing the talk button.

"Package for you, ma'am. I need your signature."

She buzzed the delivery man into the building and waited at her door. When she heard the knock, she put an eye up to the peephole before undoing the deadbolt and the chain. After all, this was New York. She took the electronic pen offered by the man in the UPS uniform. When he had gone, she examined the flat express envelope. The return address read simply, "Page, Arizona."

"What the...?" Renée pulled the tab and tossed it on the floor in haste. She reached inside the opening and removed a smaller envelope. She tore it open. "No way!" Reverently, as if she were handling an injured butterfly, Renée extracted the wafer-thin contents.

She turned the SIM card over and over in her fingers, looking for obvious signs of damage. "Hello, beautiful. I don't know how you got here, but boy, am I glad to see you."

In two long strides she was at the computer, sliding the card into the internal reader as she opened Photoshop. She drummed her fingers impatiently on the desk as her Mac accessed the card's contents.

"Please be there, please be there." Briefly, she closed her eyes as she repeated the mantra. When the computer went silent, she opened one eye to peek. The files appeared to be there. Still, she held her breath until she had clicked on, and opened, every image on the card. "Woot!"

Renée jumped up, ignored the resultant throbbing in her skull, and moon-danced several steps backward before she returned to her seat and stared intently at the series of images on the screen. "I can't believe it." She stroked the screen as if she could still reach out and touch the walls of the slot canyons.

With deft fingers, she manipulated the images with blinding speed, scrolling through, zooming in, discarding, enhancing, and moving them around on the screen.

When Renée finally sat back, stretched, and glanced up at the clock, she was shocked to find that several hours had passed. She stood and rolled her aching shoulders and neck. As she turned her head to the left, she spied the plain white envelope on the floor. She scooped it up and was about to throw it in the recycling bin when she noticed a piece of folded stationery inside.

When she touched the paper, an image of the petite woman in her hospital room popped into her mind's eye and her pulse quickened. She looked down at the page and frowned.

Thought you might want this back. It was all that could be salvaged. Hope you're feeling better.

"At least you could've signed the damn thing," Renée shouted, as she crumpled the note and threw it in the direction of the garbage. The woman had been haunting her dreams for weeks—a glimpse here, a sensation there—but every time Renée asked her name, the woman disappeared. "Damn you."

Renée stalked to the refrigerator and threw the door open, her celebratory mood dampened.

***

"Tell me again where you're going?" Ben asked, as he watched Yazhi pack her duffle bag.

"New York."

"As in Manhattan? Big city? Other side of the world?"

Yazhi paused with her hand on a leather blazer and turned to face her brother. She reminded herself that Ben had never been off the reservation and shared her people's general wariness of being outside the protective cradle of the four sacred peaks.

"Believe it or not, New York City is still part of the United States. They actually speak English there." Yazhi smiled benevolently at Ben.

"Why?"

"Why, what?"

"Why is this so important to you, this trip?"

Yazhi turned back and pretended to absorb herself in the act of folding her clothes. She didn't want to have this discussion—couldn't explain even to herself why she felt compelled to go as soon as she'd seen the announcement of the exhibit on the photographer's web site. After all, it had been more than a year since that fateful encounter in the canyon. She only knew that she had to do it.

Eventually, she heard Ben shuffle out of the room. Yazhi sat on the bed and rubbed her hands over her face. She closed her eyes and focused on her breathing. When she felt completely calm and centered, she zipped the bag, hoisted it over her shoulder, and headed out the door.

***

Renée blew an errant strand of hair out of her eyes. She'd meant to get it cut, but she'd been so preoccupied with getting the show ready that she hadn't gotten around to it yet.

"Tilt that shadow spot up a little, would you?"

The crew member to whom Renée addressed the instruction grunted and did as instructed.

Renée recognized the man's frustration in his body posture, but she didn't care. It was her show, and she wanted everything just right. She hadn't gotten to be one of the most celebrated landscape photographers in the world by worrying about the hired help's feelings. What was the point of taking spectacular photographs if they were poorly displayed?

"Why don't you get out of here? Everything's under control."

"What you really mean to say is," Renée commented, turning to face gallery owner Sabrina Devreaux, "'get the hell out of my hair and stop alienating my people.'"

Sabrina laughed. "Something like that. Besides, you look like a mutt. When's the last time you had a haircut?"

Because Sabrina was the closest thing Renée had to a friend, she resisted the urge to make a smart retort. "I was getting around to it."

Sabrina made a show of looking at her watch. "You have four hours until you have to be back here. I suggest you use the time wisely." She patted Renée on the cheek affectionately. "Wouldn't want you to scare away prospective buyers."

"Heaven forbid," Renée said as she shrugged into her bomber jacket and shouldered her bag. "I'll see you later." She kissed Sabrina on the cheek and headed for the door.

As she pulled away, Sabrina grabbed her wrist. Renée squirmed under the weight of Sabrina's penetrating gaze. "This is your best work yet, you know. It's phenomenal." She stroked her finger along Renée's jaw and then ran her fingers through her hair. "I'm very, very glad you didn't die getting these. It would've been such a loss."

Renée swallowed hard at the note of undisguised lust in Sabrina's voice. It had been a long time since she'd had sex. Renée shook her head. They'd been down this road before, and although Sabrina was an energetic lover, she wanted more of Renée than she was willing to give. Without another word, she pulled away and hustled out the door.

***

Yazhi sat on the bed in her hotel room and chewed her lip. Maybe this trip wasn't such a great idea, after all. Yes, she'd felt the pull—that intangible sense that she had long ago learned to heed. In this case, it had tugged at her insistently, urging her forward, telling her there was unfinished business that needed tending.

Still, every time she thought about it, her heart jumped and her palms turned damp.

"This is ridiculous." She pushed herself off the bed and went to the closet where the dress she bought earlier that day hung in its wrapper. "Just go, figure out what the spirits want you to do, and go back home."

***

The room was packed, and all Renée wanted to do was bolt. She hated large crowds—hated being on display and the center of attention.

"You have that look, darling."

"What look is that?" Renée discreetly shrugged off Sabrina's touch.

"The one that says you'd rather have hot bamboo shoved under your fingernails than have to endure another minute of this torture."

"Is it that obvious?"

"Not to anyone but me, darling. Stay and be a good girl, and I promise to make it worth your while later."

Renée's nostrils flared at the patronizing tone. "You can keep the quid pro quo for another client. You needn't worry. I'll be on my best behavior." Renée heard the frost in her own voice, saw the quickly hidden flash of hurt in Sabrina's eyes, and didn't give a damn. The *New York Times* art critic already had come and gone, the August edition of *Cowboys and Indians* magazine was on newsstands with her face and work on the cover, and three other magazines had run eight-page spreads. The publicity had elevated Sabrina's stature and bolstered her bottom line. She could hardly complain, now could she?

"You're a miserable, hateful excuse for a human being, you know that?"

"Yeah, I do," Renée muttered to Sabrina's retreating form.

***

Yazhi, standing several feet away and with her back turned, heard the entire exchange. She'd been admiring the extraordinary depth in Renée's photographs. The way she captured the nuances of the rocks, the textures, light and shadows—she brought the canyon to life in a way Yazhi previously had imagined only she could see.

She shook her head. How was it possible that this rude, self-centered, cruel person could show such remarkable sensitivity in her work? There was no way to reconcile the dichotomy.

Yazhi needed some air. She made her way through the crowd and stepped out onto a small balcony. The lights of the city twinkled all around her, but when she looked up, the stars were lost. She couldn't imagine a world where she couldn't find the stars.

"Enjoying the view?"

Yazhi started in surprise. "Um, yes. It is very nice."

The woman with whom Renée had been so harsh stepped up next to Yazhi and extended her hand. "I'm Sabrina. I own this gallery."

Her eyes raked over Yazhi in a way that left Yazhi profoundly uncomfortable. "I'm sure I've never seen you in here before." Sabrina ran her tongue over her lips. "I would've remembered."

"It's my first time in the City."

"Oh." Sabrina shifted her weight, putting her closer to Yazhi. "How long are you here for? Perhaps I could give you a... personal tour."

"Thank you for the offer. Maybe another time," Yazhi said, as she turned to re-enter the gallery.

"I didn't catch your name?"

Although Yazhi heard the question, she chose to ignore it.

***

Renée's shoulder blades twitched. Over the years, she'd trained herself to ignore that inner voice. This time, though, she couldn't resist following the impulse, so she allowed her senses to engage and let them take over. They led her gaze to a stunning woman with shiny, long black hair the color of midnight who was, just then, gliding across the room. Sabrina trailed behind, looking as if she would jump her bones right on the spot if she could.

It wasn't that Renée could've blamed her. The dark blue silk of the cocktail-length dress accentuated the woman's slim, strong figure. The single-shoulder cut of the frock showed off her toned arms and flawless collarbones. Perky breasts strained against the material. Yes, she made quite a picture. Although Renée wanted to believe she was assessing the woman with an artist's eye, the twinge in her loins told a different story.

When she finally lifted her gaze to the woman's face, she paused. There was something so familiar about it, but she just couldn't place her. Had she shot her back in the days when she was a fashion photographer? No, she was too short for that. Besides, her aura was phenomenal. Surely Renée would've remembered that.

"Ms. Maupin?"

"Hmm?" Renée reluctantly shifted her focus to the elderly woman with ostentatious jewelry and a pinched expression standing in front of her.

"I do so admire your work."

"Thank you." Renée offered a practiced smile and feigned interest.

"I wonder, do you ever work on commission? My husband and I are planning a trip to Kenya next month, and neither one of us is any good at taking pictures."

Renée's back stiffened. "I don't—"

The woman prattled on, "We'd pay your way, of course, and you could take whatever photos you deemed best. It would be so wonderful to have mementos of our trip."

She tried to count to ten, really she did, but Renée only got to three before her head exploded. "If you want vacation pictures, I suggest you hire a photography major from NYU, or perhaps you could hand a disposable camera to one of the chimps you're sure to see over there."

The woman recoiled. "Well," she huffed, "I'm sorry I asked." She pivoted on her heel and stalked away.

"Do you have any idea who that was?" Sabrina was at Renée's elbow again, her fingernails digging in.

"That was impressive," Renée said. "It only took you three point two seconds to get over here. I figured the way you were panting after that pretty little thing, it would take you at least a full minute."

"You think this is funny?" Sabrina's voice rose an octave. "That woman you just insulted is filthy rich. Her husband owns half of Manhattan. They are my best customers. Or should I say *were* my best customers."

When Renée merely shrugged, Sabrina's pupils darkened dangerously. "I don't even know who you are anymore. You ought to take a good, long look in the mirror, sweetheart. You're all you've got. I hope you enjoy your own company. You may be the most talented photographer I've ever known, and God knows I'll miss making money off you, but after this show is over, we're through. You can find yourself another gallery whose customers you can chase away."

Renée watched Sabrina's purposeful stride as she crossed the room and disappeared into her office. Renée couldn't remember ever seeing her that angry. She pursed her lips. Underneath that veneer of anger lurked real pain.

"You're an ass, Maupin," Renée mumbled to herself. She stuffed her hands in her pockets. "Time to go before you cause any more trouble."

***

When she arrived home, Renée stripped out of her clothes and flopped naked onto the unmade bed. She propped her hand behind her head and stared at the ceiling.

"Shit." Although it wasn't the most eloquent word she could've used, it neatly summed up the way she felt. She had no doubt that Sabrina meant what she said—Renée would no longer be a welcome fixture in her gallery. Not only that, but the friendship, tenuous as it had become, likely was ruined as well.

At least the show was a success. Most of the pieces already had been sold, and it was only opening night. Renée felt her eyelids grow heavy, and she started to drift.

The alley was dark and dank, the ground littered with crushed beer cans and broken glass. In the corner, back by the dumpster, a young boy's body lay still, his legs bent at unnatural angles, his eyes open wide and staring. A shadowy figure loomed over the child, his face covered with a sheen of sweat, his lips pulled back in a sinister smile.

Renée whimpered and thrashed, her hands bunched in the covers. She struggled to push up from the murky depths, but the weight of the vision dragged her down. Finally, with much effort, she broke free and bolted upright. She fought to orient herself. Her chest was heaving, her breath coming in gasps. Sweat pooled between her breasts. Her eyes searched wildly around the room until they lighted on a photograph of Horseshoe Bend, the sun sparkling off the waters of the Colorado river.

Even though she was staring at the comfort of the bucolic scene, it was several moments before Renée felt her familiar control slip back into place. She scrubbed her face with her hands and kicked her legs over the side of the bed until her feet touched the floor.

"Been a long time since you had one of those," she mumbled. Briefly, she considered calling the police. "What would you tell them? Start looking in every alley in Manhattan, in one of them you'll find a dead boy? Look for the man with the creepy smile?" She blew out a disgusted breath. They'd send the men in white coats.

Experience told her it would be hours before she could close her eyes again. Who knew what the next vision would be? Renée walked over and switched on the Mac. At moments like these, she would try her best to immerse herself in the familiar —images of nature—and the peace only they could bring her.

If only she'd shut herself down instead of giving in to her instincts earlier in the evening, she might've been able to keep the visions at bay. Her mind flashed on the face of the woman at the gallery. She wanted to be angry at her—to blame her for prying open a door Renée had struggled for years to keep closed. But it was no use. The woman's energy had been so pure, so light—no, this wasn't her doing.

Renée rubbed her eyes. As always after an episode, she was exhausted. With a heavy sigh, she focused on the screen.

***

A car horn sounded on the street below and Yazhi groaned. How anyone could sleep in this city was beyond her. She was in the process of turning on her side, again, when she felt it. Without warning, her heart began to race in a rhythm not her own. Before she could pinpoint the cause, her breathing quickened.

Yazhi rolled onto her back and closed her eyes, quieting her mind so that she might listen and discover the source of her agitation. Automatically, she ran through the steps to protect herself—mentally bringing golden light in through her crown chakra and allowing it to fill her being, while anchoring her feet and root chakra to Mother Earth. Then she called upon her spirit guides to enlighten her. It was a process as familiar to her as brushing her teeth, and took about the same amount of time to complete.

The first image that popped into her mind was of the photographer and, despite her surprise, Yazhi struggled not to open her eyes or break concentration. As quickly as the face had appeared, it was gone, replaced by the gruesome sight of a small boy in a cramped alley, a man standing over him.

"Oh, no!" This time she couldn't help herself. Yazhi shot up and leaned her back against the headboard, panting for air and fighting to make sense of what she had seen. Was Renée in trouble? Did the boy belong to her? Yazhi flung off the covers and reached into the suitcase beside the bed, fumbling for a pair of pants. She had one leg in before she stopped herself.

"You didn't even bring her address with you." Yazhi exhaled and sat back against the wall once more. This time, when she closed her eyes and summoned the golden light, she envisioned each of her chakras spinning in turn, beginning with the root. This heightened her awareness and she focused on allowing the information to flow freely.

No, Renée's heart rate had returned to normal, and the vision of the boy was gone. Slowly, Yazhi opened her eyes and became aware of her surroundings. She looked down and ruefully shook her head. Her pants were bunched around her knees.

"And just where did you think you were going, anyway? It's the middle of the night in a city known for crime, and you were going to…what? Run out blindly and try to find a woman who likely doesn't need or want your help?"

Yazhi removed her pants, folded them neatly, and returned them to the suitcase. She lay back down and folded her hands atop her chest. Renée certainly hadn't struck Yazhi as the damsel in distress type, despite the circumstances under which they'd met initially.

Still, tomorrow she would go back to the gallery and check on her. Just to be sure.

CHAPTER THREE

Renée sprinted the last fifty yards and bent over double to catch her breath. She leaned against a light pole and stretched first her calves and Achilles, and then her hamstrings. As always, the run had helped to clear her head.

There was no question that she owed Sabrina an apology. Antagonizing a major client was a cardinal sin, regardless of the cluelessness of the customer. Although she wouldn't have taken any less umbrage, Renée had to admit that she might have handled the woman more diplomatically.

She would go home, shower, dress, and head back to the gallery bearing a peace offering. Renée doubted it would be enough to save their friendship, but perhaps it would help salvage her lucrative business with Sabrina. After all, her two or three shows a year did provide Sabrina substantial income, and Sabrina was nothing if not a savvy businesswoman.

***

Yazhi was just rounding the corner when she saw the photographer duck into the gallery carrying a large object wrapped in brown paper. She was dressed in a pair of low-slung jeans, worn boots, and a form-fitting v-neck sweater. Yazhi wondered if she had any idea how attractive she was.

For a split second, Yazhi hesitated, wondering whether it was wise to put herself in proximity to a woman against whom her normal defenses seemed wholly ineffectual. Then she remembered the image of the crumpled boy. She shook her head, as if doing so would wipe away the disturbing picture, and took a deep breath, letting it out slowly.

Whatever it was about this woman, the spirit guides had put her in Yazhi's path for a reason. If the aim had been only for Yazhi to save her life, the connection would not still be this strong. Yazhi squared her shoulders and moved forward. She would see this through until it became clear what role this woman was meant to play in her journey. To do anything different would be to place her out of harmony with the Universe, and that was something that Yazhi would never allow.

***

"Damn it, I'm apologizing to you. What more do you want from me?"

"Right now, I want you out of my sight."

Renée threw up her hands in exasperation. "Look, Sabrina, I know you're pissed. I get that. I insulted one of your best clients. I get that too. That bloated windbag was important to your bottom line. Mea culpa. I can't change what happened, but I'm making an effort here."

"A lot too little, a lot too late, Renée. I meant what I said last night. I'm through with you. I'm sure you won't have any trouble finding some other gallery owner who'll put up with your surliness in exchange for profits. Heck, all you have to do is take that perfect ass and wave it in some poor unsuspecting slob's direction, and you'll have a new conquest in no time at all."

Renée felt the color rise from her neck to her cheeks. "As I recall, you were the one who came on to me, cupcake. So don't lay that at my doorstep."

"I obviously should have been more…selective. Clearly, it was a mistake."

"Clearly," Renée agreed. "You know where to send the check when the show's over. I hope it makes you a bundle, Sabrina. It's been real."

Renée grabbed the still-wrapped package, turned on her heel, and stormed out of the back office. She was almost to the door when she plowed into something solid.

"Oof."

Renée looked down into startled, liquid-chocolate-brown eyes. "Sorry," she mumbled. She reached the door, shoved it open, and set off down the sidewalk. It was a mistake to try to set things right with Sabrina. She had obviously miscalculated the extent of the damage she had done the night before. "Idiot."

"Excuse me. Pardon me. I wonder if I might have a word."

It took several seconds for Renée to realize that the voice was addressing her. She stopped abruptly and looked to her right to find the same woman she had nearly run over in the gallery. She frowned. "What?" She over-enunciated the "t."

"I understand that now might not be the best time, but I wanted to tell you how much I admire your work."

"Thanks," Renée said shortly, resuming her pace and expecting the woman to fall back. Instead, she matched Renée's stride. "Look, you're right, now is not a good time. But I appreciate the compliment." Still, the woman would not go away.

Renée stopped again and spun to face the annoyance. "If you're interested in purchasing something, go back to the gallery. I'm sure the owner would be happy to help you."

The woman's penetrating gaze made Renée uncomfortable. She broke eye contact and began walking again. The woman touched her on the sleeve.

"I said—"

"Who was the young boy in the alley?" the woman blurted.

Renée staggered backward as the impact of the question hit her squarely in the gut. She sucked in a quick breath and regained her equilibrium. This time, when she moved forward, she quickened her stride.

"Who was he?" The woman asked again, seeming to keep up effortlessly despite her significantly shorter legs.

"I don't know what you're talking about." Renée stared straight ahead, her heart pounding painfully against her ribs.

"I know you do. He was in trouble. Is he related to you?"

"You're mistaken."

"I'm not, and you know that."

Damn, this woman was stubborn. Renée clenched her jaw and soldiered onward.

"Please." The woman wrapped her fingers around Renée's arm. The touch was at once soothing and electric. "I mean you no harm."

"That's good to know." As always when she was frightened, Renée resorted to sarcasm. She was almost to her apartment. If she could just get inside…

"I'm glad your injuries have healed."

Renée whipped her head around. "I'm sorry?"

"I said, I'm glad you've recovered so well. I'm also happy that your work was saved."

Renée's head began to buzz. Who was this woman? She reminded herself that anyone could have read about her mishap in the canyon. Obviously, this woman was some sort of stalker. A nut job.

"I've never seen anyone who could capture the majesty of the rocks with such loving detail. I thought I was the only one who could see it."

Renée's eyes narrowed, but she kept moving.

"I'm sorry about your tripod and camera. They couldn't be saved."

Renée stopped so quickly a man ran into her from behind. "Who the hell are you?" She looked closely at the woman for the first time, a dim recognition playing at the back of her mind.

"My name is Yazhi. Yazhi Begay." The woman straightened her shoulders and jutted out her chin.

"How did you know…Wait, it's you. You're the one from the hospital room. And you were at the opening last night." *The same woman Sabrina was panting after.*

"Is there someplace we can talk?" Yazhi motioned to the foot traffic bustling all around them.

Renée bit her lip, considering her options. Alarm bells were ringing loud and clear in her head, but her curiosity was piqued. So much of that time remained a blur, and so much that she had experienced since defied explanation. This woman—Yazhi— could fill in the blanks. Besides, her aura was bright enough to light up Time Square.

There it is again, damn it. That's the third or fourth time since the accident you've seen someone's aura. As quickly as the thought crossed her mind, Renée shut it down. She shrugged. "Okay. There's a coffee shop around the corner."

"Thank you." The woman's smile was dazzling.

***

Yazhi took advantage of the opportunity to study Renée as she sipped her espresso. The telltale signs of discomfort were present, although Yazhi doubted Renée was aware of that. Her hands were steady, as one would have expected of a world-class photographer, but her eyes darted around the café and her left leg bobbed up and down to an unheard staccato beat.

"About the little boy," Yazhi began, and watched with interest as Renée's pupils dilated and she sucked in a quick breath. *She's afraid.*

"So, how is it you came to be in my hospital room? I don't remember ever seeing you before that."

Yazhi noted the evasion and reached under the table to squeeze her hand around Renée's knee to still its motion. Renée went stock still and stiffened under the touch. Yazhi released her grip. "I told you," she said quietly, "I mean you no harm. I'm worried by what I saw, that is all."

Renée opened her mouth, closed it again, then cleared her throat. Yazhi watched a series of emotions flit across her expressive face. *It's more than fear.*

"I-I don't know what you're talking about."

"We both know that's not true." Yazhi bit her lip. She would not get anywhere as long as Renée was intent on shutting her out. *Time to switch gears. Put her back in her comfort zone.* "What is in the package?"

"The package?"

"Yes." Yazhi gestured to the wrapped object leaning against Renée's chair.

"Oh. That's nothing. Just another piece I was taking to the gallery, for all the good it did me." Renée mumbled the last bit.

"May I see?" When it appeared that Renée would balk, Yazhi added, "Please?"

After a moment's hesitation, Renée unwrapped the brown paper.

Yazhi was fascinated by the care she took. It was in sharp contrast to the attitude of indifference Renée was attempting to project.

"The lighting in here is horrendous, but…" Renée held up a framed 24 by 28 inch photograph.

Yazhi gasped in delighted surprise. It was Upper Antelope Canyon just at the one moment a day when the sunlight streamed like a spotlight, illuminating the canyon floor and bringing the texture of the walls into sharp relief. She had seen literally hundreds of photographs of that same tableau, but none captured the majesty the way this one did.

"It's breathtaking," Yazhi said.

"Thanks."

Yazhi was surprised to note the subtle blush on Renée's cheeks. "I didn't see that in the show last night. I'm sure I would have noticed. Might I enquire how much you're asking for it?" Never before had Yazhi been moved to purchase a static image of something she saw every day and considered a living, breathing entity, but she was drawn to the work in a way even she couldn't explain.

"It's not for sale," Renée snapped.

There it was again, that shuttered attitude. Yazhi sat back in her chair, stung. "I see."

"Look, my memory of the hospital stay and everything that happened right before that is fuzzy. One second I thought I was dead, and the next I'm waking up in a hospital bed to see your face. I'm betting you can fill in a significant number of details for me." Renée's eyes flitted around the room again. She looked everywhere but at Yazhi.

Yazhi frowned. "I'm sure I could." She picked up a napkin, produced a pen from her pocket, and began writing. "When you're ready to answer my questions honestly, I'd be happy to return the favor. You can find me here." Yazhi slid the napkin across the table, rose, and walked away without looking back. Still, she could feel Renée's eyes on her back, and she imagined the shocked look on her face. Yazhi was willing to wager that not many people snubbed Renée Maupin.

***

For the fourth time in ten minutes, Renée fingered the napkin in her pocket. What the hell had happened back there? She shoved away from her desk, rose, and went to the window overlooking Christopher Street.

She had been wanting to know about the events surrounding her rescue for a long time. But no one she'd asked had been able to tell her anything. Something had shifted for her that day, reawakening parts of her she'd thought she'd left behind. It frightened her beyond words. Now, out of nowhere, came this mysterious woman who could answer her questions, and she wouldn't do it. Renée crossed her arms over her chest. Why was she being so unreasonable?

Out of the corner of her eye, Renée eyed the framed photograph leaning against the wall and frowned. Yazhi wasn't the only one being unreasonable. Why hadn't Renée wanted to sell the image to Yazhi? After all, she'd taken it to the gallery for Sabrina to sell.

"Because you're a bitch, that's why." Renée shook her head. That wasn't it and she knew it. Yazhi had rattled her, and Renée had done what she always did in such situations—she retreated behind an impenetrable wall.

"The best defense is a good offense. Jerk."

Not only did Yazhi hold the key to the missing pieces of Renée's recollection and the sudden re-emergence of phenomena Renée had thought dead and buried, but she was beautiful, too. So what was the problem?

Renée wrapped her arms more tightly around herself. The problem was that Yazhi somehow had known about Renée's dream—no, she corrected herself—her vision. Renée wondered if Yazhi also had picked up on anything else. She shuddered as a chill crept up her spine. She hadn't felt this exposed in years. *Damn.*

"Well, old girl, you've got two choices. You can stick your head back in the sand, hope the visions go away, and never know what happened back in that canyon. Or you can go find Yazhi, explain about the visions, risk having her think you're a raving lunatic, fill in that gaping hole in your memory, and find out what was so life-changing about that experience. What's it going to be?"

Renée walked over to the desk and snatched up the napkin. She made it all the way to the door and had her hand on the knob before turning back. "In for a penny, in for a pound." She grabbed the wrapped package and headed out the door.

CHAPTER FOUR

The knock on the door startled Yazhi. She finished folding her jeans and placed them neatly in the suitcase she was packing.

"Who is it?" she asked, her hand poised on the security chain.

"It's Renée. Renée Maupin."

Yazhi smiled. Although she'd believed Renée would come, she hadn't been sure. The photographer's fear had been so strong…it still was, Yazhi thought, as she extended her senses. She slid the chain off, unbolted the lock, and opened the door.

"Hi."

"Hello. Come in." Yazhi moved aside so that Renée could pass.

"You're packing." Renée's voice expressed surprise.

"Is it customary in New York to leave your clothes behind when you check out?" Yazhi busied herself re-locking the door to hide her smirk.

"What? N-no, of course not. I just…"

Yazhi finally turned around and allowed Renée to see the laughter in her eyes.

"You have a sense of humor?"

"This surprises you." It was a statement, not a question.

"Well, yeah."

"Why? And please, sit down." Yazhi indicated one of two chairs at the small table in front of the windows.

"No reason, I guess," Renée said as she placed the wrapped package gently against the wall and folded herself into the seat. "Do you need to leave right now?"

"No, I've got time." Yazhi sat in the other chair. "Don't tell me you buy into old stereotypes of spaghetti Westerns and the stoic, hostile Indian." Yazhi poked her tongue in her cheek; she was enjoying Renée's discomfort.

"Of course not. It's just..." Renée narrowed her eyes. "You're messing with me, right?"

"I am. Native Americans do have a sense of humor, just like anyone else. You do not have any prejudice in you, so I assume your reaction was to what little exposure you have had to me."

"How do you know I'm not a bigot?"

"The same way you know to trust me, and that I mean you no harm. It goes hand in hand with our gifts." Yazhi watched as Renée nervously twisted the simple gold band on her right ring finger.

"Our gifts? I don't know what you mean."

Yazhi shook her head. She knew she could play along with Renée's feigned ignorance, but in this instance, she surmised, directness would be best. She suspected that no amount of preparatory small talk would have made her guest more comfortable, anyway.

"Why do you fight it?" Yazhi asked. "You have been given a blessing, and yet you seem to view it as a curse."

"I'm afraid—"

"Yes. That is exactly the problem. You are afraid."

"That's not—"

"What you meant? I know it isn't. But it is the truth, and it holds you back."

"You don't even know me."

"Perhaps not. But I can see, for I am not afraid to use all the senses I have been given. You are frightened by the powers you possess that go beyond the five senses you think you should have. This limits you so much."

"I'm doing just fine, thank you." Renée jumped up and shoved the curtains aside to let in the daylight.

"Are you? Can you not see that it is the same as taking a photograph with a macro lens when you should be using a wide angle?"

"Now you're a photography expert?"

There it was again—the sarcasm. Yazhi sighed heavily. "You are ignoring your gifts, and it is causing a great disturbance in your energy field."

Renée crossed her arms and turned to face Yazhi, but said nothing.

"I'm sorry." Yazhi spoke softly. "I know you think it's none of my business, but I was put in your path for a reason, and I am beginning to think I know what it is."

Renée sat down heavily. "How did you know about the boy?"

"I saw him in a vision." Yazhi watched the emotions swirl in Renée's eyes and pressed ahead. "Who is he, this boy?" When Renée said nothing, Yazhi added, "I assume you would not have come if you were not prepared to tell me. Please, don't be afraid."

Renée bit her lower lip and took a deep breath. "I don't know who he is. I've never seen him before. I didn't recognize the alley, the boy—any of it. I'd been asleep, and then suddenly it was as if I was there, watching."

"Ah, I was seeing your vision through our connection. Now I understand."

"That makes one of us. Why am I shown things I can't do anything about? Is it just to torture me? And what connection?"

Yazhi reached across the table and covered Renée's hand with her own. "Do you feel that?" When Renée tried to pull away, Yazhi tightened her grip. She felt the energy surge between them and stared hard into Renée's eyes, until the other woman looked away.

"Yes." Renée's voice was so quiet Yazhi had to strain to hear her. She sounded defeated, and Yazhi felt a stab of pain in her heart. She couldn't tell if it belonged to Renée, or to her.

"But you wish you didn't."

"Yes, I wish I didn't. I've struggled all my life to shut out the visions, and the knowledge, and the 'feelings.'" The last was said derisively.

"You must be very tired. That kind of effort takes so much energy." A tear rolled down Renée's cheek and Yazhi reached out with her free hand to wipe it away.

"Why do you fight your power instead of embracing it?"

Renée swallowed hard and Yazhi sat patiently, aware that her guest's admissions were made with great reluctance and that fear still permeated the air. Trust clearly was not something that came easily to Renée, and Yazhi imagined that emotional displays in front of strangers were not the norm for her, either.

"You don't have time for this." Renée gestured in the direction of the suitcase. "You must have a plane to catch, or something. How about if you keep your end of the bargain, and we go our own ways?"

Yazhi raised an eyebrow but made no other move.

"You said if I was honest with you about the boy, you'd fill in the gaps in my memory of the accident. I told you what I knew about the boy. It's your turn."

Yazhi frowned. If she did as Renée asked, she had little doubt that the photographer would disappear without another word, and Yazhi would have failed to fulfill her purpose. She still was not certain she knew exactly what her role was, but it was clear that it had to do with helping Renée overcome her fear and accept her abilities.

"You're right. I must go." Yazhi stood. "I will, as you say, keep my end of the bargain, but not today." She picked up a pen from the table and wrote hastily on a nearby hotel memo pad. "This is where you can find me. If you really want to know what happened, you should see for yourself."

"You've got to be joking." Renée popped out of the chair and brought her face within inches of Yazhi's. "I came over here in good faith, answered your question, and you pull this load of crap? Who the hell are you? And why do you keep fucking with me?"

Yazhi stood her ground without flinching.

"I'm out of here." Renée spun on her heel and headed for the door. It was only after she tried to fling it open that she realized that Yazhi had reset the security chain. "For God's sake." She fumbled with the metal and stormed out, slamming the door behind her.

***

"Shit!" Renée squeezed her hand to stem the flow of blood squirting from a two-inch gash. "Stupid, stupid, stupid." She nudged the jagged edge of broken framing glass with her booted foot, rose, and hustled to the sink in her darkroom.

The water stung, but it gave her a clearer look at the damage. "Could've been worse." Renée shut off the faucet and reached into the drawer for the butterfly strips.

Just as she finished drying her hands and applying the bandages, the doorbell buzzed. "Now what?"

"Whoever you are, go away," Renée growled into the intercom.

"Ms. Maupin?" The voice was timid, tentative.

"No, it's the Easter bunny. What do you want?"

"Sabrina told me to bring this package back to you."

"Could the day get any worse?" Renée buzzed the messenger in and leaned against the open door to wait.

"Sabrina said to tell you..." The messenger, whom Renée recognized as one of the go-fers from the gallery, fished a tattered Post-it note from his pocket and shifted from foot to foot. "Your little friend dropped this off for you. Seems you left it in her hotel room."

Renée could just imagine Sabrina's voice dripping with disgust. "Perfect." She fished a ten-dollar bill out of her pocket, shoved it into the clearly uncomfortable messenger's hand, and slammed the door in his face.

It was humiliating. Really. First Yazhi gets her to give up the truth about the vision without coughing up the details about the accident, and then she goes to the trouble to return a photograph she clearly wanted. Not only that, but knowing she'd been in Yazhi's hotel room, regardless of the circumstances, would give Sabrina one more reason to hate her. Renée leaned heavily against the door. She hadn't felt this off-balance in, well, forever.

***

The sun was little more than a hint on the horizon. Yazhi closed her eyes and took a deep, cleansing breath, savoring the early morning sounds of bird song and enjoying the solitude.

"Thank you, Great Spirit, for the beauty of this day, for the gifts of sight and knowledge you have bestowed upon me, and for the wisdom to use those gifts to help others."

Yazhi smiled as the warrior she knew as Joseph appeared in her mind's eye. Over the years he had become a frequent presence in her life. He was one of three spirit guides that visited regularly, advising her and lighting her way.

Today will be an important day.

She's coming today, isn't she?

Yes. She is troubled.

I know. Her visions are more frequent and she does not sleep well. What must I do?

She is torn. She does not know what it is she seeks. Even as she doubts herself, she will trust you. You must show her the way. Teach her to use the abilities she has been given without fear or judgment.

You understand her in ways her own people do not. Her experiences have taught her to ignore what she knows. Be patient, but strong.

I understand. I am ready.

Yes, you are.

Yazhi remained still a moment more before opening her eyes. She raised her chin to the sun, which had begun its ascent. It had been nearly a month since she'd given Renée her address. At times she had wondered if the photographer would show at all.

Yazhi knew Renée's visions had become almost a nightly occurrence, for they awakened her as well. She had come to tell the difference between her own energy and Renée's. It was a relief to know that she might have an opportunity to help Renée so that they both might get some rest.

Yazhi could have shut out the visions, but in so doing she felt she would have been turning her back on Renée at a time when the woman needed her.

"Be honest, Yaz, this isn't only about assisting in her spiritual journey and you know it." From the first second Yazhi had wrapped herself around Renée and pulled her from the canyon, she had felt an irresistible connection. It was more than simple attraction—it was a recognition of a soul she had known...and loved...many times before. Renée Maupin was her twin flame.

Up until this moment, Yazhi had been unwilling to think about that, but now...now Renée would be coming to her. Yazhi's stomach did a small flip. "First things first, Yaz. Heal the spirit and the rest will follow." She stood up from the ground and dusted herself off. It was going to be a long day.

CHAPTER FIVE

Renée pulled the rented Jeep to the side of the road and snatched her camera off the passenger seat. The sun was minutes away from disappearing below the horizon, and the scene to her right was backlit so that the rocks virtually glowed. Overhead, a ripe full moon hung in the indigo sky, watching over the tableau.

"Amazing." Renée jumped out of the car and began shooting. She concentrated first on the larger landscape, then changed lenses, got down on her belly, and composed the close-up texture shots she preferred. The ripples in the red-hued sand loomed large in her viewfinder, and she snapped off a series of shots from a variety of angles.

When she was done, Renée rolled over onto her back and stared up at the darkening sky, marveling at the raw beauty of the colors, the crispness of the late-fall air, and the purity of the moment. This was what she loved, what she lived for. Out here, there were no crumpled bodies in alleys, no women cowering behind garbage cans, their clothes torn and their bodies violated. Out here, she felt calm and at peace.

A chill breeze jolted Renée back into the moment. She shivered and scrambled up from the ground. It would be full dark before long, and she wanted to reach her destination while she still could see where she was going.

She checked the car's navigation system one more time as she pulled back onto the road. If the GPS was correct, she should arrive at the address Yazhi had given her within ten minutes.

"Then what, genius?" Not for the first time, Renée's stomach clenched. She imagined what she would say to Yazhi. "Hi. I was just in the neighborhood…" *Yeah, right.* "Hi. I don't know if you remember me, but you said I should stop by if I wanted to know what the hell happened to me in that canyon more than a year ago." *Brilliant.* "Hi. I haven't been able to sleep since you left New York. Truthfully, nothing has been the same since I met you. I'm having nightly visions, I know when someone thinks about me, and I see dead people. If that isn't enough, I can't get you out of my head. So I came here to exorcise my demons. Hope you don't mind." *That ought to send her running for the hills.*

"Turn left in point two miles, then turn right." The sound of the mechanized voice emanating from the GPS on the dashboard made Renée jump.

"How the hell is it that some computer tracks all these dirt roads, anyway?" She followed the directions and found herself on yet another dirt road. There were three one-story adobe houses several hundred feet apart.

"Arriving at address, on left."

"Huh." Renée pulled into a wrap-around driveway and parked behind another Jeep. She opened her window, shut off the engine, and sat stock still. Her heart hammered and her palms dampened. "You're nervous? This is ridiculous. Just ring the doorbell and say hello. She's the one who gave you the address and told you to come, remember?"

Renée looked over at the house. Smoke curled in a plume from a chimney, and a light glowed invitingly through a window. She faced forward again, closed her eyes, and caressed the steering wheel with both hands.

"Are you planning to sit out here all night? It could get a little chilly."

Renée's eyes flew open and her heart beat double-time.

"I'm sorry. I startled you."

"How do you do that? Sneak up on people without making a sound." Renée's nostrils flared and the muscles in her jaw jumped.

"I would hardly say I 'snuck' up on you. After all, you are parked in my driveway."

"I know that, but…" Renée shrugged. She had no idea what she was trying to say. But, as always seemed to be the case around Yazhi, she felt completely off-balance.

"Would you like to come inside?"

"Sure. I guess." Renée yanked the keys out of the ignition and opened the car door. She followed Yazhi into the house, her eyes drinking in the sight of her hostess's shapely backside. Her cheeks grew hot. What if Yazhi caught her staring?

Great. This is helpful. Grow up. You didn't come here to ogle or to jump her bones, you came to get information. Renée shook her head to clear it. It was useless to deny that Yazhi flustered her in a way no woman had since her first high school crush, but that was not why she was here.

The first thing Renée noticed when she crossed the threshold was the comforting scent of lavender. It didn't take her long to locate the source—a series of lit candles populated highly polished, hand-carved wooden pedestals in the great room to the right of the entryway. More candles rested on a matching coffee table in front of a rich chocolate leather sofa. The walls were painted pale beige and boasted several Navajo wall hangings. A massive fireplace with a native red-rock hearth dominated the far side of the room. The flames licked at cedar logs, simultaneously creating a mesmerizing glow, interesting shadows, and an inviting warmth. The space over the mantle was bare.

"I'm waiting to find just the right image to hang there," Yazhi said, breaking the silence.

Renée started again. She hadn't realized Yazhi was watching her. In fact, she'd almost forgotten for a moment that she wasn't alone. The setting was so peaceful, so welcoming, that she'd become completely immersed in the surroundings. She nodded, automatically envisioning how the image Yazhi had fallen in love with in New York would look in a larger size in that spot. It would be perfect. No wonder Yazhi had wanted it.

"Um, I thought you might be hungry, so I made a stew and some fry bread. I wasn't sure, but I didn't think you were a vegan."

"How did you know I was coming?" Renée rounded on Yazhi, her eyes narrowing. She hadn't told anyone where she was going, hadn't made up her mind definitively to make the trip until the night before.

Yazhi blushed an appealing shade of deeper red.

"Dinner is ready. There's a bathroom down the hall to your left if you'd like to freshen up."

"Figures."

"I'm sorry?"

"You didn't answer me…again. You have a habit of that, you know."

"In time, I will answer all your questions."

"Do you ever speak in anything other than riddles?"

"Yes." Yazhi smiled. It was the kind of beatific expression one might have found in a painting.

"You are exasperating, you know that?"

"I know that you think so."

Renée grunted and headed in the direction Yazhi had indicated for the bathroom. Once inside, she closed the door and leaned against it with her eyes closed. *Be patient. Be polite. You remember how to do that, right? Maybe she just doesn't respond well to pressure. Or maybe she likes to have the upper hand. Don't let her think you're desperate for answers. Play it cool.* Renée opened her eyes and shoved away from the door. She washed her hands, splashed water on her face, and fixed her resolve.

When she walked back down the hallway, Yazhi was nowhere in sight.

"I'm in here," Yazhi called.

Renée wanted to ask how Yazhi knew she'd emerged from the bathroom at the other end of the house, but she thought better of it. She was sure Yazhi would only give her another equally frustrating answer. Instead, she followed the sound of Yazhi's voice and the delicious smell emanating from somewhere beyond the great room.

***

Yazhi busied herself ladling stew into two bowls and arranging the fry bread in a woven basket. She was nervous, and used the moments when Renée was in the bathroom to center herself and try to relax. It wasn't working.

By the time she heard the bathroom door open, Yazhi had dinner on the table, wine poured, and dessert cooling on the counter.

"It smells wonderful in here," Renée said, "and the table looks beautiful." She was standing at the threshold where the kitchen met the dining area.

"Thank you. Please, have a seat. I hope you like red wine?"

"I do. Thanks. And you're right—I'm a carnivore through and through." Renée sat down in the chair facing the kitchen.

Yazhi's spine tingled. Renée was watching her. She took another deep breath through her nose and released it through her mouth. "Did you have a good trip?"

"Fine. I got some great shots at sunset on my way here. The lighting in this area has a quality I haven't found anywhere else."

"I'm glad. As you know, I'm a fan of your work. I'm confident that you'll do justice to our lands."

"I hope so."

Something in Renée's tone made Yazhi stop fussing over the salad she was fixing and look. "You seem different, somehow." The combativeness, Yazhi realized, was gone. It wasn't that Renée had mellowed, per se…just that the fight seemed to have gone out of her.

"I don't know what you're talking about."

Yazhi simply raised an eyebrow and placed the salad bowl on the table. "Please, eat."

For a time, the only sound was the scraping of utensils on ceramic as the two women enjoyed the meal.

"I've never had fry bread before."

"It's a staple of our people."

"Tasty."

"Mmm." Yazhi sighed as she cleared the table. *Great Spirit, please help us to get past this awkwardness. I know I must be patient, but small talk is not natural for either one of us.* "Do you like apple pie?"

"Love it."

Yazhi removed the pie from the cooling rack, cut two slices, and brought them to the table.

"Did you make this?" Renée asked a few minutes later, scooping up the last bit of apple from her plate.

"Mmm-hmm. My mother's recipe."

"It's fantastic."

"There's more."

"I couldn't. As it is, I'll be sleeping on a full stomach. Speaking of which," Renée said, "I'm going to need a recommendation. I don't have a reservation, and I'm not really sure where your place is in relation to the hotels in the area—"

"That's easy. You stand up and go left about thirty feet, then turn right." Yazhi said, biting her lip as she watched Renée grasp her meaning.

"No. That's—"

"I insist. My guest room is all ready, it's too late to find someplace else, and I've got a special spot I want to share with you in the morning. At sun up, it is the most magical place on earth, and if you go to a hotel, you'll miss capturing it on film."

Yazhi knew it was fighting dirty to dangle an unparalleled photographic opportunity before Renée. But she couldn't seem to shake the unsettled feeling that had been with her since shortly after her morning meditation, and the stilted dinner conversation hadn't helped ease her concern. Her instincts told her she needed to keep Renée close, and Yazhi always followed her instincts. *Please,* she pleaded silently, *I don't know why yet, but I know it is important that you stay here tonight.*

"If you're sure—"

"Good. That's settled," Yazhi said, as some of the tension drained out of her shoulders. "If you want to get your things, I'll show you the way."

***

"Mama? Why is that man standing by the window?"

"What man, sweetheart?"

Renée looked from her mother, who was kneading dough on the kitchen counter, to the young man staring out the living room window.

"There." Renée pointed. Her mother swiped the back of her hand across her sweaty brow as she glanced in the direction indicated by her daughter.

"Honestly, Renée, I don't have time for your nonsense. Your father will be home any second now, and I've got to get this bread in the oven. Why don't you go read one of your books, or sit at the table here and draw."

"But Mama, he looks so sad."

"Renée Elizabeth, there is no one by that window. I swear, child, you wear me out. These fantastic stories about phantom people and the mysterious conversations you have with them in your head have got to stop. Do you hear me? Right now. Skedaddle!"

***

The hallway was dark and Renée struggled to see. She heard the murmur of voices and knew that her parents were awake. She inched along the wall until she was right outside their room. The door was open a crack and she could just make out her father standing at the foot of the bed, his silhouette illuminated by the glow of the nightlight from the master bathroom.

"She's just a young girl with a vivid imagination, Harriet. Nothing to worry about. She'll grow out of it."

"Today it was a man by the window. Wednesday it was a baby crying in Elaine's room—you know, the room we had converted into a nursery before…"

Her mother let out a choked cry, and Renée's heart dropped.

"There, there, dear. No need to think about that. We never told Renée she had an older brother who died as an infant. He never even came home from the hospital. It's just a coincidence."

"She is Satan's spawn. I'm telling you."

Renée's knees buckled, although she remained rooted to the spot.

"You're overreacting, dear. She's just a child."

"You just go ahead and ask her about it, Donald. Then tell me she's an innocent."

"I'll talk to her in the morning. Let's get some sleep."

Renée ran back to her room and dove under the covers. She cried until she had no more tears to give.

"Renée, your mother tells me you've got some imaginary friends."

Renée stared at her cereal bowl and said nothing.

"I'm talking to you, young lady. You could at least look at me."

Reluctantly, Renée dragged her red, swollen eyes away from the Froot Loops and peeked at her father. "They're not imaginary," she mumbled.

"What? I didn't hear you."

"I said, they're real." Renée glanced over toward the living room. The man was standing there again.

"Honey, I know you think that—"

"He's right over there." Renée jumped up from the table and pointed.

"Sweetheart, what have I told you about lying? You know that's wrong."

Renée felt the sting of tears. She blurted out, "He says his name is Steven and he used to live here. You bought the house from him. He says he didn't want to sell the house, but he had to because he got sick. He signed the papers from his hospital bed and died the next day. He's so sad, Daddy."

"Oh my God, Donald. Now do you see what I mean? She's a freak."

Renée started. She hadn't heard her mother come in. She stumbled backward. "N-no, Mama. I'm not. I'm really not. I promise." She crumbled to the floor and curled up in a little ball. "I'm normal, I'm normal, I'm normal…"

CHAPTER SIX

"Renée. Hey, Renée. Wake up. It's okay. Hey, wake up. You're safe here. I promise." Yazhi bent over the bed and gently shook her guest's arm.

Renée was curled up in the fetal position, whimpering. Yazhi fought for a moment against the waves of distress emanating from Renée. What she had seen in the vision through their connection was inconceivable. That parents could treat a child in such a manner—that her gift could be seen as a curse—Yazhi simply couldn't have imagined it if she hadn't seen it through Renée's eyes. *You have so much pain. I'm so sorry for what happened to you.*

Yazhi took a deep breath and centered herself, then gave in to the overwhelming desire to comfort and console. Cautiously, she climbed onto the queen-sized bed and slid up until she was sitting against the headboard.

"Renée, honey. You're all right. Come here." Yazhi reached over and enveloped Renée in her arms, maneuvering until she cradled her completely. Still, Renée didn't wake. Yazhi stroked her hair and whispered words of comfort that were as much for the little girl as for the grown woman. "Shh, no one will doubt you or hurt you here. It's okay."

"No. Please, I'll never do it again."

The words were mumbled, almost swallowed up by Yazhi's T-shirt, against which Renée's head was pillowed. The naked vulnerability was almost too much for Yazhi to bear. She leaned down and kissed Renée's tousled locks, rocking their bodies in a slow rhythm. Almost immediately, Renée settled down. Unconsciously, she snuggled into Yazhi's embrace.

Yazhi closed her eyes as her body responded to the feel of Renée against her. *Great Spirit, give me the strength to put aside my desires and the wisdom to know how to help her.* With great effort, Yazhi regulated her breathing and waited for her heartbeat to follow suit.

Eventually, she began to relax completely, and then to nod off. When Yazhi awoke, she and Renée were breathing in unison, their limbs entangled, Renée's forehead resting against the side of Yazhi's neck. Her heart thudded once, hard.

It was close to dawn. If she tried to extricate herself now, Renée surely would awaken. If she didn't slip away...*If you don't get out of here, how will you explain your presence? How will she react?* Yazhi frowned. As volatile as Renée already had proven herself to be, Yazhi didn't want to think about how the morning would unfold in that instance.

Renée began to stir, and Yazhi had no more time to contemplate her options. Instead, she relied on her instincts. With as much care and stealth as she could muster, Yazhi disentangled herself.

No sooner had she stood up, than Renée's eyes fluttered open. "Um, I just came in to wake you."

"It must be the middle of the night."

"No, actually, it's almost dawn. If you want to see one of the most beautiful sights in the world, you'll have to get up now."

Yazhi watched Renée's eyes come alive with light. "I'll be ready in ten minutes."

***

Renée brushed her teeth and ran a comb through her hair. The remnants of the previous night's dream hung over her like a shroud. But there was something else, something she couldn't quite remember, playing at the edges of her mind. She wrinkled her forehead in thought. Whatever it was, she felt more at peace than at any other time in her life. Which seemed…odd…given the circumstances.

Renée glanced at her watch. *No time to ruminate now, dummy.* She yanked the T-shirt over her head, and as she did so, caught a whiff of a light scent that wasn't her own. "Huh." She held it to her nose and sniffed. Not perfume, exactly. Shampoo? No. Lavender. Like the candles. She narrowed her eyes. "I know damn well I didn't get close enough to any of those candles—"

"Are you ready?" Yazhi called through the closed door.

"Will be in a minute." Renée hurriedly changed into a turtleneck and jeans and threw her camera gear together. When she emerged from the bedroom, she could smell freshly brewed coffee. Unable to resist, she followed her nose to the kitchen.

"I thought you could use some of this."

"Thank you," Renée said. She slung the camera bag over her shoulder and gratefully accepted the proffered thermos.

"You might want a jacket. It's pretty cool out there this time of day."

"It's in the car."

"Okay, then, let's go. We'll take my Jeep."

Renée followed Yazhi out the door, stopped and grabbed her leather bomber jacket out of the backseat of the rental vehicle, and slid into the passenger seat of Yazhi's Jeep. "Where are we going?"

"You'll see." Yazhi put the Jeep in gear and headed east.

Renée noted that Yazhi had yet to look her in the eye. "Everything all right this morning?"

"Yes. As you can see, the weather is cooperating. The sunrise will be magnificent."

Renée looked at Yazhi appraisingly. It wasn't that she was nervous, exactly, and yet...

A few minutes later, Yazhi said, "Here we go."

As far as Renée could tell, they were in the middle of nowhere. "Where are we?"

"Private Navajo lands. Outsiders are forbidden unless accompanied by one of us. Come."

Yazhi scrambled out of the Jeep and started up a rise. It was all Renée could do to keep up with her. The air was crisp and clear, and she could see her breath. In moments they crested the incline.

"Holy..." It was all Renée could manage as she looked out over an expanse as beautiful as anything she'd ever seen. Clouds streaked the horizon, and the sun was about to make its debut for the day. Without taking her eyes off the view, she dropped the camera bag, unzipped it, and removed the camera body and a lens.

She snapped off several establishing shots, repositioned herself, and got to work in earnest. "This is unbelievable." The noise of the shutter clicking and her own exclamations were the only sounds to break the stillness of the dawn.

Finally, Renée stopped to regroup. She withdrew her eye from the viewfinder and noticed Yazhi sitting perfectly still a short distance away. It was the first time Renée remembered that she wasn't alone. She was about to make a comment, when she realized that Yazhi's eyes were closed. *She looks so serene, so beautiful.* Renée raised the camera, framed Yazhi in the perfect shot, backlit by the rising sun, then paused. The moment seemed somehow too private, too personal, to record. Renée felt as though she was intruding. Instead, she lowered the camera and watched.

Remarkably, she found that she was jealous—jealous of Yazhi's ability to find such peace when all she felt was terror and turmoil.

"You can find the same thing, if only you would let yourself go."

"I'm sorry. What?" *How do you do that—get inside my head like that? Damn.*

"You spend so much time running away from yourself that you have lost your way. The only time you let down your guard is when you are hiding behind a lens."

The color rose in Renée's cheeks. "Lady, you don't even know me."

"On the contrary, it is you who doesn't know yourself."

All Renée wanted to do was to knock that tranquil expression right off Yazhi's beatific face. Instead, she stalked in the opposite direction, camera in hand.

"It is a long walk to anywhere from here. Also, there are a considerable number of rattlesnakes and scorpions. I recommend that you not go too far."

Renée merely grunted and continued in the direction she'd been heading. If she got lucky, Yazhi wouldn't be there when she got back. A little while later, she halted and took stock of her surroundings. Yazhi was nowhere in sight. *Good.*

Unfortunately, in her zeal to avoid further scrutiny, Renée had wandered farther than she intended. *Brilliant, jackass. Just friggin' brilliant. Now she can find something else to fault you for, as if she hasn't already sized you up and found you wanting. You can't follow instructions.*

Don't freak. Just look at the direction of the sun. You can do this. If you don't get lost in the City, you certainly shouldn't get lost out here.

"I can feel your anxiety. If you would but tap into a small bit of your ability, you would know how to find your way back to me. You will be fine."

Renée spun around. "What the…" She had heard Yazhi's voice plain as day. So where was she?

"Still your mind and listen. Take a deep breath and tune in to my vibration. I know you can do this. Do not be afraid."

Renée walked several steps to her right, then back to her left. Yazhi was not within view. Renée spun in a full circle—still no Yazhi. *You're hallucinating.*

"Renée, concentrate."

Okay. Where the hell are you? Renée asked the question silently and stood, arms folded, sure that she would get no reply.

"I am right where you left me."

Renée jumped. "Son of a bitch. Stop messing with me!" she yelled. Her voice echoed off the rock faces and came back to her. She sat down and dropped her head into her hands. As a child, she always had feared being separated from her parents. Once, she'd gotten lost in a department store and it had taken twenty minutes for store security to locate her mother. By the time they'd been reunited, Renée was curled up on the floor in a little ball, weeping.

"I can still feel your distress. Please, take a deep breath and focus on my energy. It really is that simple."

Renée shook her head and wiped away a tear. She knew she was being ridiculous. She was a grown woman, not a little girl, and she'd been tramping through deserts and mountain ranges for years without incident.

She looked around one more time, but nothing looked familiar. With a sigh, she closed her eyes and took a deep breath. Nothing happened. *This is crazy.*

"You can do this. I believe in you. Take deep breaths in through your nose and out through your mouth. Imagine a golden light coming down from above, filling your body starting at the top of your head. Sit still, clear your mind, and focus on your breath. The path you must take will become clear to you."

Renée waggled her shoulders to loosen the tension, then settled down and followed Yazhi's instructions. For several moments, she merely sat and breathed, feeling the warming sun beat down on her face. At first, her mind raced, but after a time, she felt herself go lax.

Renée's eyes popped open. She had no idea how much time had passed, but she knew, with a certainty that she couldn't explain, exactly where to go. She jumped up, pivoted on her heel, and walked off in the direction that felt right. Within ten minutes, she began to recognize the rock formations. Two minutes after that, she found Yazhi, sitting precisely where she last had seen her. Yazhi was beaming at her. A wave of relief washed over her, and, without thinking, Renée dropped into Yazhi's waiting arms, sobbing uncontrollably.

"It's okay. You're okay. Shh."

Yazhi rubbed Renée's back and rocked her. Dimly, Renée thought the gesture felt oddly familiar.

"I knew you could do it. I knew it. I'm so proud of you."

Renée took a shuddering breath and sat up a little straighter. "How did you know?" She accepted the tissue Yazhi offered and blew her nose.

"Because you are gifted with special abilities."

Renée shook her head.

"You are, although you go to great pains to ignore your capabilities."

"I don't know what you're talking about." The denial sounded weak, even to Renée's ears.

"Is that so? Then how did you find your way back here? Do you deny that you heard my thoughts? Or that I heard yours?"

Renée started to nod, then bowed her head in defeat. Yazhi gently put two fingers under Renée's jaw and lifted her chin until they were eye-to-eye, their noses mere inches apart, their breath mingling in the still-chill morning air.

Renée was shocked to see that there were tears in Yazhi's eyes.

"Do not be afraid or ashamed of who you are, or what you can do, Renée Maupin. Never be ashamed. You are so much more than you let on. You never need to pretend with me."

Renée swallowed hard. "I-I don't—"

"You communicated with me telepathically. That's how you found your way back."

Renée squirmed, but Yazhi held her fast. "I'm not a…"

"Freak like me?"

"Something like that." Renée blushed.

"Am I so very strange, so foreign to you? Do I frighten you?"

"N-no. No. Of course you don't. It's just…" Renée's lips formed a thin line. What did she want to say?

"You have been trained to believe that relying on anything other than the five 'accepted' senses is unsafe. That doing so makes you evil."

"That's not true."

"Isn't it?" Yazhi put her fingers over Renée's lips as she opened her mouth to answer. "Think before you speak. You may be dishonest with me, but I hope you will stop being dishonest with yourself."

Renée swallowed the automatic denial, and instead sat back on her haunches and said nothing. She was exhausted.

"Come, there are a few other spots I would like to share with you." Yazhi rose and held out her hand. Renée grabbed it, grateful for the apparent end of the discussion. Perhaps if she could just focus on the scenery once again, she could find her equilibrium.

CHAPTER SEVEN

It was close to two o'clock in the afternoon. They had gone home for breakfast, during which neither one of them had said a word. Afterward, Yazhi had taken Renée on a tour of Navajo land that had never been photographed by anyone other than a Diné. Apart from a few questions and answers about the history of the land, the uncomfortable silence had continued.

Now, they were in the Jeep on the way to Lower Antelope Canyon. "Are you hungry?" Yazhi asked.

"No. I'm fine, thanks. I really appreciate the access to your people's lands."

"You're welcome." Yazhi sighed. She wasn't sure how much longer she could stand their stilted exchanges.

"Where are we going now?"

"I promised you that I would tell you what happened that day in the canyon. Your tour started right about this time. I thought, instead of telling you, I would show you."

"Oh."

Yazhi turned into the parking lot and killed the ignition.

"Hey, I recognize him," Renée said, pointing at the man leaning against a pickup truck a short distance away.

Yazhi was already out of the vehicle. "That's my brother, Ben. He was your guide that day. We've closed the canyon to tours for a few hours, and I've asked him to help us out, since he was in the canyon with you and I was not."

As Yazhi and Renée came to a halt in front of Ben, Renée grabbed Yazhi's arm. "Wait a minute, if you weren't here, how do you know what actually happened?"

Before Yazhi could say anything, Ben spoke up. "Oh, Yaz was here, all right. If it hadn't been for her, you wouldn't be standing here."

"Ben. Hush."

"Why? It's the truth, Yaz, and you know it. You saved her life."

Renée rounded on Yazhi, her eyes filled with questions. "What is he talking about?"

"It's noth—"

"Yaz is the one who saw the storm coming." Ben talked over her. "She made me lower her into that canyon so she could pluck you out of there. We could've lost her..." His voice trailed off on a sob.

"Ben, that's enough," Yazhi said, firmly. He hung his head and walked several feet away.

"Is that true?" Renée asked, her eyes boring into Yazhi.

"That is part of the truth, yes," Yazhi answered reluctantly.

"I didn't know. I just assumed maybe I had washed out of there or been saved by snagging on a rock or something and you found me afterward. I guess it never occurred to me that there might have been human intervention in the middle of the flood."

"You would never have survived without Yaz, even if you had, as you say, 'snagged on a rock.'" Ben approached again. "You would have drowned. That wall of water was at least fifty feet high."

"Bennn," Yazhi warned.

Ben simply jutted out his chin and ignored his sister as he continued to address Renée. "She won't tell you, because she doesn't want to scare you. But I think you should know that Yaz is your hero."

"You're done," Yazhi said to Ben. She moved between him and Renée.

"I thought you needed my help."

"Not any more. I can take it from here." For a moment, Yazhi thought Ben might defy her. He crossed his arms and stared at her.

Finally, Ben shrugged. "All right. Have it your way. But I'm not sorry for telling her the truth." He motioned in Renée's direction. "If it had been me, I might have left her insufferable ass in there. But no, not you. Not the great healer, Yazhi Begay. You saved her, went with her on the helicopter flight to Phoenix, and waited with her until her family came. And she *still* hasn't thanked you. I almost lost you," Ben's voice broke, "and she has no clue."

"Get. Out. Now." It was exceedingly rare for Yazhi to lose her temper, but it was all she could do to maintain self-control. She did not break eye contact with Ben until he stalked off and jumped in his truck. He peeled out in a haze of dust.

Yazhi paused to collect herself before she turned to face Renée. "I'm so sor—" Yazhi stopped talking mid-sentence. Tears streaked Renée's cheeks. "No. No, please don't cry." *This was not the way I wanted you to find out.* Yazhi closed the distance between them and took Renée in her arms.

"You risked your life for me. I didn't know."

"Of course you didn't," Yazhi said, stroking Renée's back in comfort.

"Oh my God, you could have died in there. And for whom? An asshole like me? Your brother is right—I'm not worth a quarter of you."

"Don't say that," Yazhi said, heatedly. "Please, don't say that," she added, more softly. "You have no idea of your worth."

"I'm a miserable excuse for a human being, and I have been for a very long time. That's just a simple truth," Renée said.

"That is not the truth," Yazhi tightened her arms around Renée to emphasize her point, "but you have allowed others to convince you that it is so, and that saddens me. You have always tried to be as others define you, instead of trusting the truth that lives inside you."

"How many times do I have to tell you—you don't know me." Renée tried to pull away, but Yazhi held her fast.

Yazhi could feel the waves of misery flowing from the woman in her arms and it nearly destroyed her. "I know you much better than you think. I have known you, as you have known me, over many lifetimes." She leaned back until she and Renée locked gazes. Slowly, Yazhi rose up so that her lips brushed first Renée's chin, and then her mouth.

It was the briefest of touches, and it sent sparks shooting through every one of Yazhi's nerve endings. She gasped. When she opened her eyes, Renée was staring at her, slack-jawed.

"I-I'm sorry," Yazhi stammered, as she dropped her arms to her sides and stepped back. "I shouldn't have—"

"Shouldn't you?" Renée asked, pursuing her.

"I—"

Renée covered Yazhi's mouth with her own before she could say anything else. Yazhi's knees buckled, and she felt strong arms come around her. Fire streaked through her veins, and she yielded as Renée sought entry, her tongue stroking Yazhi's, the beats becoming increasingly insistent as the kiss deepened.

In the recesses of her mind, Yazhi heard a desperate groan. With a start, she realized the sound had emanated from her. Her body surged forward, pressing against Renée until they were wedded all along their lengths. Hungrily, she returned Renée's kisses, dropping any pretext at control.

Finally, regretfully, she pulled away to catch her breath. For several seconds, the only sound Yazhi could hear was the thudding of her heart.

"What the heck was that?"

Renée's question snapped Yazhi back to reality, but she couldn't seem to find her voice.

"I mean, I've kissed my share of women, which is perhaps not a good thing to be pointing out right now," Renée said, her tone filled with wonder, "but nothing has ever felt like that. It was as if we were one…"

At first, Yazhi could manage only to nod. Eventually, she managed, "In many ways, that is true."

"I don't understand."

"We are twin flames—destined in many lifetimes to find each other—and always to be intertwined, like two halves of a whole."

"I'm sure what you just said made sense to you, but I have no clue what it meant."

"I will explain later." When Renée looked as though she would object, Yazhi reached up and kissed her softly—just a touch of the lips. "I promise." She lowered herself back down and took Renée's hand. "Right now, I really want to show you what happened that day, while we are still within the time span that you spent in the canyon."

***

Renée's mind was spinning, and her body tingled all over. What she'd told Yazhi was true—she'd never felt anything like what had overcome her when their lips touched. It was as if their souls fused together. It was disconcerting, and confusing, and oh, so deliciously exciting.

"Can you show me where you were set up before the accident?"

Yazhi's question forced Renée to focus. They were walking through the middle of Lower Antelope Canyon. Although she wanted badly to bring her camera along, Yazhi had asked her to leave it in the Jeep.

"I was standing over there." Renée pointed to a spot roughly fifteen feet farther into the canyon.

"Okay." Yazhi walked to the indicated spot and turned in a circle, her expression pensive.

"What is it?"

"Huh?"

"What are you looking for?" Renée asked as she came up beside Yazhi.

"I'm calculating where I was above ground in relation to where we are now."

"Oh." Renée thrust her hands in her pockets. "Is that...is that what you did? Follow the crevice from up top?"

"Yes," Yazhi replied. She seemed distracted. "I asked Ben for his last position fix, and then I tried to estimate how far the force of the water would have swept you, and the point where the fissure would be wide enough for me to rappel down in time to reach you before..."

A chill ran down Renée's spine as she filled in the blanks.

Yazhi, whose back had been turned, pivoted around and took both Renée's hands. "Don't. It didn't happen. You're here and you are fine."

For several seconds, Renée simply allowed herself to get lost in the security of Yazhi's compassionate gaze. "How do you know what I was thinking? Is that just a hunch, or…?"

Yazhi shrugged, but maintained contact. "I am empathic. I can feel what you feel. Because we are twin flames, this would not be hard, in any case. If you look inside yourself, you will find that you have an equal sensitivity to me."

Renée dropped her hands and wandered over to examine the striations in the rocks.

"This notion makes you uncomfortable."

Renée shook her head, but did not turn around to face Yazhi. "It's not something I've thought about. It's foreign to me."

"Is it?" Yazhi's question was asked softly, but for Renée, it's implication reverberated off the walls.

"Of course. Not everyone has your abilities or can do what you can do."

"No. That is true. But you can."

"What makes you so sure?" Renée turned to find that Yazhi was standing right behind her, essentially trapping her against the wall. She squirmed. "You're really short, you know that?"

"So my name says. But you are changing the subject."

"Your name means short?"

"No. Yazhi is Navajo for 'little one,' and you are still avoiding the topic at hand." Yazhi stood within inches of Renée, her arms crossed and her legs shoulder-width apart.

"All right. What makes you so damn sure I have any sort of supernatural powers?" Renée made air quotes around the last two words.

"Have you forgotten how you found your way back to me this morning?"

"I was desperate and bound to find my way."

"But that is not what you did, and you know it. How do you explain how it feels when we do this?"

The end of Yazhi's question echoed inside Renée's mouth as she kissed her hard, her tongue demanding entry. Renée felt the searing heat, then the same sense of oneness she had experienced before—as if she finally had come home. Somewhere in the deep recesses of her mind, alarm bells rang, but she was powerless to know why.

When Yazhi released her, Renée staggered backward into the wall, where she gasped for breath. "That doesn't prove..." Renée flared her nostrils and narrowed her eyes as the source of the alarm bells became clear. She pointed her finger accusingly at Yazhi. "Lavender."

"I'm sorry?"

"Lavender. You smell like lavender. The same scent I smelled this morning when I took off my sleep shirt."

The expression on Yazhi's face told Renée everything she needed to know. "You were already in my room. You weren't coming in to wake me. You were sneaking out."

Yazhi sat cross-legged on the ground and bowed her head. "You were in such distress. Your memories gave you such pain. I only wanted to take away the pain."

"How the hell do you know about my memories?" Renée towered over Yazhi menacingly, her whole body trembling.

Yazhi looked up directly into Renée's eyes. "The same way I knew about the boy in the alley, the young woman on the Ferris wheel two nights after that, the elderly gentleman walking home from the store..."

"No." Renée put her hands over her ears. "You have no right."

"I have never tried to intrude, Renée. The Great Spirit sent me to help you. To teach you the ways, so that you might reclaim who you really are and live a life in harmony—"

"My life is none of your damned business! Screw you and The Great Spirit. Get out of my head!" Renée stormed past

Yazhi and sprinted toward the end of the canyon. She didn't stop running until her sides cramped. She bent over and vomited, then slid down behind a large rock. Her whole body shook as she sobbed uncontrollably. "Leave me alone," she whispered. "Just leave me alone."

CHAPTER EIGHT

Yazhi paced back and forth across the small office. She peeked out the window at the impending darkness and bit her lip.

"Do you know where she is?" Ben put his hands on Yazhi's shoulders.

"No."

"But you could figure it out just by focusing if you wanted to. Why won't you? I can see that you are worried."

"No." Yazhi shook her head. "She must come to terms with who she is and decide that she wants what I am offering. It would be wrong to tune into her energy when she has made it plain that she does not wish to let me in."

"Yaz, I don't want to point out the obvious, but it'll be full nightfall in less than an hour, the temperature is dropping, she has no idea where she is, and she has no food or water out there. This is a safety issue."

"I know." Yazhi balled her hands into fists. "I have reached out only far enough to know that she is safe. Ben, she is more frightened of herself than she is of the obvious dangers."

"That's crazy."

"A child's fright can be very difficult to overcome, especially when it has been instilled by adults who reacted out of ignorance and their own fear."

"But she's an adult now."

"Yes, but we all carry within us the lessons of our youth, however misguided, until we learn a better way."

"And you think leaving her out there by herself will teach her a lesson?" Ben asked.

"As a child, she was taught that it was not safe to be who she was—she got the message very early on that awful consequences would ensue if she used her psychic abilities. That mentality still persists for her. That is her reality."

"So I repeat, you think leaving her out there will teach her a lesson?"

"The lesson is within her. Renée needs to overcome her fear and look inside. That will not happen if I intervene. My telling her she should not be afraid is not good enough, though I wish it were. This is her journey." Yazhi rubbed her eyes with the heels of her hands.

"Why don't you go home? I'll stay around for a little while in case she comes wandering in."

"She won't."

"All the more reason for you to go home. Nothing will be gained by you wearing the carpet out in here."

Yazhi considered Ben's suggestion. If Renée hadn't strayed too far from Lower Antelope Canyon, Yazhi could reach her just as quickly from the house as she could from the office. At home, she could light a candle and meditate. It might help ease some of the tension that was eating away at her insides.

"You're right. I should go home."

"I'll stay for another hour or so. Just in case you're wrong."

Yazhi kissed Ben on the cheek. "You are a good brother. I think I'll keep you."

"I'm a lucky guy. Now get out of here."

Yazhi lingered for a moment more. She closed her eyes and focused on her third chakra—the seat of intuition. Yes, going home was the right course of action. She grabbed her keys off the counter and headed out the door.

***

Renée shivered inside her jacket. The warmth of the day had disappeared with the sun several hours earlier. She jumped up and down and slapped herself to restore circulation. "I am not cold. I am not cold. I am not c-c-c-cold." *Damn, it's freezing out here.*

Although she couldn't see the hands on her watch, Renée knew it had to be after nine o'clock. She wondered where Yazhi was and what she was doing. Was she worried? Was she out searching?

Renée shook her head. "You're pathetic. Why should she care? Didn't you tell her to butt the hell out?" A tear leaked out and rolled down Renée's cheek and she angrily wiped it away. She'd shed too many tears already. She put her fingertips to her lips and imagined that she could still feel the warmth of Yazhi's mouth on hers. "Oh, God."

She wanted nothing more than to be lying in the comfort of Yazhi's embrace. But the woman scared her silly. "If you're going to be honest about it, fool, it isn't Yazhi that scares you, it's what she said and what she knows."

For perhaps the tenth time since she had run out of the canyon, Renée replayed the events of the day. Everything had been going so well, until…"Until you realized that she knew about what happened with Mom and Dad." Renée felt her cheeks go hot with shame and embarrassment at the memory.

"What bothers you more, idiot, the memory, or the fact that Yazhi knows about it?" Renée punched at the air in frustration. She'd been through this so many times over the past few hours, and still, she had no answer. Disgusted, she sat down on the flat rock she'd chosen for her perch. *Hope to God you're not sitting on some rattlesnake's home, jerkball.*

Renée felt the panic well up inside her as the reality of her situation sank in. "Okay. No reason to freak here. You can't see two feet in front of your face, you're hungry, you're thirsty, you've resolved exactly nothing, and you're in the middle of nowhere. No problem." She took a deep breath. What was it Yazhi had said to do when she'd been lost that morning? Rhythmic breathing had been a big part of it.

Renée closed her eyes and breathed in through her nose and out through her mouth. Immediately, she felt the fear begin to recede. She imagined a golden light shining down on her, flowing through her and filling her until she glowed from within. Her shoulders began to relax and her mind started to drift.

You're asking the wrong question.

Renée furrowed her brow. She did not recognize the voice in her head, yet she was not frightened.

What question should I be asking?

Why do you fear who you are? Why do you run from the knowledge? Why do you deny your true self?

*I do not…*Renée let the thought trail off. She did, and she knew it. She had spent the better part of her life running—running from thing to thing and from person to person—never standing still long enough to quiet her mind unless she had a camera in her hand. Looking at life through the filter of her lens was her comfort and her shield. She was tired, so very, very tired of running.

What must I do? This is the only way I know how to be. How can I change?

Take the hand being offered.

Renée frowned. What the hell was that supposed to mean?

Yazhi. The answer came not from the voice, but from within. Renée's eyes popped open. Yazhi. The thought of her brought a smile to Renée's lips. Yazhi seemed so comfortable in her skin. She accepted her gifts so easily. Hadn't Yazhi said she would teach her? Yazhi could help. Yazhi, with her patient eyes and enchanting mouth. Yazhi, who already knew the truths Renée had denied but had not turned away or judged. Renée wanted to jump for joy.

Then she remembered that she had shoved Yazhi away—had treated her badly—as she had so many others in her life. She had permanently alienated them all. Had she done the same with Yazhi? The thought made her sick to her stomach.

Please, God, if I've ever done anything right, please let me fix this. She closed her eyes again and focused. There was only one way to find out.

Yazhi, if you can hear me, I sure could use your help.

***

Yazhi's eyes fluttered under her lids. She'd been meditating for nearly an hour.

Yazhi, if you can hear me, I sure could use your help.

I'm right here. How can I help?

Please, I know I don't deserve it, but I want another chance. Can you forgive me?

There is nothing to forgive.

I have so much to learn. I want you to teach me.

Nothing would make me happier.

I know something that would make me incredibly happy right now.

What is that?

Being held by you.

I can arrange that.

But I don't know where I am.

It doesn't matter. Focus on my energy. I will find you. Stay exactly where you are.

Yazhi? Is this going to be all right?

I promise you it will.

Yazhi opened her eyes, sprang out of the chair, and scooped her keys off the hook. Within seconds she was in her car and headed toward Lower Antelope Canyon. Her heart was racing. *Calm down, Yaz. She's fine. Just keep it light for now, nothing too heavy. She's had an emotionally wrenching day. She doesn't need to know how frantic you've been. It won't help her.*

When Yazhi turned into the visitor's parking lot, she put the Jeep in park and closed her eyes once again.

After several seconds of quiet concentration, Yazhi nodded. She removed a large flashlight from the glove compartment and checked her handheld GPS. Although she knew every inch of this ground, the darkness had a way of transforming the landscape. She didn't want to take any chances.

Yazhi marked the starting point on the GPS and turned to her right. Although there was no trail, the flashlight offered sufficient illumination, and she had little trouble finding her way. She traveled soundlessly for nearly ten minutes and then extinguished the flashlight before continuing another fifty yards.

I'm almost there, Renée.

How do you know?

"Because I can see you." Yazhi laughed with relief and turned the flashlight back on as Renée spun around on the rock and gaped at her.

"Very funny." Renée jumped down from the rock, lifted Yazhi off the ground, and swung her around. "Boy, am I glad to see you."

"Me too."

For a while, they simply held each other and rocked in place.

"Thank you for coming to get me," Renée said as she buried her face in Yazhi's hair.

Yazhi could feel Renée shiver. "I always make it a point to rescue damsels in distress. If you've ever watched old Westerns, you must know it's what we Indians do. I wouldn't want to ruin our reputation."

"I didn't know you people were so concerned with PR," Renée said.

"Only when dealing with extra special VIPs," Yazhi answered.

"Am I one of those?"

Yazhi tightened her grip. "Oh, yes, you are most definitely one of those."

"Yaz?"

"Hmm?"

"Take me home, please."

The raw note of pleading momentarily cut through Yazhi's resolve to keep the reunion lighthearted. "Yes. Of course." She stepped back and took Renée's hand. "You must be thirsty."

"And hungry. Don't forget hungry."

Yazhi chuckled. "I think I can help you out there." She tucked the flashlight under her arm, reached into her coat pocket, and produced a small bottle of water. When Renée had taken it from her, Yazhi reached back into the same pocket and pulled out a protein bar. "It's not exactly filet mignon, but it will replenish your energy," she said, apologetically.

"Thank you, thank you, thank you."

The two women walked on hand-in-hand as Renée consumed the protein bar and washed it down with the water.

"Better?"

"Much. Thank you," Renée said.

"Part of the job."

"What? To come out in the middle of the night and search in the dark for idiotic hot-heads who lose their way?"

"Please, don't do that." Yazhi squeezed Renée's hand more tightly.

"Do what?"

"Demean yourself in that way. Thoughts are real things, Renée. When you call yourself names and think about yourself in those terms, you send a message to the Universe that that is the sort of treatment you expect and deserve. You attract that behavior to yourself."

"How did you get to be so wise?"

Yazhi shrugged. "I've had good teachers, a lifetime to learn, and lots of practice."

They walked on a bit farther.

"Your brother called you a great healer."

"My brother is premature."

"Are you a healer?"

"My mother is the healer for my people. She has been grooming me so that one day I might take her place. I hope that day is far in the future." Yazhi released Renée's hand. "Here we are." She directed the flashlight beam toward the passenger door handle and opened the door for Renée.

As they pulled out of the parking lot, Renée said, "You know what happened with my family, right? I mean, you saw it last night?"

Yazhi noted that Renée was no longer looking at her, and that her knee was bouncing nervously. She sighed. "I did experience your memory with you last night, yes."

Before Renée could say anything else, Yazhi continued, "But I want you know I didn't ask to see that. I would never intrude intentionally. I respect your privacy. The subconscious mind takes over during sleep and it is more difficult to control what we are privy to."

"It's okay, I guess." Renée chewed her lower lip. "My parents weren't bad people, really."

"I make no judgments, Renée, except to say that they did you a disservice by making you feel the problem was with you. That you were somehow abnormal."

"Wasn't it? Wasn't I?"

"No. You saw what you saw. Children are far more open to psychic experiences and abilities because they have not yet been taught to fear such things or to disbelieve. All you were doing was describing your reality," Yazhi explained. "Because your parents' perspective was so much more limited, they could not see as you did, and that unknown frightened them. It is unfortunate that they chose to deal with their fear by isolating and stifling you instead of educating themselves and encouraging you."

"You are angry with them."

"I don't know them," Yazhi said, simply and without rancor. "I am angry that a beautiful young girl with so many gifts was brought up to think that she was 'less than,' and that she believed she had to hide her true self in order to survive."

Yazhi turned into the driveway and cut the engine, but made no move to get out of the Jeep. Renée had her hands in her lap. Her eyes were downcast.

"You keep talking about my true self, but I have no idea who that is."

Yazhi reached across and covered Renée's hands with her own. "When you are ready, I will show you. You are more beautiful than you can imagine."

"How can you be so sure?"

"Because I can see the real you—the person Renée Maupin was born to be. And you will see her too. She's very special. You do know that your name means, 'reborn,' right?"

"I hadn't thought about it, but you're right."

"And so you shall be," Yazhi said. She released Renée's hands and got out of the Jeep.

"Yaz?" Renée asked, as they crossed the threshold into the house.

"Yes?" Renée's use of her nickname brought a lump to Yazhi's throat.

"Will you hold me tonight?"

Yazhi smiled brightly. "It would be my pleasure."

***

Renée, cocooned safely in Yazhi's arms, began to drift. "Yaz?" she mumbled.

"Hmm?"

"How come I went so many years without any visions or anything else happening?"

Yazhi sat up a little straighter. "Your fear allowed you to suppress your abilities. You ignored or lost touch with your guides. You filled up your life with noise and drowned them out."

"Yeah, that makes sense. But then why did the accident in the canyon change all that? I still had just as much noise in my life."

"Yes, but before you resumed that life, you had a near-death experience. You spent time in a coma, which is a subconscious state. You were suspended in a place where you were closer to your guides, with no defense mechanism or filter standing between you and them. The channel you'd closed was reopened. Your spirit guides brought you back so that you could be the woman you were truly meant to be. You got a second chance."

"Yaz?"

"Yes."

"Thank you for saving my life and for not giving up on me."

"Never."

Renée slid into slumber with a smile on her face. When next she awakened, it was still dark outside. She was curled up against Yazhi's side, her head pillowed on Yazhi's chest, her arm thrown possessively across Yazhi's middle, and her leg sprawled across Yazhi's pelvis.

For the first time since she'd awakened in the hospital after the accident, Renée hadn't had a single vision, or even a dream that she could remember. She smiled and sighed happily.

"Are you usually giddy in the middle of the night?"

Yazhi's voice sounded sleep-filled and incredibly sexy to Renée's ears.

"Not usually, no. But in this case, I'm making an exception." Renée lifted her head. She could just make out Yazhi's exquisite features in the moonlight sifting in through the window.

"You are, huh?"

"Oh, yes." No longer able to resist, Renée traced her fingers along Yazhi's chiseled cheekbones and full lips. Renée heard Yazhi's sharp intake of breath and it sent shock waves directly to her center. She swallowed hard and cleared her throat. "This twin flame thing…"

"Mmm?"

"You said we've been together in many lifetimes, right?"

"Yes."

"How does that work?"

"We are all made of energy. Energy never dies, it merely reconstitutes. Our energies, in whatever lifetime, always have, and always will, seek each other."

Renée absorbed that information. "So we were destined to find each other?"

"That's complicated. I believe in destiny points."

"Destiny points?"

"Yes, in other words, there are certain events that are outlined in the map of our lives. But because we have free will, once we get to those points, we can choose to take the destined path, or head in another direction. If we head in another direction, obviously it can change the way the rest of our lives unfold."

"That makes sense. So, my accident in the canyon and your saving me was a destiny point?"

"Exactly."

"And what happens next is free will?"

"Mmm-hmm. Just because you find your twin flame, doesn't mean you cannot walk away."

Renée did not need to hear the hitch in Yazhi's voice—she felt Yazhi's heart lurch as if it was her own. She scooted up until she was perched over Yazhi, their faces inches apart. "I've been walking…no—running—away, all my life. For the first time, I believe it wasn't what I was running away from, it was who I was running to. I'm not going anywhere, unless you want me to."

Afterward, Renée was never sure whether she had lowered her mouth to Yazhi, or Yazhi had risen up, all she knew for certain was that in each other's arms, they'd both found home.

The End

Balance

By

Georgia Beers

I know it's there. I feel it the second I open my eyes, and the wave of familiar dread washes in, then recedes just as quickly. I should be used to this by now, but there is always that split second of fear before the acceptance that inevitably follows.

I swallow and turn my head. Six-forty in the morning. What is it that makes us wake up five minutes before the alarm goes off? Next to the clock is the small piece of notepaper I'm expecting. I inhale deeply, exhale slowly. Five more minutes, and then I'll deal with it.

I roll onto my right side, prop my head up on my hand, and watch the rise and fall of her chest as she continues in the safety of slumber. She'll have work to do when she wakes, just as I will, so I let her sleep, and I watch. Her dark hair is tousled and adorable, the creamy-smooth skin of her shoulder teases me, dares me to touch it with my fingertips, my lips. The heat coming off her never ceases to amaze me; I call her the Human Radiator. It's why she sleeps naked...not that I mind. Pajamas make her overheat. As I study her, she pouts subtly in her sleep; her full lips pull down slightly at the corners, give me a glimpse of what she might have looked like as a child, and I smile.

At 6:44, I turn the alarm off before it can sound, and I give in to that teasing shoulder, pressing my lips against it tenderly, marveling, always marveling, at the softness of her. She inhales that deep, just-about-to-wake-up breath, and her eyes flutter open, their color nearly startling me as it does every time. They're green, not quite a sea foam, closer to the leaves of a delicate fern, and they're ringed with black and surrounded by lush, dark lashes. I swear I can lose myself in those eyes. I have.

"Morning, gorgeous," Hayley says as she stretches her arms above her head.

"Hey, you stole my line."

She glances at the nightstand, a habit she's picked up from me, and sees the note. "Got work to do today?"

"I'm afraid so." I distract us both from the moment by nuzzling the warmth of her neck.

"Where are you off to?"

With a sigh, I peel myself away from her and reach for the note, give it a glance. "North Carolina, apparently. Rebecca Cassidy."

"Rebecca Cassidy," she repeats, rolling it around in her mouth like a piece of hard candy. "Good, strong name." Throwing off the covers, she gets out of bed. "Better pack a bag, sweetie."

"You know," I say as she pads past me in all her unclothed glory and into the bathroom, "it's really not fair that you parade around me all naked and pretty like that when I've got to get up and moving."

She responds by giving her tush a cute little shake. "Hey, you had me last night. That should hold you over."

"Nothing can hold me over," I tell her, laying it on so thick that she rolls her eyes and laughs. "I can never get enough of you, baby."

"Well, go take care of Miss Cassidy and then come home to me. Maybe I'll have a present waiting for you when you get here."

"Maybe? Maybe you'll have a present? That's not much incentive, really."

"Pack a bag, whiner," she orders, then steps into the shower.

I, of course, do as I'm told.

Two hours later, she's dropping me off at the airport, my boarding pass printout to Raleigh-Durham, North Carolina, gripped in my hot little hand. The routine has become old hat to us, as it happens two or three times a month on average, and we've become quite efficient. She pops the trunk, and we meet at the back of the car where she kisses me tenderly on the mouth, hugs me tightly, and tells me to call when I land. Then she's off to the office to start on her research, and I'm off to a hotel room in the South, wondering how long it will take me to locate Rebecca Cassidy and what kind of help she needs from me.

CHAPTER TWO

The first time it happened, I was fifteen. I woke up one morning and there was a small notebook on my nightstand that hadn't been there when I went to bed. It was opened to a sheet of paper. In my handwriting, the note said, "Janine Barber, Poughkeepsie, NY." The name was vaguely familiar, and I lived in Poughkeepsie at the time, so I was nothing more than mildly confused by my inability to remember writing it. I have learned since, that as we get older, we forget things constantly, so I suspect that's why it began when I was young. Otherwise, I might have simply considered myself scatterbrained and never thought about Janine Barber again. As it turned out, hers is a name I will never, ever forget.

First things first. You really need to know a few things about me. My name is Norah Ellison and I'm thirty-one years old. I grew up in Poughkeepsie and my family is, to put it bluntly, filthy stinking rich. I'm not exactly certain how my father and grandfather made their fortunes, but I suspect it wasn't all on the up-and-up, which is a big part of why I do what I do. I am not close to my parents. My father isn't a warm and fuzzy guy, and his acquaintances are questionable, as is the way he bends things to his will. My mother was a sweet woman once, I believe, but I think she's had to look the other way when it comes to my father on so many occasions, her gaze has ended up permanently focused on the bottom of whatever bottle she's drinking from. I still worry about her, but you can't force help on those who don't want it, can you? My big brother, Porter, is following in my father's footsteps, which I suppose was to be expected, given that he's the eldest son of the eldest son. It will forever disappoint me because I've always wanted to believe that Porter is a better man, but maybe I'm wrong. I just don't know any more.

When I turned twenty-one, I gained access to my trust fund and my inheritance from my grandparents so, like my family, I am also filthy stinking rich. But gaining access to all that money also gave me something I'd been waiting for since Janine Barber's name showed up on my nightstand: freedom. I took my money and moved upstate, knowing my parents would have no desire to visit me there. Upstate? I might as well have moved to the slums! All visitation would be my responsibility, just the way I wanted it. That's when I began Balance, Inc.

But I'm getting ahead of myself.

Let me get back to Janine Barber because she's the starting point. After her name appeared on my nightstand, and after I puzzled over it for a morning or so, I forgot all about her...until a week later when I happened to be walking by my father's study and my stride was slowed by the sound of heated voices from behind the closed doors. I stood there with my popcorn and Diet Coke in hand and eavesdropped like any teenager: without a shred of guilt.

"She's a nobody, Dad," I heard Porter say. "She's only at our school because her mom's in administration so her tuition's free. She's white trash."

"White trash can make just as much noise as anybody else, Porter. Sometimes more."

"Don't worry. It's her word against mine."

My father's voice became hard as granite, a tone that told you if you took one more step, you'd cross the line with him. "You're not listening to me, son. I have no intention of seeing my name dragged through the mud because you couldn't take no for an answer."

Porter started to speak, but was cut off mid-word, and I could absolutely envision my father holding up a hand and, with one glare from his ice blue eyes, killing Porter's voice before it even left his mouth.

"There is one language that trash speaks better than most other people...the language of money. I will handle this problem, Porter, but mark my words. This is the last time I clean up your mess for you. Next time, you'll be on your own. Are we clear?"

"Yes, sir."

"Good. Now. Do you know her father's name?"

"Bill, I think. Bill Barber. He works in a factory or something."

"Good. Good. I'll take it from here. You do nothing. And I mean *nothing*. Keep your mouth shut, your pants zipped, and stay away from the girl. Understood?"

"Yes, sir."

Porter's voice was suddenly closer, so I knew he was approaching the door. I scooted up the stairs and into my room before I was seen. Once there, I lay on my bed, staring at the notebook paper. Janine Barber. Bill Barber. It couldn't be a coincidence, could it?

It didn't take me longer than a day or two to figure out exactly who Janine Barber was. Solving the mystery of what had happened to her was even easier, judging by the way she carried herself through the halls of school, her arms wrapped tightly around her books, her books held in front of her chest like body armor, her head down, her pace rapid. Her auburn hair was stringy, her clothes so baggy they must have been three sizes too big. The whispers and snickers as she passed were so obvious, they might as well have been shouts and finger pointing.

I watched her scurry past my locker one morning and felt a pang of sympathy for her. My friend Amy was standing next to me and gave a snort before I could say anything. "She's such a loser. She should consider herself lucky to have been with somebody like your brother instead of crying about it."

And I knew. Just like that, I knew exactly what had happened.

I was a smart fifteen-year-old; I could add two and two, and if I knew anything for sure, it was how my brother operated. He saw, he desired, he took. Simple and base and completely justified as far as he was concerned. After all, he was an Ellison and Ellisons got what they wanted. Always.

My gaze stayed on Janine Barber's back, and I felt ill as she hurried down the hall, her shoulders hunched like some sort of shell, as if she were trying to shield herself from the gossip, the stares, the blame.

Three days later, she was dead, having slit her wrists in the bathtub.

Her name still stared out at me from the notebook paper, but this time, it felt less like a mystery and more like an accusation. I felt like I hadn't paid enough attention. That guilt haunts me to this day. Janine Barber. I wonder if I could have saved her. I wonder if I was supposed to. I wonder if I failed my first test. I still do. Every day, I wonder.

It was three months later, and I had turned sixteen before the second name showed up on the nightstand. Megan Stevenson, Poughkeepsie, NY.

Again, a vaguely familiar name, but one I couldn't place, and I became a little frantic, wondering if Megan Stevenson had been raped by my brother and was about to down a bottle of sleeping pills. I had no idea where to start, and it frustrated the crap out of me.

Let me pause to add this little factoid about myself: I love books and always have, since as far back as I can remember. I still have my original copies of *Green Eggs and Ham* and *The Velveteen Rabbit* on a shelf in my bedroom. This is important because in the early 1990s when I was a teenager, the best way to surround myself with books was to get a job, much to my father's dismay, at the local library. And in the library, in addition to books, there was a computer system. It was new and slow and a behemoth compared to today's models, but it stored the names and addresses of everybody in Poughkeepsie who had a library card. Megan Stevenson turned out to be one of them.

I had her name. I had her address. I had no idea what I was supposed to do with either of them.

I decided to take a walk by her house which wasn't all that far from the library. What I would do once I got there was anybody's guess, but I headed out one afternoon after school. The house was modest, but neat and tidy, a small Cape Cod with yellow siding and a deep green front door. I strolled up the street on the opposite side, watching, not a clue what the hell I was supposed to do now that I found Megan's home. I continued to pace up and down for the next half hour, wondering how much longer it would be before a concerned neighbor called the police to report an apparently disoriented teenage girl wandering the neighborhood.

It's a good thing I gave up when I did. Frustrated, I was heading around the corner back toward the library when I heard voices on the other side of the hedges that ran along the sidewalk. Kids' voices.

"But…it's mine," a small, female voice said, shaking.

"Well, it's mine now." This one was male, still a kid, but older.

"No." The girl's tears were apparent in her tone. "Give me my bike."

"I told you." Sneered. "It's mine now. Go home to your mommy and tell her you lost it. And if you rat me out, I'll sneak into your house while you're sleeping, and I'll kill your cat. Got it?"

The girl's gasp told me she was as horrified as I was, and I stepped around the hedges to put a stop to the harassment.

I recognized Megan Stevenson immediately. Her name had rung a bell because her mother had been my English teacher the previous year. She'd brought Megan to school with her for Bring

Your Daughter to Work Day. She was about nine years old and was sitting on her butt, her knee skinned and her face tearstained. Her red hair was bowl cut and the sprinkling of freckles across her nose made her look more like a rag doll than the tomboy she was. A large boy stood over her, his hands clutching the handlebars of a very sleek-looking electric-blue bicycle with blindingly shiny chrome and thick tires. He was dirty and mean looking and had to be at least three years older than Megan, if not more. He jumped when he saw me, which gave me a little tickle of satisfaction.

"What is going on here?" I asked, trying to sound menacing. I had suffered a growth spurt that year and had already reached my current height of five-seven, so I towered over him.

"I was just taking my bike home, ma'am," the boy said. *Ma'am? Wow, he's good*, I thought, watching his face as he thought up a story.

"No!" Megan jumped up. "That's *my* bike."

"This?" the kid said, stretching his arms to their full length as if examining the bike for the first time. "No, this is mine. I mean, look at it. Does this look like a little girl's bike?" He posed the question to me, and I narrowed my eyes at him. It certainly *didn't* look like a little girl's bike. He was right about that.

"It's *mine*." Megan started crying, which she tried to hold in, judging by the look of embarrassment that crossed her face and the angry way she swiped at her own tears.

"Well, why don't we walk around the corner to Megan's house and ask her parents if this is hers? Okay?"

The first cracks in the bully's veneer started to show then, and I knew I had him. "Oh, no. I don't have the time to do that. I was supposed to be home by now. My mom isn't going to be happy with me if I'm any later." He started to turn the bike and wheel it toward the sidewalk.

"My name!" Megan said with a gasp. The bully whipped his head around and glared at her.

"What?" I asked.

"My name. It's written in Sharpie on the bottom of the seat. My daddy did it in case I ever lost it."

I raised one eyebrow and stepped toward the bike. The bully swallowed audibly, and I managed to stifle a chuckle. A quick duck and I saw it, clear as day. "Megan Stevenson" in big, black letters. I could tell by his breathing that the kid wanted to make a run for it, but I grabbed him by the front of his shirt.

"Megan, take your bike and wait right here for a minute. This young man and I are going to have a little discussion." I hauled him out of Megan's earshot, enjoying the fear I could smell on him. There is something about a bully terrorizing somebody younger or less powerful that just makes my blood boil, even back then. I yanked him up onto his tiptoes and brought my face down to his. When I spoke, it was a low growl through gritted teeth.

"You'd better hope I never catch you messing with her again, you understand me?"

He nodded vigorously, his brown eyes wide.

"I don't want to catch you messing with *anybody*. Any. Body. Because if I do?" I pulled him closer and changed my voice to a hissing whisper. "I'll sneak into *your* house while *you're* sleeping, and I will cut off your tiny little dick and feed it to you. Got it?"

The strangled whimper he made while he nodded some more gave me what I can only call a perverse sense of satisfaction. When I let him go, he ran at the speed of light. I never saw him again. I don't think Megan did either. Neither of us ever even knew his name.

After that, I at least had an inkling of what the names might mean. And when I realized that Megan's situation was *not* life or death, the relief I felt was palpable. It took half a dozen more before I was clear on the fact that they were all people who needed some kind of intervention, and that they weren't going to stop showing up on my nightstand. Sometimes, I'll get two names in a week. Sometimes, months will go by with nothing. I don't know where the names come from. I don't know why or how they come to me. All I do know is that I was put on this earth to help. I was given more money than I know what to do with so I can help. The only way I feel I can undo some of the bad things my family has done is to help.

So, I help.

CHAPTER THREE

After an unavoidable three-hour layover in JFK, my plane lands uneventfully, thank goodness, and I pick up my rental car not long afterward. The Raleigh-Durham airport is small by airport standards, and I've been in the area on three other cases, so finding my way around will be easier than it would be if it was my first visit—which is not to say that it'll be easy. Durham is a fairly large sprawling city. If New York City is a clump of peanut butter on the middle of a piece of bread, then Durham is a thin layer of it, spread over the entire slice. The streets weave in all different directions, change names in the middle, and are confusing as hell. You can be going east one minute and then suddenly, you're going south on the same street. It's kind of ridiculous, and a good map is a necessity. Having grown used to the compact downtown and distinct suburbs of my adopted city of Rochester, New York, driving around such a spread-out area as Durham seems to take forever, but I'll manage.

The Hilton Garden Inn is in the southern part of Durham, across the street from the Southpoint Mall, which has anything I could possibly want or need during my stay. This will be my headquarters for the duration, unless I'm told Rebecca Cassidy lives way the hell on the other end of town. Then I may have to consider a change of location for the sake of convenience.

I check into a nice, generic room, drop my stuff, and hit Speed Dial 1 on my cell.

"Arrive in one piece?" Hayley asks, and I can envision her sitting at the desk in her office off the back end of our house. The windows look out onto the woods in the backyard—we back up to a county park—and she'll be gazing out at the numerous bird feeders she's hung from various trees. It's still only March, and though the snow is gone, it's chilly. The bird population consists of only winter birds yet—blue jays, cardinals, sparrows, and Hayley's favorites, chickadees. My heart constricts as I'm hit with a wave of missing her.

"I did. Uneventful flight."

"Always a good thing."

"What have you got for me?"

"Interesting stuff." I hear papers sliding around on her desk as she lines up her information. "I had to call on Officer Jefferson from the Raleigh police department. Remember her?"

My brain does a quick memory search and I vaguely recall a female cop a couple years earlier whose partner was in up to his eyeballs with the local drug dealers. Tricky case, but everybody came out intact. "I do."

"Well, I needed her help because I couldn't find an address for Rebecca Cassidy. Seems she's had four of them in the past two years, along with six phone number changes, and then went invisible. The only thing Jefferson could give me was a post office box. I've got Megan on it now. I'll call you as soon as I hear from her, which should be any time now."

"Four different addresses in two years?"

"Yup. You thinking what I'm thinking?" Hayley asks.

"Stalker."

"Bingo. Listen to this: Jefferson's got seven police reports and two restraining orders that Rebecca filed in the space of twenty-six months. Guy's name is Todd Bennett. He violated the first restraining order and went to jail for three months. Came out, found her; she filed a report, then another TRO; he violated that, went to jail again for six months. Now he's out again. No current address, but Megan's on it."

"When did he get out?" I'm jotting down notes as she talks.

"Looks like late December." She's quiet for a second or two. "What are the chances he gave up?"

"Slim to none. More likely, *she* thinks she got away from him this time."

"Ugh. Poor thing."

I release a breath loudly. I hate stalker cases. They're unpredictable and rarely end well. Cops—male cops especially—don't understand that a man can intimidate a woman, can scare the bejesus out of her, without actually breaking the restraining order. He doesn't have to be closer than five hundred feet to terrify his victim. I'm hoping maybe this case will be different, but I've got a bad feeling already. "All right. Send me pictures of both, so I'll know them when I see them. Let me get settled in and get something to eat, and you give me a shout as soon as you hear from Megan, okay?"

"Will do. Talk to you soon. Love you." Hayley's voice softens on that last note, and I pretend I'm bathing in the light of those green eyes instead of standing in a hotel room alone.

"Love you, too."

There's not a lot I can do before Megan comes up with an address. I know you're wondering right now if I'm talking about the same Megan. I am. Megan Stevenson went on to MIT, if you can believe that, and is frighteningly smart. I think she was one of twenty-six women in her graduating class, and I don't even know what her degree was in. She's some kind of engineer that works with computers and math theorems and other numerical things that make my head hurt. All I know is she can find just about any piece of information on any person with nothing more than a few keystrokes. She lives in Manhattan and is an independent consultant for half a dozen Fortune 500 companies. I keep her on retainer for when I need something like today. Finding Rebecca Cassidy's current address will take Megan all of ten minutes, I'm sure.

In the meantime, my BlackBerry buzzes, and I pull up the pictures Hayley sent of Rebecca Cassidy and Todd Bennett. Both are standard DMV photos, and both faces are somewhat unremarkable, which can be said about most people in general. Rebecca is a strawberry blonde with a plump, round face and kind, gentle green eyes. With thinning brown hair and round, wire-rimmed glasses that shield startlingly blue eyes, Todd looks like any guy I might run into in Home Depot. Sometimes that makes cases like this even harder: everybody looks so freaking *normal*.

I sigh at the same time my stomach rumbles. I really need to eat. My hotel is near a plaza that has a Chili's, so I call over and order myself some food to go. Their nachos are so loaded down with cheese that they're really just a heart attack on a plate, but I can't resist the melty, stringy, greasy goodness of it. I go for the comfort food when I'm away from Hayley. I won't tell her, of course. She'd scold me, then make me eat nothing but salad for a week.

Hayley.

It scares me sometimes how much I miss her when I'm away. I still can't figure out if that's a sweet thing or an enormous weakness. And as usual when I dwell on my feelings for her, my mind reverts to five years ago.

Hayley Ryan Grafton was born Anna Elizabeth Ryan in a small suburb outside of Cleveland in 1979. She was the only child of Donna and Ken Ryan, who had tried throughout their entire marriage to have children and weren't blessed with their daughter until Donna was in her mid-forties. Anna was a good baby, quiet and easy. She remained that way throughout her childhood and into her teen years when she studied hard, played on the volleyball team, and graduated fourth in her class. She went to college at Marietta, but dropped out in the middle of her senior year after losing her father to colon cancer. Less than a year later, her mother died of a massive coronary, and Anna found herself all alone, with no family at all, at twenty-two years old.

Being suddenly solitary can do weird things to your head, and I firmly believe that's why Anna fell for Brant Collier. Of course, there was also his ability to be devastatingly charming, a characteristic he used to his advantage, one that he could turn on and off as it suited him. He won Anna over completely before the first time he hit her, so much so that she was utterly shocked and ran through the catalogs of her mind to figure out where she had screwed up so badly to deserve a black eye and split lip. Surely, it was her fault; Brant was a great guy, *a cop*, for Christ's sake. He was sworn to serve and protect. She must have done something horrible for him to sock her one.

It's a path of warped logic that has become all too familiar to me since I started this mission of mine. You'd be surprised how many very intelligent women are victims of abuse by their husbands, boyfriends, or partners. It's staggering the kinds of games that can be played with your mind in order to make you feel small and worthless. Anna was far from stupid, and she didn't come close to naïve, but she was with Brant for nearly three years before her name showed up on my night stand. *Three years* being knocked around by a police officer. By that time, she was trapped, broken, and terrified. It's hard for me, even now, to think back on that time and have my mind's eye conjure up the bruises on her lovely face. I have to consciously unclench my jaw and force myself to stop grinding my teeth.

One thing an abuser makes sure to do is keep his victim isolated and that actually worked to my advantage when getting Anna away from him. Because he was a cop, there really were no other options. All I had to do was stake him out for a short period of time and have Megan do a little research on his life, and I had all the information I needed about what kind of obsessed lunatic he kept hidden beneath his blues. He'd never let Anna get away from him, never. He'd hunt her forever, and she'd never be free of him; of that I had no doubt. The fact that

I'd practically fallen in love with her on sight only stoked my creative fires and my desire to rip her out of his possessive grasp.

The right amount of money can buy you just about anything in this country, including a bogus car accident, a doctored death certificate, and a new identity. That's how Anna Elizabeth Ryan died and Hayley Ryan Grafton was born. She said she'd always liked the name Hayley, Sue Grafton is her favorite writer, and she wanted to keep one small piece of her parents with her always. How I managed to win her trust and her heart is another story altogether, and it often leads me to long, internal conversations with myself about things like destiny and greater purpose and if Fate started me on these missions so that I'd meet the love of my life, and blah, blah, blah. It's enough to give me a migraine and has on more than one occasion.

I'm munching on the last bite of my artery-clogging nachos when Hayley calls me back with information from Megan. Nobody ever calls me directly except for Hayley. It might seem a little paranoid, but there are many times during my cases that I'm sort of flying under the radar of the law, and the last thing I want is for any of my contacts to get caught in the crossfire. Anonymity is key to what I do. Most of the people I've helped never see my face and many barely know my name, which is kind of interesting given that any time I've called one of them for their assistance later, like Officer Jefferson, for example, they've never hesitated. The human spirit is amazing that way, more liable to pay it forward than you'd think.

"Rebecca Cassidy lives in the Windy Oaks Apartment Homes. I MapQuested it, and it looks like she's not that far from you." Hayley gives me an address that's only about ten minutes from where I currently am, according to the map I have spread out on the second bed in my room. "Megan found Todd Bennett in another apartment complex about four miles down the street, if you can believe that. Under a false name."

"Terrific. She probably has no idea he's that close."

"Why can't men just take no for an answer?" Hayley asks, and her tone is such that I wonder if she's asking me or simply asking the universe.

"I wish I knew, babe."

"Megan's still working on details of Bennett...financials, employment and such. I'll call you when I hear from her."

"You're the best. I'll set up a stakeout so I can get a lay of the land."

"Did you get dinner?" She changes the subject, her voice moving from employee to wife.

"I did."

"Something decent?"

"I'm full. Does that count?"

She chuckles and it makes me smile. When I first met her—and by "met," I mean "started following"—her smile was completely different than it is now. She smiled often; it was her disguise, the only way to keep people from wondering if something was wrong. But the smile never reached her eyes. It sounds kind of corny, but there is little that depresses me more than the thought of those amazing eyes of hers looking flat, dull, and lifeless. The first time I made her laugh—a true, genuine laugh that crinkled the corners of those eyes—I almost burst with the satisfaction that flooded me. There's nothing more wonderful than the warmth of Hayley's smile.

God, I'm a sap. I know that's what you're thinking, so let me just put it out there for you.

"It doesn't count if it was greasy and more than five hundred calories," she gently scolds.

"Oh. Oops."

"Norah, honestly. What am I going to do with you?"

"Love me forever? It's really the only solution."

She snorts, and I can almost see her shaking her head in exasperation. "Fine. I suppose if I have no other alternatives..."

"You don't. That's the only option." We banter a bit more, then I realize I need to get down to business. Time is often of the essence on my cases, and I never know for sure until I can get an overview of the situation. "Okay, babe, let me get some supplies, and then I'll go stake out Ms. Cassidy and see what I can see."

"I'll call you when I have more. Be careful."

"Always."

CHAPTER FOUR

A stakeout is much less comfortable and way more boring than the cop shows on TV would have you believe. They always show two people, sitting in their car and shooting the shit, drinking cups of coffee, until, as if on cue—and of course, it *is* on cue; it's TV—the person they're staking out suddenly shows up, and they can grab them/follow them/report on them. In reality, it never happens that quickly. Also, the coffee? Yeah, you have to be careful of that because lots of coffee not only gives you the jitters, but makes you have to pee. Not a lot of parking lots are equipped with Port-a-Potties, in my experience. And stakeouts at night are the worst because sitting there in the dark with nothing to do but stare at somebody's door is a good way to bring on the drowsies.

Hard candy helps a lot. If I suck on a vibrant, punchy flavor like lemon or pineapple or mint, it helps keep me from feeling sleepy. I keep a stash with me; Life Savers are my current favorite. Given how much I can go through, I went sugar-free a while ago, afraid I'd rot out my teeth.

Rebecca Cassidy's development is nice, as most of them are around here. From what I learned during my last stay, the Raleigh-Durham area of North Carolina is one of the fastest-growing sections of the country, and in order to handle the influx of people from out of town—or more accurately, out of state—there has been a high percentage of new rentals built. When you move from one state to another, you don't know the area, you don't know the market, and buying a house blind is a risky prospect. So, most people choose to rent for a while until they get a feel for the place. I flash back to Hayley's telling me that Rebecca has had four different addresses in less than two years, and I wonder how much money she's spent buying her way out of her leases. Even a six-month lease will cost you bunches of money if you break it.

I coast gently into her parking lot, slowing way down for the damn speed humps that seem to be everywhere in this town, and find number 612. I continue on by, paying close attention to the other cars in the lot, as well as to any people walking around. It's not quite dark yet and the mild weather has pedestrians out in droves, walking their toddlers, their dogs, and themselves. I did a GoogleEarth search on my laptop before I came, and I saw that Windy Oaks is laid out in a horseshoe shape, with the clubhouse and community pool nestled in the curve. Beyond that—and on the other side of a chain link fence—is a small office park, which is sort of also in the curve of the horseshoe, but farther up. The office park is notable because it allows me to cruise into that parking lot and see the backs of the apartment homes. Each two-story unit looks to have a sliding glass door and a small concrete patio off the back. Off each patio is a door that I assume is for outdoor storage. Unfortunately, that outdoor storage is only one story high and has a nice flat roof that would make an easy step for anybody who wanted to break into a second-floor window. If Todd Bennett wants in to Rebecca Cassidy's home, it won't be hard. I continue to coast through the lot, weighing the pros and cons of staking out the front versus the back.

At the little pavilion that houses the apartments' mailboxes, I get a glimpse of a familiar shade of strawberry blonde hair. I slip my rental car inconspicuously into a nearby spot so I can watch. Sure enough, when the woman turns to respond to the greeting of somebody near her, I see that it is Rebecca Cassidy. The smile she gives to her neighbor is sweet and kind, but the wariness in her eyes is obvious only to somebody who's looking for it. Somebody like me.

I pretend to be looking through some papers in case anybody notices that my car is unfamiliar, though I'd be surprised if that happened. Because of the comings and goings I mentioned earlier, the turnover in places like this is pretty high, and many people aren't around long enough to recognize those living in the same building. I watch peripherally as Rebecca slides her key into her mailbox and retrieves the contents. She must be feeling secure since she's getting mail here at her apartment complex, rather than at the PO box Hayley mentioned. As I subtly keep watch, Rebecca's pale brows knit together as she studies one piece, then slices the plain white envelope open with a finger. Her face drains of color before my eyes, and her head snaps up, her gaze darting around, landing on me for an extra second, then scanning the rest of the vicinity. She crumples the paper and throws it angrily into the garbage can that's tucked into the corner of the little pavilion. With quick, staccato steps—her head up and continuing to scan—she heads back toward her apartment as fast as she can go without actually running.

I watch in my mirrors until she turns the corner, and I notice nobody following her. When she's completely out of my sight, I exit my car and pull the crumpled paper from the garbage. It's simple, plain white notebook paper, and the message is written in letters cut out of newspapers or magazines, so cliché that I roll my eyes. The message itself, though, sends a chill up my spine:

See you soon.

No wonder she freaked. Like any stalker worth his salt, Todd Bennett probably lets Rebecca settle into her new place. He probably leaves her alone for a certain length of time, allows her to drop her guard and maybe even start to feel safe. And once she does…once she starts to think, "Hey, you know, I may finally be okay now," *that* is when he strikes, effectively tearing down any progress she feels she's made in her life, taking away any confidence in her own safety, making it clear to her that she can never, ever get away from him. It's brutal and it's cruel and it does the job.

Have I mentioned how much I hate stalker cases?

I pull out and drive back around to where Rebecca's front door is, passing just in time to see her enter. The parking lot is lined with units on both sides, cars parked facing the doors, and I decide that it's too open for me to park and sit here. Somebody could notice. All it takes is one neighborhood busybody to find my car suspicious, and I could waste precious time talking my way out of a police inquiry. No, the office lot overlooking the back is going to be a much better place for my stakeout, and I've worked enough of these cases to understand that Todd Bennett will probably feel the same way.

I noticed during my first drive-through of the office parking area that there are two CPA firms in the building, and I thank my lucky stars. That means, of course, that there will be people working late, which means cars will remain in the lot after hours, which means I won't look so conspicuous sitting there all alone. It's a hard decision, but I finally find a spot two rows back from where I'd park if I wanted to look directly onto the back of Rebecca's unit. I do this because I have the sneaking suspicion that Todd Bennett will show up tonight, and this is the most likely place for him to park his stalker ass. Just the idea of the way he'll watch her, spy on her, record her every movement, makes my skin crawl, and I have to take a deep breath and force myself to remain calm, to do things in an orderly fashion, to not let myself get too emotional about it. Hayley's boyfriend stalked her in a way. Yes, they were a couple, but he still kept tabs on her, monitored her every move, approved of or disapproved of any shopping trips she took or time she tried to spend with friends—some of the same things a stalker does—only she'd let him into her life willingly which made it worse for her.

I shift my focus and concentrate on getting a pineapple Life Saver out of the packaging and into my mouth, consciously unclenching my jaw. I tend to tighten it, grind my molars together, whenever I get to thinking about how badly Brant Collier mistreated Hayley. Visions of strangling somebody with your bare hands will do that to you.

Dusk will settle within the next half hour or so, and I hunker down in my seat, feeling less obvious as the light fades and the sky goes from bright blue to soft indigo to near black. I plug in my earpiece and give Hayley a call.

"Are you slouched in your seat in a dark parking lot?" she asks as a greeting.

"Your psychic abilities never cease to amaze me."

"I was just going to call you, babe. How's it going?"

I fill her in on the note and the set-up of the complex.

"Wow," she says when I finish. "Some pretty amazing timing on her name showing up, huh?"

"I'll say. I wish the Fates or the Universe or whatever wouldn't cut it so close." It's happened before, the name showing up on my nightstand within a day or two of when the person is in desperate need of help. I haven't always been on time.

"Todd Bennett drives a navy blue Ford Ranger pickup."

"Dark, nondescript, perfect for going unnoticed."

"Exactly. Megan says the only record of employment she can find is a part-time job with Time Warner. He barely makes enough money to cover his rent."

"Ugh. That doesn't bode well." I've learned from experience that when a stalker begins to pare down things that need his attention, like work and home, it most likely means he's focusing all that attention on his victim. Not good news for Rebecca Cassidy.

"I thought the same thing." The tone of Hayley's voice has changed, and I can picture the little divot that appears between her eyebrows when she's concerned about something. "Norah, please be careful. I've got a bad feeling about this guy."

"I will, sweetie, I promise." I don't tell her I have the same bad feeling.

After a little flirting and a tongue-in-cheek offer of phone sex to keep me awake, we say our I-love-yous and hang up. I hunker down in my seat once again and wait, my mind drifting to my past cases.

In the years I've been doing…what I do, I've had three other stalker cases, not including Hayley's. I only count one of them a success, the one in which I was able to reason with the stalker and get him to back off with the promise that if he ever harassed his victim again, I'd be back and it would be very, very unpleasant. Luckily, he was a bit of a Poindexter, not at all a tough-ass like most of them. I do keep tabs on him, and he's currently living four states away from his victim and, from what I can tell, he doesn't have a new one. So, he's my Stalker Success Story.

The other two, I don't like to think about, but at times like this, my mind doesn't listen. Kara Bonavilla from Wichita stabbed her stalker to death with a letter opener as he tried to rape her. Thank God she wasn't charged, and it was ruled self-defense, but killing somebody will scar you for life, and I wish I could have spared her that. I could have if I'd shown up three minutes sooner than I did.

Jennifer Meyers was raped and murdered by her stalker twenty-four hours after her name showed up on my nightstand. I took the first flight the next morning, got lost in downtown Houston, and by the time I arrived at her apartment, the police were already there, wheeling her out in a body bag. I threw up in the bushes when I realized I'd failed. I was inconsolable. It was my first mark in the loss column since Janine Barber, and I did not handle it well; it still makes me nauseous to think about it. The only upside to the whole thing was that her stalker was caught and is sitting in jail with a life sentence. After that case, I started booking the very next available flight to wherever the note sends me. So far, so good.

Of course, not every one of my cases is life or death, and thank God for that or I'd have gone insane long, long ago. Some of them have had very happy endings, and some have actually been almost fun. There was Pam Easton in Allentown, Pennsylvania. She was a high school senior who needed to be in the top ten of her graduating class in order to get a scholarship, which was the only way she could afford to go to college. She was number eleven when her name appeared on my nightstand. It didn't take long for Megan to help me figure out that the number six guy was hacking the school's computer system and fixing his own grades. Pam ended up number ten of ten and should graduate from college *magna cum laude* next year. Then there was Carla Cavanaugh in Bangor, Maine, single mother of two who'd been laid off. She looked for work for six months and was in danger of being evicted from her apartment with her kids and nothing else. She was well qualified for the jobs for which she'd applied, but her timing was lousy, and she always seemed to be "a day late and a dollar short," as my Uncle Skip used to say. A quick after-hours trip to a particular office that was looking for a receptionist was all it took to move Carla's application and resume to the top of the pile. She was hired three days after my visit and two days before her time ran out on her living arrangements. Melanie Taylor in Atlanta worked in a law firm and was being sexually harassed by one of the lawyers. When she spoke up about it, she was summarily fired, and honestly, had a good case for a lawsuit. Of course, who has the balls, or the money, to sue a lawyer, let alone a firm of them? So Melanie left it alone and went looking for other work, but continued to receive harassing e-mail and phone calls from the lawyer, so much so that she began to worry about her career and whether she'd be able to find another job in the field, never mind find relief from the constant pestering. That's when I received her name. A well-placed phone call to a friend of my father's at the Georgia State Bar, along with copies of the threatening e-mails the lawyer had been stupid enough to send, was all it took to put an end to that. Last time I checked, the lawyer was under investigation and in danger of being disbarred, and Melanie happily had a lucrative new job with a much bigger, much more successful firm.

So, see? It's not all bad. It's not all life or death, and there are bright spots amid the darker times. Like I said, not every case is a stalker case.

I pop another Life Saver into my mouth and notice Rebecca's second floor light come on; it's the only window I can see from my vantage point. A glance at my BlackBerry tells me it's nearing nine o'clock. I know Todd will be showing up soon; I can feel it in my gut. That's the thing about stalkers—I've learned this from experience—they think they're in the right. They think what they're doing is perfectly okay, and that it's ridiculous for somebody to call them a stalker. They're insulted by that term. The constant e-mails, nonstop phone calls, demands of time and acknowledgment, picture-taking that isn't consented to, following on foot or by car, they think all that is perfectly acceptable, and they don't understand why they creep people out. They don't get that what they're doing is wrong on so many levels. They can't wrap their brains around the fact that the object of their desire has *no interest* in them, and that they need to just back the hell off.

Sorry. I tend to get a little emotional about this subject. After all I've seen, I don't care if it's some kind of sickness that needs to be treated; I don't care if therapy could possibly help. I see these men—and they are, overwhelmingly, men—as pimples on the face of society. They need to be squeezed out and gotten rid of. I know, I know. There are laws in place for this sort of thing, and you think maybe I'm being a bit harsh. But you know what I've found doing what I do? That a stalker doesn't give a shit about laws. He doesn't care that he's breaking them, that he's got no right to each and every minute detail of his victim's life. *He does not care.* His focus is on one thing and one thing only: her.

And he will stop at nothing until he possesses her, or kills her so nobody else can.

I sigh, irritated at my train of thought. Just as I'm trying to come up with something else to occupy my brain, a dark pickup pulls quietly and slowly into a parking spot exactly where I predicted, two rows up, right where he can watch the back of Rebecca's townhouse. Point for me.

I'm slouched down enough where I'm pretty sure he won't see me. Not that he's interested in his surroundings. He's all about Rebecca. By looking at him through *my* binoculars, I can see that he's looking through *his*, focused on the bedroom window. I smile when the mini blinds flip closed. Because my spot is a bit raised, I'm looking slightly down on him and I can see that he's jotting notes. I don't like that at all—notes usually signify plans—but there's not a lot I can do right now other than watch him and make sure he doesn't make any moves beyond spying.

It's going to be a long night.

CHAPTER FIVE

Turns out Todd Bennett isn't nearly as adept at stakeouts as I am because by four-thirty in the morning, he's sound asleep in his truck. I can tell by the angle of his head, which is tipped backwards against the seat's headrest, as well as by the fact that, using my binoculars, I can see his wide-open mouth in the truck's side mirror. I give a little fist pump of thanks for the golden opportunity. I suspect Rebecca will be getting up for work before long, and I don't know what kind of time Todd normally spends ogling, but I assume he'd want to bail before the day's employees begin populating this parking lot. But I've got to get to his place and see what I'm dealing with in order to plot a course of action. I need to know where his mind's at, where he is on the danger scale.

I reach into my knapsack where I've stashed the supplies I purchased earlier, and I pull out the brand new hunting knife, still in its leather sheath. The polished pear-wood handle is cool and smooth, and my fingers slip into the grooves as if the damn thing was made for my hand. The four-inch, stainless-steel blade gleams in the dim light of the parking lot, and for a moment, I'm mesmerized by it.

No, I'm not going to kill him. What kind of person do you think I am?

I slip out of my car as quietly as I can, not closing the door all the way to avoid any noise, and I slither along the asphalt like a reptile, staying low and out of sight. My gaze is riveted to the back window of the truck, looking for any sign of movement, but there is none. Todd Bennett is out like a light.

He'll be in for a treat when he does wake up. The blade of my knife pushes through the sidewall of Todd's rear tire like a shark fin through water, silently and effectively. I give the other rear tire the same treatment, as I want to keep him here longer than a quick change, and I'm betting he doesn't have *two* spare tires.

Back in my rented Toyota, I leave the headlights off, start up, and pull out. Seeing no movement, I assume Todd Bennett is a heavy sleeper. I grab my notebook, look up his address, and head that way.

Todd's complex is owned by the same management company as Rebecca's, and they look weirdly similar. The difference looks to be that Todd's is mostly apartments rather than townhomes, so the buildings are three story and have small balconies with white railings. The lot is quiet, but well lit, which makes me a little nervous. I find his unit, then cruise back out and park my car down the street, returning on foot with a small pack over my shoulder.

The Universe is smiling on me for a change—it often doesn't when I'm on a case. Todd's apartment is on the ground floor, and his lock is a cheap piece of crap that I pick open in about fifteen seconds. I scoot inside, unsurprised to find no dog and no alarm system. Stalkers are kind of stupid that way. Their focus is so intent on their victim that they fail to think about protecting themselves. I guess that's a good thing.

As I stand still and allow my eyes to adjust to the darkness, the first thought to hit me is that it smells like a single man lives here. Sweat and pizza and unwashed socks are the main players in the aroma, reminding me of what Porter's room smelled like when we were teenagers. I think about how women smell so much better, and my sense memory reminds me of the peaches-and-cream scent of Hayley's hair. With a quiet sigh, I extract a small Maglite from my pack, click it on, and wave it discreetly around the tiny apartment.

My blood runs cold.

There's very little furniture; an old, beat-up recliner in front of a modest television set sits in the middle of the living room. Next to it is a cheap, pressboard TV tray with a dirty paper plate and three empty beer bottles. The white wall the chair faces is papered—literally *papered*—with pictures of Rebecca Cassidy. None of them show her posing or smiling at the camera, so it's glaringly obvious to me that they were taken without her knowledge. Many of them are grainy, telling me they were shot with a telephoto lens of some kind. The beam from the flashlight confirms my suspicions as it illuminates the rickety table standing below the pictures. Various lenses and camera equipment litter the surface. My stomach rolls sourly as I scan the photos again, notice the variety of locations, of activities. Walking, riding her bike, in her car, at a restaurant, in the grocery store, on a beach, everywhere. I notice the changes in her hair style and the maturing of her face and comprehend with a sick, sinking feeling that he's been following her, photographing her, for years. *Years.* It was probably years before she even realized it, before she got scared and called the cops and filed the restraining orders. I wonder how long he followed her before he actually made contact, because it's the contact that brought in the police; I have no doubt about that. I wonder if he's kicking himself now, if he's angry for not being able to resist.

I make my way through the rest of the apartment, and my question is answered when I get to the bedroom.

The room resembles the Spartan style of the living room, with only a double mattress on the floor, draped with rumpled, probably unwashed, sheets. A trail of wrinkled clothes leads, like Hansel and Gretel's breadcrumbs, to an overflowing laundry basket in the corner.

The walls are bare; I scan each of them with my flashlight and notice the closet door is ajar. When I open it, I'm stunned.

Inside is covered with images of Rebecca—side walls, rear wall, back of the door—but these are different. This is where the anger lives, hidden away in the closet where only Todd Bennett can access it.

There is red everywhere. Across her face in many of the photos, livid red slashes slicing her image. Her eyes are gouged out of several, literally gouged, as if he used his fingernails to do it. A handful of them are torn, ripped or lacerated, and I have a sudden vision of him standing here with a knife, hacking at them, hacking at her, his anger and emotions completely out of his control.

I remember Hayley's phone call. She told me that there were seven police reports filed by Rebecca in addition to the restraining orders. Until yesterday, she probably didn't know Todd had found her again. Since no police showed up, I can only assume she hasn't called them yet…she might be in shock or completely freaked out. Without her report, they have no way of knowing that he's not only up to his old tricks, but also dangerously close to going off the deep end. I wonder how long it was, after his release from prison the last time, before he took a knife and a red marker to the walls of this closet. I wonder how long it will be before he plans to kill her. I wonder if he's planned it already.

I wonder because that's the next step. It's always the next step. I've worked enough of these cases to understand that. My brain tosses me an image of a black body bag, zipped up tight, anonymous, though I know Jennifer Meyers is inside. The spectrum of stalker mentality always ends there: with a death. "If I can't have her, nobody will." I spend several more minutes looking at the closet, trying not to feel the anger and sickness that seem to have coated me like some foul oil, slick and sticky.

I only know two things for sure: Todd Bennett is a ticking time bomb, and I have to stop him.

CHAPTER SIX

What I've seen continues to make me nauseous even hours after I leave Bennett's apartment, and I'm staring at the ceiling of my hotel room, trying to catch a couple hours of sleep while Rebecca is at work. She works at a lab in Research Triangle Park where, it seems, half the local population works. Megan was able to hack into the security system's computers there, and now she can tell me when Rebecca's ID pass is swiped, letting me know she's safely inside where she is surrounded by people and her stalker isn't able to get to her. My memory sends me continuous flashes of his photos and the sickening red slashes through them. This case has taken a turn down the path I was hoping it wouldn't. I know what has to be done; it's as clear as a full moon on a cloudless night. But I'm not ready to make that call just yet. I have to let things absorb for a while. I have to ruminate, to ponder, to roll it around. I will inevitably come to the same conclusion, but this is the process I must follow. It's the only way to hold on to my sanity, my self-worth, my sense of right and wrong.

I sent Hayley a text on my way back from Bennett's little "art gallery" and told her I was going to try to grab a few hours of shut-eye. She worries about me getting enough sleep when I'm on a case, but I think my adrenaline kicks in and keeps me going. Once I get home, I usually sleep for twelve or fifteen hours straight. She'll give me time to rest, but then she'll call. I hope I'm ready to talk to her by then. I wish she were here now to hold me, to whisper in my ear that everything will be okay... that I'm a good person who does good things for people who can't help themselves...to make love to me, just for a while, just long enough to quiet the thoughts in my head.

But Hayley isn't here. I am alone with my thoughts.

The heavy hotel curtains are pulled tightly closed and the room is dark, but my eyes are wide open, and I turn onto my side and stare at the red numbers of the bedside clock—9:45 a.m. I've been awake for more than twenty-four hours and I sigh, knowing the only way I'll get any sleep is if I give in to the mental churning.

Is there another way?

That is the main question and I have to—I *have* to—explore every option, look at every angle, think of every possibility. It's only right. It's only fair. I am a good person; that's what a good person would do, isn't it?

Seven police reports. Two restraining orders. Two stints in jail. And he still came back. He still found her. He still tracked her. He still stalked her. Visits from the police obviously had little effect. Months in prison have made no difference. I think about his barren apartment, the fact that Hayley said he barely works enough to pay for the roof over his head. I flash on the photographs all over his living space and realize that I don't recall any other items there that might take up his time. There were no books, no magazines; I didn't see a computer. There was no weight equipment, no bike. He has nothing to occupy his time but Rebecca. I don't imagine I have to tell you what bad news that is for her. The newspaper-letter note comes back to me and I suppress a shudder at the creepiness of getting something like that in the mail, no matter how stereotypical of a Lifetime movie it might be. I remember the look on Rebecca's face, the way she turned pale, how her eyes darted around like she was a cornered animal. At that moment, she must have been thinking exactly what I'm thinking now: he will never, ever leave her alone.

I snatch my BlackBerry off the nightstand and send another quick text to Hayley. I need information on Todd Bennett. Specific information. I can't make a decision without it.

I press Send and immediately feel more relaxed. It's my body's way of telling me I've worked out the details, gone over everything I can, everything I need to. It's time to rest. Once Hayley's reply comes, there will be a lot to do.

Sleep claims me.

***

I manage to get almost four hours of rest before my BlackBerry alarm wakes me up at 1:30. Sitting up against the headboard, I scroll through the e-mail that arrived as I slept and see the information I'd asked for from Hayley. Apparently, Todd Bennett has a brother in Seattle and his mother lives in Florida. Doesn't look like he has much contact with either of them. I can't really call what flows through me relief, but it's something along those same lines.

As I sit and think about calling Hayley, the phone rings in my hand and it's her, which spreads a grin across my face. We've always had this weird connection. We can finish each other's sentences, know what the other is thinking, stuff like that.

"Hi, sweetie," I say as a greeting.

"Did you get some sleep?" I can hear the love in her voice, even after so long together, and it grounds me.

"I did. More than a couple hours, even."

"Very good. And did you get my text?" When I hum my positive response, she continues. "Megan couldn't find any records of Todd having taken a flight to see either his mother or his brother, and there's nothing to indicate either of them have been to visit him. There aren't even any recent phone calls. Last time he spoke with his mother was from prison last year."

"Sounds like she got fed up with him."

"Wouldn't you?"

I snort my answer, not mentioning that it's been nearly two months since I last spoke to my own mother.

"So? Are you going to tell me what the deal is?" She knows me so well and, if I'm honest, it's actually almost liberating that she does. I don't have to try to hide things from her because I couldn't even if I wanted to. She can see right through me like I'm some clear stream, and my innermost thoughts and fears are just variously colored stones on the bottom. Fighting her is nothing more than a waste of time and energy, so I don't bother. I tell her all about Todd Bennett's apartment, the pictures, the camera equipment, the lack of anything other than his very basic needs for survival. She listens quietly, not interrupting, taking in the information. "Ugh," she says finally, and hilariously, it's the perfect word. It's exactly how I feel.

"I think we should call Pax." There. I said it. I don't feel any better, but at least it's out in the open.

"I think so too," Hayley says, her voice grave, and again, something like relief floods my system. Hayley doesn't move without thinking. She doesn't make snap decisions or judgments, and she knows how hard it is for me to say the words I just did. "I'll make the call."

"Okay."

"It's all right, Norah." Her voice is softer this time, gentle, soothing. "It's all right. Just think about the balance."

"Okay."

We hang up with her promising to get right back to me with the results of her call. I feel heavy, which is not unexpected, so I drag my ass out of bed and open the curtains. Sunshine pours in on me, warm and peaceful, and I rest my forehead against the cool glass of the window.

Just think about the balance.

I've never really told anybody but Hayley about the names that show up out of the blue in the middle of the night. However, I did sort of gingerly approach the subject with my mother once, when I was in my early twenties and felt I might be getting the hang of the whole weirdness. We spoke in the morning near the holidays when I still visited on a regular basis.

"Mom? Do you believe in God?" We were seated at the dining room table and enjoying the breakfast that was being served by Mrs. James, our cook. I bit into a strawberry as I studied my mother's once-beautiful face and, if she was surprised by such an out-of-the-blue question, she didn't show it.

Her light eyebrows furrowed as she thought, and I was grateful to have this time of the morning with her, all to myself. It was a mere hour or two before she'd indulge in her first cocktail and become unreachable for the rest of the day. I loved that she was seriously contemplating my question. She finally turned her gaze to me, softly blue and intense, eyes that I've been told are exactly like mine.

"I'm not sure about a god, but I believe in the Universe," she said, choosing her words carefully.

"The universe?"

"With a capital *U*. I believe that the Universe has a plan and the Universe makes things happen...or doesn't."

I must have looked puzzled because she went on, speaking slowly, as if trying to come up with the best explanation for me to understand what was in her heart. "When I say 'the Universe,' I guess I mean, the World, or maybe Destiny is a better word. Or Fate. Whatever the correct phrase is, I think the Universe makes sure that the world has balance."

"Balance."

"Yes. Like…a balance of opposites. I think there's a balance of dark and light, a balance of right and wrong, a balance of good and evil. And there are often times when it feels like things are terribly off-kilter, that one side is alarmingly heavier than the other, but then the Universe steps in and corrects the balance." She made a face, part frustration and part question, obviously wondering if I grasped what she was saying.

"And how do you think the Universe corrects the balance when it needs to?" I liked the theory; I liked it a lot. It made some weird kind of sense to me, especially given my lack of explanation for what I was apparently expected to do with my life.

"I don't know for sure, Norah. But I think some things happen for a reason, and I think some people are put on this earth to help maintain the balance. Doesn't it put the smallest bit of clarity on things like natural disasters and murder and execution and birth and death?"

It did. She was right about that. I'd always had a problem with the idea of an all-knowing, all-seeing, all-loving God because I was never able to wrap my brain around the idea of innocent suffering. Yes, I got the concept of faith and free will and humans choosing their paths. I understood that the child molester has free will and chose to abuse the three-year-old, but where does the three-year-old fit in? Is she merely a prop? Why does she have to suffer because the child molester has *chosen* to be a sick son of a bitch? Why do innocent animals die horrible deaths because men *use their free will* to wager on dog fighting? Where does free will come in when we're dealing with terrible illnesses like AIDS or Huntington's or Parkinson's? It has never made any sense to me that a supposedly all-loving God would allow his "creations" to endure such pain or do such awful things to each other.

After that discussion, I began to wonder if I was some "instrument of the Universe," and it was a concept I could actually embrace and be okay about. I like the idea of helping to maintain the balance of things and for the most part, I enjoy it.

But not today.

My phone buzzes and it's Hayley calling me back.

"Pax will be on the next flight." She gives me the flight details and a meeting place, and I jot them down. Pax always sets up these things, and I just go along. I understand why she needs to maintain complete control of every aspect of her situation—so she can be gone in a heartbeat if need be—and I don't argue. I'd do the same thing in her sizable shoes. And in a way, I *am* in her shoes, which freaks me out a little bit.

"Don't worry," Hayley says.

"I'm not."

"Yes, you are. You're not saying much and that means you're stuck inside your head. Don't worry. You're doing the right thing."

"Yeah? According to who?" My tone is bitter, and I don't mean to lash out at Hayley, but who else would understand?

"Well, I can imagine Rebecca Cassidy would agree with me."

That shuts me up because, as usual, Hayley is right.

CHAPTER SEVEN

Pax is one scary bitch, and you can tell that everybody in her path thinks the same thing. They can't move fast enough to get out of her way. As I watch her head in my direction, I can only imagine what kind of picture she made as she lumbered silently through the Raleigh-Durham airport, a modest building full of well-mannered, friendly southerners who wouldn't want to stare, but probably couldn't help it.

I used some very questionable contacts of my father's about six years ago to make my first and only contact with her. She scared the crap out of me then, and I realize that hasn't changed at all as she makes her way to my car in the parking lot of Southpoint Mall near the movie theater. This section of the lot is set away from the rest of the mall, so nobody walking the street of shops can see us, or at least, not clearly. Pax is at least six feet tall, if not taller, with impossibly broad shoulders and the most enormous hands I've ever seen on a woman. Her face is chiseled, all sharp angles, and her smooth skin seems almost out of place. She wears her dark hair very short, and I've never seen her without her leather jacket and Doc Martens. She's literally a walking stereotype, which would make me chuckle if I weren't so busy trying to keep my knees from knocking in terror. I know for a fact that behind the ever-present sunglasses, her eyes are a startling blue; I've only seen them once, but they shocked me speechless, they were so pretty, surrounded by what I can only call very feminine dark lashes. Regardless of the intimidation factor, there is something about her—a hum or an aura or something I can't quite put my finger on—that almost resembles sex appeal, which feels so wrong to me given how she makes her living.

It's just after five o'clock and according to Megan's digging, Todd Bennett actually has to work for a few hours this evening, so I have a reprieve from worrying about Rebecca's safety, at least for a little while. Pax slides effortlessly into the passenger seat of my rental, which should be impossible considering her bulk, but she moves like a cat…a really big, fearsome cat, but a cat just the same.

There's no small talk. She nods a greeting, and I hand over the file I created for her on my laptop in my hotel room and printed in the business center off the lobby. It has all the information she needs about Todd Bennett, Rebecca Cassidy, their history, their addresses, the police reports and restraining orders, any tidbits Megan happened to dig up, all of it. I sit silently and give her time to absorb each piece, which she does very quickly.

"How do you want to play this?" she asks, and I'm just as surprised as I was the first time I heard her voice. She sounds like a woman, like any other woman in the world. I expect her to have a voice that goes with her appearance, something sinister and rough, like gravel in a blender. Instead, she sounds like... well, me.

I outline my plan and give her my thoughts, being completely honest about everything that's been rolling around in my brain for the past four hours. It's one thing to understand and accept what Pax does as a career, but that doesn't mean I can't express my own reservations about likely taking such an irreversible step.

She listens quietly, nodding on occasion, but not interrupting until I finish. Then she surprises me by removing her sunglasses and looking me dead in the eye. Mentally, I squirm and part of me worries that if I look directly at her, I might turn to stone or a pillar of salt or one of those myths.

"Seems like you don't have any other option." Her words are simple, her voice matter-of-fact, but I'm hit with the weirdest sensation that she gets my turmoil, and I don't know quite what to do with that.

"I'm hoping that when we give him the chance, he'll change my mind."

"I guess we'll see." Doubt shades her tone. She grabs the door handle with her huge, powerful mitt and asks, "He works until nine tonight?"

I nod.

"I'll meet you there at eight-thirty. Just come to the door. I'll already be in."

With that, she's gone, and I have never been able to figure out how somebody so big and imposing can just slip away into the ether so fast. I exhale loudly, only now realizing that I'd been taking shallow little breaths to calm my apprehension at being that close to someone so deadly. "Jesus Christ," I mutter and rub at my tired eyes.

I hate stalker cases.

***

"Talk to me." My command to Hayley is gentle, but she understands. I want to feel normal, average, everyday. I just want her to talk about mundane, boring things we share so I can stop dwelling, if only for a moment, on the crazy circumstances that make up my life.

"Hmm. Let me see." I flop back onto my hotel-room bed and picture her, stretched out on our leather sofa in her sock feet, probably under the forest green afghan. "I found a squirrel in our squirrel-proof bird feeder today. Or rather, Duncan did."

Duncan is our terrier. We rescued him from the shelter three years ago. He's about eighty pounds of sheer attitude crammed into a twenty-pound body, and we love him fiercely.

"Did the poor squirrel die of heart failure?" I ask, a smile in my tone.

"Luckily, no. I still can't figure out how it happened, but when I unhooked the feeder and lowered it toward the ground, he slipped out and ran away like a shot."

"I'd run, too, if Duncan was on my scent." We laugh together, and I'm starting to feel the slightest bit better. "What else?"

"I made him an appointment with the groomer for next week."

"Thank God. I don't know how he's not walking into walls by now." His wiry hair grows like a weed and flops over his eyes. It's adorable, to say the least, but I suspect there comes a point where the poor dog can't see a damn thing. "What else?" The tension is seeping away from me, like water sliding off my body.

"My dress for the fundraiser came." The lilt in her voice tosses me a vision of the twinkle that is surely sparkling in her eyes. Despite the thousand times I've told her she can absolutely go shopping at any real store she wants, Hayley prefers to shop online. Frankly, I think she likes getting packages in the mail, and she giggles like a little kid when one arrives, so who am I to criticize?

"Which one did you go with?" She showed me her three final choices early last week—a royal blue satin number with puffy shoulders, a black one, sleeveless and sleek, and something in jade green with subtle gold trim. I cross my fingers.

"The black."

"Yes!" I pump a victorious fist in the air. Go ahead and call me simple. I can't help it; black is damn sexy. "And? How does it look?"

"Get your ass home and I'll model it for you. I might even let you take it off me."

Her flirtatious tone relaxes me more, and a little thrill surges through me when I think about the envious looks that will be thrown my way next month. The fundraiser is for a local children's hospital, one with a wing named for me. I have donated millions of dollars to them and will continue to do so as long as I draw breath. The gala event happens once a year in the spring, and it's a who's who of wealthy New Yorkers. Many of them—most of them, really—will be absurdly rich, older, white men who would pay almost any price to have a woman like Hayley on their arm. The fact that she'll be on mine will make most of them gnash their teeth and wonder what I have that they don't. The answer to that question, of course, is her.

"I'm hoping to be home very soon," I say, snapping back to the conversation. "And I will take it off you. With my teeth."

"Promises, promises." We're quiet for several seconds, just basking in one another's presence. When Hayley speaks again, her tone changes with the subject. "I know she freaks you out a little bit, but I'm glad Pax will be there tonight. I don't trust Todd Bennett. He reminds me too much of Brant." I can almost feel the shudder run through her body.

"He's definitely got some screws loose. Honestly, Hayley, his apartment gave me the heebie-jeebies. Obsession is definitely not sexy. It's frightening."

"You're preaching to the choir, babe."

"I know." If anybody understands what it's like to be the sole focus of another person—and not in a good way—it's my Hayley. A glance at the bedside clock tells me it's going on eight. "I'd better get my ass in gear."

"Do you need a pep talk?"

"Never hurts."

"Okay." She takes a theatrical deep breath, and I laugh, loving her with every fiber of my being in that moment. "Buck up, babe. You're a tough-ass. You're way tougher than this guy. He's a creep. He's a menace to Rebecca Cassidy, and you need to convince him that it's in his best interest to *back the hell off*."

I admit, it sounds a little corny, but her tone is hard, and the fact that she's been in Rebecca's shoes makes her that much more credible. I stand, bolster myself, pull my shoulders back, and puff up. Todd Bennett can't see how much he scares me, how intimidating it is to know what he does. I have to be strong and tough and a badass. And Pax will be there if I need her.

I clench my fist and will strength to flow through me. I'm always a little surprised when it does.

"The Universe picked you for a reason," Hayley continues. "Because you can handle it."

That's always her parting line, and it never misses. I feel power surge through me, a certainty that what I'm doing is not only right, but necessary.

"Thanks, babe," I say softly.

"Anytime. Call me later."

"I will."

"I love you, Norah. Be careful. That's an order."

"Yes, ma'am."

***

The door opens before I can even raise my hand to knock, though Pax stays out of view as I slip quickly inside. I'm thankful for me, but not for Rebecca, that people around here don't seem to pay a lot of attention to the comings and goings of their neighbors. When you won't be sticking around, you tend not to reach out to those nearby. Getting to know who lives next door doesn't matter because you're leaving anyway. I've never been to this development before in my life, but now I've broken into this apartment twice in two days, and nobody seems to have noticed.

I haven't really bothered with much of a disguise, but I took a little bit of precaution. I'm not famous by any means, but if you were to do a thorough enough Google search, you could find me. I have no idea how Todd will react to me, and the last thing I want is for him to find my real identity…not that he'd have any idea where I've come from or how or why, but still. I've tucked my blonde hair up into the Seattle Seahawks baseball cap, figuring the least I could do is send him to the wrong coast, and I've got on black-rimmed glasses with slightly tinted lenses. Combined with how dark he keeps his apartment, he probably won't be able to make out a single detail about my face. My clothes are plain and indiscernible, worn jeans and a plain, navy blue sweatshirt with no logo or markings. A glance around the room tells me nothing's changed from the night before.

"How do you want to play this?" Pax asks me, her standard line, and I jump just a bit, having almost forgotten she's here with me. It briefly crosses my mind that I need to have her teach me how to move so quietly and be so unobtrusive. Then I remember that I hope never to have to call her again, and that idea zips right out of my head.

I explain my plan to her. Whether she thinks it's a good one or complete crap on a cracker, I have no idea, as her face remains impassive and her eyes are shaded behind the ever-present sunglasses. How she can see in the darkness of this place, I haven't a clue. She gives one quick nod of her head and positions herself near the door to wait. For the first time, I notice the small duffel bag she has with her, and she sets it near her feet. I look away, not wanting to know anything about the contents or where they came from, since I'm relatively sure they're things she wouldn't have been able to get on the plane. My stomach rebels, and I try to remind myself of what Todd Bennett has put Rebecca Cassidy through over the past years. Taking my position in the bedroom, I open the closet door to help that reminder along. I'm assaulted once again by the insanity of the photos, and I have to tear my eyes away. I lean against a nearby wall and try to mimic Pax's patient silence.

Thank God I don't have to wait long or I very well may have pulled out my own hair from the nervous anticipation, but I'm saved when I hear a key in the door. There's a brief scuffling sound, almost like the shuffling of feet, a thump, and a groan. I hear them approaching the bedroom, and I quickly flash back to my college drama class, when my teacher, Professor Zeigler, taught us to grab from our own experiences in order to get ourselves into the right mood for a scene. My mind unspools a film reel of every wronged, mistreated woman I've ever dealt with and shows them all to me in quick succession. I can almost feel myself hardening as my fists clench at my side and my jaw muscles tighten. I snap my head to one side, then the other, and hear cracks come from my vertebrae, a release of tension, and suddenly I feel every bit the tough-ass Hayley said I am, every bit the savior Rebecca needs me to be.

It's hard for me to describe how this persona comes over me. I don't often have to deal face-to-face with the people I handle for my clients. As I've explained to you, a lot of what I do consists of strategically placed phone calls, covert B-and-E's, making sure somebody is in the right place at the right time. It's not a lot of person-to-person interaction. Only in the extreme cases like Hayley's or like this one. And when it comes down to it, somehow, I manage to find the power I need to change into somebody that I'm really...not.

Or maybe I'm completely full of shit, in complete denial, and this is *exactly* who I am.

Todd Bennett is dropped to his knees at my feet. His bottom lip is bloody, his hands are cuffed behind his back, and Pax has a thin strap around his neck that she's holding tightly from behind him, like he's her dog and she's the abusive owner.

"Good evening, Mr. Bennett," I say, and my voice is as steady as if Todd and I are two old business associates meeting for drinks.

His eyes dart around the room, seeing the open closet with its light on, and I'm sure he's trying to put the pieces together. The truth is, though, he has no freaking clue who I am, and I like it that way.

"I'll get right to the point, Mr. Bennett, because you're looking a little...peaked. You and I have a common acquaintance." With that, I give a Vanna-White-like sweep of my arm toward the closet. "Ms. Cassidy."

His eyes widen ever so slightly before he catches himself. "I...I don't understand," he croaks.

"Of course you don't. That's because you're a psychotic prick who can't get a date without stalking one."

That hit a nerve, and his eyes narrow at me. His upper lip crinkles just a bit, but it's enough to give me a glimpse of the real man inside. I can absolutely see that he *is* psychotic, and there is not a doubt in my mind he will kill Rebecca sooner or later. In this moment, seeing that glimmer, I already know where this is going to go, but I have to make sure to examine all angles.

"You and I both know that you've been stalking Ms. Cassidy for years. I know you've gone to prison and that it apparently had no effect on you. I've seen the police reports. I've seen the look on her face when you send her one of your little love notes. And you know what, Mr. Bennett? It's going to stop. Right here. Right now. Enough. You are not to contact her again. You are not to call her answering machine or her cell phone or her number at work. You are not to mail her anything. You are not to park behind her townhouse and spy on her all night."

He's looking a little freaked right now, probably because I've listed all his covert ops like I'm telling him what groceries I'm about to buy, and he's wondering if he saw me and didn't pay any attention. I bet he's kicking himself for being so careless. He struggles, and Pax tightens the strap around his neck, sending him into a coughing spasm. I squat down so I'm eye-to-eye with him.

"Let me use little words, so you'll be sure to understand." I drop my voice to a menacing whisper and speak very matter-of-factly. "I will be watching. And if I find you anywhere near Ms. Cassidy again, *anywhere at all near her*, I'm going to skip the slashed tires and the handcuffs and I'm simply going to have you taken out, and that will be the end of that." I stare into his eyes, looking for the fear of understanding, the realization that I'm not fucking around, that he'd better heed my warnings and hit the road, but it's not there. I try not to sigh in disappointment, instead maintaining my ominous tone. "Are we clear, Mr. Bennett?"

He manages to nod even as he glares at me, all dagger eyes and anger, and I stand up in order to pull away from his negative energy. He looks up at me, and the hatred he sends my way is almost palpable. With no idea how, I manage *not* to step back in alarm, in fright. Instead, I arch an eyebrow at him, not letting on for a second that he's scaring the crap out of me.

"I'm not kidding around here," I warn him. "Don't test me."

I step past him and give Pax an almost indiscernible nod. As I reach the front door, I hear the zzz of her Taser and feel confident that we won't have to deal with Todd Bennett for the rest of the night.

Tomorrow, however, is another story.

CHAPTER EIGHT

When I was a senior in high school, I dated a boy named Nelson. Don't let the wimpy name fool you, he was beautiful. This, of course, was before I realized how much *more* beautiful women are. He was lean and muscular and handsome with light hair and smiling blue eyes. We were terrific friends, and I often think about him and wonder where he is now, how his life turned out; my memories are fond. Anyway, we were goofing off one day after school and we got into a friendly wrestling match. Being the sweet guy that he was, he let me have the upper hand for a while before smoothly taking control and pinning me to the floor flat on my back beneath him, my arms stretched over my head. I will never forget that moment. There was a split second where, all at once, it was absolutely crystal clear to me how strong he really was, how much stronger men are than women, inherently. It's a fact of life. In that instant, I understood that if Nelson wanted to hurt me, if he wanted to have his way with me right then and there, he could and there wasn't a damn thing I could do about it. He was just too strong for me to fight him off. Luckily, he had those smiling eyes, and I trusted him and everything was fine, but that realization will stick with me for the rest of my life. Men are strong and they can be scary and, if they want something from a woman physically, chances are, they can take it. Not that they would; I don't mean to generalize. I am well aware of the fact that most men are *not* creeps and scumbags and psychotic killers and rapists. But it's in the eyes; there's a reason people say the eyes are the windows to the soul. Nelson's eyes allayed my fears; Todd Bennett's terrified me.

"I don't like it, Norah." Hayley was trying hard to be calm and not let the trickle of fear into her voice, but I could hear it.

"I know, sweetie. But you said it, Pax is here. I'll be fine."

"He scares me. He sounds so much like Brant."

I shouldn't have told her about Todd Bennett in quite as much detail as I did; I know that now. I just made her worry. But I've never felt right about sugar-coating the specifics of a case for her. In fact, she asked me early on not to. She believes in what I do, knows it's necessary, and that most of the time, the women I help have no other options. So she's never shown any kind of reservation before. I think this case is hitting a little too close to home.

"You keep Pax close. I know she weirds you out a little bit, but she can protect you. This guy is a loose cannon, and it sounds like nothing you said to him today is going to make any difference." Her tone has moved from concern to certainty. She talks like she knows her shit, which, of course, she does. "He's gone into if-I-can't-have-her-nobody-can mode. That's the next logical step. If Pax didn't make him soil his tighty-whities, he's not going to be convinced."

She's absolutely right, but I don't tell her that. I don't tell her that I'm actually thanking my lucky stars Todd Bennett has no way of knowing who I am, what hotel I'm in, that he couldn't possibly find me. That's how much the look on his face scared me, and it makes me angry to admit it. I'm a strong woman, stronger than most I know, both physically and emotionally. I don't take kindly to being terrified in my own skin, but I can't seem to shake the creeping willies that crawl along my arms and the back of my neck like tiny insects every time I flash back to earlier.

It's after ten now and I wonder if Todd Bennett is still unconscious from the zapping he took. I hope so. I try hard never to take anybody's safety for granted, especially after doing what I do for more than ten years. But I realize that I was a bit too lax in my investigation of Rebecca Cassidy. Not that I could have done much differently. I have no control over the timing. I never know when the names will appear to me or how much time I have before somebody could be in danger, but I'm not pleased with the nonchalant way I searched for Rebecca. Todd Bennett could have killed her that first night, and I'd have been sitting on my ass in the parking lot wondering why he wasn't showing.

"Stop it." Hayley's voice pulls me out of my reverie.

"Stop what?"

"You're doing it again. You're getting stuck inside your head. You had no way of knowing what a danger this guy is."

I feel the corners of my mouth quirk up just a bit, almost against my will. "How do you do that?"

"Do what?"

"Know exactly what I'm thinking?"

I hear her release a breath, and I can picture her making herself more comfortable on our bed, sinking into the thick down comforter, her naked body sliding along the cool sheets. "I know you. I know your heart. After that, understanding what you're thinking isn't that much of a leap. Besides, you always go there when a case is more difficult than you expected it to be. You always beat yourself up, wondering how you could have done things differently to change the outcome when the truth is, you couldn't have. So stop it."

"Yes, ma'am." I say it tenderly, and I hope she can hear all the love I feel for her in that moment. She's much too good for me.

"Just do what you need to do, finish this up, and come home to me. I miss you."

"I miss you too."

We talk for a few more minutes about silly, trivial things before we say our goodnights. After we've hung up, my mind wanders back to thoughts about the Universe my mother spoke of. I honestly don't know what I believe. The Universe, heaven, hell, reincarnation, nothingness. I haven't a clue what happens to us when we die, whether we each have a destiny that's already written, whether we come back to fix mistakes we made the first time around. I don't get any of it, and I try not to dwell. Given what I do with my days, with my life, I don't think I want to know if there's a higher power all set and ready to judge me when my time comes.

Often, these are the thoughts that swirl in my head when I'm submerged in a case. Sounds like fun, doesn't it?

***

The next morning, Pax sends a text to Hayley letting her know that Rebecca Cassidy is safe at work, the front door to her townhouse is unlocked, and Pax is tailing Todd Bennett, who is just returning to the land of the living after his surprise meeting with the business end of a Taser. I have no idea how she manages to get so many things done in such a short space of time without anybody noticing. Does she have a clone? Does she have underlings who do her bidding in various cities? I'm sure I don't want the answers to these questions, but I'm curious just the same. Inarguably, this is why her fee is exorbitant. She certainly earns it.

I park down the street from Rebecca's development and stroll into her parking lot, trying to be as nonchalant and unnoticeable as I can. I'm once again wearing my Seahawks hat and the glasses, and my clothes are just as boring as they were yesterday: jeans and a long-sleeve Tar Heels T-shirt. Everybody in this city who's not wearing a Duke shirt is wearing a Tar Heels shirt, so it's not like I'll be standing out.

The sky is robin's-egg blue today, and the sun is shining cheerfully. It all seems so strange, all bubbly and happy, unmindful of the turmoil that some people are no doubt going through today. The sun warms my head gently, the bluebirds flit around looking for debris with which to build their nests, and spring flowers bloom in bright colors, despite the fact that Rebecca Cassidy's life is in danger and has been for years. Nature is blind like that. Hell, *life* is blind like that.

I nod silently to a young man I pass as I walk, but I'm relieved that nobody is around Rebecca's unit. I act like I know exactly what I'm doing, like I'm totally supposed to be there, as I reach her door. I learned that lesson early on. Unobtrusive is the last thing you are when you're constantly looking over your shoulder, skulking around like you don't belong. *That* makes people notice you. Instead, I simply walk up to Rebecca's door, turn the knob, and walk in, then close and lock it quickly behind me.

It takes a couple moments for my eyes to adjust to the dimness of the room, and the pounding of my heart in my ears is temporarily distracting. No matter how long I do this, I don't think I'll ever feel easy about being someplace I'm not supposed to be. I'm a good girl at heart and sneaking around like this makes me a little ill at ease. I tend to think that's a good thing. Frankly, the idea of not being the least bit bothered about breaking into somebody else's home freaks me out.

Rebecca Cassidy is neat, but not obsessively so, and a quick glance around her living room makes me like her right away. There aren't a lot of froo-froo items lying around, no dust-collecting knick-knacks, or scary collections of weird stuff like nutcrackers or Precious Moments figurines, but there are a lot of books, several well-worn throw pillows, and a really nice stereo system. Lots of fiction, comfortable lounging areas, and great sound…Rebecca is obviously a girl after my own heart. If there's mint chocolate chip ice cream in the freezer, I might have to marry her. Don't tell Hayley. She has nothing on the walls, which gives a little bit of a stark feel to the place, but two things occur to me. One: she hasn't been here that long. Two: she has probably grown used to being ready to flee at a moment's notice, which just makes me sad, because judging by what I can see, she'd do a really nice job decorating a living space she knew she'd be staying in for a while. My sympathy for her wells up a bit, and I sigh, wondering not for the first time why stalkers can't hunt annoying, high-maintenance bitches instead of nice girls. A stupid thing to think, I know, but I think it anyway.

I like the smell of Rebecca's place. The air doesn't reek of violence or anger or fear, like the situation warrants. It's simpler. Sweeter. Welcoming, even, like cinnamon or freshly baked bread. It invites me in, tells me to pull up a chair and stay for a while. And I want to.

Her tastes lean toward feminine—more flowers and paisley than I would pick for my own home—but the furniture speaks of comfort, and the atmosphere is warm. Rebecca Cassidy is probably a fabulous hostess. I imagine sinking into her floral-print couch while she brings out bold, rich coffee in kitschy mugs and a plate of warm chocolate chip cookies. Yes, I realize I'm making her into a fifties housewife, but I can't help it. That's the image this place hands my brain.

The presence of Pax, of course, puts a damper on my fantasies. How could it not? She's like a hulking harbinger of doom, so completely out of place in this setting, it's almost laughable. She's like an angry, dark scab on an otherwise perfect ass, and I have to look away to hide my grin at the comparison.

Since there's not a doubt in my mind that the bedroom is always the room of focus for somebody like Todd Bennett, I head up the stairs. The second floor is nicely laid out with two good-sized bedrooms, a bathroom, and a washer and dryer hidden smartly behind folding doors, which stand open now. The smell of Downy tells me Rebecca was doing laundry this morning.

Her bedroom is where the personal items are, and I'm strangely relieved to see them. The protection I feel for this woman I've never met isn't new to me—it actually happens a lot in my line of work—and the lack of photos or anything that reflects her personality in the living room made me sad for her. Here on her dresser, though, is a pewter-framed black-and-white wedding photo of a couple that can only be her parents. A smaller frame outlines two teenage girls with the same strawberry-blonde hair, their arms wrapped lovingly around one another's shoulders. Rebecca and her sister. I have trouble pulling my eyes away as I wonder where these family members are and why they haven't helped her. Then I realize it's more than likely she hasn't told them much—if anything—about Todd Bennett. There are any number of reasons why—

embarrassment, not wanting to worry your loved ones, miscalculation of the danger—and they all seem silly to me now.

I move to the bed, neatly made and covered with throw pillows as if they were candy sprinkles on ice cream. The colors are cheerful primaries—reds, blues, oranges—and the room is the perfect marriage of teenage girl and grown woman. I take a seat on the mattress that's a bit too soft for me, close my eyes, and try hard to clear my head.

I wish Hayley was here.

And then I'm glad she's not.

I hate that she's touched at all, even fingertip-lightly, by this life of mine.

There is no sound from the rest of the townhouse, and I know Pax is practicing her own waiting ritual. I have no idea how long this will take, and I concentrate on visuals of things that help me relax—a warm, sandy beach, a gentle rainstorm, the lull of a silent car ride—and soon, my heart rate slows, the pace of my breathing evens out, and I talk each muscle into loosening, letting go. It's a long process, which is why I do it. I could be sitting on Rebecca's bed all day, for all I know.

Such will not be the case today, though, and at the sound of the front door, my muscles spasm suddenly with tension like so many overextended rubber bands. Hoping Rebecca returned home for something she forgot, but knowing instinctively that it's Todd Bennett, I hold my breath and marvel at how frighteningly easy it is to break into somebody else's home. How horrified would Rebecca be to know that at this very moment, there are strangers wandering through her space and looking at her things?

I brace myself as whoever it is climbs the stairs. I don't blink. I don't breathe. The emotional mix that floods my system— anger, disgust, fear, hatred, and disappointment—narrows and pinpoints until it's only disgust. My expression hardens; I can actually feel it do so, and my eyebrows draw together. At this moment, there is nothing else in this world. Just this. Just me and this piece-of-shit man who will never terrorize or terrify another woman again. I gave him the chance to change his ways and he blew it. Game over. He is a boil on the skin of humanity. I am the lance.

His shock is plain as he steps into the bedroom. He sports jeans and a black, tight-fitting T-shirt, a non-descript duffel bag dangling from his shoulder. Blue eyes widen behind the wire rims, then dart around the room in apparent confusion. I cock my head to the side and watch him, wondering what's going through his head. Is he kicking himself for not being more patient and waiting longer before making his move? Is he calculating his chances of making it back to the door and escaping? Is he wondering if maybe he can take me out with his bare hands? Or does he already know how this will end?

When his gaze settles back on me, it almost seems questioning, as if he thinks we're at an impasse, as if asking, "Now what?" My answer to him is quite simple.

"I warned you."

The only visible change in his expression is a small twitch at one corner of his mouth. In the next second, he's convulsing on his feet, the second bite of a Taser in twenty-four hours coursing through his nervous system. I didn't even see Pax, had no idea she was so close. As Todd Bennett collapses to the floor like a heap of wet towels, Pax shoots me a quick glance and no-nonsense command.

"Go."

She doesn't have to tell me twice. The deadness on her face, the utter lack of any kind of emotion at all, is enough to propel me up off the bed and out of the room. I don't look back as I maneuver down the stairs, hoping I don't trip over my own freaked-out feet. My hand grips the doorknob so tightly, my knuckles go immediately white, and I have to close my eyes and force my ragged breathing to steady. I can't sprint out of the townhouse, much as I'd like to. I'm supposed to be discreet, subtle, unnoticed. Like I'm preparing to go onstage and give a speech, I take a deep breath, count to five, and open the door. I exit Rebecca Cassidy's home calmly and unobtrusively, as if I've done it a million times before.

I don't look back.

CHAPTER NINE

I drive for a while; it's the only way I'm ever able to really clear my head. My brain goes into this weird zone of thinking-but-not, and I'm barely conscious of things like stopping and turning. I am truly on autopilot.

At some point, more than an hour later, my subconscious must just turn control back over to me because I'm tooling along down highway fifty-four when I register something round and brown in the road about a hundred yards ahead of me. Luckily, traffic is light on the two-lane road. A great blue heron soars by as I brake to a gentle stop, put my car in park, and get out.

The turtle is the size of a dinner plate, which is a little intimidating. From what I've read, it's very common for them to wander into the road and get squished by fat rubber tires as they roll on by. There are wetlands on either side of this stretch, and it's much greener and lusher here at this time of year than it is at home in New York. I breathe in the scent of nature as I approach the turtle, and he pulls in his feet and head to ward off my likely attack.

"Hey there, big man," I say softly to him as I gingerly grasp him by the sides of his shell. "You got a death wish or something?" He's surprisingly heavy as I lift him and carry him the rest of the way across the road in the direction he was facing, then set him down in the grass.

A car slows as it passes, bless the polite heart of the true southerner, and the driver gives me a smile and a nod of approval for my actions. Isn't that ironic? Here I am, rescuing a turtle in distress, not two hours after ordering and *paying handsomely for* the extermination of another human being. Would the woman in the car be so quick with her smile if she knew that? I can almost envision the horror as it washes over her face once she has all the facts. I am a murderer just as surely as Pax is a murderer. Just because I don't do the actual killing doesn't mean I don't have blood on my hands. I'm painfully aware of this fact, believe me.

Later that afternoon, I go to a movie. I can hear you making judgments, thinking, *You just had somebody killed and then you went to see a flick? What kind of a cold-hearted bitch are you?* I've asked myself the very same questions, I promise you. But I need something to hijack my focus for a while, something to make the time go by, because I have one more thing to take care of before I can head home. Just bear with me, and you'll understand. The film is an above-average romantic comedy starring Sandra Bullock and some impossibly handsome guy. Frankly, Sandy could be on the screen doing absolutely nothing for two hours, and I'd gladly fork over my money to watch, so it's a good choice for me. By the time it's over and I emerge, blinking rapidly in the blinding sun like somebody trapped for weeks in a dark cave, it's nearly five o'clock. I give my BlackBerry a glance, and there's a text from Hayley that says simply, "Done." She hasn't called or left any other messages because she knows I need time. I'll contact her when I'm ready.

***

I knock on the front door, no shaking or sweating or nerves, not once showing any signs that I was in this very same place illegally not six hours ago. The development is bustling now, people returning from work, kids home from school. The change in atmosphere from this morning is almost jarring.

This is the part I love. The impending conversation—if it goes well—is what will allow me to sleep tonight, to look at myself in the mirror tomorrow morning, to understand why Hayley isn't repulsed by me.

"Hi," Rebecca says. "Can I help you?" Her smile is genuine but hesitant, as if she's expecting me to try to sell her something or offer to save her soul.

"Rebecca Cassidy?" I ask, even though I know I have the right person.

"Yes?" Maybe a bit more hesitant now.

"My name is Norah, and I'd like to talk to you about Todd Bennett."

Her complexion immediately drains of color, and she tightens her grip on the door. Her smile doesn't falter, it merely drops right off her face.

"Please," I say, rushing to reassure, but keeping my voice down. "Please, don't be afraid. I'm on your side."

Forever and a day go by as she studies my face, looking for... what? Sincerity? A trick? I can only guess and wait. Finally, she steps aside and lets me in, then waves me into the small eat-in area of her kitchen.

"Can I get you anything? Coffee? Tea?" Ever the hostess, I see, and I bet she was raised that way, always to be polite even if she's so scared she's about to crap her pants.

"No, thank you. I'm good." She motions me to the table and chairs, and we sit.

Her green eyes are just as friendly, just as kind in person as they are in her driver's license photo, and I know that she's easily liked. A person like Rebecca has many friends and tons of acquaintances. She is the kind of woman you want to be around, just hoping you can suck up some of her positive energy. I wonder how much of that Todd Bennett has sucked out of her over the years. I pretty much have my answer when I see the worry on her face. I rush to alleviate it.

"This is going to be very hard for you to believe," I begin. There's no standard, easy-to-absorb wording for something like this. I've done it more than once, and I always seem to stutter and stammer and fumble for the right words. "First, you need to understand that I know all about Todd Bennett, the troubles he's caused you, the police reports, the restraining orders, all of it. I know about all of it."

I give her time to absorb that. Her pale eyebrows furrow slightly, and I'm sure she's trying to figure out *how* I have all this information as her hands clasp and unclasp on the table between us.

"I'm not a cop," I go on. "I'm not a detective or in any kind of law enforcement. But I have sources, and I'm privy to information in cases like yours." I've found it best to leave the details vague. Most of the time, people are too stunned or confused to ask for them anyway. I've also found that it helps to get right to the point. "It's important that you know and understand that Mr. Bennett will never, ever bother you again."

At that, her eyes narrow, as if she's certain I'm lying to her, that this is a sick joke and she can't believe I'd do something so cruel.

I shoot her a half grin. "Told you it'd be hard to believe."

"I—I don't understand." It's the most common phrase uttered by my clients after I tell them such a thing. I don't do face-to-face very often at all. In fact, I prefer to stay behind the scenes, cloaked by shadows and unseen, like the Wizard of Oz behind his curtain, except way more competent, I'd hope. But in cases like this one, it's important for the Rebeccas of the world to know they can take a deep breath and go on with their lives without having to constantly look over their shoulders, without wondering if they'll have to flee their lives at any given moment...again. I feel I owe them at least an attempt at a conversation about it.

"I'm afraid I'm not at liberty to go into great detail," I say, which is, of course, a big lie. "But let me assure you that I know exactly what you've been dealing with where Mr. Bennett is concerned. Exactly." I look her dead in the eye when I say this, and I think it helps my credibility. She's listening intently, her focus solid on my face despite the gentle trembling of her hands. I cover them with my own. "Listen to me. I'm sure you know you're not alone in the world, that many other women around the globe have been terrorized, stalked, afraid to be alone in their own homes, because of some sick pig like Todd Bennett. You also know that the authorities can only do so much to help, especially if the asshole is familiar with the law."

"Or doesn't care about it," she adds softly.

"Or doesn't care about it." I tighten my grip on her. "Those extreme cases? The ones that seem hopeless? The ones like yours? That's where I come in."

Rebecca squints at me. "So...you're a private investigator or something like that?"

"Something like that. Let's just say Mr. Bennett is not the first of his kind with whom I've had...business dealings."

I sit quietly and let her examine my words, my thinly-veiled hints. She seems like a smart girl. She'll get there.

"But...how do you know about him?" she asks.

"I have sources."

"Did somebody call you?"

"I really can't say. I'm sorry."

She studies my face, searching for clarity. Her eyes narrow just a touch, then open a little wider as she puts the pieces into place. "You said he'd never bother me again."

"That's right. He won't."

"Never?"

"Never."

"Is he...dead?"

I hold her gaze for several seconds. I can feel her probing mine for the answer. "He will never bother you again, Rebecca. I promise you that. He will *never* bother you again."

Tears well up in her eyes, and she lets out a little whimper-gasp. "Oh, my God," she whispers. "Oh, my God. It's over? It's really over?"

"It's really over."

"Oh, my God."

A combination of near-disbelief and utter relief takes up residence on her face, an uncertain smile topping off the expression. I've seen it before on other women, on Hayley. It's beautiful, and it makes every doubt that plagued me earlier absolutely worthwhile.

It takes a few minutes for belief to settle in completely, but I know when it does because Rebecca Cassidy is suddenly in my arms, great wracking sobs of relief tearing out of her body.

"Thank you," she says in my ear with such emotion that I feel the surprise of a lump in my throat. "Thank you, thank you, thank you…"

I hold her tightly, relishing the moment, and in that snapshot of time, I don't care what anybody says or how harshly you might judge what I do. For Rebecca Cassidy, the balance has been restored, and for that, I am proud.

CHAPTER TEN

I open my eyes and squint in the pre-dawn gray of the bedroom. A smile spreads its way across my face as I realize I slept all the way through the night. No two o'clock wake-up. No nightmares. No flashbacks. I release a deep, relieved sigh. It's been six weeks since my return from North Carolina, and last night was the first night my sleep hasn't been disrupted by my guilt.

Don't misunderstand. I'm not asking for or expecting your sympathy. I know that I walk a very fine line of ethics and morals and right and wrong. But until I—or you, for that matter—can come up with a better way to help the women I help and save the women I save, I do the best I can. If it takes my sleep, my appetite, my sanity, so be it. The balance must be kept. Of that, I am certain.

Hayley stirs next to me and opens her eyes.

"Why are you awake?" she mutters.

"Because I slept," I tell her. She gets it immediately and grins at me.

"That's great babe. No scary dreams?"

"Not a one."

She snuggles close to me, her gaze focusing beyond my body. "We've got another one."

"I know." I've sensed the presence of the name on the nightstand since I opened my eyes, but I wanted to savor the peace and warmth of our bed for just a little while longer.

"Have you looked?" Hayley asks.

"Not yet." Her naked heat presses against me, and I revel in it. Both of us drift along in that luscious, warm, half-asleep haze for several long moments. Hayley's patience runs out first.

"Okay, let's look." She stretches across my torso—I nip at her as she does, and am rewarded with a cute little squeak—and grabs at the paper. "Who have we got here? The winner is Candace Murphy of Poughkeepsie, New York. Candace Murphy, come on down!" She flops back onto the bed. "Your old stomping grounds, right? Honey?" She gets back up on an elbow and looks me in the face. "Norah? What's wrong?"

I can barely hear her. The sound of her voice has gone fuzzy, like she's talking to me through wet gauze. I blink rapidly, squeeze my eyes shut, blink some more, trying to bring her into focus.

"Norah. *Norah.*" She shakes me, and the fog suddenly lifts, as if it was never there, save for the acidic taste of bile in my mouth. "Are you all right? What the hell just happened?"

"What—" I clear the fear from my throat and try again. "What was the name again?"

She makes a show of reading carefully. "Candace Murphy in Poughkeepsie." My expression is scaring her; I can tell by *her* expression. "Do you know her?"

I nod slowly, not wanting to.

"Who is she?" When I meet Hayley's eyes, her voice softens to a frightened whisper. "Norah, who is Candace Murphy?"

My voice is equally low as the reality hits me full force.

"She's my mother."

The End

Triskelion

By

JD Glass

There is a secret that no one knows, but everyone lives. There is more to us than the body, more to the mind, more to our emotions. There is above and below, and there is also without and within. And in the middle, there is something different. Therefore, things are never simply easy or hard, hot or cold, right or wrong. In that between place, there is a third state of being and it is in that state—the place that is neither completely one nor the other but shares the qualities of both—where we find balance.

"Arigato," I said into the mouthpiece, the sum total of the Japanese I'd absorbed in the last few months, and hung up the phone. I stared at it for a long second as it rested, charging in its cradle, before glancing up to see humor-filled eyes gazing back down at me.

"Hey, Steph...you think this'll work?" Bear asked me with a nervous grin.

"It better," I said fervently, not certain if I was hoping or praying. "If this doesn't help, I don't know *what* will."

Three years. It has been three years of working together and with them, learning each other and the personalities. Bear and I have been friends since high school, and we both were in Nina's first band, so that part was easy. Fran, we thought we knew, but learned better, and over time, learned better again. Samantha had, in the beginning, been the newcomer, but again, three years later, that wasn't the case anymore.

It was also possible to see, after all this time, the toll everything has taken on mine and Bear's buddy, our pal, the reason we still worked together in the first place—Nina.

Yeah, sure, we observed that there was some tension for a while, but nothing that couldn't be handled, something we even very occasionally teased Nina about. I mean, hey, it's not every person that has two people in love with them and each other and everyone being oh-so-polite about the whole thing and, in Nina's case, maybe even deliberately ignoring it.

Until about two or so weeks ago. Something happened, something that took the smile from Nina's eyes, and weighed Samantha's shoulders down whenever she thought someone couldn't see. Even Fran, who was spending a *lot* more time lately in the New York office, was affected.

At first, Bear and I thought we knew what it was. It wasn't a secret, at least not to us, since we knew Nina so well. Caught still between Sam and Fran, she was either unaware that she had options, or unable to get to that place to think about them. The way she and Fran looked at each other, or Fran and Sam...and now it was worse than ever.

Bear and I had had it. If Nina couldn't figure it out, we already had, and this time, we were in a position to help. Because really, she needed it, a little help, a little push in the right direction, and after all, when everything was said and done, well, me and Bear? We were Nina's friends...and we had her back.

***

"You're kidding!" It was under her breath, but Samantha heard Nina's exclamation anyway as she stepped through the door. Samantha hefted her instrument case from where she'd leaned it against the frame moments before, then followed and took in the sight before them. A small corridor, with another door for the bathroom on the right, ended several feet ahead. From there, the room opened to the right, the bed completing the corridor with its head set against the wall of the bathroom, a sofa perpendicular before it.

Nina put her guitar case down at the other end of the sofa, and walked past the standing mirror to peer out the window. "At least it's not a bad view," she observed. "Not that we'll probably get to see much of it otherwise." She turned and gave Samantha a bright smile. *Too bright*, Samantha considered, *forced*. What they had discovered in Fran's apartment, not two weeks ago, the shock of it—

Fran bumped up behind her, tumbling Samantha's thoughts. "So...I'm either next door or...oh. Sorry."

"It's okay," Samantha grinned as she turned, then glanced down at the key Fran held. "Uh...not next door—the *same* door."

Nina stepped across the space and examined the key Fran gave her. "The place must have—"

"Double booked," Fran finished as Nina handed it back.

"All right, we'll just pile our stuff here and work the rest out. It's only for a few nights, anyway," Samantha said into the awkward silence as the porter arrived and wheeled the rest of the luggage into the room.

"Yeah, I'll just take the sofa—not that I'll probably be here much, anyway," Fran added with a cheer that matched the smile Nina had given Samantha earlier. "It's a full schedule, and Ren's here. I'm sure we'll spend time catching up."

This time it was Samantha's turn to force good humor. "Hey! That's right," she agreed heartily. She hated the way her voice sounded. She busied herself with rummaging through her travel bag, hands buried between shifting layers of silk, cotton, and leather, unsure, unaware, and uncaring of what moved where. "It's been, what? Three, four years?"

"Five," Fran answered quietly, her eyes focused on the items she removed from her own case. "We haven't seen each other in five years."

"Long time," Samantha commented in a noncommittal fashion, but mentally she winced. She really should have known better, she chastised herself. Five years ago meant Samantha had been, albeit briefly, in New York. *That* was when she'd "officially" met Ren, which meant Samantha's arrival and Ren's departure were probably—

A drawer slammed abruptly, shocking both Samantha and Fran. Eyes drawn by the sound, they stared at Nina as she straightened. "I'm going to the venue," she announced, guitar case already in one hand as she swung her jacket over her shoulder with the other, then strode past them to the door.

Samantha didn't have to ask if something was wrong. As tightly reigned as Nina kept herself, the discord she felt was a haze that surrounded her, and the connect that existed between them carried it as well, despite what Samantha knew were Nina's best attempts to prevent that. What had caused it, some of it she thought she knew, but the rest, however, she could only guess. While she did have some good ideas, ideas they would remain until Nina was ready to tell her. Samantha would never force her for the answer.

"We've got sound check in three hours. Hang a bit, and I'll go with you," Samantha offered to Nina's back.

"'S'all right," Nina answered, her hand on the door latch. "This"—she waved about to indicate the room but kept her gaze focused directly ahead—"got messed up. Gonna check if our sound setup's okay. Three hours is *not* enough time if something's missing." She swung the door open and stepped through.

"But—" The door closed with a click of finality on Samantha's protest. She shook her head and stared down at her bag again. This time she noticed that she'd severely mixed up her clothing. "Fuck," she muttered softly.

"Is she angry with me?" Fran asked in a low tone as she removed the contents of her luggage and claimed a spot in the closet.

"No." Samantha breathed the word out as she carefully untangled her things, then pushed behind her ear a stray dark lock that had fallen across her sight. Samantha just as carefully worded her answer. "She's a little nervous, which is pre-show normal...mad at herself, probably...and at life, *definitely*. I know for a fact that, crazy as it sounds, she's *still* hurting. But mad *at* you or *with* you? No."

There was a slight rustle as Fran shook her head. "I don't..."

Samantha could hear the breath Fran took as the full meaning hit her.

"Sam...Sammer?"

The warm weight of Fran's palm came to rest on Samantha's shoulder, and Samantha smiled gently at the sound of her old nickname.

"What do you mean, she's still hurting? Hurting over what?"

"Are you telling me you really don't know?" Samantha countered as she folded the final item and placed it in her drawer. She closed it methodically, before she finally turned her gaze on her friend, the friend she loved as much as she loved Nina. She found Fran's eyes golden on hers and as warm as the hand that rested on her shoulder.

She covered Fran's hand with her own and searched the gaze that held hers. She watched as the earnest concern on Fran's face shifted, became a flash of hurt and dismay as understanding dawned.

"You don't mean because I...I mean...she was—Sam, you *know* why...why I did that!" Fran exclaimed, her shock palpable. "I was—" She broke off and shook her head again, then took another deep breath as she weighed her next words. She let it out slowly into the heavy silence between them. "Done is done, Sam," she said with quiet firmness as she glanced up again to meet Samantha's eyes. "It was—"

"The wrong thing to do," Samantha interrupted as she moved closer. "I told you then, I'll tell you now," she said as she gently caught Fran's cheek in her hand and cradled it in her palm. The familiar and welcome feel of it brought the automatic rush and flow of the connect between them and combined with the new knowledge gained over the last few weeks; it made Samantha's eyes smart and her heart clench within her chest. "You should have *never* done it, or you should have fixed it," she told Fran quietly. "But either way?" Samantha paused to catch her breath, to speak past the fist that grabbed her heart. "You shouldn't have left Spain the way you did, you..." She took another breath before she continued. "We could have worked it out, it would have been okay…we should have—" She broke off as the fist in her chest climbed to her throat even as she choked it down. "You shouldn't"—it broke her voice anyway—"you shouldn't have left us."

***

All the way through the corridor and into the elevator, through the controlled fall to the lobby and her passage across it, until she found the concierge and got the first available taxi to the venue, Nina kept her mind stoically blank and her back rigidly straight. It was only after she was safely ensconced in the black vinyl seats—guitar safely tucked, the door firmly closed behind her, and her destination confirmed to the driver—that she let her shoulders sag. Nina rested her head back against the seat and closed her eyes beneath her sunglasses, ignoring the sights of the city she rode through. *It figures*, she thought, frustration the emotion that topped the rest, *it just fucking figures*. The cab hailed for her just so happened to be a carbon-copy of one she'd ridden in a few years ago with Fran.

The memory played through her mind. It was a different coast, a different day, the same day she'd gotten into some stupid physical altercation with someone at the bar she worked in then and Nina had taken a solid blow to her face, complete with bloody nose. Her boss sent her home early, and on the ride back to Fran's place she…they'd—

Nina opened her eyes and leaned forward. It was a mistake to let her mind travel there, to remember how she and Fran had touched and loved, how on that same day, that day now almost four years gone, she'd spoken to Samantha for the first time in a long time. And it had spelled the beginning of the end for her and Fran.

The picture in her mind *hurt*. It made her ache in ways she hadn't in a long time. It had been fast, a whirlwind of the

143

unexpected—to meet up with Samantha again, to have that cause her breakup with Fran, and then, before she had time to adjust to Fran's removal or Sam's renewal, to have left the continent for her first tour with her first band.

The cityscape flew by unnoticed as her mind played its relentless movie. The tour, the dissolution of *that* band, and the lack of communication from home—from either Sam *or* Fran—then the insane, unexpected, and ultimately confusing reunion in Madrid, Spain. During the months they literally lived together, they were friends, good friends, even best friends, until *that* night, that first time between them.

Nina's shoulders involuntarily twitched and she shifted uncomfortably, her skin too warm, the jacket too heavy on her shoulders. She removed it, knowing it wasn't only the mercurial San Francisco weather responsible for her discomfort.

The memory—correction, *memories*—were more than merely mental reflection: they carried emotional and visceral reality, a reality that felt more vividly three-dimensional than the cab she rode in.

"You're the only one I've ever let touch me, love," Nina said to her that night, her last night before the first tour.

"No, baby, no," Fran corrected, and Nina could still feel the kisses Fran gave her in between the words even as she said them, a warm trail along her neck, then a fiery branding that tracked across her jawline. Nina again felt Fran's thumb draw along her chin. "I'm your *first*."

And it was true: Fran had been her first, her for-real-and-true first, and Nina had known from the start that Samantha would be the last, but— *Dammit!* She slapped her palm on the edge of the door. Her eyes, normally light blue with a surrounding silver ring, were the same muddy grey they'd been for the last two weeks. They stared unseeing at the streets streaming past the streaked and scratched glass. *None of that matters now.*

The thought was a forlorn one as Nina let her body rest against the door, done fighting with herself for the moment. She'd not been truly alone since she and Samantha went to Fran's apartment to find some paperwork Fran asked for while stuck in the hospital—"Just some routine tests," Fran told them on the phone. "My doc's being overly cautious…"

Among the documents they searched, they found an unexpected surprise, a secret that Fran had held for a few years. But before either one of them could truly ask her about it, the diagnosis came, shocking them all.

I'm scared, Nina admitted to herself. *I don't want to lose her—not again, and not like that—it's too soon.* It was a good starting point, that admission, it opened the doors for other reflections and thoughts. But still, her mind skirted around the edges of deeper truth, wading in a step at a time.

Just the thought, the idea, of Ren makes me angry, and it's not as if I've ever even met *her. Samantha,* Nina thought, *Samantha and Fran love each other. It's just not fair. I don't even know why it's Samantha and I, and not the two of them. And the truth?* Nina took a deep breath, because it was a deep truth, one that she'd not wanted to face. *I guess…the truth is that it's kinda my fault. The first, and the last. I never counted on "always," never knew I'd been in—*

"Here ya go, Miz," the driver announced, interrupting her thoughts.

"Yeah. Thanks," Nina answered as she fished mechanically into her pocket for her wallet, pulled out a few bills, and handed them to the driver before once again donning both jacket and sunglasses. Grabbing her guitar case, she stepped out onto the curb and walked toward the open double doors that led to the back stage.

Nina watched for a moment as two people struggled to push a large wooden box through the doors. Some of the lighting rigs, she surmised. That was all the confirmation she needed that she had the right entrance. She had a job to do and, forcibly putting all her musings aside, "Now is now," Nina told herself firmly. She readjusted her guitar and stepped in.

***

It's only for a few days, Fran reminded herself as she examined her reflection in the mirror. Big eyes stared back at her. *Warm as caramel, bright as gold.* Both Nina and Samantha told her that many times in many ways, over the years.

Right now, she—and they—just had to get through it, and that was critical. She was painfully, almost terrifyingly, aware that there was yet another hurdle to be faced very soon after, but this, this here and now? She resolutely turned her mind from it, focused on her breath, on her hands, on the tasks before her. *I am in this room. I feel the air as I breathe it in and out, feel the soft and supple leather beneath my fingers. I hear the sounds of the air in the vents, feel it as a nice cool breeze on my still damp back. I can smell the soap from the shower, and outside, the sun is getting ready to set.*

She ran careful fingers through her hair, long curls and waves the color of wheat mixed with strands of burnt sugar. *Water, air, earth, and fire,* she continued as she readied herself and breathed with focused intent, *part of and with the energy that is the Universe, the energy that flows through me,* is *me, right here, right now.* Centered and calm, Fran allowed herself to review what she knew and what she had to do.

This night, this first night of three with its attendant party afterward, was in reality part cross-cultural celebration and part business meeting, or perhaps "audition" was a better description, since outside of the performers themselves, the audience would be a limited one. In essence, it would be a witnessed rehearsal. The combination of performance, audience attraction, and crowd response were all critical to the future that the three of them, Nina, Samantha, and Fran, had begun to plan—the creation of a new label, their own label, outside of the confines and schedule their current label had them under.

It was supposed to be a secret, so of course the news of that traveled in the usual way through the usual channels. Samantha spoke with Graham, who was not only a close friend, but also one of the acts they wanted to sign. Graham, of course told his wife, Maeko, and Ren...well, Ren *was* Maeko's cousin. There was, Fran thought ruefully, no avoiding the Tokyo connection.

Under the pretext of holding a Japanese Moon Festival for a private select party of both audience and investors, Ren brought her dance troupe to perform, as well as her lawyer and her accountant. Her company was, after all, the primary one interested in investing the funds a new label start-up would require, and it was a matter of proving to the purse-string holders that the investment was a sound one.

Instead of merely performing for the investors, it made business sense for the band to recoup the expense of both the travel and the personnel by having an actual show. Ren's group, traveling in from Tokyo, agreed.

As for Ren...Fran couldn't stop the sigh that escaped her. Five years *was* a long time to not see or be in true contact with someone, and the practicality of geographic distance aside, the reasons were sound ones. During Fran's year in Japan, they'd been joined because of mutual study and interest, before it became...

Well, Fran reflected, it had never been love between her and Ren, not really, not in the soul-binding way it was between her and Samantha, nor, only a few years later, the blood-bond between her and Nina. Her connection to Ren had been an association of comrades in arms before it became a way to distract and even somewhat block the unbreakable and powerful link she had to Samantha.

Fran shook her head as she examined herself one last time. Despite that, Fran was very aware that she and Ren could and would have made a powerful team: they were mutually aware of and comfortable in the recognition of the type of love they *didn't* share, they were comfortable with one another. They were also aware that although they did not have the same devotion that they had with others, their loyalty could have equaled it.

It would have been very easy to do, and it *was* tempting: after all, between the genuine care and respect, the tacit familial approval, and the financial backgrounds they both came from, life between them would have, in many ways, been easy. But that life would have come at a cost Fran was unwilling to pay.

It was no secret, either to Fran or to her circle of friends, that her father was a local politician with ambition for greater things. The approval and the outright encouragement he'd shown toward the growing closeness between her and Ren had taken Fran by surprise…until she learned his reasons behind it.

At the time, Ren had only recently been recognized and legitimized by her father—"I am my father's daughter because he has no son." *Her* father was a man much like Fran's father. He had similar standing in their own community, as well as the same sort of ambitions and connections to achieve them. Ren's father—was *Yakuza*. And Ren worked for him.

The discovery of Ren and her father's direct involvement with the underworld and Fran's own father's connections to something similar led her to break free from it all—from her father, from Ren, from anything that would tie her and obligate her in ways she didn't want to things that were not right.

The ethical and legal breaches committed by her father and her lover felt like the deepest sort of betrayal; they violated Fran's ethics, her sense of self, and the image of her father she'd been made to believe. Fran simply could not pretend that this aspect of their life didn't exist.

That was ethics—a full half of her decision. The other half was love. Fran knew very clearly what she and Samantha shared was something so real, so damned *true*, it was transcendent.

No, they weren't—and at the time they *couldn't*—be together, but it made no difference. For Fran, any relationship that could not equal or exceed the connected intensity of her and Sam was ultimately a sham; for her to willingly suspend her knowledge of that would betray what love is all about. She was capable of all sorts of compromise, but not with these parts of herself, things that defined who she was at core. When she found Nina another year or so later, she knew she'd been right.

But before that reintroduction happened, Fran wanted, she *needed*, to escape, to free herself from a web of deceit and worse that she wanted nothing to do with. She needed a solution, and quickly, before she was completely ensnared, with no way out. *That* life, the one her father and Ren promised her, was one Fran had in fact taken vows to fight against.

That was when she made the decision to—

She shook her head once more as she took her jacket from the closet.

When Fran left Tokyo after a year, she flew across the Pacific unsure of where she'd eventually go or how she'd manage to maintain her studies and create her financial independence. A brief visit to her parents' home and an even briefer visit with the items she'd left there revealed the answer.

The brochures in an old packet of "how to afford your college degree" given to every high-school senior made it seem so simple, so easy, attractive even. "Come to the Coast," they seemed to say to her then-New Yorker heart. "All expenses paid. And it's such a small thing on your part, while it's a huge gift to someone else."

Those ads appealed to her, the mix of altruism and profit was the perfect combination, and so after a little investigation, she decided to give it a go.

For a while, it seemed that the pitchmen were right—she was ostensibly helping people out and able to do something for herself at the same time. At first she didn't mind the paid trips to California, the strict medical regimen; she even found she tolerated the side-effects quite well until...Until she was with Nina.

And *damn* Samantha for bringing that up! But then, she never really told Samantha how much that break had hurt her too.

The only thing Fran found she was able to do at the time was admit to Nina that she'd overreacted. But she didn't reveal some of the reasons behind the "why" of it, the *true* reasons behind. And so, done was done, and through her own actions, so were she and Nina. By the time Fran truly realized that perhaps something different was possible, not only was it too late, but also she had made a decision based on what she thought were very sound reasons, and they had settled into the roles that now ruled their lives.

Except...except...it was Nina and the secrets and scars she carried that Fran was thinking of when not allowing things to develop in different directions. Well, not one hundred percent, because there was also Sam to consider, and Fran's intimate knowledge of the things Samantha had been denied for so long. Knowing Sam, her Sammer, the way she did, Fran believed her withdrawal from the situation would give back some of those things.

But now, Fran's long-held secret was coming to light, and the tension between all three of them was reaching a painful point, especially since the "big C" came into their world.

Fran shrugged the light jacket across her shoulders and slid the room key into a side pocket, then quickly double-checked her soft-sided attaché. She took a deep breath, squared and set herself before she reached for the latch.

She was afraid but, she suspected, not in the way most would be. She didn't know if she could kick the illness, didn't know what the treatments, starting soon after her return from this trip, would do to her. What she did know was that forming their own label was a dream dear to those precious to her, and no matter what tomorrow held, it was up to her today to do her best to ensure that dream came true. That was something that would last, whether or not she did. That was what mattered. She closed the door behind her.

***

No way over but through, Ren thought as she observed the chatting group that stood next to the bar. The dim and atmospheric lighting obscured most features at this distance, but time and distance aside, there was no mistaking Fran, the set of her shoulders, or the toss of the hair she'd let grow so long since the last time they were together. Nor could she miss the pair that stood near her within that crowd. After her dance group ran through their routines, Ren watched the band sound check, then put on the rehearsal performance for the investors and self-important industry suits that made up the select audience.

Cray she knew, or at least had met during a trip to New York when the former Londoner made an unexpected visit. She never learned the full story behind the surprise arrival, but it was obvious that Fran had something Cray needed, and equally as obvious that Fran wanted to provide it.

Ren wasn't certain if it was those days and that…that *interruption*…that prevented a full reconciliation with Fran, nor was she sure if she considered Samantha Cray a rival. She did, though, recognize an equal when she met one and, even prior to that day, had been *very* aware of Cray's initial claim, as well as the depth of her tie, to Fran. Either way, one thing was for certain: that was the last time Ren had actually, physically, seen Fran.

Going into this new venture, Ren at least knew *them* to varying degrees. The person who was truly new to her was Nina, and Ren was also very aware that she had once been a seemingly impossible dream for both Fran *and* Cray. Back then, when Nina and Fran were together, Ren thought Nina was the only person in the world capable of making Fran isolate herself from her friends, for she neither answered nor returned letters and phone calls during that time. That alone was enough to convince Ren of how deep in it Fran was. It also made her wary of this "Nina."

"Hey, can I give you a hand with anything?" Nina asked her not more than eight hours ago.

Ren had observed the pretty girl—woman, she corrected herself—when she entered the backstage area behind the crew pushing the crate with the lighting rig. It took a moment to recognize the face, given the casual clothes and sunglasses and the nonchalant pony-tail, but when the woman with the guitar took those sunglasses off and smiled as she introduced herself to the crew chief, recognition from photos and videos, along with the brightness of the mega-watt grin, struck Ren.

She's taller than I expected, Ren noted as she turned away and focused mostly on the sets she and her crew were assembling. "Mostly" because every now and again, her attention returned to the cipher that was the only person Ren had every truly considered a threat to her own intentions.

Oh, she was over it now, really and truly, but Ren had concerns for her friend, concerns about the amount of love she knew Fran held for Nina, for Cray, and what all of that might mean both personally and professionally.

She hadn't expected Nina to walk over and offer to lend a hand and was surprised at her own acceptance of it.

"Yes, that would be wonderful," she answered, and quickly grasped the hand held out to her for introductions.

"Nina Boyd," she told her as they shook briefly.

"Toya," Ren responded automatically, the habit of using her surname long ingrained. Now, as she approached, she realized that might have created some confusion. Ren did not appear "typically" Japanese. With her straight dark hair pulled back into a working ponytail to reveal a high and clear forehead, Ren's mixed ethnicities sculpted her face, leaving delicate outlines that would be described as classic in more than just her father's culture. Blue eyes revealed not only her mother, but also the presence of *gaijin*—foreigner blood—in her father's line.

"Can you swing a hammer or play with a paint brush?"

"Sure, either or both." Nina laughed. "And I can help you assemble those flats over there too."

Sometime later, flats and sets painted, assembled, then disassembled for later return to the stage, Ren was again surprised—she hadn't expected that she would sincerely like Nina. She objectively knew that boded well for a future if they worked together in any capacity, but it also made it harder for Ren to be as equally objective when it came to observing Nina in connection to Fran. It didn't matter if Ren harbored anything more than an abiding friendly love and an honest admiration for the woman whom she secretly admitted was probably the one person she'd been closest to in her life.

She had very good reasons for pursuing this deal: in addition to providing a forum for artistic expression with business control, it was a public declaration to her late father and to the remnants of the clans that once rivaled his. It would tell them that the Door-into-the-Valley, the Toya clan, was truly dead: Ren herself delivered the fatal blow, then turned her back on the underworld.

And it was a legitimate venture; the money she invested in it came, *not* from her work for her father, nor from her inheritance. No, it came only from the success of the efforts she and her troupe put into their fledgling company, and this was something Ren was deservedly very proud of. But finally, too, and perhaps most importantly, it was both her apology as well as her thanks to Fran…for everything.

Ren took a deep breath and stepped toward the circle. This was her first opportunity since arriving to truly meet and greet everyone outside of the troupe. She addressed her first hello to the person closest to her, pitching her voice to carry just slightly over the background music.

"Hello, Cray. It's been a while."

"Toya." Cray spun and held her hand out for a quick but firm handshake.

The smile Ren observed was not merely a formal one, but it was not much more than that, either. "Yes, it has. You traveled well?"

"Smoothly enough." Ren nodded.

"Glad to hear it," Samantha said politely. "Have you met Neil, house sound engineer?" she asked with a wave of her hand to the gentleman she'd been talking with.

"Not officially," Ren answered with a small grin, "I got caught up with—"

"Ren!"

Fran's voice was bell-clear, her smile genuine and warm, and Ren couldn't help but respond with an equally genuine expression. She restrained herself as she leaned forward and, instead of an embrace, caught Fran's hand, smooth and cool, with both of hers.

Ren was again surprised at the sudden rush of emotion that physical proximity brought with it; she'd not expected that. Suddenly, she was twenty again; she was finally recognized and, if not loved, then at least needed, by her father, by Fran. Outside of Maeko, who was cousin and kin, she had made her first true friend.

"It is wonderful to see you, my Hope," Ren told her in Japanese, unable to stop herself from either the expression or from using the name she'd always used for Fran: *Nozomi*, hope. Such was what Fran had always been to her.

"It's good to see you, too," Fran answered in English and took her hand back to reach for the arm of the person who stood slightly turned away. "Have you met Nina?"

"Toya," Ren told her as they shook hands for a second time that day. "Ren Toya." For one brief moment, she regretted the revelation, because it meant the almost-anonymous observation of Nina she enjoyed was gone.

Ren was taken aback by the expression, the pure emotions that flew through the dark grey eyes that looked down and back at her. They reminded Ren of where she was and why she was there. And as Nina murmured the required social nicety in ritual return, Ren learned several things: the confident, nice young woman with an unassuming air who had helped her construct sets and then gone on to her own sound check and performance was not merely a pretty face with a voice, nor was she someone who was kind but essentially stupid with a softness at core that made for weakness. This was someone who did not appreciate deceit or the appearance of it.

No. There were two things Ren learned, and the first was that she had grossly underestimated whom she met and whom she was dealing with, for in that grasp that reminded Ren of a gauntlet and the now-visored gaze that reviewed her, Nina revealed her core—it was steel.

***

Samantha's head was tight with an uncomfortable tingling numbness she'd not felt for a long time. Part of it she recognized as the weight of too many minds, too many emotions after a high-level, important, performance. But the rest of it...

This particular meet-and-greet function was similar to so many others she attended, but the differences were critical and were not so well hidden below the surface. She kept a practiced smile on her face as she moved from group to group. The first held a discussion on cultural impact and relevance of the project —this was really a metaphor for how much do you think we'll make off this. The next was full of effusive praise for how timely, how daring, how cutting edge it was to include a performing troupe such as Toya's, a troupe that mixed original works with classics and standards and featured an all-female cast in both male and female roles. Such appeal to the avant garde! And of course, there was Samantha's and Nina's band, too, featuring real, out lesbians! And they had a "look" as well as sound that would have mass market appeal! Plus, they already had solid indie cred and support.

Samantha smiled politely through all of it, answered questions about production frequency, current audience reach versus projected, and thinly veiled inquiries about additions and changes to the current stage show, how to kick it up a notch.

"After all," the talking head in the suit blithely continued, oblivious to the warning glance given him by his less obtuse clone, "ya got hot music, hot chicks. Hold on there, Greggs!"— he shook off the obviously cautioning hand laid on his forearm by his colleague—"Ya get a little action going and you're looking at being in the solid black for the next ten years!"

It was that last, said with a slight raise to the eyebrows, too-wide eyes, and uncontainable smirk that snapped at the last of her reserves.

You slimy fucking bastard, Samantha thought, *no one's having on-stage sex for your viewing or other pleasure.* "You've got the wrong party or the wrong idea. Either way, this conversation is over."

She paused a moment for the clone-companion's attempt at an apology. "I've traveled for hours, sound checked, and performed. You *will* excuse me, won't you?" The smile she gave him before she moved on was mostly teeth.

Seemingly interminable moments later, Samantha was at the bar signaling for a bottle of water. When the plastic with its condensed-water skin touched hers, she ripped the cap off and took a slow, long sip, then allowed herself to relax against the wooden ledge.

The music in this area wasn't quite as loud as it was in others though it wasn't completely muted, and as Samantha listened, she wondered if Nina had made suggestions for the play list—it bore her "style."

The melody played well to Samantha's feelings, and she attempted to rid herself of the anger and irritation from the last conversation. The sweet dark tones over hard rhythm brought her back to the things that carried much more weight for her, and she let herself process through them, from least to most important.

The performance had gone well, and from her place in the wings, she enjoyed watching the troupe that preceded them. The next two nights sold well; no matter how discussions went, the event, in and of itself, was a success.

Samantha lit a cigarette and inhaled. She had a view of the larger room, including the area reserved for dancing. The rest of the band, the dancers from the troupe—all still in their various stage-wear, just as Samantha herself was—mingled with the other guests and seemed to be enjoying themselves.

She exhaled slowly and considered Toya's figure striding off the dance floor in search of whatever through the smoke. The dark suit she wore through the last part of her performance fit her beautifully, accentuated the strength of her shoulders, the narrowness of her hips, let the length of her legs show. The look was sharp, strong, and Toya had left her hair loose, let its straight ebony length brush her shoulders. That touch of softness, the malleable flow of it, was a stark contrast to the unyielding lines and angles. It highlighted them, but instead of clashing, they melded: softness and strength, grace and power.

It was that melding of contrasts, Samantha admitted, that pointed to the similarity between them, almost as if they were two sides of the same coin—or perhaps the same side of different coins? She didn't know.

Samantha's feelings about Ren were mixed at best; Ren's presence brought memory with her, memory of a time of pain and confusion. *Fucking ironic*, Samantha considered as she tapped the red glow between her fingers against the ashtray. *Ren's here, and there's more pain to deal with.*

Samantha did not know the entire story between Fran and Ren, but she did know that Fran's turning to Ren back in those days was very much a direct result of Samantha's own actions.

Fran was the source of both the discomfit and the uneasy peace. The truce between Samantha and Ren, hastily hammered into place after they finally met, was a strained thing at best; it was an association forged through ties of friendships and the relations of others. Samantha didn't really know why but she also held a sense of debt to Ren. And she had no idea how to repay it.

All those paths of thought ended in the same place as her eyes found, then tracked, Fran crossing the floor, arm in arm with her old friend. She took another sip, watching the dark head draw closer to the golden one as together they stepped onto the dance floor.

Has Fran told her what's going on? Samantha wondered as she ignored the increased beat of her heart and left her cigarette to burn in the ashtray. She noted the way they moved, the slight distance between their bodies, and as one song slipped into another, she was unaware that she, too, was being observed.

A wordless emotion filled and welled up through her, strong enough to make her blink, to turn away for a moment. When she looked once more at the dancers, she stared at the last thing she expected to see: Nina approaching the pair as the song changed once more. Samantha put her water down on the bar and unconsciously leaned forward as she watched, the music that filled the air gone beneath the beat that hammered her within. The exchange was brief and seemingly polite, even friendly, but the conclusion shocked her: Nina cut in and was dancing—with Ren.

Samantha leaned back, released the breath she didn't realize she held, and blindly reached for her water once more. Her fingers trembled slightly as she raised it to her lips, and took a long pull. The water soothed and cooled on its way down, and a feeling flooded through her as it did. The emotion increased as she saw Fran look for her, then make her way over—it was relief.

***

"How do you prefer to be addressed…Toya or Ren?" Nina asked as they moved through the opening bars of a tune that she had requested earlier. She had, in fact, arranged the majority of the set list, since she wanted it all to be right.

Eyes, slate-blue and shiny, stared back at her and the slightest of grins—or was it a smirk— played in their corners.

"It depends on the situation."

Nina paid attention to the tone, where the tension was and wasn't in the body before her, as well as the expression she could see.

"This situation," Nina told her, her own smile sharp and angular as it cut across her face and she acknowledged the game they played. "This here and now."

The hint of a grin became a smile that mirrored Nina's as the rhythm that sounded around them changed. "Are you always so…acquiescent?"

"Hardly," Nina retorted. "I'm being polite…allowing you a choice before I make one for you."

It was very confusing. All Nina truly knew about Ren Toya previous to this day was her first name, that she was related to Graham's wife, Maeko, that at one point she and Fran were something more than friends and, after viewing clips of her group's performances, that Ren had a great concept going with even better execution. And it turned out now that person was someone she spent a few hours with earlier, working very companionably.

The name confusion she could mostly excuse—mostly. In the few times that Ren was mentioned over the last years, both Samantha and Fran probably assumed they'd mentioned it, but she never picked it up. When they were once again introduced just a short while ago, she remembered the cultural difference, but still…*She enjoyed the confusion. I* know *she did*, Nina reflected, her conclusion based on what she felt in that hand shake earlier and saw before her now.

Between that time and this, Nina was also caught up with the same meet-and-greet niceties as Fran and Samantha. Although social obligations separated them, Nina still kept an occasional eye out for them during their various wanderings.

When Nina spotted Samantha by the bar, her first intention was to put arms about her beloved partner, ask how she was, then plan their exit, but there was something about Samantha's demeanor that stopped her. Nina read a tension to Samantha's shoulders, stress in the lines of her back, as she watched *something* and Nina honed in on that.

For a moment, she saw what Samantha saw, felt what Samantha felt, as they watched Fran and Ren move together. Nina didn't stop to think, she just did. And now she was dancing with—"Toya," Nina decided. It was how *she* met her, *her* first association. If she thought of her as Ren, she couldn't consider her objectively at all. Ren was someone who'd been connected to Fran in ways Nina didn't want to *think* about. Ren was someone that Nina instinctively knew had hurt Fran as well. Toya was someone Nina worked beside, was someone she could get along with. Maybe someday, Nina would be able to call her Ren. Today was not that day.

"You're letting me lead."

"I'm *letting* you think that." Nina laughed outright, and with the slightest twist of her leg and a shift in her hand position, proved it.

Toya laughed back. "Touché," she agreed, and moved in tandem. "And do you always...how does that phrase go...switch hit that way? Isn't that...deceptive?"

"I am what I am—I don't pretend to less, more, or other," Nina answered as the space between them narrowed for the next step. "What are *you*?"

"I am whatever I want to be, whenever I want, with whoever wants me to be it." Toya's body, quickly, briefly, brushed against

Nina's and despite the layers they both still wore from the stage, Nina recognized clearly the subtle protuberance that bumped against her thigh. She pushed slightly away.

"Thank you for the dance," Nina excused. "I should—"

Toya stepped closer, this time deliberately leaving the slightest breath of space between them. She brought her face closer to Nina's shoulder. "Does this scare you? Play with your sense of who you are?"

"*You* don't scare me," Nina said pointedly and turned away.

Toya slid into step behind her and gently touched Nina's shoulder. "What about that?" she asked softly and inclined her head in another direction. "Does *that* scare you?"

Nina followed Toya's gaze through the crowd to find Samantha and Fran, sitting together on one of the many scattered sofas. They were so close their knees touched, crossed over into each other's body space. The way they leaned into each other made Nina's heart smile, and that smile grew while she watched Fran reach across the space between them and brush the hair off Samantha's cheek.

The palpably obvious emotion in Fran's lingering touch, the expression that played across Samantha's face, was discernible to Nina even from where she stood. It once again filled her heart to ache with the beauty of what she saw, stretched it with the intensity of how so very much she loved them. Those emotions were netted in with the fear of losing either one of them, for Nina was very aware of the crazy reality thrust upon them that might make that happen all too soon.

But in this here and now, Nina gratefully welcomed and allowed her true feelings for Fran and Samantha to rule her.

Love softened her mouth, cleared her eyes to true blue and made the almost-silver ring that surrounded them flash. Nina worked her jaw and swallowed down the fear. She let love fill and square her shoulders, set her spine with pride. "No," she answered with uncensored honesty, then faced Toya's raised-brow appraisal. "That I embrace."

Nina neither saw nor cared about the open-mouthed reaction she left behind her as she walked away.

***

Fran was delighted. Preliminary buzz for the performance was better than good; it was *damn* good, and some of the casual discussion she'd had with the potential investors and partners had gone from cocktail chitchat to opening-round negotiations. Although she knew much better than to take anything other than officially agreed-upon and signed contracts as guarantee, it augured for a strong and positive position, especially when she considered the verbal promise she'd received from one of the larger interested backers in the presence of Ren's own representation.

She'd not noticed when either Samantha or Nina had left the party and so, full to brimming with excitement that she half-expected her skin to vibrate, Fran thought of nothing other than the news she had and the discussions they would have over the next few days. *They're probably sleeping*, she reminded herself as she carefully slid her key card into the lock then quietly opened the door.

Music played, loud enough to hide the sound of the door as she shut it but low enough not to be heard in the hallway, and light glowed from just around the corner where the room opened into larger space. Fran stepped quietly forward.

The image froze her, stunned her mind into complete immobility as well, leaving her able to do nothing other than witness. Sight and sound melded, swelled in her throat and became the air she breathed, stopped her heart and took over with an almost painful rhythm as the mirror played its unblinking image for her.

They moved together and they were one. They moved again and revealed open heat and hunger. The movement continued and they already possessed each other; now they possessed *her*.

She had known and deeply loved them both, and when Samantha pressed her face to Nina's back, rubbed her cheek against the soft skin that covered the sharp angle of the shoulder blade, Fran viscerally remembered. She could taste Nina's skin in the place where Samantha's lips touched, felt Samantha's open kiss there, right *there*.

Nina's head turned, exposed her throat and the length of her body. She arched her neck and the mirror lay bare the reflection of raw desire even as Samantha filled it. The intensity that flowed between them overran and filled the room, and the aching twist of love followed a whisper that Fran saw but could not hear, turned Nina's head once more until her eyes, their eyes, reflected back to the glass, to bounce and lock with Fran's, frozen as she watched and loved and missed and wanted.

It was too late for her to move, too late to stop for them, no way to pretend or undo. Love and desire together spun a web, sent their net through the air and caught her within. Now Fran could feel Nina's body yielding to hers, the delicate taste of Samantha on her tongue. Her own hands curved and curled, landscapes of love alive in her palms and under her skin, electric and knowing, until it seemed as if the very knowing itself was what made her blood flow, her heart beat.

Yes, Fran was caught in those eyes, wrapped in the energy that blanketed and made her one with them; the pleasure pushed, edged to pain, a tearing burn into her heart, her body. The fine line point of Light closed in, tightened, rendered time and distance meaningless, and when the moment came, it took them all.

***

Ren was restless. The time zones played havoc with her sleep schedule, and unable to stay still any longer, she dressed and left the room.

"Isamu," she addressed the guard outside her door, "I'm going down to the lobby for coffee and possibly a paper—I would prefer if you stay here." There was no need for him to protect her in what she was sure would be a lightly peopled lobby, and if there *were* to be any danger, it would more likely occur somewhere much more private, somewhere like her rooms. To leave them unattended as well as unoccupied was foolish.

Isamu silently nodded acquiescence and displayed the press-button pager he held. Its indicator light glowed a solid green. Ren touched the pendant she wore. Should she need to, the press of it in just the right place would cause the device Isamu held to silently vibrate and change the light from green to red—the signal that she needed immediate assistance. Since the final dissolution of her father's operation, she had yet to need it.

Precautions in place, Ren took the elevator to the main lobby. The hotel had a small twenty-four-hour café where Ren could do exactly as she planned: find the cup of coffee she wanted, obtain a copy of the most recent *Wall Street Journal,* and ensconce herself in a comfortable spot in the ample seats that made up the lounge next to the café.

Ren sipped and read at her leisure. The lateness of the hour was no deterrent to the occasional murmur of voices from people coming and going to the concierge or the reservations desk. Porters with loaded trolleys walked behind her at random intervals and it all combined to become a soothing background noise.

Though it was not addressed to her, a familiar voice cut through her pleasant reverie, and Ren craned about to see Fran at the reservations and check-in desk. Surprised, Ren got up from her seat and walked over with her cup. "You're up late," she said over Fran's shoulder.

Fran turned to give her a brief but troubled smile, and Ren saw instantly the mark of tears. In that same instant, Ren's friendly surprise gave way to concern, and the clerk returned.

"I'm sorry, ma'am," he said with a properly apologetic shrug, "but the first available space won't be until tomorrow, after one in the afternoon."

"That will be fine," Fran answered as she reached into her bag for her wallet. A second later she pulled her credit card and slid it across the counter.

"That's unnecessary," Ren interrupted, covering Fran's hand with her own. "I've extra space...you're welcome to share it."

Fran shook her head. "Ren...I appreciate that, but I really can't. I—"

"No, nothing like that," Ren quickly interrupted while the clerk coughed politely and attempted to make himself unobtrusive. She quickly curled her fingers about Fran's, then let go. "Where will you sleep?" she asked simply. "You can't stay down here." She pointedly stared at Fran's lack of luggage. "And you'll need your things, too."

Fran gazed about the lobby. "Shit," she exclaimed quietly.

"Why don't you join me for a cup?" Ren suggested, hoisting her own into view. "You don't have to tell me anything," she added hastily, reading the objection in Fran's reddened eyes. "Just think a bit...and then I can help you move your things if you'd like."

The clerk coughed loudly. "Shall I hold this for you, then, while you think on it?"

"Yes, yes. Please do," Fran answered, still clutching her card.

"Come," Ren said again and offered her hand. "Take the moment."

Fran rubbed her temple. "All right, yeah. Sure." She dropped her card back into her bag as she followed Ren the few feet to the sitting area, and just as carelessly dropped herself onto the thick seat, then buried her face in her hands.

Ren considered from where she still stood before her. "Will you be all right for a moment? You still take your coffee the same way?"

"Ren, don't. It's…*I'm* okay," Fran lifted her face to answer. "Things…they're just…they're complex right now."

"I'll be right back with that cup," Ren told her, then took hurried steps to the café. As she ordered at the counter, she realized she didn't really know what Fran's sleeping arrangements were. *But something has happened, something that's upset her and if I can't literally offer her a place to rest, then at least I can do so metaphorically.*

Besides, tomorrow was bound to be a big day: she had meetings in the morning with her team, with Fran's, and then later they would all meet with the other investors. She already met the drunken man who had strange ideas about what this venture was about, and Ren wanted to come to an agreement with her team as well as Fran's about how best to cut him and his company out of it. Also, she wanted Fran to be at her best, for all of their sakes, especially her own.

She handed over a few bills to the cashier and accepted the cup placed on the counter. Ren took careful steps back toward the lounge area and, in an action born of very necessary habit, quickly surveyed the area.

The main lobby was quiet, though not completely devoid of people, as yet another couple walked through on their way to the elevator. It arrived just as her gaze landed on it, and she was only mildly surprised to see Cray, in a half open shirt over jeans and bare feet, step from its open doors. Ren didn't stop to think about why she found that only mildly surprising but followed the direction of Samantha's gaze, expecting to find it on Fran.

Nina's back was to Ren, but she too, had bare feet and wore what was more than likely a hotel robe that hit the carpeted floor as she knelt before Fran. Their heads touched as they spoke, and from the tremble that ran down Nina's back and into the fingers that reached for, then caught, Fran's face, Ren knew that she cried. That *did* surprise her, so much so that she halted sharply, causing the cup in her hand to tilt dangerously.

She muttered a curse as she righted the cup, then strode forward again. Whatever this was, it couldn't be good for any of them, not if there were so many tears involved, not if it had people running about in the middle of the night for reasons other than jet lag. *This has* got *to stop*, Ren resolved grimly as she walked.

She was close enough to hear the broken words Nina spoke. "Please...I *know* we have to talk—we will—I promise. Just... please don't leave."

The pain that wove between them was a living thing, an open wound that bled freely and visibly. It built a wall around them that halted Ren once more, and she felt the pain reach through to her own heart, an echoed repeat of days long gone.

"Leave them," Cray said urgently into her ear, catching up to her just a few feet before the perimeter. She pulled gently on Ren's arm.

"This...this is unacceptable," Ren said indignantly as she followed Cray. Together they found a table and had a moment's silent negotiation as to which would get the seat with the view of the lobby. Ren conceded the claim. *Why does that always happen between us?* she wondered fleetingly, but in truth, she knew why. Ren passed the cup to Cray, then angled her own chair for a better view.

Cray signaled the lone waitress for another cup for Ren, which was quickly deposited and they both sipped in quiet.

Ren's gaze kept shifting back and forth from Cray to the two seated not more than twenty feet away. *Why is she just sitting here?* Ren wondered. *Why doesn't she do something, say something?* The calm stillness from Cray baffled her completely. Earlier, Cray very clearly had shown her feelings for both Nina and Fran, who were now experiencing some sort of emotional connection that easily rivaled what Ren had seen before. "How can you stand it? How can *any* of you stand it?" Ren finally broke into the silence as she watched Cray brood into her cup.

"Stand what?"

"That," Ren answered, "them...the whole thing. Where is your pride? Possession? Something? *Anything?*"

Cray's eyes looked steadily and unblinkingly at her. "What would you have me do? Yell? Beat my chest? Glower and threaten? I don't feel those things, nor the need to do them. Pride and possession have no place in love."

Ren returned her gaze to the scene before them as she thought about what she'd heard and what she'd witnessed earlier. She understood jealousy, rivalry, respect, had seen them all at play in various guises throughout the night. She understood power and its subtle increases when coupled with restraint. She understood friendship and undying loyalty, but this—

"I don't understand *any* of you," Ren said quietly as she watched Nina take Fran's hands in her own and stand. When Fran followed, Nina held Fran to her, heedless of the fall of her robe that revealed a glance of very pale bare skin.

Ren glanced at Cray who gave her a wry grin, then said, "Is this one of those cultural things, like first names versus surnames?"

Ren shook her head and, despite herself, grinned in return. "You tosser. That was an easy accident...you know that. And no," she continued, "it's not *cultural*." Ren held her fingers up in quotes. "I grew up in the UK until I was twelve or so, so it's not some great East-West mind divide."

Are we actually joking? Ren wondered. *Have we ever done this before? This* , she decided, *is the result of too many odd and discordant things jammed into one day. Or*—Ren narrowed her eyes in thought—*it's Cray's way of distracting us both.*

She turned serious again, and faced Cray. *Eyes the color of a summer storm,* Ren decided, not knowing that her own could be described similarly. "You love her," Ren said quietly, indicating Fran with a nod of her chin where she stood still wrapped in Nina's arms, the return embrace so close they seemed entwined.

"You *married* her...and then broke her heart! *You're* the reason we were ever together at all, and now..."

Ren took a breath. "And now," she continued with a slight shake of her head, "you and *Nina* are together, and yet..." She glanced back again, only to see that Nina and Fran had gone.

"And yet...perhaps I know something that you don't," Cray answered then sipped calmly as Ren stared at the now-empty space.

Returning her attention once more to Cray, she contemplated the woman before her. This time, Ren really looked and saw what she had missed before.

Cray was pale; her eyes held a dark burn over bruise-colored smears. The way she angled her head, held the nearly-empty mug. This was more than jet lag combined with over-confused emotions and nerves. This was something *other*, this was—

"Samantha," Ren said quietly, carefully addressing Cray by her given name for the first time ever, "what's *really* going on? What don't I know?" A chill raced across her shoulders when Samantha's gaze rose once more from the depths of her cup to meet hers.

Those eyes gleamed with the emotions they held in check, and the shine of them seemed to cut with their intent. Ren found herself leaning forward.

"You don't know how much I *never* wanted that—*any* of it—to break with her, to hurt her, but it kept her safe." Samantha's voice was low and harsh, a vehement whisper of a growl. "You don't know *why* she broke off with Nina. You don't know *how* she lived, you don't know *why* she did it, and you *don't* know—" She turned her head away, the words seemingly caught in her throat as she breathed around them.

The coffee sat neglected on the table and the waitress who approached hesitated when once again Samantha faced Ren. The visage that confronted Ren made the chill that had raced across her shoulders earlier grab a firm hold. Samantha's face was stone, stone broken only by the flow of a single tear down her cheek. She made no move to brush it away, and she made no sound. She barely breathed.

Samantha's broken stoicism turned chill to fear in Ren. But Ren was no stranger to fear, so she embraced it and let it flow through her while tears continued to silently fall from Samantha's eyes.

Ren took a deep breath and let it out in a controlled flow as she reached out and lightly rested her fingertips on Samantha's fist where it lay on the table. Her decision made, she said the only thing she could.

"How can I help?"

***

It was the last thing I expected, especially at six in the morning, eastern standard, which meant it was three a.m. in California. The timing didn't bother me, either; I'd already been up for an hour, and that was a habit everyone was aware of. It was just that I thought the first discussion I would have with any of them might be about how the initial events had gone, a joke about some of the people they were dealing with, and even though I winced to think of it, maybe even a complaint about the sleeping arrangements.

I definitely did not expect a request for the itinerary over the next six months, any copies that could be obtained from the home label of their HR policies and benefits, and a double-check of their passports. And especially not at that hour.

"No problema, Sam," I promised, and began to tally the items I needed, and the number of calls I'd have to make as I quickly jotted down the essentials. It definitely seemed like today was going to be one of *those* days. "I'll get that all together and to you. Bear will have it when he gets there at"—I took a quick second to dredge up his itinerary and calculate—"uh, four in the afternoon, your time. If you think of anything else while he's traveling, I'll have it faxed or overnighted."

Her voice was rough as she thanked me again. Damn, but she needed to sleep. There were two more nights of full performances and I knew how important they were.

"It's all right—don't worry about it. Just make sure you both get some rest so you can knock 'em dead later," I told her through her apology for the hour and the thanks. "Oh, and keep me posted on how the deal's going," I reminded her before we clicked off.

I took a quick gulp of the coffee I'd poured while balancing the phone and a pencil, then dialed Bear.

"Is it a new label yet?" he asked. From his tone, I guessed he was halfway through his first cup of caffeine.

"Good morning to you too, and I don't know yet. I think we're still in labor. But dude, Samantha just called and I need you to get to the office as soon as you possibly can. There's a bunch of stuff Sam asked for that's got to go with you. I'll explain when you get there, *and* I'll get you to the airport on time."

A muffled crash followed by a not-quite-as-muffled curse sounded in my ear. "I'll see you in twenty. Everything okay?" he asked, his voice and mind now definitely wide awake. "What's going on? Do you think—"

"I've no idea," I interrupted, as anxious as he was and impatient to get started, "but something *big's* on the move."

I offered to bring more coffee, he promised to help me make phone calls, and I knew in between, we'd both speculate a little about what we did know and worry a lot more about what we didn't.

As I swept my keys off the table and grabbed my jacket where it hung by the door, I wondered what I'd helped set in motion and sincerely hoped it hadn't been a mistake.

***

"Thank you, Isamu," Samantha said to the slender man who accompanied her and saw her securely into the elevator when she left Ren's room. He nodded silently as the doors closed, and she pressed the button for her floor.

This can work, this can work well, Samantha reflected as the car rose through the building. She was tired, but for the first time since she and Nina had walked into Fran's apartment those weeks ago, she felt calm. There was a plan, there were possibilities, there was *hope*, and she had Ren to thank for opening that door.

She had no doubts as to Stephie's ability to find what they would need to help make this happen. All Samantha had to do was present these ideas to the women she hoped were safely ensconced in the room they shared. She wondered about them when the doors opened, depositing her on her floor.

She was careful as she stepped over the elevator's metal edge, not wanting to cut her bare feet, and the carpet scratched at them as she walked down the corridor. She pursed her lips as she deliberated. She highly doubted Fran and Nina had gone beyond a talking stage...or if they even got past anything but the past itself. She paused by the door to pull her key card out of her pocket, then shook her head ruefully as she unlocked the door. *The answer's so simple, Nina,* Samantha thought as she walked in, half afraid and half hopeful of what she'd find.

The low light by the bedside was on in exactly the same way it had been when she'd left the room moments behind Nina, and the mirror, that mirror that had caught and captured them all so clearly earlier, now reflected only the low light and the silent still forms on the bed.

Samantha stepped forward quietly and gazed down at the reality before her. Nina was propped up against the headboard; Fran's head rested just in the hollow of her shoulder. In their sleep they held each other closely, legs and hands entwined, and while Fran's cheek had found the soft warm skin in the *V* of the robe, Nina's lips rested a breath away from Fran's brow.

The sweet vulnerability of their repose made Samantha's breath catch as she filled with the weight and the warmth of how she so very much loved each of them. That love further gentled her eyes, manifested itself as tenderness in her fingertips when she stroked, oh so lightly, through Fran's hair and touched her lips to Nina's. Long lashes flickered sleepily open and Nina gave her an equally sleepy smile. "Hey, baby," she whispered and attempted to adjust.

"Shhh…stay there," Samantha quieted, then kissed her again. "Go back to sleep. Tomorrow's a really big day."

"All right," Nina returned. "Are you okay?" The gaze she held on Samantha was as smoky as it was tired, and Samantha smiled as she removed her jeans.

"I'm fine—you? Is she?" She eased into bed beside Nina and took a moment to get comfortable, then slipped an arm over Nina's waist and rested her hand over their interlaced fingers.

"For now, I think." The look Nina gave her was troubled and sad and as tired as Samantha was. The rigid control she kept herself locked down with had eroded.

Sadness crept back through Samantha, sadness for the rift that had sprung between them and between Nina and Fran, as well as for the dark possibility that loomed in their combined future.

"I *love* you," Nina whispered, her voice tight, intense, her eyes full. "You know that, right?" Emotion warmed Nina's skin, floated over her, was a flow Samantha could feel.

Samantha tightened her hold. Except for when they made love, the rapport between Samantha and Nina had suffered since they'd walked into Fran's apartment those weeks ago. But for the first time since, the connect was solid and strong.

"I love *you*," she whispered back just as intently, her gaze focused on the beautiful blue eyes that swam before hers. "And I *never* doubt that…I never doubt *you*." They shared another kiss as the gaps between them reduced to nothing. "You shouldn't either."

"I'm…Sam, I'm so sorry. I didn't know—"

"Don't apologize. You did the right thing," Samantha assured her. "We'll get this all sorted out…I promise." She kissed Nina once more, sealing her intent. "Please, love…sleep."

I don't want to be your reason for holding back, Samantha thought as they snuggled in closer. *And I don't want to push you into* anything, *especially something you're not ready for, or that you don't truly want.*

Whatever happened next—even Samantha's proposal— would hinge on Nina's decision, and, in the end, it could be Nina's decision only. But it had become increasingly, even painfully, clear that Nina wasn't truly aware of all the choices she had. The not knowing was tearing her, tearing all of them, apart. That Fran had decisions to make as well didn't enter into Samantha's musings. For a very long time, she and Fran, her Frankie, had been very clear about their feelings for each other, what they would and wouldn't do about them, as well as what they would do about Fran's feelings for Nina.

In fact it was Fran, Samantha remembered, who had the stronger knowledge of Nina back when this all started, who cautioned and even occasionally coached Samantha. The memory made her smile. There were two occasions when they disagreed about her approach to the strong but still secretly and deeply scarred woman they both loved. One occasion had turned out well, and the other, Samantha considered ruefully, they were seemingly all paying for now.

How do I tell her without pushing her in any way? How can she make a decision that's free and wholly her own if she's not fully aware of everything?

It hit her suddenly. She didn't have to tell Nina anything, because such a telling could force things and that forcing was anathema to them all. *But I can let her know!* Samantha realized, eyes growing wide. *I can do that without pushing or forcing anything!*

A subtle hint, Samantha decided, that's all it would take. Well, given what Nina had already shown, perhaps not too subtle, but still, it would probably give Nina all the information she needed to make her own decision.

Tomorrow was a full day. There were meetings, there was a gig, there was the party at some club they had to go to since it was being thrown for them by the venue owners and, of course, there were the plans that Samantha had begun.

She didn't know how or when she would do it, but as she closed her eyes, Samantha knew exactly what she had to do next.

***

All Nina could remember of her dreams the next day was that they were a confused medley and muddle of image and emotion. She fell asleep sitting up on the bed with Fran held close, woke up when Samantha came in, and when next she wakened, she had a few moments of warm peace hearing the low conversation between Fran and Sam—Frankie and Sammer, as they called each other quietly.

She let the soft murmur of their voices fill her drowsiness with a satisfied calm for that little bit of time before the regret that she'd ever come between them rose and filled her eyes. Then she remembered the demands of the day and jumped out of bed. There was a quick round of good morning affections, and she hit the ground running.

A hasty breakfast meeting took place in Ren's rooms where they quickly discussed and agreed to cut out an interested party. Nina was aghast to hear the conversation that Samantha had had the night before. "A small man, uh, mind," Samantha began, "with big ideas." But there was no time for anything but that quick review and an even quicker agreement on how they would proceed during the official meeting that would take place in an hour.

They all promised to meet again the next morning and discuss final details before any official signings or promises were made. There *were* hints of something more to come in that conversation, but then before there was an opportunity to ask… the next meeting was underway. There was, at its start, the rapid, polite-but-firm dismissal of the rejected party with its attendant brief explanation euphemistically positioned as incompatible differences but in reality, ethical ones. "We have them. They don't," as Fran stated in their earlier, private meeting. Then it was onward with outlines and plans, stats and projections, and the tentative assignments of rights and responsibilities.

Bear had to be picked up from the airport and there was a flurry of activity with instruments and stage-wear. Then it was back to the venue for yet another sound check now that Bear was there to run the sound and lighting boards since this, as opposed to the dress rehearsal of the night before, was a real show with a paying audience.

The performance lasted longer than Nina thought it would. The audience was more enthusiastic and responsive than usual, and the band responded in turn. That was followed by the truly unavoidable, entourage-encumbered journey and entrance to the club. Nina rolled her eyes at the memory. It was only now that Nina had a moment of silence and solitude, although standing at the bar surrounded by strangers still high from the concert could hardly be called either of those things.

As she sipped at her cup of juice, Nina allowed her mind to wander where it would, then let her eyes do the same. She spotted regular club-goers and the rest of the band, Toya's troupe and the venue administrators, and even some of the suits that she'd met with earlier, milling about, drinking, dancing, having what seemed to be a good time. More than likely, she decided, some hand-picked press was there too.

She let her gaze continue to drift until it finally found Bear, who was heartily enjoying both his beer and an animated conversation and dance with Fran. Nina focused on her, the way she angled her head, the flow of her hair, the brilliant flash of her smile, and the beautiful curve of her lips when she laughed. Nina's eyes traveled further down the elegant length of Fran's neck, rested on the glorious rise of—

Samantha's warm presence announced itself half a second before she wrapped herself around Nina and leaned her cheek against hers. "She really is amazing, isn't she?" Samantha asked quietly. Nina thought she sounded wistful as well.

Guilt over coming between Samantha and Fran twisted through Nina, but the wistful note in Samantha's voice and the real love and comfort that radiated from her, opened Nina to a new awareness as together they watched the wonder that moved before them.

It was in that stillness, with Fran before her and her Samantha wrapped around her, that the words finally floated free, easy and clear in Nina's mind. *I love* her—*I'm* in *love with her.* She'd always known the first part, and the second, she supposed she ignored, out of fear, out of ignorance, and perhaps a thousand other stupid reasons. But there was a third part left to acknowledge, and it made itself clear the second she saw one of the members of the dance troupe cut in to dance with Fran. *God! I* want *her.*

The knowledge of it hit her hard, threaded through the guilt with shame, and slammed into her with heated and heavy urgent fullness. It stole her breath and pounded with bruising force against her heart.

Nina's whole world tilted. Had Samantha not already held her, Nina was certain she'd have fallen. As it was, she couldn't prevent leaning harder into Samantha's embrace.

"Go dance with her," Samantha encouraged softly. Her breath whispered against the sensitive skin behind Nina's ear. It felt the same way it had when they made love the night before, when Samantha asked her to look up, to see them and the reflection of the love they made. One physical memory brought others, and Nina, already off-balance, felt the ground beneath her cant further.

The minute shake of her head rubbed Nina's cheek against Samantha's. It took effort to breathe, to speak. "Maybe later." The words were faint, even to her own ears.

Samantha loosened her hold and slid around to face her. She took Nina's now half-full cup from her hand and placed it on the bar. "Then dance with *me*...it's been a while." She smiled and, despite her turmoil, Nina couldn't help but smile in return at the lips she frequently and freely admitted she was addicted to kissing.

She glanced up and was caught in the placid blue glow of Samantha's gaze. Love and desire flowed from it, and Nina's heart raced. "Yes, it has," she agreed, and for the first time, perhaps ever, Nina allowed herself to be led to the dance floor.

For a little while, Nina was lost in the rhythm. She let the music and the motion cascade over and through her and released all the tension to the dance. Samantha's raw sensuality, coupled to the heavy beat, played well to her state of mind.

Here and there, a flash of light went off. *Wonder if that's private or for the press.* Nina shrugged the thought away. It didn't really matter, either way.

"Hey, good party, huh?" Bear asked as he bumped into her. "Better than Prague."

Nina shared a laugh with him. "But not quite like London."

"But neither of those would ever beat Madrid," Samantha said, her voice mischievous and light in Nina's ear.

Nina raised an eyebrow as she faced her partner. "Don't you mean Ibiza?" When it came to parties and party towns, as much as she loved her native city of New York, so far as Nina was concerned, Ibiza beat the world.

"'Biza totally rocks!" Bear seconded, his head bouncing in time to the rhythm that surrounded them.

"For parties, Ibiza, sure," Samantha agreed, "but for amazing, beautiful, wonderful? Madrid. Absolutely." She wore an enigmatic smile.

Nina stared. Madrid brought memories with it, memories that beat through her already heightened state with both an emotional and visceral reality that very much resonated in the present. Nina's world was again a-swirl; the dance haze was gone.

"What do you mean?" she asked carefully.

Samantha laughed lightly as she gazed about the dance floor, then found who she was searching for in the direction of the bar. "Why don't we ask Fran?" she asked, as she waved her over.

Nina's every nerve jumped into hyper-alertness. "I'll take your word for it," she answered, but Fran was already there.

"Hey, they did a really good job with this party, don't you think?" she asked, her voice pitched to rise above the din of the music and the crowd. Her face wore the incredible smile Nina now clearly knew she still was—and had probably always been —very much in love with. Even had she wanted to, she couldn't stop staring. With that smile before her, all Nina could think was that she wanted nothing more than to touch its corners, round its curves, taste its depth.

"Awesome!" Bear agreed as Samantha reached for Fran's hand and pulled her closer to them. "And Sam here is saying that Madrid beats 'Biza for parties. What do you say?"

"That's not it exactly," Samantha corrected him with a laugh. "I said Ibiza was great for parties, but for sheer wonder, Madrid. What do *you* say?"

Nina wasn't sure exactly when any of them had stopped dancing. She cast her gaze downward, and her eyes caught and loved the elegant, sensual fit of Fran and Samantha's hands together. She vividly remembered how that joined touch had felt, remembered too, how hers blended with it, and heat joined memory.

Nina glanced up, and watched a flush, visible even in this erratic light, rise on Fran's cheeks. The world stopped and for a moment; Nina thought her heart might too.

"Madrid." The answer was low, barely audible, and Nina wasn't certain if she'd merely read Fran's lips. But they were closer now, so perhaps it didn't matter. "I *loved* Madrid," Fran continued. "And you're right, Sammer," she said, directing her gaze to her, "I should *never* have left like that."

The music, the rhythm, the party, even Bear, were forgotten as Nina stood there, shocked by the admission, by the real discussion they were finally having under the surface conversation. Fran took her hand, brought it to her lips, and kissed it. "I'm sorry."

Every moment, every touch, every word, the offers and promises both Samantha and Fran had made when they'd last been together in Spain replayed and lived in Nina's mind, a thundering tumble that beat with her blood.

Nina reached delicate fingers to touch Fran's chin, brushed her thumb along her cheek. With Samantha's hand firmly in hers, Nina didn't wonder or worry about anything at all as another light flared near them. She followed her heart and kissed her desire.

***

The car ride back had been…interesting. It was not the sensual make-out fest of porn fantasies, nor was it filled with the casual rough banter of friends and teammates. There were long silences occasionally punctuated by intense short questions, followed by even briefer answers—exchanges that were in essence the confirmation of very necessary permissions, accompanied by the affirmation that, yes, they were *really* going to *do* this, because they wanted to, because they needed to. Sober. Clear.

"It's not…it's not because of—this isn't just some sort of strange sympathy thing?" Fran asked into the tense silence that grew as they traveled back to the hotel, her nerves and fears at the surface now.

The answer was quick, almost vehement in its reassurance, from each of them. The situation was the catalyst, not the cause, and while there was a half-embarrassed admission from Nina that perhaps things between them might have dragged on a bit longer before resolution without it, there was also the firm promise that whatever tomorrow held, they'd face it together.

Despite these assurances, tension in the car escalated, and they each grew quiet, almost still, as they neared their destination.

Expectation, anticipation, and even a touch of fear, twined and grew so thick between them, that it seemed palpable. It made the walk through the lobby almost silent and the elevator ride found them all avoiding both touch and even random glance.

Fran's heart shook the way Nina's hands did when she unlocked the door. She felt the tremor that ran through Samantha's arm when it accidentally brushed against her back as she reached to flick the light switch.

They stared at each other solemnly in the warm glow, the color of their eyes indiscernible to one another through the flames that danced within them. Samantha smiled at her, a tiny gentle quirk of her lips as she took Nina's hand and embraced Fran with the other arm, but it was Nina who closed the circle between them.

And then…and then it was easy, just oh so very easy.

The shake Fran felt from within moved through her when Nina leaned into Samantha and kissed her. "I *love* you," she told her, voice low and deliberate. "I will *always* love you." She turned her gaze on Fran, her eyes now luminous and deep blue, the silver that outlined them so clear, as clear as the emotion that poured from her touch with her words. "I have *never* stopped loving you—and I won't." She edged closer, her lips a breath away. "And *I'm* sorry," she whispered. "I should have known—should have told you before."

Fran's body pulsed with what her heart and mind could no longer contain or restrain. She was alive with the taste of Nina's mouth in hers, Samantha's whispered declaration confirmed with her lips on Fran's neck. The bond that ran between them was open and strong, the one from her to Nina free and clear.

Naked in ways she had never been before either of them and they to her, Fran allowed her heart full reign as she embraced them both and together they lay down.

She had thought it was enough to remember, or at least had tried to make it enough, to cherish what had been the past, to let it remain there. But surrounded by the scent and sight and sound of the present, Fran knew she'd only tried to fool herself.

This moment, this very *now*, with Nina's body once more melded to hers, the pulse and flow, over and under and within, while Samantha's breath floated under her ear, cascading down her neck and shoulder only to become a kiss that heightened the hunger it satisfied…Now was all that mattered.

The kiss itself grew, traded, shared, until Fran lost all sense of difference between one lover and the other, and her body became the instrument through which they played the music of love and desire in a rhythm that made up for lost time. Then time itself erased.

Whispered words that came from the depth of each self—felt and known before even being spoken—preceded each deep touch, and the welcoming heat of even deeper embraces brought the sweet song of such profound satisfaction that Fran felt its jolt with her entire self, body and mind lifted even higher. She never knew who made it first or echoed it next. It didn't matter —Fran herself was part of the refrain.

The days and nights of longing, of rigid restraint, were banished in a dance that called for unconditional release; it demanded a complete surrender to its rhythm and rhyme, and in that surrender, gifted them all with an absolute freedom new to each, as they remembered and relearned, renewed and rediscovered.

Fran could feel Light grow, expand, spread through her until she was made of it. Even behind closed eyes, Nina and Samantha glowed with it too, as the melody they built between them swelled.

Each note eased into the next, every empty space was filled and full. Point and counterpoint wove a harmony through a chorus that held Fran firm and hard and fast. Between the two women she loved perhaps even more than she loved herself, Fran was brought face to face with the source of that Light, her soul the witness, her body the testament as it filled her, a burgeoning lift until it overflowed and she knew, she *knew*—

She was loved, she was loved, she *was* love. This was her family. She was finally home.

***

"...and that," Ren said, "is the final offer. Ladies"—she looked over where Fran, Samantha, and Nina sat nearby at the long conference table—"we are certain?"

The question was as rehearsed as it was rhetorical, but it was necessary that it and its answer be public so that there would be no doubt. Ren was chosen to present the final proposal so that both the reality and illusion of unity were firmly upheld.

Fran, who spoke for Nina and Samantha's part of the deal, quickly answered to the affirmative. "We are. And we would, of course, prefer to wrap this within the next twenty-four hours, before the needs of business require we all be out of country."

Ren leaned back in her seat and impassively observed the other participants over steepled fingers. There was quick scowling over notes on pads, frantic crossings-out of eliminated terms. Quiet discussion took place among scattered pairs. "We can reconvene in an hour, so you may have the time you need to check with your various home offices," she offered, and the hasty agreements were accompanied by the hurried push of chairs across the carpet.

The hour of time had also been pre-agreed upon between them; it permitted for a fair response to the issues, while keeping the meeting itself within acceptable time constraints. This would allow Nina, Samantha, and Ren herself time to rest before tonight's performance. She smiled over at them. "Shall we get some coffee?"

Not more than two hours earlier, Isamu announced the prompt arrival of the triad for their private pre-meeting, and during it, Ren allowed Samantha to lead the discussion. There was, Ren observed when they all first sat down to eat and discuss, a definite change between them.

Even had Ren not witnessed both the exchange between Fran and Nina, nor the kiss at the party the night before, the change would still be evident. It was obvious to Ren in the brightness of Nina's smile and the softness in the corners of her mouth when she looked at Fran or Samantha. Ren read it in the clarity of Samantha's eyes, the openness of her hands that touched one, then the other. She saw it in the set of Fran's shoulders, the way her body leaned toward one, her head angled to the other.

Should I tell them about the young woman with the camera? she wondered, then decided against it. Considering the gravity of what they were about to discuss, Ren felt no pressing need to tell them about the after-show party attendee who'd snapped a photograph of the brief but intimate scene between them. Besides, Ren herself had taken care of it. Under pretense of examining a camera model she'd not seen before, she "accidentally" exposed the film and had Isamu efficiently dispose of the rest.

Ren rapidly assessed the information she had: she was comfortable with Samantha, had decided that Nina was both more than capable and trustworthy, and Fran...well, she would always love and respect her friend, as well as frankly admire her abilities. If Fran was happy—and given the warm glow that suffused both her skin and her smile, Ren was certain she was— then Ren would do nothing to harm that, and certainly do quite a bit to aid it.

Aid, in fact, was what this breakfast meeting was about, though of those there, Fran and Nina did not know that yet. There was no need, Ren concluded, to mar their new union with concerns outside the ones they already had, and she enjoyed the quiet conversation that flowed between them.

When the time was right, Samantha outlined the proposition to them. "…so this covers the bases, and lets us truly focus where we need to, while providing for future expansions."

"I love it, it's perfect—let's do it!" Nina agreed immediately.

"You *can't,*" Fran protested almost simultaneously, "you've all worked too hard to let this opportunity go."

Nina turned in her seat to touch Fran's cheek and gaze into her eyes. "No, baby," she said, her voice soft but firm, and her eyes over-bright as she spoke. "Nothing is more important than *you* right now—not music, not business…not even us. Nothing."

Samantha grasped Fran's hand over the table. "She's right. And since you have to do something anyway, let's do it this way —and it'll take a lot of stress off your shoulders during the process. Besides," the half grin Samantha gave as she spoke made Ren certain Samantha had forgotten anyone else was there, "you've always said you wanted to spend a few months living in Tokyo again and see the *sakura,* the cherry blossoms."

"I would have you stay in my apartment in Kichijoji," Ren interjected. "And it would be completely yours, for as long as you wanted. I myself will stay in my father's"— she faltered a moment—"my place in Seijou. Besides, you can see the *sakura* in Inokashira Park—just make sure the three of you don't take boat rides together on the pond. Then again," and here Ren paused to allow herself a small grin, "you're a triad, not a couple, *and* you've moved beyond courting, so perhaps Benzaiten's spell won't work."

Ren's grin grew into a full smile at Fran's shocked expression.

She knew full well that Fran was surprised not only by the allusion to their relationship, but also by her reference to the park's legend of a vengeful goddess who placed a curse on courting couples who ventured out on the pond in a boat. But in her warning of it, Ren was also affirming her support and approval, and when Fran finally returned a watery smile, Ren knew her message had gotten through.

"You can't do this," she said finally. "I won't let you—you can't all give up the things you love so much for me. Ren, you *love* that place! Nina, Sam," she said and looked at each of them, "the *point* of this entire trip—the meetings, the shows, all of it—was to create a new label, *your* label, your *future*. All of you."

Ren glanced quickly at Samantha, then Nina. Permissions granted and clear, she leaned across the table, then placed her hand over the warm knot of their entangled hands. "And what future do any of us have without our Nozomi? You have taken care of everyone else. Please, Fran, let *us* take care of *you*. Then the future will take care of itself."

Fran took a shaky breath as she stared down at the table and considered. "All right," she said quietly before she looked up.

Tears filled Fran's eyes, glinted from her eyelashes, but didn't fall. For a moment, just a single moment, Ren felt an answering smart in her own, and a brief clutch of regret that things had not turned out differently. But destiny, Ren knew, could not be avoided, only made worse. And so, Ren let that feeling go as she leaned back and released their hands from hers, secure in the knowledge her beloved friend was exactly that—beloved.

"And what's the plan for the meeting later today, then?"

The plan Samantha and Ren presented to her and Nina had been relatively easy to create. The night before, when Samantha apprised Ren of the true situation with Fran, the solution became apparent, and was surprisingly simple: Japan had some of the best cancer facilities globally, a national obsession given their historical experiences. Ren had both the money and the connections to access the care Fran needed, as well as heart enough to know that through the recovery process, Fran would need those dear to her as close as possible. And though they did not speak of it, underneath was the silent acknowledgement that the closeness would be critical should the worst occur.

The new business venture could be put on hold, but a lot of money and effort had gone into arranging the meetings and events, so face, for both them and the interested parties had to be saved, and the future—a future that they were firmly certain must and would include Fran—had to be provided for. With that in mind, they created a list of proposals that would work to everyone's ultimate and increased benefit, though it would perhaps take a bit longer than expected. Should they be rejected, the plan would allow each party to walk away knowing they'd done their best and not feeling they'd wasted their time.

On the personal side, it would let Samantha and Nina focus their energies and attention where they wanted over the next several months—on Fran during her treatment and recovery process in a place she loved. On the business side, there would be a new entity that joined East and West and the time spent in Japan would allow them to build a firm Pac-Rim foundation.

Both Nina and Fran approved.

Now, with their proposal before the investors and the initial meeting over, they once more companionably sipped coffee together, discussed their upcoming travel plans, and called Stephie in New York to make more phone calls and send faxes to numbers Ren provided in Tokyo.

By the time they walked back into the conference room, nervous excitement buzzed through them all, and Ren realized that within the excitement that filled her, she also felt something else, something she'd not felt in a very long time. It didn't matter how the meeting went, whether the terms were agreed upon or not. *I'm happy*, Ren thought as she walked to her seat. *I'm actually happy.*

Not only was she finally going to be able to build something of her own, she would perhaps also redeem some of her father's legacy. Already, she was able to help a friend. Friends, she amended to herself with a secret small smile as she looked at them: Fran, in her suit and her papers set neatly before her on the table, Samantha with her air of casual indifference as she leafed through hers, and Nina, with her studied cool as she placed her own report down and stood to face the rest.

"Welcome back, ladies and gentlemen," Nina began with a smile. "So...have we reached an agreement?"

***

"Oh my God, Stephie! I totally can't believe it! Hey Steph—do I have a passport?" Bear asked, his excitement and confusion clear to me across three thousand miles.

I couldn't help but laugh as I answered. "Dude, I sent it with that package you brought with you, just in case. But you don't need it yet. You're not traveling for about another month. Better start learning Japanese now, *gaijin* boy."

"Yeah, yeah, I know, I know," he answered. "But I know they can be a total bitch to get! And hey, I know how to ask for the bathroom, Fran told Nina and me—and that's a good start," he insisted. "But, omigod, omigod, omigod—Steph, it worked, it so totally *worked!* You're a total freakin' genius!"

Even though he couldn't see me, I blushed at the compliment. "Nah," I said, "it came from something you said, anyway."

"I said something? When did I say something?"

I could imagine the expression on his face and it made me smile as I answered him. "About two, maybe three weeks ago? Oh hey"—this time I interrupted myself—"have you seen the logo design Nina created for the new project?"

"I think they're faxing it to you later, but I can tell you what it is—it's gorgeous. It's a triskele set within the Japanese naval-ensign-styled sun. Hey, maybe I'll get that as a tattoo!" he enthused.

"We're not there yet, bud," I reminded him. "Only two of the investors agreed to all of the terms, and one of them was Toya's group. It's gonna take a little bit, maybe another full year or so before we're completely up and running."

"True that," he conceded, "and there's also the whole thing with Fran and her...d'you think she'll be okay?"

With both Fran and Samantha's agreement, Nina had filled us both in—separately, of course—on what caused the black cloud that invaded our work space before they went on this trip.

"Yeah, I do," I answered, nodding because I forgot he couldn't see me. "There's too much love, too much hope, and too big a tomorrow for her not to be all right."

Bear sighed into his end of the phone. "I guess...I hope, anyway. I might try praying. Couldn't hurt, right?"

"You do all those things, and I will, too," I promised.

A companionable if slightly melancholy silence filled the miles between us.

"Steph?"

"Yeah, bud?"

"What did I say?"

"Huh?"

Bear sighed a long-suffering sigh. "You said I said something a few weeks ago that gave you an idea. What was it?"

That knocked the melancholy right out of me as I remembered. Bear was partially right. I wasn't a freakin' genius, but I occasionally had a good idea. "You said 'just lock them up in a room together with a bathroom and enough food to get by for a few days. They'll either work it out or kill each other.'" I couldn't help grinning. "I figured they wouldn't kill each other."

Bear laughed so hard I had to hold the phone away from my ear, and two seconds later, I joined him.

The End

Blackout

By

Susan X Meagher

The Vagaries of Fame. The Perils of Celebrity in a Starcentric World. Laurie Ambrose stood on the corner of Sixth Avenue and Eighteenth Street, devising titles, as she often did, for quotidian events in her life. Her underpaid and over-used assistant Libby stood at her side.

"I wouldn't normally care if they saw me, but I look so bedraggled that I'm afraid they won't believe I'm me." Laurie's body was on Eighteenth, but her head was peeping around the building so that she could spy on a neat queue of people waiting in line.

The ninety-degree temperature, the very high humidity, and the fact that Laurie had just finished a yoga class combined to make her look almost nothing like her publicity photo. Her sandy brown hair, normally sleek and full, was wet with perspiration and had sprouted a short halo of humidity-induced strays. Her blue-and-green print, sleeveless V-neck top and leaf green yoga pants rendered her far too casual to properly represent her brand to her adoring fans. But Libby knew the bigger problem was that Laurie had been running very late, and when she was late, she was nervous. When she was nervous, her underarm protection sometimes failed her. Today it had failed her completely, but Libby did not want to be the one to mention this. Using the skills that made her a very good assistant, she proposed, "My gym is just two blocks away. You look enough like me to pass. Take my ID and you can have a shower and a nice place to change."

"I'm fifteen years older than you are!"

Libby did not remind her that their age difference was a bit over twenty years. "It doesn't matter. Just swipe the card through the reader and head down the stairs. The women's locker room is on the left." She pushed the garment bag into Laurie's hands. "I'll go into the store and make sure we're set up properly. Your agent should be there already."

"My agent," Laurie growled. "She's nothing more than a pimp."

"She can help me get organized. And, if somebody from your publisher is there, I'll wheedle some books out of them to give to your fans. If you give them something for free, they won't even notice if you're late."

Indecisively, Laurie's eyes shifted from the crowd of about a hundred people back to the garment bag she held. "Are you sure?"

Libby took her by the shoulders and turned her in the direction of the gym. "I'm positive. It's only three thirty-five. You can easily be back here in twenty minutes, and you'll be five minutes early." They both knew that was a ridiculously optimistic timetable, but Laurie started running towards the gym, and Libby headed for the door of the bookstore.

***

Libby had no idea how she had accomplished it, but Laurie stood next to her at 4:05, looking and smelling fantastic. She wore a very simple sky-blue-and-yellow sun dress which showed off her enviably toned arms and long legs. Her hair was in order once again, held back from her face with a tortoiseshell band, and she'd applied a little bronzer to her cheeks, making her look more like a model for a high-end women's clothing catalog than a mystery writer. But that was the "Laurie Ambrose" look, carefully chosen for the brand.

Laurie smiled gracefully and shook hands with her agent and a rep from her publisher. The table was set up, large signs with her publicity photo were properly placed, and the books were not only on hand, it looked as though there were enough of them. Libby discreetly said, "It took some doing, but I pried ten books out of your rep's greedy paws."

"Good for you. Did you give them out?"

"Yep. I went outside and made people answer trivia questions about the series. Some of those people must do nothing but read your books."

"I hope so," Laurie said, her throaty laugh making not only Libby but everyone nearby smile at her.

"I'm not crazy about where they've stuck us," Libby said, looking worried.

"I've had worse. I had to sign in front of the pool toys at a Wal-Mart in Mississippi right before the Fourth of July. I barely sold a book, but I learned a lot of Southern insults."

A kind-faced woman approached and addressed Libby, "Are you ready?"

She turned to Laurie, but before she could speak every light in the store went dark. All five of them looked at each other for a moment, then Laurie said, "It's so quiet." Indeed, it was. Every person in the store seemed to come to a standstill, waiting to see what happened. But the lights didn't come back on, and the shoppers began to look to Laurie and her group—as though they were in charge.

"Nothing to worry about folks," said the bookstore manager. "We must have blown...something." She took off, heading for a door at the back of the building.

"Now what?" Libby asked.

"We can't sell books in the dark," Laurie said. "Besides, if the lights aren't on, the cash registers won't work."

"The air conditioning is off too," a woman behind Laurie said softly. "It'll get hot in here soon."

Laurie turned to find an exotically lovely woman gazing at her. Laurie found herself strangely calmed just by looking at the woman, whose reaction to the power outage was devoid of emotion. Always seeking out the calmest-looking person in times of strife, Laurie said, "How can you tell that?"

"It was blowing on my neck. Now it's not." She smiled, showing even, white teeth that nearly glowed in contrast to her tanned skin and straight, black hair. "I bet the demand for power blacked the whole neighborhood out."

"No," Laurie said confidently, then asked in a softer voice, "You really think so?"

"Yeah. If it was something in the building, they'd have it fixed by now."

"I'll go look outside," Libby said, dashing away.

"I wonder what she's going to look for?" Laurie asked.

"Traffic lights would be a good start. If they're out—the neighborhood's out."

"Oh, shit," the rep mumbled. "I'll go see what I can do to help," then he walked towards the front of the store.

"Does he have the ability to bring life to the power grid?" the woman asked, showing a sly grin.

"Hardly. He's in publishing." Laurie turned to her agent. "Call someone in another neighborhood. See what's up."

The agent did as she was told, leaving Laurie to roll her eyes at the stranger. "It's hard to find good help." She extended her hand. "Laurie Ambrose."

The woman shifted the large format, hard-cover book she was holding, turning it so the cover faced outward. "Taj Medina." They shook and Laurie spent a second looking at the book.

"The book you're holding has your name on it."

"The books on that table have your name on them. You've got more than I have." Taj walked to the table, resting her hand on the large, neatly arranged stack. "How many on your backlist?"

"Thirty-five."

"You're kidding!"

"Nope." Laurie smiled, her grin still easy to see in the darkened building. "I crank out...I mean...craft three a year. Have been for ten years."

"I guess I should have heard of you, but I'm sorry to say I haven't."

"Oh, I'm only well known in the genre. I'm not big enough to make most airport kiosks." She walked over to Taj and tugged at the book she still held, taking it into her hands and peering at the photo. "This is a lovely book." Their eyes met briefly. "I bet you get more than one dollar and five cents per copy for every one you sell."

"Yeah, I do," Taj agreed. "But I bet I sell fewer than you do. A lot fewer."

"So...tell me about *Emerging Womanhood: Girls Becoming Women in Afghanistan.*"

"I can tell you about the photos. I didn't write the text." She pointed at a name above the photo of an achingly beautiful young woman. "She's a writer from Afghanistan. I just trailed her for a couple of months, taking pictures."

"You make that sound like a routine job. Taking pictures in a war-torn country can't be easy."

Taj shrugged. "It wasn't bad. I've been in worse places."

Laurie's agent shuffled back towards them, panic etched on her sharp features. "There's no cell service! None!"

"That's common during a blackout," Taj said, her voice calm and reassuring.

But the reassurance didn't work on the agent. "I've got to get to my office. I've got to be able to use a phone!" And with that she was off, heading for midtown.

"I wonder how she thinks she's going to get anywhere." Taj said.

Libby approached, looking concerned. "We're screwed. Traffic lights are out. Every building on the block is out. People are getting freaked."

"Freaked?" Taj asked. "Because of a power outage...? Oh, right. I forget how accessible electricity is here."

"No, they're saying they think it's terrorism."

"Fuck!" Laurie kicked the table, sending books scattering across the surface. "If those fuckers fuck with us again...I'll... fucking wring their fucking necks!"

Taj and Libby stared at her, mouths slightly agape.

"Sorry," she said, hurriedly piling the books back into a poor semblance of their former order. "I just don't know of a lower form of life than terrorists. Such fucking chicken shits," she mumbled, just loud enough to be heard.

"Knocking New York off the grid would be a feat," Taj said thoughtfully. "But I think it'd be awfully hard to accomplish. My guess is that this is just a blackout from demand. I'd bet money on it."

"Shit." Laurie took off, heading towards the front of the store. "I'm not going to let those people stand out there in the blazing sun for another minute."

***

A few minutes later she was busily signing books while the store manager and a couple of clerks hand-wrote charge slips for people who didn't have cash. Taj had gone out in search of credible information and had found the closest fire station. She'd learned that the city didn't think terrorism was involved, but they were on tactical alert just the same. She withheld that last bit of information and shared only the first when she returned to the store.

She, Libby, and the publisher's rep worked the line, reassuring people that they would get a book and that Laurie would stay until every one had been signed. It took until almost six o'clock, and they were all hot and thirsty by the time the last customer left.

"I'm going to head home," Libby said. "Is that cool?"

Laurie said, "Sure. No problem. How far is your apartment?"

"Maybe fifteen blocks. How about you?"

"Mine's a lot farther than fifteen blocks. But I'll get there. Thanks for all your help, Libby."

Libby said her goodbyes, then the rep declared he was going for a drink. Taj deferred as did Laurie, who now stood in the

199

nearly empty, stuffy store, both seemingly at a loss for words. "Where do you live?" Laurie finally asked.

"I don't have a permanent address right now. I'm staying with an aunt and uncle up in Riverdale. How about you?"

"Park Slope...Brooklyn," she explained, when Taj looked puzzled.

"Oh, right. I know where that is. I don't get to New York very often, but I know of a couple of women who've moved there. Is there a pretty big lesbian community there?"

Laurie shrugged. "Yeah, I guess. I mean, there are lesbians everywhere in New York." She saw Taj giving her a questioning look and continued, "There's another lesbian in my building. Besides me," she tacked on, inelegantly.

"So...maybe we should find a different bar to have a drink in. I'm not opposed to having a drink. I just didn't want to spend the evening with that guy."

"Ditto. I'd love to have a drink." She stopped short. "But no place will be open."

"Of course they will. You don't need electricity to sell liquor. Just ice. And that's actually optional." Taj grinned, showing those remarkably white teeth again, and Laurie found herself following the lovely woman through the darkened aisles of the store and into the blinding sunlight of the New York August afternoon.

***

The heat was stunning in its intensity; it was as though the concrete had become an oven, sending the heat right through their shoes. The sidewalk was clogged with people, some heading uptown and some down, with traffic at a complete standstill on Sixth Avenue. Horns blared, drivers yelled, and pedestrians and bicycles threaded their way through the stalled cars. The side street was just as bad. Some of the drivers had simply turned off their cars and were sitting on the hoods.

"This is strangely...exciting," Laurie said, her pale eyes showing generous hints of glee.

"I guess it would be, if it didn't happen to you very often. I got used to having electricity for just a couple of hours a day in Afghanistan. It loses its allure," she said, smiling.

"But it never happens here. Are you sure it wasn't terrorism?" Laurie's self-assurance seemed to vanish in a heartbeat. She looked at Taj as though she were desperately seeking solace.

"Positive," Taj replied, even though she was merely guessing. "Why would you think a power outage was terrorism? I've been in thousands of situations like this and it's never occurred to me that it was anything other than demand overcoming supply."

Laurie's eyes narrowed and she shivered, despite the intense heat. "You weren't here on Nine Eleven, were you." It wasn't a question. More of a statement of fact.

Taj winced. "Right. Right." She looked down for a second, then seemed to compose her response carefully. "I wasn't here. Nine Eleven seems like it was a very long time ago to me."

"Not to me," Laurie said, her voice tight as she tried to control it. "It seems like it could happen again at any time. It's just been over a year, you know." She sounded a little defensive, and Taj didn't mention that it was almost two years.

"Were you in the city?"

"Yeah." She blinked, her eyelids fluttering for a moment. "I had to walk home in air so thick with dust and dirt and incinerated...everything...that I developed a cough that lingered for months."

"I'm sorry." Taj gently squeezed her shoulder. "It must have been horrible."

"It was. And this puts me right back there."

"I'm really sorry. It must be hard to get past it."

"Damn right it is. The police are still on tactical alert, they still randomly search us at the subway, and you'll see fifty police cars screaming down the street for no reason at all. It makes you nuts."

"The city does seem different to me. Changed, somehow. This is just the second time I've been back since it happened and, even though I can't put my finger on it, things are different."

"They are. Mostly we're edgy." She laughed. "Like we weren't before? But now there's an edge to our edge. Mild-mannered women like me start cursing like a lunatic in a bookstore."

"Don't give that another thought. My uncle says *fuck* is conversational vocabulary in New York."

"Are you sure this isn't terrorism? Really sure?" She looked at Taj with a childlike need for reassurance.

"Positive. This is just urban living."

Laurie smiled at her, relieved at having gotten some of her feelings out. "I wonder if the outage is only in this neighborhood or the whole city?"

"Well," Taj said thoughtfully. "There won't be television, and cell phones aren't working, but land lines should. My agent is in Soho. We could go down there and use his phone."

"Mmm, okay. What subway?"

"Subways won't work."

"Sure they will." She paused. "Won't they?"

"Ever heard of the third rail? It's electric."

"Eww. I guess this isn't that much fun. So we have to walk to Soho?"

"No, we don't have to. When I'm in a situation like this, I usually find the coolest bar with the coldest drinks and listen to gossip until I have a handle on the situation."

"I like the way you think. Let's find one."

***

It took a while to find a place where they could sit outdoors, but they finally spotted a small bar deep in the West Village. The garage-style doors were wide open, and there was a table tantalizingly close to the sidewalk. They nearly ran for it, each grabbing a chair and flopping into it with finality. It was considerably cooler now that they weren't in the sun, and the noise was greatly reduced away from the lamentations of the cabbies. "I'd kill for a vodka and tonic," Laurie declared.

"Do you have cash? They might not take charge cards." Taj pulled her wallet from the breast pocket of her cocoa-colored linen shirt. Her sleeves were rolled up, exposing skin just one shade lighter than the fabric. "I've got...forty dollars."

Laurie took her wallet from the gym bag and counted. "Forty-eight. That's not gonna go far."

"How much do you think drinks are?"

"At least ten. Maybe twelve." She laughed. "Maybe fifty. We're not known for our civic mindedness."

"Oh, sure you are. I think people have been behaving extraordinarily well."

"Yeah, you're right. We're still in good Nine Eleven mode in some ways."

A harried waitress approached. "What'll you have?"

"Two vodka and tonics," Taj said. "I'll get the first round," she added to Laurie.

When their drinks were delivered, Taj managed to convince the server to let them run a tab, promising to show her how to handwrite a charge slip if the power didn't return before they'd finished. "Smooth," Laurie said admiringly. "You're very good at that."

"I've had to talk my way out of a lot of situations. I guess I'm getting better at it."

Laurie took her glass and clicked it against Taj's. "So, tell me about you. How do you get by without a permanent address?"

"Oh, I use my aunt and uncle's house as my mailing address. You can't get anything in this country without a mailing address. A post office box won't do."

"You've obviously tried."

"No, but my parents have. We're all semi-homeless, but in a positive way."

Laurie's mouth dropped open. "Are your parents Richard and Sonya Medina?"

Grinning, Taj nodded. "You've heard of them?"

"Oh, yeah! I'm a huge fan of travel writing. Literary travel writing, that is. They're the best!"

"I think they're awfully good, but I'm prejudiced."

"So, you do the photography for their books?"

"Yeah. I've been doing most of the photos since I was about fifteen. That lets my parents write and not have to worry about lugging cameras around."

"This is so cool! I can't tell you how much I've enjoyed their books. But the book you showed me didn't have their names on it."

"They only do a book every three or four years. I can't live on as little as they do, so I do as many independent projects as I can."

"Fascinating." Laurie took a long drink and smiled. "This is the best drink I've ever had."

"Deprivation does make you appreciate the little things. I have been known to worship porcelain."

"Porcelain?" She nodded slowly when the answer dawned on her. "Bathrooms."

"I won't give you the details, but I've had to go in places that just the thought of can make me retch." She took a drink and shivered. "There are a lot of times that I wish I had an apartment with a bathroom."

"How long have you been semi-homeless?"

Taj considered the question for a moment. "We had fairly permanent places until I was about five." She smiled at Laurie. "So I guess it's been about thirty years."

Stunned, Laurie said, "You honestly haven't had a home since you were five?"

"We really didn't have one up to that point. But we stayed in the same country for a couple of years, which is as close as we've gotten to having a home."

"Where were you born?"

"In India. We stayed there until I was two. Then we lived in Thailand until I was five. Since then…it's been one place or another."

"That's remarkable. Truly remarkable."

"It seems pretty normal to me, but I guess that's because many of our friends are wanderers too. Photographers are a peripatetic lot, and a lot of American writers that you meet in Asia also have wanderlust."

"But how do you…have a normal life? How do you form relationships? Things like that?"

"That's not so easy." For the first time, Taj's dark eyes were tinged with sadness. "It would be easier if I were straight, but I'm not."

"It can be hard to meet women in New York. It must be a lot tougher when you're moving around a lot."

"Especially when you can be put to death for being gay." She smiled again, but the sadness remained. "Execution is surprisingly effective at squelching gay pride."

"You're not always in places like that, are you?"

"No, not always. I've spent a lot of time in Afghanistan in the last few years, though. To be honest, I'd rather be sitting in an apartment overlooking the Champs Élysées, but that's not where the action is."

"Isn't it dangerous?"

"Very," Taj said solemnly. "I've never met a member of the Taliban that I'd turn my back on. But somebody has to record their destruction of the ancient world. Nobody cared until Nine Eleven, but at least we'll have pictures." She sounded bitter but oddly resigned.

"You're risking your life for this."

"I've been within a day's drive of Kabul for the last couple of years and things are better with the army there. Before that…" She let out a low whistle. "It was hell."

"Who do you work for?"

Her smile was back, and this time it had an impish quality to it. "Anyone with a generous expense account and lax bookkeeping."

Laurie observed the lovely, somewhat laconic woman for a few moments. She was having a hard time figuring her out, but she was intrigued. "Are you a huge thrill seeker?"

"Not so much. I had fun when I was in my twenties and feeling invulnerable, but I'm feeling more vulnerable with every year. I'd prefer to just work with my parents since I'm afraid they only have a couple more books left in them and they work faster when I'm pushing them. But they can live on the equivalent of ten thousand dollars a year. I can't."

"You have more expensive tastes?"

"Yeah. Definitely. And I'm also more realistic than they are."

"Realistic…how?"

Taj took a drink and leaned back in her chair. The chair was a standard wooden bar seat, but the way she draped herself upon it made it seem like a chaise longue. "Maybe the word is practical. There won't be anyone to help me out if I break a hip when I'm sixty. I've got to have some money put aside if I'm disabled and, given my line of work, that's not out of the realm of possibilities."

"Can you put enough away to provide for yourself?"

"Probably not. And I don't save as much as I should."

Laurie looked at her well-made linen shirt and snuck a glance at her big backpack. "How do you blow your money? I'm always interested in people's spending patterns."

"I don't blow much, to be honest. But I'd like to come to New York more often and spend some time in my home country. My parents lived here until they were in their thirties, but it's new to me."

"That must be odd. To not really have a home country."

"Not very," Taj said, shrugging it off. "I like not having a ferocious attachment to any one place. The world might be more peaceful if we all felt like earthlings."

Laurie narrowed her eyes, considering whether to proclaim her love of America and all that it stood for. She decided to keep her feelings to herself for the moment and find out more about Taj. "How else do you spend your money?"

"Well, I like to be able to stay in hotels and buy my own meals."

"Versus sleeping on the street and stealing?"

Taj's smile was warm and made her even more beautiful. "It's not that bad, but my parents are more than willing, hell, they're eager to bunk with strangers and share whatever the people can spare. But I've had it with that. I want some privacy and some"—she frowned and paused a moment before she finished —"dignity. I don't like to take from people who have so little."

"I can understand that. Is that a bone of contention between you and your parents?"

"Not too much. They're not the types to argue with me or try to change me. They've simply decided I'm a spendthrift because I like to go to Singapore every year or so to buy some clothes and have a few great meals."

"Ooo…a great meal. I could really use a great meal."

Taj looked at her watch. "It's almost eight. Let's take a walk. I can take some photographs now that the light is really good and we can look for a place to eat."

"You've got a deal."

***

Their path was a meandering one, with Taj dashing off several times, looking for a good image. Laurie kept walking down Seventh Avenue, keeping her pace slow so Taj could catch up after her forays. The evening light had faded by the time they reached Soho, and it was now dark. As dark as Laurie had ever seen New York. Taj carefully put her camera into various protective appliances inside her backpack. "I wish I'd brought my tripod so I could keep shooting, but I think I got some good shots. As soon as my cell phone works I'm going to call my agent and see if he can find a buyer."

"I hope that's soon. I keep turning my phone on but I'm not getting anything. All I'm managing to do is run my battery down."

"My battery is full, so I'll turn my phone off to save it. We don't know how long this will last, so we'd better conserve."

"We're not in the third world," Laurie laughed. "They'll have this fixed in no time."

"I hope you're right, but I wouldn't count on it. I heard some people saying that the blackout is covering the whole Northeast. If that's true, this could go on for quite a while."

"No way. They've got some plan in place to make sure we'll get power. This is the twenty-first century."

"Uhm-hmm," Taj said, nodding while maintaining her sardonic grin.

***

"Who has the best sushi in town?" Taj asked. They'd passed four subway stations, each closed, and had given directions and advice to at least forty people during the amble.

"Mmm, probably Hiro. It's not very far from here, but I've never eaten there. It's far too expensive for me."

Teasingly, Taj said, "An author with…what…thirty titles? You must be flush."

"I do all right, but I'm not rich enough to eat at Hiro. I think their omakase menu is three hundred bucks."

"Not tonight it's not," Taj said confidently.

***

Laurie stood near the entrance of the very high end Japanese restaurant watching Taj work her magic. The bits Laurie heard were persuasive, but she was confident that it was the way Taj presented herself and her arguments that carried the day. After a good five minutes of negotiation they were shown to a table. The manager stood there for a moment and said, "I can't offer our traditional service because most of our waiters went home, but we'll do our best."

"We'll take whatever you have. There isn't anything I won't eat," Taj assured him.

He gazed at her suspiciously for a moment then left to head for the kitchen. "I'm not as adventurous as you are," Laurie said. "There are lots of things I won't eat."

"Then there's more for me. Don't worry, we'll eat well tonight."

"How will we afford it?"

"We struck a deal. If the power comes back on, we'll pay half of the usual. If it doesn't, it's free."

"Free?"

"That's why I wanted to come for sushi. Everything will be spoiled by tomorrow, so they have to move it or throw it out. I'm pretty confident that the power isn't coming back on anytime soon, but even if it does I figured it would be worth a hundred and fifty dollars if the food is really extraordinary."

Grinning, Laurie said, "I think you might be a spendthrift."

"No, but I *am* a gambler."

***

By nine thirty the restaurant was half full. The manager had offered Taj's deal to anyone who'd come, and people were happy to be there, even though the room was now hot and stuffy. The sake was still cold, and they had a couple of glasses along with their fantastic food. The chefs had done a masterful job preparing everything they had in their walk-in cooler and the freezer. Laurie had sampled things she'd never heard of, much less tried, and even though some of it was a little exotic for her, she managed to keep up with Taj bite for bite.

It was eleven thirty when they were finally too stuffed to eat another bite. The manager assured them that the restaurant's insurance would cover the cost of the food, so they ignored their guilt at having eaten hundreds of dollars of sushi, but left the majority of their cash for tips. They walked out into the still steaming night, with ten dollars between them. "Want to try to hitchhike to Brooklyn?" Laurie asked.

"I guess it couldn't hurt. Brooklyn is closer than Riverdale, isn't it?"

"I think so, but don't quote me. I've lived almost every place in the New York area but I'm not great at measuring distances."

They started to walk again, the sidewalks still jammed with people. Traffic had hardly moved, and people looked less happy and more harried. "First worlders don't take well to discomfort," Taj said. "It makes them question all of their assumptions about being in control."

"Very philosophical. I've got my own Margaret Mead."

Raising an eyebrow, Taj said, "Did that offend you?"

Laurie surprised herself by saying, "Yeah. It did a little bit."

"I'm sorry. I was just making an observation, but I should have kept it to myself."

"No, I don't want you to do that. You're a very interesting person, and I want to hear what you have to say even when you *are* making fun of me and my ilk."

"I'm not making fun of you at all. We're all products of our environment. If a guy from the Taliban saw the dress you're wearing, he'd probably stab you." She grinned. "I think he'd be making a very big mistake because you look fantastic, but he wouldn't see it that way."

"I think there was a compliment in there. If there was, thank you."

"There was definitely a compliment. You really look lovely. It's been a long time since I've seen a woman's…legs," she said, her eyes fixed considerably higher on Laurie's body.

"How long have you been in New York?"

"I just got in yesterday. I'd been to see my agent in Soho, and I stopped in the bookstore to see if they had my new book. I don't get to see my stuff in bookstores very often. It's a treat."

"The circumstances aren't ideal, but I'm really glad you were there. Are you any good at hitchhiking?"

"My family has never owned a car, a scooter or a bicycle. I think I've hitchhiked ten times more than I've bought a train ticket."

"I don't know about anybody else, but I feel very, very lucky tonight. I couldn't have picked a better companion to travel with."

***

They tried for almost an hour, but no one would consider giving them a ride across the bridge. They discussed walking across along with thousands of others, but Laurie thought there were safer places to sleep in Manhattan than there would be if they couldn't make it all the way to Park Slope.

They walked over to West Side Highway, trying to get a breeze from the river. They weren't successful, and the noise from the traffic was even worse than it had been downtown. But there was something nice about walking near the river with only the lights of furious drivers to illuminate the night. "How is your hand?" Taj gently lifted Laurie's right hand and tried to get a good look at it.

"It's fine." She was tempted to pull it away, feeling embarrassed about punching a car window when the solo driver wouldn't make eye contact, but it felt nice to have Taj's hand hold hers. "I thought people would be more generous. We were really nice to each other after the attacks."

"People are still being nice. I haven't seen any rioting, and that's what I would expect in a city of this size."

"I guess you're right. And people are talking to each other more than normal."

"Absolutely true. We've gotten a lot of information from people on the street. It's all been bad," Taj admitted, "but people are really interacting."

"It's hard to believe that there isn't one form of public transportation working. I thought you'd be able to get home on Metro-North. Doesn't it run on diesel?"

"I thought it did, but that guy we talked to said he was certain none of the trains were running. I guess we could walk over to Grand Central and check..."

"It's only a couple of miles, but I feel like I'm gonna drop. I'd love to sit down and rest my barking dogs."

"Those sandals are cute, but they've got to be pinching by now."

"They were pinching when we were still at the bookstore. If I knew you better I'd be whining."

"You don't seem like the type. As a matter of fact, I can't begin to figure out why you're single."

"Yet another compliment. Keep them coming." She smiled and squeezed Taj's hand. "I've only been single for a year. Before that I was in a relationship for over five years."

"What happened?"

"My girlfriend decided that she wanted to have a baby. I'm leery about getting a goldfish. Too much responsibility," she said, grinning. "To be honest, having her break up with me wasn't the worst thing."

"How come?"

"I'm still not sure. We got along fine, but...it was all too... predictable?"

"Is that a question?"

Taj smiled, the look so attractive that Laurie's breath caught for a second. There was a pause, then she realized she was supposed to answer. "Oh! No, I guess I know the reason. I might be a little embarrassed about it."

"Come on." Taj's voice was low and teasing. "Don't hold out on me."

Laurie sighed. "Okay. She didn't challenge me. That's probably not the best reason in the world to break up, but it's all I've got. Life got boring."

"That would be enough for me. More than enough. Maybe that's why I'm single too."

"What's been your longest relationship?"

"For a full-time girlfriend? Six months. But I had a long-distance relationship that tortured me for almost three years."

"Six months? That's—"

"Embarrassingly short. Even more embarrassing is the fact that I was fourteen when it happened."

***

They made it to Christopher Street, to Pier 45, in the far West Village. The pier was under construction, part of the reclaiming of the Hudson for a park that would span the length of Manhattan. They found a bermed area where Laurie could put her yoga mat on the dirt and sit with some back support. Taj took a rain poncho from her pack and stretched it out next to her. They sat watching a few boats plying the dark water.

"Tell me all about this adolescent love affair," Laurie said. "I barely knew what sex was when I was fourteen."

Taj lay on her side and supported her head with her hand. "I didn't know much. We were in the Kalahari, doing a book on the !Kung San in Namibia, and I came down with a lung infection."

Laurie's eyes grew wide. "That sounds serious."

"Yeah, it could have been. A lot of that tribe's people die from lung problems. They don't have any antibiotics or modern medicines, and the desert winds can force a lot of nasty stuff into your lungs. But we used our first world privilege, and my parents got me transported to Gaborone in Botswana. They went back as soon as it was clear that I was going to be all right."

"They left you?" Laurie's tone showed how amazed she was.

"Yeah, but that was fine. There was a school run by missionaries, and a lot of the staff spoke English. My parents were only half done with the book we were working on, and they didn't think it was wise to take me back there and risk getting another infection."

"But they left you," Laurie said again, her voice softer this time.

"I was a very independent kid. I didn't mind at all." She took Laurie's hand and squeezed it. "Really."

"You stayed with a bunch of missionaries?"

"Yeah. It was fun. I didn't speak the local language, so I couldn't be in a regular class, but I sat in on math class. It was cool to go to a real school."

"You'd never been to school?"

"Nope. I was home schooled, but my parents didn't follow a curriculum or anything. They just taught me things as they came up."

"Wow. That's remarkable. Did you go to college?"

"Oh, no. I don't even have a high school diploma. My parents were in their anti-government period when I was in my teens, and they didn't conform with any of the rules for home education. I think they feel bad about it now, but I guess I could talk my way into a college if I wanted to go. But I've never felt the need."

"Now *that's* remarkable." She looked at Taj's placid expression. "Come on, you've got to admit that's rare."

"Yeah, I guess it is. I didn't generally care that I'd never been to school, but I definitely wanted to stay in the missionary school, especially when I met Rebecca, the daughter of the people who ran the mission." Laurie could see her eyes twinkle even in the very faint light of the moon. "I was in love in no time at all."

"Cool. Coming out stories. My favorite thing. Did this girl feel the same way?"

"Yep. Only problem was that she wasn't a girl. She was twenty-two."

"And you were fourteen?" Laurie squawked. "That's a crime!"

"Yeah, I suppose it was. But she was no older than I was emotionally. She'd lived in Botswana her whole life and the only books she read were religious. They didn't have TV, and they didn't go to the movies or anything. They were very simple people."

"Still…"

"Yeah, my parents were none too happy. They came to get me after about seven or eight months, and I immediately told them that I'd fallen in love. I honestly had no idea that it would upset them."

"Oh, you poor naïve thing. What were they most upset about?"

"The age difference. Definitely the age difference. They packed me up and we left the next day. We went all the way to North Korea, with me crying the whole time. I'm still sure that was a wild goose chase." She chuckled softly. "I was very dramatic about being separated from Rebecca, but they held their ground. It wasn't until I was older that I realized they were only trying to protect me. We had a tough month or two in North Korea, then we went to Burma which had its own challenges." She smiled, then added, "Do you know Burma?"

"No, I'm not sure I could find it on a map. Why's it tough?"

"It's a kingdom and the royal family was pretty much in charge in those days. It was hard to get in and even harder to interact with ordinary Burmese. We wasted a whole year there and never got enough material for a book. But that's when I started really pursuing my interest in photography, so it wasn't a total waste. When all you have is a camera and hours to kill, you can get pretty good at composing pictures."

"Were you being held against your will?"

"No, we wanted to be there. At least, my parents did. I wanted to be in Botswana with Rebecca. The authorities just kept us wrapped up in red tape for months on end. They want you to go with an official tour group, but we didn't want to do that. As I said, my parents were in a very confrontational mood in those days, and they were as hardheaded as the Burmese authorities were. I just wanted to go somewhere. I almost died of boredom."

"Damn. That sounds horrible. Especially for a fourteen-year-old."

"It wasn't too bad. Of course, that's from my perspective today. I'm sure I felt different about it then."

"You seem very...tranquil. You have an inner peace that I find appealing."

"Maybe it's from being in India for so many years. I find Indians more accepting of their circumstances than most. At least the people in the areas we worked in were. The people in the cities might be different."

"Are you Indian?"

"I have an Indian passport and an Indian name, but my ethnicity is"—she paused—"complicated. I'm a mongrel, to be honest. I met a guy who worked for a firm that did DNA typing, and he tested me. I had just about everything—except for South Asian. So, even though I can pass for and have an Indian name, that's one of the things I'm not." She gave Laurie a happy grin. "I've got some genes from Bedouin people. Maybe that's why I need to move around."

"Whatever you are, it's a very nice combo." Laurie put her hand on Taj's bare arm. "You have the most amazing skin tone. It's truly beautiful."

"I like my color. I'm much darker than either of my parents. My mom's father is from Puerto Rico and we think he's African, Taino, and a little Spanish. I think my skin got a good dose of the African genes."

"It's lovely." She gently stroked her skin, amazed at its softness. "This is the smoothest skin I've ever felt."

"Thanks." Taj's dark eyes followed Laurie's hand, avidly watching it move across her skin. "The woman I had the long-distance relationship with was Scottish. She was as pale as milk. I loved the way our skin looked when we were lying next to one another. We hardly looked like the same type of animal."

"Do you miss her?" Laurie asked, extending her touch to Taj's shoulder, then down to her hand.

"Sure. We got along really well and we were very attracted to each other. But she couldn't stand to be in the same place more than two weeks. It was exhausting."

"Two weeks is too fast a pace for you?"

"Yeah. Much too fast. She came from a small town in the north of Scotland, and she'd been itching to leave since she was a girl. I figure she'll need twenty years to get that out of her system."

"It sounds like it's leaving your system."

"I think it's starting to." Taj laughed softly. "I don't want to be too settled, of course. I could never stay in one place permanently. But I'd love to have a home base. Somewhere that I could keep things and know that they'd be there when I got back." Her eyes grew unfocused. "Somewhere I could have a nice bed and a comfortable chair to read in." She met Laurie's eyes and said, "I've never had that. Everything we own travels with us."

"How many bags do you have when you move someplace new?"

"Not that many. I have a lot more stuff than my parents do. I probably fill three crates, including my photography gear. My dad could get everything he owns into a backpack." She laughed. "He usually has two pair of pants, one pair of shorts, three T-shirts and two regular shirts. He wraps that in a rain poncho, sticks it into a backpack and he's ready to go."

"No coat?"

"Nope. They stay in the tropics now. It's never below twelve degrees. Centigrade," she added, when Laurie's eyes widened briefly.

"You didn't mention underwear."

Taj laughed again. "He wears it, but he usually buys a couple of pair when he gets to where he's going. He wears his shoes until they fall apart, then gets whatever the local people are wearing. It wouldn't bother him to go without, either. He's the simplest man you'll ever meet."

"I feel like I know your parents from their writing. I'd give anything to be like they are—real writers."

"You're not a real writer? Why not?"

"I'm a hack," she said, sounding disgusted. "I crank a book out in a month."

"Why do you write if you're not proud of what you do?"

She looked so ingenuous that Laurie could feel tears of shame come to her eyes. "I'm good at it. I make a nice living from it, and I like plotting the books out. That part is a lot of fun. But doing the actual writing has gotten so formulaic." She practically moaned the last sentence.

"Then make it less formulaic."

"I can't. My publisher wants me to keep repeating the formula until sales fall off. Which they are definitely not doing," she added, chuckling. "I convinced them to let me do another series, but now I'm stuck doing three different formulas. I've got my original series, the one I write under my own name. That's set in the current day."

"That seems most logical."

"Not for mysteries. I got smart and put my next one in the seventies, which allows me to write without having cell phones and computers and all of the things that make mysteries easier to solve."

Taj's eyes twinkled with interest. "Very smart. I've never considered how technology would make it harder to write a tight plot."

"It can, but it can also help. My latest is in two thousand forty, which lets me make up all of the stuff I want."

"That's pretty clever."

"Yeah, it kept me interested for a couple of years. But I really want to try to write something more…literary."

Taj rolled onto her belly, her head propped up by her braced hands. "Then do that."

"I guess I should."

"I used my sharp powers of observation to discern that you're not crazy about your agent. What does she think?"

Giggling, Laurie said, "I really showed some fantastic attributes today, didn't I?" She shook her head ruefully. "She wants me to chug them out and never call her."

"That's not uncommon."

"I know. I just wish she'd help me try to find my voice." She shrugged. "I guess that's unfair of me to expect. That's not what her interest is. I'd need an agent that can sell what I'd like to write."

"Let me introduce you to our agent. He's great at finding homes for books that won't ever be in the airport kiosks."

With a smile slowly blooming, Laurie nodded. "I'd love that. But I still need to put out new mysteries to earn a good living. Literary fiction doesn't sell."

"Then live with less. You could cut back."

"Yeah, I guess I could, but my father…kinda depends on me."

"Oh." Concern colored Taj's expression. "Is he ill?"

"No, he's fine. He's just…my aunt says he's a user, but he says he's never gotten a break."

"Who's right?"

"My aunt." She sighed and lay down, looking up into the amazingly clear night. "Look at the stars! I've never, ever seen this many stars!"

Taj looked, not mentioning that there were places in Africa where the sky was nearly white from the vast number of visible stars. "It's nice. Tell me more about your dad."

"Well, he's always asking me for money, and I tend to give it to him. My aunt, his sister by the way, says he's always been a mooch and that I'm only rewarding him for his bad behavior."

"I'm glad I'm an only child. I'd hate to have my sister say that about me."

"Yeah, me too. There's no love lost there. But my aunt's been like a second mother to me."

"Your mom…?"

"Died when I was twelve. Blood poisoning."

"What? That's a pretty third-world cause of death. What happened?"

"We didn't have health insurance and she didn't go to the ER until it was too late."

Taj flinched in sympathy. "That's horrible. Just horrible."

"It was," she agreed, her voice soft and shaky. "I blame my dad for not providing for us, but I blame her too. She married him," she added, disgust in her tone.

"That sounds very hard." Taj reached over and took Laurie's hand, chafing it gently. "My parents had their faults, but I always knew they'd protect me. It must make the world a scary place when you don't have that."

Laurie turned her head just enough to let Taj see that her eyes were bright with tears. "The world was a scary place for me. We moved all the time, and each time was worse. Eventually, I stopped even trying to make friends."

"How did you learn to be so friendly? So easy with people? You interacted with your fans as though you didn't have any barriers at all. You seemed really genuine." Taj had been tenderly stroking the skin on the back of Laurie's hand. Her eyes seemed so focused on making out all of the details of that single piece of her body in the dim light that Laurie felt freer to talk about her feelings. It was always easier for her when she didn't have to look another person in the eye.

"Thanks for saying that. I'm not sure exactly when it happened, but I came out of my shell when I started writing. Having that vent allowed me to start being who I guess I really am." She smiled sadly. "The person I would have been a lot sooner if I'd had a more stable home."

Continuing to gaze and play with Laurie's hand, Taj said, "Sometimes I play around trying to figure out who I would be if I'd been born to a couple of regular stay-at-home people in Chicago or Minneapolis or someplace normal." She let out a low chuckle. "It's impossible. There are so many factors that go into making each of us unique that it's folly to try to add or remove a variable."

Laurie had a sudden need to see Taj's beautiful eyes. She gently touched her cheek and their eyes met. "You don't speak like a woman who didn't graduate from high school."

Grinning, Taj said, "I don't know if that's a compliment for me or an indictment of formal schooling."

"I think the latter. Your parents did a good job."

"Thanks. I'm pretty happy with my education. The only thing I know nothing about is popular culture. I've seen a lot of television, but most of it has been overseas."

"Did you ever own a television?"

Taj laughed. "No. Not by a long shot. But just about everybody else on earth has one and when we'd stay with other people we'd sometimes watch."

"So if I talk about *The Sopranos* or *Seinfeld*, you don't know what I'm talking about?"

"I've seen an episode or two of *Seinfeld*. My uncle really likes it and I think it's on once or twice a day when I'm at their house. I'm aware of *The Sopranos*, but only from reading references to it." She looked thoughtful for a few moments. "It's kind of like hearing about a very close friend's family. You know a lot of things about them, but you couldn't necessarily pick them out in a crowd. That's how I feel about most popular television shows. As for the less popular ones, they never cross my radar."

"But I bet you know a zillion things about a bunch of different countries. I think I'd trade my TV trivia knowledge for some of yours."

Taj's eyes shone brightly even though only the starlight and the glow from the traffic on West Side Highway provided illumination. "You don't have to trade away your knowledge. If you want some of mine all you have to do is travel and keep your eyes and ears open."

Laurie's smile betrayed her embarrassment. "You probably won't believe this, but Canada is the only foreign country I've been to."

Taj didn't look particularly surprised. "That's not uncommon. When I tell people that I'm American quite often they ask me why I bother coming to their country. People often say that they'd never leave America if they could only get here."

"I'm very interested in other countries and other peoples, but I've always found it satisfied me to read about them. I have to travel around the country for book tours at least once a year. I honestly hate every day I'm away from home." She rolled her eyes. "You must think I'm a real rube."

"Not a bit. I'm a firm believer in doing what makes you happy. Now, if you were unhappy being at home, I'd think you were selling yourself short. But if you like it, no one has the right to tell you to live differently."

"I like the way you think. My friends are always telling me that I don't know what I'm missing by not traveling."

Taj's smile was wicked. "I agree with them on that. You can't really know what another place is like until you go there. But a lot of people prefer their own space to any other. So, you'd know what Botswana was like by going there, but you might hate every minute of it."

Laurie looked at her for a few moments, clearly seeing that she was teasing. "Do you think I'd like it?"

Taj pursed her lips and her eyes narrowed in thought. "I'm not sure. The Kalahari Desert covers the majority of the country. How you feel about deserts?"

Getting into the game, Laurie said, "Hmm, I feel pretty good about them. Especially if they have animals I wouldn't get to see anyplace else."

"You can probably see most of the animals they have at the Bronx Zoo, but if you want to see them running free, you've probably got to leave New York."

"What else do they have?" Threading her fingers together, she put her hands under her head and scanned the star-filled sky while waiting for Taj to respond.

"If you get tired of the desert, there is an area up in the north of the country that has a few good-sized hills and more varied terrain. That part isn't tropical, so the weather is more… interesting. That's where most of the really good basket weavers live too. Do you like baskets?"

"Who doesn't like a good basket? So far it sounds like I would like Botswana."

"I like it. Things have been good for quite a while now. The economy has been growing and people seem to get along well. They're trying to increase their tourism, so they'd be happy to have you."

"If I were to go somewhere, somewhere exotic, where would you send me?"

"That's a big question. I've spent most of my time in Asia, South Asia, and Africa. So my view of the world is definitely skewed."

"It has to be less skewed than mine is. I went to the trouble of getting a passport to go to Canada. I wanted to make sure I could prove who I was in case I got into a scuffle and was thrown into one of those Canadian jails."

Taj had been discreetly studying Laurie's face and she started to smile when the corner of Laurie's mouth twitched. "I've heard about those jails. People in Turkey often say they'd go to North America if it weren't for the threat of being thrown into a Canadian prison."

"You can't be too sure."

Taj furtively moved her hand across the space that separated them and gave Laurie a playful tickle. "I think you *can* be too sure. You have to tolerate some uncertainty to see the fun side of life."

"Do you really think that's true?"

"I'm afraid it is. Life is brutal, painful, demoralizing and tragic. And it's over in the blink of an eye. I believe you've got to find pleasure and take it whenever you can."

"My mom wouldn't have liked you," Laurie said, her smile looking a little sad. "She thought that life was all about having a little security and holding onto it as tightly as you could. Don't ask why she married a man who had bill collectors chasing them all over New York."

"Was that a rhetorical 'don't ask,' or do you really not want to talk about it?"

"I'm happy to talk about it. I truly don't know why she picked somebody so ill suited to what she claimed she wanted. For that matter, why would my father pick a wife who disapproved of almost everything he did?"

"That's a tough one. I think a lot of people don't know why they pick the person they partner with. I'm very cavalier about where I travel, but I'll never be that way about picking a partner. I know exactly what I want, and if I can't have it, I'm perfectly happy being alone."

"You can't make a statement like that without providing some details."

"I can do that. If you're interested."

"I'm rapt. Give me what you've got."

"Okay. My parents are so alike that they've almost grown into one person." She gave Laurie a mischievous grin. "I don't want that. I want a partner who has her own life, her own likes and dislikes, her own opinions. I don't need someone to complete me. I want someone to complement me."

"That's a very good way to put it. I don't think I've looked at it in those terms, but that's kind of what I meant about my ex. She wanted to be in *my* life rather than share her life with me. Does that make any sense?"

"It might. What did she do for a living?"

"Don't think I'm an ass, but I'm not sure. She worked for a big company, but she didn't seem to know a lot about it. She didn't make much money, so I don't think her position was very responsible. But I had to guess about a lot of things. If she wasn't interested in something, she acted like it didn't exist. I can tell you a lot about some of her coworkers, but that probably wouldn't hold your interest."

"I guess it depends on who the coworkers were."

"They were mostly other people who were also treated badly. There was always some plot by management to make some or all of them miserable."

"So she didn't like talking about her own work. Did she want to hear about yours?"

"Oh, yeah. She was a little jealous of the fact that I worked from home, but she was genuinely interested in my life, and my friends, and my family, and my interests. If I had taken up bow hunting she would have been at the sporting goods store buying arrows and camouflage clothes."

"That sounds kind of nice. I think everyone wants to have a lover who's interested."

"Be careful what you wish for. It was almost like having an imaginary friend. She was always there, which was nice, but she didn't have any depth."

"You're gonna think I'm psychic, but I'm going to guess two of her qualities." She held up a hand and tapped her index finger. "One, I bet she was very good-looking. And two, I bet the age difference between you was more than five years."

Laurie sat up and fixed her narrowed gaze at Taj. "How did you know that?"

"It's common for younger women to glom on to a lover and act more like a shadow than an independent person. Plus," she added, grinning, "it's good for the ego to have a beautiful young woman look up to you like you're terribly intelligent and so fascinating that everything you do is worth mimicking."

Laurie slapped her hand over her eyes and peeked out through a tiny hole she made between her third and fourth fingers. "Am I that transparent?"

"You're not unique. It's easy to mistake sycophancy for respect. You were pretty well known when you got together, right?"

Laurie's other hand covered the first one, completely hiding her eyes. "She was a fan."

"Oh, no. That's the kiss of death."

She moved her hands so they bracketed her eyes. "Yeah, I see that now." She lay on her side, watching Taj raptly.

"You can't have a real relationship with someone who sees you more as an image than a person. It's not fair to her."

"That's the awful truth. The things that first attracted me to her were the things that I began to resent. I should have known better."

"But you didn't. If you made the same mistake again you'd be an ass. But I bet you don't."

"I'm doing my best not to. I will never again pick up a woman from a book signing."

Taj gave her a smile so filled with innuendo that it was as though she had boldly propositioned Laurie. "You don't have to be doctrinaire about it."

Laurie felt herself moving slowly in Taj's direction. They were soon on their sides facing each other, their breath heating the small space that separated them.

"There's nothing wrong with picking up women in bookstores. Just make sure they don't think you're god's gift to women. Choose someone who's been around the block...or even the world."

Laurie leaned forward just enough to be able to reach Taj's lips. They kissed briefly, then Laurie moved back to look into Taj's eyes where she saw clear sparks of interest. "That's damned good advice."

"I have another piece of advice." Taj's voice was low and sultry. "Life is short. Never stop at one kiss."

***

It took Taj just a moment to feel comfortable kissing Laurie. The fact that she felt so comfortable made her slightly uncomfortable. She tried to ignore the plump tenderness of Laurie's lips, the suppleness of her body, and the delicious sensation of once again holding a woman in her arms. Pulling away, she spent a few moments looking into Laurie's welcoming eyes, puzzled as to why she didn't feel her usual trepidation. Deciding that the adult thing to do was to give voice to her fears, she said, "It normally takes me a while to feel comfortable with someone." She used her fingers to flip a lock of hair from Laurie's forehead, then she kissed the now bare spot. "Why does this feel so natural?"

Laurie's tone was teasing, but in a gentle way. "Maybe you're a lesbian."

"Yeah," Taj smiled at her. "But I've been a lesbian for a long time, and I usually have to know a woman a lot more than I know you to feel comfortable kissing her."

"What would you rather do? Think about why I'm different, or keep kissing?"

"The way you phrased that begs the answer. Very clever." She kissed her again, briefly this time. "My poor body wants to dive into you like a cool pool on a hot day. It's been two full years since I've kissed a woman and I think I've forced myself to forget how fantastic it feels."

Laurie sat up and put her hand on Taj's cheek. "But you'd still rather talk about why this feels different, wouldn't you?"

Taj felt compelled to be completely forthright. "That's not normally how I am, but for some reason I'd rather talk."

"Then we'll talk." Laurie hiked her skirt up until it would have been indecent, but it was so dark out she was confident she wouldn't shock Taj. Then she quickly twisted her body into a lotus position, resting her hands palms up on her knees. She took in a deep cleansing breath and let it out slowly. "Start any place you'd like."

***

They didn't talk about anything too complex. In fact, it seemed to Laurie that Taj was treating this evening as she would any first date—a first date in which she was very, very interested, that is. There was no question in Laurie's mind that Taj was not only interested in her, she could tell just how much she wanted to stop talking and get back to kissing. But it was also clear that Taj was a disciplined person and that she had an agenda even if she wasn't able to express it.

Laurie had the sense that they'd been talking for a couple of hours, but she was surprised when she caught a look at her watch to see that it was two a.m.

Taj said, "I can't believe I'm still yacking away. I haven't been to bed in thirty or...thirty-five hours. My internal clock is totally screwed up."

"Do you think you can sleep?"

"If I can brush my teeth, I think I can sleep."

"Your teeth? You've been up for more than thirty hours, and you can't sleep unless you brush your teeth?"

With a guilty-looking grin, Taj opened her backpack and showed Laurie two boxes filled with a product called Quick

Brush. "I don't know why, but I have a real thing about brushing my teeth. Every time I'm in the US, I buy a couple boxes of these, since I haven't found them in Asia or Africa. Whenever I'm going to be out in the field, I waste precious space carrying these around. People think I'm crazy, but they make me happy." She tore open one of the tiny packages which was about the size of a Band-Aid. Inside was a piece of gauze impregnated with toothpaste. Taj took the piece of gauze and started brushing away, looking perfectly content.

"You don't need water?"

She shook her head, continuing to brush. Watching her with amusement, Laurie started to dig through her own carryall and produced something called EZ-Pic. She took one of the tiny toothpick-like devices out and handed it to Taj. "I hate to have things stuck in my teeth."

They spent the next few minutes giggling at each other as they thoroughly flossed and brushed with neither water nor sink at their disposal.

***

Taj carried an amazing number of small items to aid in her comfort. She pulled out a large watertight bag that she used to store her camera when it was raining. It self-inflated, and she carefully opened the valve to make it into a fairly comfortable pillow. She also had a plastic container filled with earplugs which she offered to Laurie.

"I don't think I could relax enough to sleep if I couldn't hear someone coming up beside me."

"That's a good thought. I'm not going to use them, so feel free."

There was a lot of noise, mostly from the cars that were still gridlocked. "Are you sure?"

"Yeah. I only use them when there are bombs going off." She gave Laurie a half smile. "I wish I were kidding."

Laurie took her hand and brought it to her lips, kissing it gently. "I wish you were too."

"Do you think you can sleep?"

"Maybe. I think I'll put my gym clothes back on. I'm sure they smell horrible, but I'll be able to relax better if I'm not worried about showing every passerby my hoo-ha."

"You have a hoo-ha?" Taj grinned mischievously.

"So do you, but your shorts cover yours. I'm gonna go behind those shrubs and change."

"Don't be surprised if I sneak over there and spy on you."

Laurie leaned over and kissed her teasingly. "All you have to do is ask."

***

Once Laurie had changed into her damp, admittedly foul-smelling gym clothes, she lay back down on her yoga mat and tried to get comfortable.

Taj watched her struggle and pushed her backpack over towards her. "I've got a lot of stuff in here, but you could move things around until you could make a pretty nice pillow out of it."

"But your camera's in here."

"I know. But every lens is in a protective case and the camera body is wrapped in foam. I take care of my prized possession. Besides, if you're sleeping on it that's another level of protection."

"I don't know if I'll be much help if somebody tries to take it away from me."

"I'll protect it—I mean you," she teased. "I'm pretty good at self defense."

"You don't look like you would be. You seem very, very gentle."

Nodding solemnly, Taj said, "I am. I've never started a fight, but if someone brings one to me I won't run. I think most people are like dogs. Once they know you're afraid, they take advantage of you. The best thing to do is face them head on."

"Have you had to do that often?"

"No, not often at all. But I often have to bluff my way out of situations. That's another time that you can't show fear."

"I'm not sure I'd be very good at that."

"You won't know until you're put into the position. You might surprise yourself."

"Or get killed."

"That would be a surprise too." Taj leaned over and gave her fresh, clean-smelling mouth a kiss. "I think you'd be a good traveler. You have a quick mind and I can tell how thoroughly you study people. That's a critical requirement. So, I think you're set."

"I think I do better at reading travel books than traveling. But it feels good to have you say you think that I'd be good at it."

"For what it's worth, I think you'd be good at just about anything you tried." With another quick kiss, Taj lay down on her poncho and fussed with her waterproof bag until she had it just as she wanted it. "I don't think we'll need it, but I have some insect repellent from China that I assume is a carcinogen. But it kills bugs like nobody's business." She laughed softly, nudged her pillow with her shoulder a couple of times, then reached out and took Laurie's hand.

Feeling strangely cared for and completely safe, Laurie lay on her back and watched the stars for a long time, fearing it might be the first and last time she saw them so clearly.

***

The sun warmed her face, and Laurie turned her head to avoid opening her eyes. She was stiff and uncomfortable, and briefly wondered how her relatively new bed had gotten so firm. Then she heard a long, baleful horn bleat, and she shot up and stared. She was about a hundred feet from the end of the pier, safely nestled behind a stand of shrubs which protected her from the bike path and, further on, West Side Highway.

Her memories returned and she looked around for Taj, spying her at the end of the pier, doing what looked to be tai chi, or some other form of martial art.

Taj was, to Laurie's pleasure, dressed in only her underwear —silky-looking pewter-colored briefs and bra that could have passed for a swimsuit on a beach where Laurie could easily spend the rest of her days. Taj wasn't particularly muscular. In fact, she was lean, almost wiry, but her sleek body was as flexible and fluid as any Laurie had ever seen. Taj had clearly been practicing her routine for a very long time. She moved effortlessly—as if suspended in water—in one slow, beautiful and graceful motion.

Laurie had often seen groups of Chinese men and women doing tai chi in public parks around the city, but she'd never watched anyone perform the art as raptly as she now did. She was transfixed by Taj's peaceful elegance and power, unable to take her eyes from her.

She watched until Taj finished, then walked slowly back down the pier and, seeing her, waved happily. When she was close, Taj said, "I've had my exercise. Now I need breakfast." Her cocoa-colored skin was glistening with perspiration, and she ran her hands across her forehead, then smoothed her dark hair back.

Laurie wasn't sure she could speak without her voice breaking, so she stood up and grasped the end of her yoga mat. "I was going to limber up a little. Do you mind?"

"No, no, do what you normally do. I'll sit here and cool down."

Laurie was a long way from cool, but she ignored the desire she felt for Taj and focused on centering herself so she'd be ready for whatever the day had in store for them.

It took her a few minutes to feel loose enough to get into her usual routine, but she managed. After a while she was rolling through the downward dog, the crane, the half-moon, the dancer and all of the rest of her daily program, until she stopped and looked over to see Taj gazing at her with what could only be called lust.

Laurie averted her gaze just before Taj's eyes met hers. She took a few deep breaths and walked over to her. "Guess what I see?"

"Electricity?"

"No, but almost as good. There's a bubble fountain right down the path. We can cool off and at least start the day feeling a little less grungy."

Taj grabbed all of her things and followed Laurie down the bike path to the fountain used by kids in the playground to stay cool. "I don't think this was made for adults, but I'm loving it." Taj walked right into the cool water, her nipples hardening so quickly that Laurie had to tear her attention away.

She ran into the water beside Taj and shrieked at the cold. It was already a warm morning, but the water couldn't have been more than sixty-five degrees, far too cold for her. But it was so nice to see the water glinting off Taj's beautiful skin and clinging underthings that she quickly forgot her discomfort and relished the pleasure the water brought.

After jumping around to try and get warm they realized they'd never reach that goal, so they dashed out of the spray and stood shivering in the sun. "We're gonna want to be this cold later today," Taj predicted. "It's gonna be a scorcher."

***

They were both surprised that the electricity had not come back on, but they realized how bad things were because even their cell phones were still not working. Their first goal of the day was to find food. Since there were more stores and restaurants there, they crossed over to Tenth Avenue. The pickings were very slim, with every restaurant and diner closed. There was a very nice market in Chelsea that Laurie had been to, but the front doors of the old factory that housed the little shops were locked tight.

Despite the disappointment, Laurie took Taj's hand as they continued to walk up the avenue. "You seem very cheerful this morning," Taj said.

"This is still kind of fun. I feel bad for all of the people who can't open today, and I know a lot of people are going to lose a lot of money, but from my single perverse perspective, I'm enjoying myself."

"I hate to keep bringing this up, but that's the key requirement for being a good traveler. I think you have unexplored talents."

"God, I hope so," Laurie said, laughing. She caught sight of a man walking down the street with a grocery bag. "What's open?" she asked.

"The bodega on Twenty-fourth, if you have cash."

"Thanks," she said, already rummaging through her pockets. Gleefully, she produced a five and two singles. "I bought an Italian ice yesterday after my yoga class. Good thing I didn't bother putting my change in my wallet, or I would've left it at the restaurant last night." She shook her three bills in the air. "We're livin' large!"

***

The seven dollars didn't actually buy them much. Laurie considered buying two energy bars and a bottle of water, but Taj spent ten minutes walking around the tiny store surveying their options. She finally picked out a twelve-ounce jar of peanut butter and a decent-sized bag of raisins. "We'll get the most calories and the most protein from this. If this is the only thing we can buy it'll hold us for two days."

"Two days!" Laurie shrieked. "This is New York City. If the electricity isn't on by tonight, the federal government will start airlifting in tapas and Pinot Grigio."

Taj snapped the bills from Laurie's hand and put her purchases on the counter. "The energy bars are easier and might taste better, but I'm not counting on an airlift."

***

The bodega had a few plastic spoons left, so they sat in a pocket park eating spoonsful of peanut butter topped with as many raisins as would stay attached to the mound. After just a few spoons, Taj held the empty utensil in her hand and looked at the jar like she had no intention of eating another bite.

"Peanut butter isn't great without jelly," Laurie opined.

"I don't need the jelly, but I'll admit this isn't going down too easily. I wish we had a big glass of milk."

"Forget milk. I crave coffee."

"I kicked my coffee habit, which had become pretty bad, when I was in Afghanistan."

"They don't drink coffee?"

"Yeah, they like coffee, but they love tea, or chai as it's known locally. I started drinking green tea and now that's what I'm addicted to."

"I'll get you a chai the second Starbucks is open."

"I've had their chai and it doesn't bear much resemblance to what I've had in Afghanistan. But I'll gladly take it. You don't know of a good Afghani restaurant, do you?"

"No, but I bet there's one in Queens. Queens has everything."

"I don't have a confirmed flight out of New York, so I could hang around for a bit. I'd love to take you to Queens for dinner."

Smiling brightly, Laurie said, "It's a date."

***

It was just nine, but it was already hot and muggy. Not many people were out, even though no one had air conditioning or a fan. "Isn't it odd that people aren't heading to the parks? It's gotta be cooler outside than it is in."

"Maybe they're all standing under a cold shower."

"If their building is more than four or five floors, they don't have water." Laurie pointed at a big, wooden barrel perched atop a nearby building. "We have water towers if we're over five stories. Our water pressure only goes that high."

Taj surveyed the tower for a moment. "Why wouldn't the water still work?"

"It would, if it doesn't run out. But no one will conserve. Every native will assume the lights will be on in the next five minutes."

"Sounds like someone I know," Taj teased.

"It'll be back in no time. But I really don't like being broke. I have an idea of how to make a few bucks, but I have to change back into my dress."

"Sounds good to me. You look great in that dress." Taj's dark eyebrows popped up a few times, making her look like a teenager.

***

It took some teamwork, but Laurie was back in her dress, hair combed and lipstick applied by ten. They walked another ten blocks, winding up in front of Penn Station.

There were hundreds of people loitering in front of the entrance, with weary-looking police officers informing people that the Long Island Rail Road was still not in service. Nor was New Jersey Transit. But the A-C-E subway was back up, and people streamed into the hot building to wait for the subway.

"Will the A-C-E get us to your house?" Taj asked.

"Yeah. That's my normal train, but I won't have water or electricity. My apartment is hot when it's over seventy, so we're probably better off here."

"Then let's try to scare up some cash. How many do you have?"

Laurie checked her bag. "Five."

"Okay. I'll do my best." Taj stood near the entrance to Penn Station and started her pitch. "Get the latest from Laurie Ambrose, best selling mystery novelist. She's right here, a local girl made good. Let's hear it for Laurie Ambrose." She made an exaggerated circle with her arm and then pointed towards Laurie, who waved at the puzzled group of people.

Laurie held up her new book, acting like a spokesmodel for a new detergent.

"Yes, it's the book you've been waiting for," Taj continued. "It's in hardcover…and, in honor of the blackout, Laurie is selling the book for a mere twenty dollars. That's seven dollars off the list price, folks. And she'll autograph all copies. She'll even take a picture with you. Come on now, don't be the last person to get in on this deal. The blackout could be over in five minutes and you'll have missed your chance."

The nearby police officer snickered at Taj's prediction.

A few people stopped and regarded both women, clearly trying to figure out what kind of scam this was. But a flushed-faced woman tentatively approached and said, "Are you really Laurie Ambrose?"

Laurie turned the book around and put it next to her face. "I'm as close to being me as I can be in this heat."

"Ahh!" The woman started pointing and jumping up and down, and a few more women approached. "We're big fans!"

"Wonderful!" Laurie acted as excited to see them as they were to see her. "My book just came out yesterday, so you'll be the first to have it."

The woman looked at her three friends. "Do we have any money left?"

Laurie caught Taj's eye and they both sighed. "I won't charge you twenty dollars. I'm just stuck in the city and I'm out of cash. If you can spare a few bucks you can have a copy."

They talked among themselves, looking into wallets and bags, then produced sixteen dollars, which Laurie gratefully accepted. She signed the book for the first woman, then wrote down the names and addresses of the other three, promising to send them complimentary copies once she got home. She walked over to Taj and said, "Well, that only cost me about forty dollars. I'm gonna have to buy copies from my publisher."

"Yeah, but we've got sixteen dollars. That'll buy us... something."

***

They decided to walk to Central Park, even though it was so hot they had to walk in the shadow of buildings to keep even marginally cool. Once they reached Fifty-ninth Street, the whole city seemed to cool off by ten degrees. They entered the park at Columbus Circle, and immediately spent five of their scant dollars on a bottle of water and a giant pretzel, which they consumed in seconds.

"I've never known water to taste so good," Laurie moaned. "It's like rare wine."

They found a shady spot under a grove of trees and sat on Laurie's yoga mat, just watching people wander around. No one seemed to have an agenda. "I've never seen New Yorkers amble. No one's in a hurry for a change."

"They're probably worried about sunstroke," Taj said dryly.

"Hey! That guy's Blackberry is working." Laurie got to her feet and approached the man as soon as he hung up. "Is there any chance I can use your phone? Just for a minute?"

He eyed her for a moment, then asked the question that identified him as a local. "How much?"

"Two dollars."

He shook his head. "No deal."

"Okay. Five." She took out the bills and showed that she had them.

He grabbed them and handed her the phone. "Make it snappy."

She turned and called one of the few numbers she knew by heart, spending a good five minutes speaking. When she hung up, she said, "Someone's gonna call me back. You get another five if you let me take the call."

"How long will it take?"

"Not too long. Why? Where've you got to go?" She delivered this with her best New York attitude.

He nodded and sat back down on a bench. When Laurie went back to Taj, she said, "I might have had a brilliant idea."

"What?"

"I'll let you know if it turns out to be brilliant. I don't like to advertise dumb ideas."

***

They sat on their mat, watching people roller blade and bike ride in the blazing sun. As she looked around, Laurie noted that the cell phone holder was wearing a suit, obviously one he'd slept in. She started to feel a modicum of sympathy for him, but when he waved the phone at her, she jumped up and ran back to him, holding out the five dollars, which he took and pocketed.

A few minutes later she walked back to Taj, clearly with very good news. "Guess where we're going?"

"Brooklyn?"

"Better."

"Riverdale?"

"No. Even better. Even closer."

"Tell me!" Taj was on her feet, holding Laurie by the shoulders as she resisted the temptation to shake her.

"An apartment on the Upper West Side. One of my fans is letting us crash there. And," she said, delivering the news with the authority it deserved, "we can eat everything she has in the place!"

***

During the fifteen-block walk, Laurie told of calling Libby and having her use her Blackberry to place a notice on Laurie's internet chat group. A fan from New York was traveling, but she offered her place and the contents of her cupboard.

"That's really remarkable," Taj marveled. "She doesn't know you at all, but she's gonna let you use her apartment."

"She knows me." Laurie blinked, surprised at her own statement. "My readers know me pretty well. Heck, there are thirty writers I can think of that I'd let use my place. When you really follow someone, you know them better than you know most of your friends."

"And you say you're a hack," Taj scoffed.

"No, I'm not really a hack. I write good stories. I can just do more. That's what's been bothering me."

"Then do more."

"My publisher will only publish three books a year for me. Even though I could easily write four or five. As a matter of fact, I've got four books ready for editing right now."

"Then write under a different name. Find another publisher."

"You make it sound so easy," Laurie said, smiling warmly at her.

"It is. If you want it badly enough, it's easy."

***

They reached the apartment moments before they were ready to expire from heatstroke. The building was, blessedly, a brownstone of a mere four floors. A neighbor had been alerted and gave Laurie the key.

When Laurie opened the door, the remarkably hot air hit them like a blow. She took a breath and dashed for the windows, flinging them open as quickly as she could. Then she leaned out of the nearest window and sat on the sill, smiling at Taj who did the same at the adjacent window.

After resting for a few minutes, Laurie went to the refrigerator, pulled out two liters of water, and handed one to Taj. They drank until they were full, then Laurie said, "I call dibs on the shower."

"After you," Taj agreed, flopping onto a loveseat. She stayed right there, trying to will herself to cool down. But in a few minutes Laurie stood behind her and dripped cool drops of water on her head. "Don't stop," she said, her head lolling on the back of the loveseat.

"Go take a cold shower. You'll feel fantastic."

Taj got up and saw that Laurie was wrapped in a towel that barely covered her hoo-ha. "I love blackouts," she said, grinning lasciviously.

***

After two showers each and clad only in towels, they sat on the loveseat, a repast of cheese, crackers and olives on a platter between them. A cool-ish bottle of white wine rested against the corner of the loveseat and they each sipped a glass, savoring the crisp sensation as though it were the finest French import.

"This is the life," Laurie said, raising her glass.

"You'll get no arguments from me. I can't remember the last time I had a nicer day."

"Hey," Laurie said, looking down at an olive that had fully caught her attention. "Why do you think you didn't want to keep kissing me last night?"

241

Taj put her cool hand on Laurie's shoulder. "I did want to. But I'm…gun-shy, I guess. I get my heart broken easily."

Their eyes met. "Really? That's really the reason?"

"Yeah. Really. It would have crushed me to get…closer…and not be able to see you again. I try to keep my distance until I know there's a chance of…something happening."

"Like what?" Laurie moved the tray away and scooted closer.

Taj smiled warmly. "Like seeing what you'd say to having me stick around for a couple of weeks. I'd love to spend some time with you. Riverdale isn't very far from Brooklyn, all things considered."

"You know what's even closer?" Laurie scooted even closer, so close she could feel Taj's warmth.

"What?" Her voice was soft and tender.

"Brooklyn. Come home with me."

Taj's face lit up in delight. "Really?"

"Definitely. I haven't been this attracted to a woman in years…maybe never. I'm gonna find your passport and confiscate it so you can't get away."

"Well, I don't have an assignment lined up. I was gonna go to Mauritius for a little R and R."

"Mauritius? You say that like I say I'm going to the grocery store."

Taj shrugged. "I love it there. I know a place where I can stay for about fifteen dollars a night. It's right on the beach, no tourists." She moved closer, closing the distance completely. "It's warm and sunny and tropical. A nice rain every afternoon, cool drinks while you lie in a hammock with the wind rocking you. I'd recommend it to anyone who wanted to start traveling."

"I'll give you two weeks to convince me," Laurie whispered as she grasped Taj's shoulders and pulled her in for a long kiss. "Then I'm going with or without you."

The End

Billy Boy

By

Susan Smith

It was all Achilles' fault. Heel. Achilles' heel was redundant, according to Joan. She, Joan, much against her own good will and sense, was suckered, shanghaied, press-ganged into covering Sheila's class for her. Sheila had gone and diabolically done the one thing that Joan could not resist, she'd asked politely, backed up by more than twenty years of friendship. That was Joan's Achilles' heel; the sacrifices on the sacred altar of friendship had to be immediate, grand, generous and without thought, qualm or regret. A friend asked, an Old Friend, and it was done. Whatever it was. Now, it was Sheila's summer writing seminar.

It is important to have a place where emotion carries against all sense, where it is honored and respected and let run free. For Joan, that was friendship. Relationships, for her, never seemed to touch that profound intimacy. Something about the flesh ruined everything. Friendships—we ride out into the hail of bullets together, we fight back to back, I will die in your place, blood brotherhood—were central to Joan's heart. She just didn't have many male friends. That was complicated by the severe case of lesbianism she'd discovered in grade school. Girls were mystery and excitement and terror. Boys were safe, nonsexual, staunch friends without complication or threat. Until later.

It was this growing up that gave Joan her only taste of acceptance and relief, male friendships. Before high school, they were her saving grace. They were devout, uncomplicated, robust, and doomed to end in tragedy. For what is adolescence, for those unready and without place to hide, but a tragedy? Adolescence, the poverty of puberty, threw into high relief the differences she'd been trying to suppress. Her male friendships, as staunch and joyful as she'd imagined them, as bold and free as she was sure they saw her, changed forever. Once the secondary sexual characteristics hit, Joan's world ended. No more playing outside with the boys, in a tank top and shorts, just as they wore. No more running around in the woods until well after dark. No more riding bikes deep into the wilderness, into the farmland and away from everything manmade. No more. Outside the boundaries of civilization was danger. No longer was she the gay, bold adventurer. Now she was a girl, and the boys noticed.

Joan was gob smacked. What was wrong with them? Why did they keep staring at her shirt? Why didn't they touch her as they used to, hand clasps, shoulder slaps, punches, and now try to touch her in different, side-eye ways? Like there was something sly and ugly, but deeply interesting about her now. And she, the center of her, no longer mattered. They stopped talking to her. You can't look and talk at the same time, Joan thought.

So her refuge ended with puberty. Girls got more mysterious and terrifying, and boys became drooling predators. Joan did what many fine queers faced with the same intolerable situation did, she retreated into a passionate interest and pretended that sex, and sexuality, dating, boys, girls, and all that sweaty horror didn't exist. She rejected the experiences that had pre-rejected her. So in adolescence, when most are stewing in the hormone bath, Joan became a monk.

A bookish monk, which helped her sail into college and later, grad school. She was a professor of classics by the time she was thirty-two. She was intellectually brilliant, driven, reserved, arrogant, or so it was whispered. Joan had learned her lesson in high school and stopped trying to be friends with men, or please them at her own expense. The severe, exacting precision she radiated kept everyone at arm's length, and what was insecurity at the core got interpreted, as it often is, as arrogance. The monkish look suited Joan, with the subdued, tailored clothing, the uniform simplicity. The lack of any makeup or jewelry gave her face a strange naked impressiveness, a mountain crag washed by rain. If her eyes were too shadowed, if her lips were held tight from habit, it added to her grim dignity. Pain, well tamped down, reads as strength. Her dark hair was first cut into a Caesar when she was twenty-three, and never varied from that. Gray now, at forty-two, crashed against her widow's peak and temples, but the stability of the cut remained. This was an area of her life where long ago she'd achieved a sense of peace, or armed truce, and she wasn't about to threaten that.

There were other areas like that, sealed off places, airless, in her that she'd learned to brick over and retreat from. Rarely did she take a pick axe to those doors. Friendship had been one of those airless places, until Joan hit eighteen and went away to college. Freshman year, she'd roomed with a girl that ended up becoming her best friend. Sheila. In those days Sheila was a vegan Marxist radical lesbian feminist. Now she was a Democrat pescetarian yoga enthusiast married to a lovely man, Chris. The span of time between eighteen and forty-two, those twenty-four years, had welded Sheila and Joan together.

When they'd first met, Joan had been astounded and thrilled at Sheila's in-your-face boldness and activism. At her prodding, Joan joined the campus gay and lesbian alliance and dipped a toe into political waters. Experimentations with recycling, not shaving, Patchouli oil, and sex followed. Joan ended up liking the sex best.

As a brand-new, young dyke impatient for life now that she'd caught a glimpse of it, Joan decided to kiss Sheila. Sheila was her roommate, which made things potentially disastrous, and Sheila was her friend, which seemed more complicated still. So, one night, after smuggled bottle of Rolling Rock, and because she was sure despite how she felt about it, that this was a cultural imperative, Joan kissed Sheila, who promptly giggled hysterically. This did nothing for Joan's budding romantic sense of self.

"It won't work, Joan. We're friends."

Joan, stung, humiliated, sat down on the bed with her hands hanging between her knees. "But how do you know? We're both gay. We get along. Aren't we supposed to date?"

Sheila allowed that this was likely true. So they tried for a week. The anemic handholding added nothing to the conversation, and tension over the eventually dared kiss kept

Joan from enjoying Sheila's company. They agreed to give it up and went back to being friends, to a much-relieved Joan.

After that, Sheila started introducing Joan to every girl she knew. Sheila and Joan worked out the standard tie-something-to-the-door-handle-to-indicate-mating-rituals code. At first it was a rainbow plastic lei, carried back from a protest against Army recruiting on campus. Joan liked that signal. She giggled every time she put the rainbow lei on the doorknob.

So her second adolescence began, and at eighteen, brilliant and monkish, Joan became a fourteen year old boy. Girls were still a paradox, but now they were individual paradoxes Joan could touch with her hands, with her lips, try to decipher the questions of why this sweet wet destruction of her dorm bed was so incendiary to her. Flesh and friendship were still separate realms.

Joan's devotion to Sheila was threatened, over the years, but always held true. When, at thirty, she'd been confronted with her weeping friend's coming out to her as bisexual, Joan had stood by her when many in the dyke community tossed her off. Joan felt the initial denial, the stab of sadness that Sheila was leaving her, leaving their whole world, jumping the fence and grabbing fistfuls of that heterosexual privilege. She'd escaped the prison. Thinking of her life as a prison made Joan recoil internally, so she shoved the whole uncomfortable mess aside and reduced her reaction to the simple, classic. Sheila was her friend; therefore, whatever Sheila did was to be understood and defended. That was what Joan did...eventually. There were awkward moments along the way—getting used to meeting Sheila's boyfriends, double-dating, realizing, even as she didn't want to be right, that Sheila wasn't coming back. She was with men.

This sawed at Joan's deepest convictions. If Sheila was with men, she wasn't with Joan or their people. Joan smothered the reaction when around Sheila, but was convinced, convinced, that Sheila would keep going away, piece by piece, now that her loyalty had shifted. If that could shift, anything could, and there was no certainty or security in the world. Joan was left alone on the shores of a world Sheila had guided her into. Her friend was leaving her. Joan tried not to let that show, but how could she not to the one person who knew how to read her? The one person who knew how to interpret pained silence and false, determined smiles?

It put distance into their friendship. That shoving away was needed; it let in air, movement. They took jobs in different states. Joan learned to make friends on her own of a sort, a painful, awkward stage to be in when you are in your thirties. Eventually, Joan learned humility, when she called Sheila and told her that she missed her. The friendship grew closer again, and Joan made such an effort to like and get to know Sheila's boyfriends that eventually, she liked them. It was an effort that needed much soul-searching and determination on her part, to climb back over that fence to her younger self, even a little. She'd stood apart from men for years. It wasn't like her early friendships; there were too many chasms to breach at one leap. Yet, this was for Sheila; therefore, it would happen. Chris, thankfully, she'd liked from the first, bonding with him in a simple, masculine way. They never got particularly close; their friendship was good, but not the fiery romantic adolescent blood brotherhood. When Chris and Sheila got married, Joan stood as Sheila's best man. Pleasant years followed, jobs taken back in the same state, same city. Houses purchased nearby. Long-term relationships came for Joan, two that gave an added stability to their time together. Joan relaxed into her own open-mindedness—even congratulating herself on it—forgetting the early years of wrestling like Jacob with her soul. What was more important, belief or love? Love asked compassion and understanding. Not forgiveness, as there was no need. What had Sheila done, really? Shown great courage as she always did, faced things head on, been true to her own desire, and trusted her friend, Joan, to be an adult. Eventually, Joan earned that trust and their friendship thrived. Joan hoped that she'd covered her early turmoil.

Her last relationship, with Cody, had ended months ago. After seven years, they'd drifted apart. What else could Joan say? There was no argument, no fire, no yelling. It burned itself out. Without the deep friendship to buoy it up, their relationship vanished like smoke. Cody left, and Joan was sad, but not too much and not for too long. There was her work, there was the summer stretching golden and endless before her, and there was Sheila and Chris. She'd be fine.

Joan hadn't wanted to take over Sheila's writing seminar, but Sheila had asked. That was all there was to it; her friend needed her. Not that Joan would be a saint about it; she'd grumble and bitch until she was sure Sheila had suffered along with her, then she'd let it go.

"One class a week, Wednesday nights, for a non-major, summer creative-writing seminar, mostly chock full of Women's Studies majors," Sheila had said to a pouting Joan.

"I hate creative writing. More like adolescent masturbatory exercises. I don't give a damn about the content of their souls, the depth of their personal insights. They are teenagers."

"You are such a curmudgeon, I want to pinch you. Most of them are grad students, and two of them are our age."

"What do I do with them?"

"Enflame their minds. Ignite their souls. And do a basic write-a-letter-to-a-mythological-figure writing exercise."

"Can I include Jesus and Santa Claus?"

"No. You're a classicist. Do Zeus and that junk."

"Lovely. Do I talk about your work this way?"

"All the time. Blame Chris. He got me the stupid dog that decided to lay down on the stupid second step in the dark, and thus helped me along to my stupid torn tendon. We could say it is his fault."

"No, I'm not willing to do the bloodguilt back seven generations. I'll do your letter thing. Is there anyone I should watch out for?"

"No troublemakers. There is one standout, reminds me of you actually. A young you, brilliant and focused, but unlike you in personality. Impish. I won't tell you who, I want to see if you spot them."

The art annex was supposed to provoke creativity with the rusting insectoid welded sculptures in the courtyard and the muddy local bucolic paintings. Joan's nostrils flared slightly, unconsciously. The modern world offended her aesthetic sense. For Joan, the world ended with the fall of Rome. Her dissertation had been on Hadrian.

It was always the same, walking into a new class. She had to remember to smile after she set her briefcase down, or they would stay closed off, unsure of her, until well into the second hour of the class. These weren't her students; she didn't need them to be scared of her. This was a creative seminar, what Joan imagined to be as touchy-feely as an empowerment weekend. So she was expected to make them feel good, not her normal burden. It gave her an awkward sweetness of which she was entirely unaware.

There were fifteen people in the class in a room designed to seat fifty. The chairs were arrayed on risers in a circle, ascending from the central stage. Joan noticed that the students tended to map out a great deal of space for themselves, even after entering together in friendly bunches. This class was used to working alone. Good.

"Good evening. I'm Dr. Ligurious. I'll be covering the seminar for the next two weeks. Dr. Cross will return after that." Joan picked up the stack of assignments and started handing them out.

"What happened to Sheila?" The boy sat with his feet hooked over the back of the chair in front of him, retro canvas sneakers artfully untied, which annoyed the living hell out of

Joan. She didn't bother to look at the rest of him; she swatted his sneakers off the chair.

"Dr. Cross is attending to some personal matters."

Most of his head was a baseball cap, pulled low, brim rolled but at least, Joan thought, facing forward. It was summer; nearly everyone wore the uniform of t-shirt and jeans or shorts. He had jeans on, and two t-shirts, layered despite the heat. Foolish things we do for fashion, Joan thought. The edge of his jaw was spiky with stubble, days' worth. With the cap tilted back his eyes were as disturbingly blue and large as a child's picture on a bottle of mashed apricots. He grinned and held out his hand for the assignment.

"I hope Sheila feels better soon. Her ankle, right?"

He brought out the stern in her, in that instantaneous animal bristling she could neither explain nor address. It was the type of thing teachers never tell their students. They strive to confront and root out their own biases, be aware of treating students differently, of favoring or disfavoring any individual or group. Despite all that, when two people meet, and for reason neither of them might be able to explain, there might spring up an instantaneous reaction light years ahead of rational thought, where liking or disliking is sealed. He evoked such a reaction, though guarding against it, Joan wasn't sure which. He was used to being liked, she could tell that at once, much as a puppy is used to being liked. His sunny lounging body language didn't change; he seemed unfazed by Joan's scrutiny.

"Tendon." Joan answered automatically, walking away.

The boy mumbled something that might have been, "Can't count on Achilles in the clutch." He might have said "The Achilles"; Joan wasn't sure.

"Your assignment for tonight: write a letter to a mythological figure. You may ask them the truth about a myth or legend; you can praise them, warn them, and scold them, as long as you interact on a personal level with the figure," Joan said evenly. There, it should be quiet for a while. Joan went to sit at the desk.

"What do you mean by mythological figure?" This was one of the older women, clearly returned to school after her kids were grown and gone. Joan addressed her with careful respect.

"Why don't we stick with the Greek gods for ease? Zeus and the Olympians primarily."

The woman nodded, satisfied, and Joan was pleased.

"Can we be mythological figures too, writing the letter?" It was the sneakers boy. This was why Joan hated creative writing. You could argue for endless exceptions to any rule. It was all arbitrary. If things did not have the decency of being evidently true, they should at least be overwhelmingly possible and most plausible.

"Fine," Joan said, not giving a damn. He seemed to take this as a triumph, grinned again, and set to work.

It was blissfully quiet for more than an hour. Ten minutes for coffee and cigarettes and cell phones, then back to it with a vengeance. She had to hand it to Sheila, these were devout students. That spoke well of the environment she created. At the end of the class, sunlight going from gold to bruised orange crept across the rows, turned the students in that moment into castings, bronzed like baby shoes in Joan's memory. The end of day in summer always brought out her melancholy, brought out the yearning for the brief golden years of noble friendships, the unified trunk of humanity before it is split into men and women. "Are we nothing but the scars left on us by love's passing?" Joan thought, very much in the creative writing mood, influenced and buoyed up by the enthusiasm and seriousness of the class.

Students dropped their papers off on the desk as they headed out, nodding to Joan, most shyly. They hadn't had any time or interaction to bond; they were being polite for Sheila's sake. But when sneakers boy came up to the desk, last and five well-documented minutes past the end of the class, he was more than polite. He held Joan's gaze longer than necessary, smiling broadly as he handed the paper in as if they were already old friends, no time or distance between them. It was an inclusive camaraderie—warm, fast, generous. Familiar. He didn't respond to any of Joan's distancing signals, as if they weren't directed at him. They were coconspirators already. Joan looked down at his paper. His scrawled name, in a broad and careless hand, was Billy. Joan glanced back up and saw as he exited in profile, backlit, the clear outline of breasts beneath his shirt. Joan nodded to herself, feeling foolish. Of course. It was the instant intimacy of the tribe. He read her, and was letting her know he was family. He'd seemed very happy about it.

Joan brought the papers over to Sheila's two nights later. Chris was cooking and Sheila was recovering and refusing to sit still, so Joan was imported to keep her entertained. This ended up being reading student papers while Sheila was altered on pain meds and Joan on a few glasses of wine.

"What have you got?" Sheila asked, tossing a paper on the pile.

"Oh, an eco-fable about Gaia. Polemic, but good. As far as I can tell. How do I rate these stories? By how much I like them?"

"In vino veritas," Sheila said, pouring Joan more wine. "You don't have to grade them. I'm just flaming bored. I'm glad to hear that they were well behaved. You met our Billy, I take it."

Joan frowned. "Yes. Bit too casual for me. This was the student who reminded you of me?"

"Not the grim, dour Puritan you, the remarkable force of your mind. Strip the flesh away. He doesn't think like anyone I've ever met, except you. You can tell him anything, and he will listen, and nod, and smile, and go do whatever he was going to in the first place. He's following his own drummer."

"Better than his own Pied Piper. Still think it's funny that golden retriever of a boy reminded you of me. He's trans?"

"Yes. His voice is starting to crack; I'm surprised you didn't notice."

"I wasn't looking for it. He needs a shave."

Sheila poured Joan another glass of wine. "He's pretty enough for a boy band."

"He probably looked great as a girl too. Why are so many young dykes changing these days? Is it just me? In our day, half these kids would have stayed in the community, instead of leaving us."

"Funny you can say 'us' while my husband is in the kitchen. Once upon a time, you wouldn't have been able." Sheila's tone was even, but there was a hint of reserve in it, a hint of pulling back, that Joan missed.

"You know what I mean. The lesbian tribe, which you still belong to. You're a better dyke than I am."

"He's still in the community, he IDs as queer. Ridiculously open. Enviable. Kids these days."

Joan put her wine glass down and tossed the papers in her lap onto the couch. "Kids these days forget what it was like, a generation ago. Queer indeed. Don't you wish we had the internet when we were coming out? God, one dog-eared copy of *Rubyfruit Jungle* and a videotape of *Desert Hearts* were all I knew of lesbianism before college."

"Billy might have been in the lesbian community, Joan, but he wasn't a lesbian. He wasn't a girl. He was a boy; he just wasn't public about it yet."

"Sheila, I felt like a boy at that age, if you recall. From twelve to twenty-five, I'd say. I hated being a girl." Joan wasn't sure why she was getting heated, but she was. Her blood started to kick up, moving from a walk to a trot.

"You hated being treated like a weak fool, as I recall. You can hate women's oppression and be female or male. Hating being treated as an inferior doesn't make you trans, it makes you sane."

"So what does? I've always felt more masculine in my interest and pursuits, and I don't fit any of the basic female requirements. I don't relate sexually to men. No husband. No kids, and more heinous still, no desire for kids, of my body at least. No biological clock. If that can be disconnected—and not through effort, I never remember having one—then why am I still female? Am I some in-between thing now, by the queer definition?"

"By the queer definition you get to tell us, sweetie, we don't tell you. And if you change your damn mind in a week, you get to tell us that too. Your identity, your sense of being in the world, is mined from within, and then expressed externally. Tell me, Joan, if there were no impediments, and you could do it relatively painlessly and quickly, would you transition?"

"Men have it differently. I would think about it. But, no. I don't think I would. It took me a long time to learn to live in this body, but I think I've achieved that. I wouldn't want to change."

"Then you likely aren't trans. But Billy has already answered that question publicly. It isn't easy or inexpensive or without consequences to change. Quite the opposite. With all that, knowing all that, he chose to pursue it. For him, it was worth everything to be himself. I know you respect courage."

"Of course I do. I liked the boy, Sheila, I did. I don't begrudge him his path. It makes me wonder how I ended up where I am, and if I'd have made a different choice if I were coming up now. I was so relieved when I found out there was a place, no matter how small or hard to find, that respected and admired women like me, masculine women, butch women. That I could be both a member of a community and a desired romantic partner."

"You were so damned serious. It was adorable. An eighteen-year-old girl trying to look like a forty-year-old man. A priest, with your black coat that you never took off, and your face above it pale as bone, library pallor. I knew you read yourself to sleep every night of your life."

Joan tilted her wine glass and looked down at it. "Why, though? Why did you talk to me? I was a monk, a wallflower. I noticed you right away, you were laughing. I'd never heard anything so lovely. I would never have approached you. If you hadn't spoken to me, I'd still be waiting to come out."

"Total crap, you were a lesbian from the time you could walk."

Joan smiled, a relaxed, easy smile, a transformative one. Years fell away from her face; the deep grooves at the corners of her mouth were hidden in the smile. Like many faces designed for sorrow, designed to stab the heart of the watcher with the translucent suffering in great dark eyes, in a mouth made firm by habit, not nature, a genuine smile transformed Joan. Beauty strode out, all the more potent as it was mixed with relief that such a vehicle for pain—that pale, suffering face—could host such unguarded human joy. The rarity of the smile made it a spear.

"See, that's what I mean. You see me. That's always startling to people who feel like windows."

"It takes no special insight to see the dyke in you, Martina."

"Very funny."

"Butcher than Steve McQueen, if he were playing St. Francis." Sheila fished through the pile of papers, selected one, and tossed it to Joan. "Ouch, too much movement. Here, read his."

Joan took up the paper. Dear Zeus, she read.

Dear Zeus,

Hey, how's it going? Yeah, it's beautiful here on Mt. Ida, and I'm totally having a ball hanging out and being a shepherd and all, but people tell me I'm far too pretty for this farm-boy life, and I should get my blond self off to a city, so I can be appreciated for my beauty, grace, and charm. How's about it, Sugar Daddy?

Kidding, Cloud-gathering Zeus! Put the bolts down. Let's just talk, man to man. Man to twink. You are a hot, commanding, masterful, older man. You are the authority in your realm. Me, I'm just a pretty boy hanging out in a sunlit field, royalty that doesn't know itself. Exposing every inch of my smooth, golden flesh to the bright light of Apollo, my thighs causing more duels than Hyakinthos. Waiting to catch a fierce eagle's eye and be borne up to Heaven. We're Greek; you can see where this is going. I've always had a thing for kings, for the majestic masculinity, strong, experienced, protective, honorable, leaders and shepherds of their people. Oh, Daddy!

But that's not what I wanted to ask you. Why, Lord Zeus, do men and youths who meet in love have example in the divine ranks, such as Apollo and Hyakinthos, Herakles and Hylas, Hermes and, well, lots of folks, but women and girls do not? Experience and guidance met with beauty and eagerness, Eros and Anteros, love given and returned in that most noble of loves, the love that is sacred friendship, the love that defeats tyranny and builds cities, the love that pleases the gods with its fidelity, the love that creates honor and glory for the lovers and the people. Is this not what the gods themselves envy— love from the soul, love that recalls us to our wings?

I see you, sitting at the desk, with your dark eyes holding the look of eagles, proud, commanding, under your Caesar's hair. Send for me. Have a drink with me, Zeus; I'll pour. Let me be your cupbearer.

- Ganymede

"I think the little bastard is playing with me." Joan set the paper down and then picked it back up.

"If he is, it's your game he's playing and your language he's speaking,"

"Is he always like this?"

"No. He wouldn't talk to me like that, I wouldn't follow it. He's very good at reading people. You must bring out the best in him."

Joan took up the red pen of judgment and answered Billy in precise handwriting on the bottom of the page.

Ganymede,
Can't spare the eagle.

Regards,
Zeus

It would do. It handled him by cutting him short, but it answered him in kind. If he were playing with her, it was now done. If he'd been asking what Joan thought he was asking? No, it was part of the exercise, and he was merely being young and clever and a bit of an ass. He wasn't actually asking to be Ganymede and comparing her to Zeus. Absurd. She was a woman, a dyke, twice his age. He was a brand new boy. It was the camaraderie of the tribe he was invoking. In that case, no offense to take, he was just young and likely lonely. Though why youth should be lonely made no sense. It had youth. The loneliness she carried she'd earned over years of trial and error, honed at last to a distance that kept even in relationships. No lover had ever known her the way Sheila did. Flesh and friendship did not mix.

Meeting someone who spoke her language was rare. There was loneliness in it that approached the separation of growing up queer, for Joan, and made the wasteland between friendships worse. If she was made of ice, or filled with, after years of distancing herself until it became reflex, she'd unlearned how to open up. Perhaps that was why she yearned so for the fast and easy camaraderie of boys, from her own boyhood. Girlhood, Joan corrected. She'd been a girl. As much as she'd felt like one of the boys, as much as she felt part of the group, puberty gave it the lie. There was a gulf between her and the boys, a parting of ways, a split in the path. Now, and looking on, she'd have to go on her own. It would melt her heart to be able to simply belong without having to explain herself.

The conversation with Sheila kept ringing round her head after Joan went home late in the night. She was forty-two, and the lesbian world had changed somewhere along the way. There wasn't anything new in that, really. The boundaries, which were always slippery in the women's community, were just shifting along the coastline. Joan had long thought of the community as biological unit, a cell, with a permeable membrane. Sometimes, women passed through that membrane and joined the community, moving away from husbands, bringing kids with them. Sometimes they set up shop and stayed forever; sometimes they went back, and forth, and back again. You could cross the membrane as often as you needed. Thinking of it like this helped her adjust to Sheila's dating men. If it had happened the other way, if a woman had started dating women for the first time, there would be congratulations all around. Not in reverse. The sense of loss had to be overcome first. Sheila had mastered still being culturally a lesbian, despite her husband. She saw herself as queer, not straight. Bisexual, to queer the lesbian space, lesbian to queer the straight, words she was able to take on, back and forth through the membrane. Sheila said she felt, thought about, and experienced the world as a queer person. Not an ally, though she was that, a member of the community. That was as much a modern identity as any other, Joan thought. If Sheila accepted Billy so readily, why was she having trouble?

Joan was alone, sitting with her chin on her hand, lit by her wire-armed desk lamp, eyes hooded, staring out into nothing. She sighed and admitted it. Part of her conflict with Billy was his age, part was his boyhood. Then there was the way he wrote to her. She wasn't sure what to make of him yet. Joan found herself looking forward to Wednesday, to the seminar, to hand back the papers. Even if he was an imp, as Sheila called him, Billy was interesting.

Wednesday came, and the class filed in, and Joan looked around the room, disappointed, though she didn't want to admit it. Billy hadn't made it to class. Joan handed out the writing exercise and tried not to think about it. He didn't come storming into class after twenty minutes, nor did he show up at the break. The sun was down. It was too late. Joan collected the papers and said goodbye to the students, assuring them that Dr. Cross would be back next week. That was her stint as a creative-writing babysitter. It wasn't that bad; she'd have to apologize to Sheila for griping on about it. Parts of it were even pleasant. At least it was over, and she had the rest of the summer to herself. She dropped the papers off at Sheila's and washed her hands of it.

Days later, sitting at her desk on the second floor by the tall window overlooking the long green space that divided Bidwell Parkway, Joan felt the silence weigh on her. The windows were open to catch the breeze, the smell of cooking meat, propane, and cut grass was intoxicating. Maybe she should go for a bike ride. She didn't own a bike. Maybe she should buy a bike. It had been years. Maybe decades. Summer used to be about the endless—endless afternoons, endless bike rides down endless roads, through green and amber fields stitched by falling-down stone walls. Finding a brook hidden deep in the forest, and dipping your feet into the ridiculously cold water in a shaded pool by a pockmarked rock. It was summer, as she'd longed for, and she was bored. There was nobody to share things with.

Maybe this was about missing Cody, Joan thought. That was an idea worth exploring. So she got out the photo albums and leafed through, looked at seven years of holidays, dinners, trips, events. There was happiness, sure, especially in the first album, when Cody's red hair was still hippie long and wild, when they went barefoot in the garden and laughed and held hands. By the second album, the handholding went away. She and Cody were still in the same frame, but often looking in different directions, talking with different people. Joan noticed, for the first time, that when she was standing next to Sheila, her body language was relaxed and intimate; they stood closer than she and Cody ever did in front of the lens. You could see, looking back, the album where they drifted apart. What was it? No shared interests, once the infatuation wore off? Lack of a shared language, shared understanding of the world? Having shared flesh, they couldn't ever be friends? Joan missed having a new friend, the way she did when she and Sheila were new. Joan put the albums away. Too much thinking. She wanted to go and do something, but had no idea of where to go or what to do.

Sheila called on Friday to thank her. "The students said nice things about you. Maybe I should get my tendon operated on more often."

"They are just being nice. I didn't do anything."

"I gave Billy back his paper with your note."

"Oh?"

"He laughed."

That was all there was to it, then. He laughed, and the matter was closed.

The first e-mail came on Sunday.

Zeus,
Sorry I missed you. I can take a cab, if you are out of eagles. How's 8 pm?
Besos,
Ganymede

Joan wrote him back promptly, starting the exchange.

William,
How did you get my e-mail?
Dr. Ligurious

Z-dog,
Sheila gave it to me. 8 sounds bad for you. 7 it is. How's Tuesday? I've got the cup and am ready to pour.
Hugs,
Gany

Billy,
I'll have to have a talk with Dr. Cross. No, Tuesday doesn't work. This has been fun, but I'm done.
Joan

Three days went by, and Joan was convinced that Billy was finished with his game. Which was all just as well, Joan told herself. She didn't need that kind of attention. The next e-mail came on Wednesday after midnight.

Hadrian,
I read your dissertation, "Sharing a Couch: Intimacy in Hadrian and Antinous' Iconography." Sheila recommended it. Now I get why you were standoffish when I called you Zeus; clearly you are Hadrian. So then, Imperator, be thou my lord and I shall be thy Antinous. Friday, perhaps?
Antinous

The nerve of the boy. And Sheila! Handing out her private e-mail, encouraging the boy to read her dissertation was out of line. Yet, he had read it. That was flattering. But she couldn't encourage this kind of behavior.

Billy,
You couldn't keep up with me.
Joan

She regretted sending it as soon as she clicked. That was going too far, and sounded like she was encouraging him. When he didn't e-mail back right away, Joan decided that she'd clearly crossed a line, frightened the boy, and he'd run off. Thursday, nine a.m. came his reply, irrepressible as ever.

Hadrian,
You'd be surprised. I'm young, but supple and lithe. Antinous followed Hadrian at the hunt, one of their favorite pastimes. The beloved is supposed to keep up with the lover, think of all you have to teach me. Take me with you on your travels, we will see the world. We'll just stay out of Egypt; I have a thing about boating on the Nile.

Antinous

Joan smiled when she read the last line of the e-mail, one of the smiles that brought such astounding beauty to contrast the severity of her usual expression. So Billy knew how Antinous died. If this were any other situation, Joan might be enjoying it a great deal. If this were, say, a woman. It sounded almost flirtatious, but maybe was only playful. Either way it was fun but inappropriate, and it was time to shut it down.

> *Billy–*
> *You seem to be laboring under a misapprehension. I'm gay.*
> *Joan*

> *Hadrian,*
> *Well aware of it. So? Saturday might be nice.*
> *Antinous*

She had to stop herself from typing "Antinous"; it was catching.

> *Billy,*
> *Saturday is out. So this is fun, but I don't want to give you the wrong idea.*
> *Joan*

> *Hadrian,*
> *I've got lots of ideas, and most of them I come up with on my own. Sunday perhaps?*
> *Antinous*

> *Billy,*
> *I'm also 42.*
> *Joan*

Hadrian,
Then you are the answer to life, the universe and everything! I'm having a geekgasm here. I'm 24, you're 42. The symbolism is awesome, no? I'm holding your mirror, you are holding mine.
Don't panic, I have a towel.
Antinous

Billy,
I have no idea what you are talking about, more than half of the time.
Joan

Hadrian,
That's why you need to hang out with me. The rest of the world feels like that around you all the time. You need to run with a pack that can keep up, but you can't command the good and the beautiful to just appear in your life. You take what is given, with joy. I think I taught you this. Sunday it is!
Antinous

A.,
You are presumptuous, aren't you?
H.

Hadrian,
Ouch, I know why you are famous for building a wall. Single malt and video games. Come out and play. Hadrian loved to play with Antinous. Don't you remember?
Antinous

Antinous,
Fine. I'll play. I'll drink Scotch and play video games with you if you can answer this, and convince me of your answer: did Antinous drown accidentally in the Nile, did he sacrifice himself for Hadrian, did he commit suicide, or did I have him sacrificed?

Hadrian

There. That would take care of the boy. If he wanted to play, he'd better play on her level or she'd have none of it. Plus, it would keep her from having to drink scotch and play video games. Thursday she had a meeting with the Feminist Film Festival committee, something Sheila had talked her into after Cody left. It was staffed almost entirely by lesbians, so naturally it had to be called "Feminist" so nobody would be scared off. The treasurer of the committee, Carol Eisenberg, had a wicked crush on her and Joan was uncomfortably aware of it. While Cody was still living with her, Carol kept her distance, while following Joan with barely concealed romantic longing in her eyes. Sheila, in a reversion to old habit, tossed Joan in Carol's way, or Carol in Joan's, but no sparks were struck from Joan's flinty hide. Sheila explained it to a crushed and crushing Carol that Joan was just grieving from the end of her seven-year relationship. Not true, but plausible, and a pretty lie that spared Carol's feelings. It helped that Joan normally looked like she was in mourning, even when getting coffee. It helped that she hadn't dated in months, either.

This year, the theme for the film festival was celebration of the personal, so women were being encouraged to bring in their personal footage and photos from Michigan. Joan was curating the Michigan Memories event, as she had video going back ten years of her and Sheila at Michigan, every summer, lovers or no, husbands or no. It was set to open the last week in July, and run through the end of Michigan in August. It was the only deadline Joan had left for the summer, now that Sheila's writing seminar was done for her at least.

Joan heard Sheila's high pitched whistle and looked up, puzzled. Sheila was on the far side of the room, leg propped on a rolling chair. She wasn't supposed to be out, but she'd gone batty, as she said, being home. Why had Sheila summoned her? Then she saw. Carol was bringing her coffee, coffee in a Styrofoam cup, with an obscene dollop of powdered petroleum product kreemer languishing on the surface, flaking off slowly into the muddy orange liquid. This was a lovely gesture, Joan had to remind herself, and she should not, under any circumstances, flinch away from Carol's hand when it ended up on her arm.

"How have you been, Joan?" Carol asked, transferring the coffee to Joan with lingering fingers.

Carol was a perfectly lovely human being, Joan would argue to anyone but Sheila, who read the recoiling in her whenever Carol came around. Joan wasn't able to explain it, when questioned. Being around that woman was just nails on a chalkboard to her. Unconscious, animal reaction, she didn't like Carol for any sound reason. Carol was perfectly nice, if a little showy with her laugh and hand gestures. She was nice. She was very, very concerned with people around her, involved. From a distance, beautiful, in a whippet-blonde way, slim, elegant, high strung, seemingly delicate. She loved looking delicate so she could lean on Joan. That was a base and bitter thought, so Joan tried not to let it show on her face, while Carol was staring at her, waiting for her to answer and maybe take a sip of that loathsome coffee.

"Fine, good. Thanks." Joan took the cup awkwardly. It was too hot.

Carol drew her lips down in a comical mockery of sorrow. "We worry about you being so alone."

"We?" Joan asked, looking up from the cup. It was too full, and she was trying to keep the balance needed between motion and pain.

Carol looked around the room and rested on Sheila, implying the universal concern. "Everyone. You seem too lonely, it can't be good."

"I'm fine, really."

Sheila's high pitched whistle came again, and Joan stood up with relief. "Sheila needs me. Would you excuse me?"

Carol moved out of Joan's way to keep from getting burned. Joan put the coffee down as soon as she was seated next to Sheila. "Thank you."

"You looked like you needed a rescue."

Joan struggled not to smile. "Carol is a lovely human being."

"Man, you always say that as such an insult. What did she ever do to you?"

"Nothing, but I bet she'd like to do a few things to me."

"You're full of piss and vinegar tonight."

"Yes, meaning to talk to you about that. What are you up to, giving Billy my private e-mail?"

Sheila looked at her. "Oh, did he write? Good."

"And encouraging him to read my dissertation?"

"Look, he reminds me of you. That means he's too smart for his own good, and struggling with it. Nobody around him reflects him and it has to be lonely, like it was for you. I want to spare him some of that. Plus, I think you two need to have a meeting of the minds."

"You want me to mentor this kid?"

"Not exactly. I just think you should talk. I think you'll be friends."

"Friends?" Joan said, in layers of melting skepticism.

"Friends. How many do you have, really? How many people do you know who know you, all the way, to the hilt, to the bone, no walls? Everyone needs that, and you, I think, more than most, because you long for it more and have less of it."

"Why do you think we will be friends?"

"Because I saw Billy the week after you left. He was all lit up when he spoke about meeting you. Broke his heart that he had to miss your last class. He seemed so genuinely upset that he wouldn't see you again that I gave him your e-mail on impulse. I assumed you two had just clicked, like sometimes happens with a student. That magic, when you find you are speaking the same language, using the same symbols, reaching for the same ideas, sharing the hunger. It was a gut thing," Sheila said, adjusting the rolling chair under her cast.

The secretary, Belinda, called the committee to order. Carol gave the treasurer's report, and Sheila and Joan tried to look like they were listening carefully. When Carol paused to grab a different set of books, Joan leaned in to Sheila.

"He did write."

"Oh? Good!" Sheila whispered back. Carol started presenting again. They were silent for the rest of the agenda. When everyone was packing up, Joan was deeply grateful for Sheila's infirmity and the stainless steel excuse it gave her to cut and run before Carol pulled her aside. She shouldered Sheila's bag, and held her arm out for Sheila to lean on. Carol came over, looking surprised and sad that they were leaving.

"Oh, are you off already? Joan, I was hoping we could talk about the Michigan reunion party. Debbie did it last year, so it is my turn to host. I was thinking maybe we could combine efforts. What with your portion of the exhibit and all, we could work together on contacting the usual suspects and have them bring their Michigan memories video and such to the potluck in July."

Joan froze, trapped like Prometheus between the eagle and the rock. Sheila groaned piteously and doubled over.

Carol started. "My goodness, is she okay?"

Joan bent over to see Sheila grinning behind the curtain of her hair, so Joan shook her head.

"No, she's not. It's a reaction to the pain medication. Makes her very ill."

Sheila groaned explosively, promising colorful expulsion. Carol stepped back.

"We'll talk about this another time, Joan?"

"Another time," Joan agreed, half carrying her friend out the door. When she got Sheila in the passenger seat of her car, she finally laughed.

"You missed your calling. You are wasted on Women's Studies," Joan said. She interpreted Sheila's small wince as one of pain.

"Yeah. So, Billy wrote? He wasn't too much of a pest?"

Joan shook her head. "No, not really. Impish, as you said. But it was fun."

"Fun?"

"We wrote back and forth a bit. He asked me to play video games and drink scotch with him, and I told him only if he answered a question for me. Historical stuff."

"What kind of historical stuff?"

"Hadrian and Antinous."

"Joan."

"Not my fault, on my mother's grave. He started it," Joan started the car. "Isn't that why you gave him my e-mail?"

"I suppose so."

"Well, doesn't matter. He hasn't answered my challenge, and I expect he won't. We have really very little in common. I'm sure I scared him off."

"Cheer up. I might have given Carol your e-mail."

"You're walking home."

It was the blink of an eye until Friday, and Joan was able to suppress any disappointment that her e-mail was empty. Of course it was, as she'd intended it to be. Maybe she missed his sunny tone a little. It was easy to get used to, the romping canine warmth that admitted no impediments or distance. He was a golden retriever of a boy. She, Hadrian, was simply splendid, as was he, Antinous, and why not bask in that? Or so he seemed to say, between each line of the e-mails she reread. Come and play, Caesar. Aversion to boating on the Nile. Joan smiled, again, and wished she hadn't been quite so stern. It was intoxicating talking to someone who could both keep up and challenge her, who came at her with ready camaraderie and no barriers. Familiar in that lost old way, longer ago than the hurt. It became something that argued for itself, that emotion, that thread of familiarity.

She liked the way he made her feel. All this was quite beneath her reason, gathering like guests around a fire at an inn on a wintry night. Waiting to justify itself when the time came.

No e-mails on Friday, and by ten p.m. Joan was able to admit to herself that her house was too quiet, the night hanging too still, and her e-mail was too empty. It is unfair of certain types of people, Joan thought, to go gamboling through life wagging tails and licking faces and charming their way past your defenses. Because they go gamboling right off again. What doesn't stay doesn't matter, she reminded herself from the quarry of her past.

Saturday morning, as she was drinking her expensive organic, shade-grown and ethically-harvested coffee and reading the *ArtVoice*, her laptop, which just happened to be on, dinged at her announcing e-mail, which just happened to be open.

Hadrian,

Very well, I accept your challenge. And to make it look like I'm serious and deep and shit like that I thought about it for a few days first. You ask me, how did Antinous die? We'll do this in your language. To answer that, I have to speak of how Antinous, I, lived, and what effect my passing had on the world. We know that I was Hadrian's favorite and constant companion, from my boyhood until the day of my death, if not the very moment. Everywhere he went, the wandering Emperor, I went with him. We visited every corner of the Empire, we hunted, we feasted, and together we shared initiations into the Mysteries. You, yourself, wrote that the iconography of Antinous left behind, both from before his death and after, argue for a great love co-mingled with a great passion, not just a Greco-styled lust from an avowed Hellenophile susceptible to such loves and understanding of their potential and nobility. From his profound and inconsolable grief after my death, documented worriedly as excessive in his own time, we can say Hadrian loved me. But did I love him? Antinous is recorded in statues so plentiful we know his beautiful, sullen face under the mop of spilling curls, the downcast eyes, hooded and Dionysian, languid athlete's form, a young

Hermes at sport, from early boyhood changing along as he advanced toward nineteen. His representation in marble can be seen as a sign of his great importance to Hadrian, not just at the end of their affair and his death, but from the first. A companion beloved not just for his beauty, which is so overabundant that it cannot be factored out—face it, I was hot—but also for his company. That sullen, fleshy beauty changed over the years, a moving target. What was loved was more than the flesh, though that too was loved. Because this other thing was loved, this intangible, we can say that the love of the flesh was only a part of it, and the rest was friendship. Strong, companionable, intimate, active, vigorous masculine friendship, sometimes teaching, sometimes pleasuring, and coupled with love. How can I assert this? Look what was left behind me. Not just the statues that Hadrian commissioned all over the Empire. The temples. The Emperor had me, his beloved dead Bithynian Greek boy who was drowned in the Nile, created as a god. I was worshipped, taking on aspects of Osiris, of Dionysos, of Hermes. Hadrian couldn't face eternity without seeing me again. Longing like that speaks of love given and love returned. There were other pretty boys, it wasn't just flesh. Hadrian, you, couldn't go on without the perfect friend, the divine companion. So, it doesn't matter how I died. What matters is a love existed between the Emperor and the favorite, the lover and the beloved, the eagle and Ganymede, a love great enough that it pushed back the borders of mortality and is remembered today when the Empire that birthed it has passed away.

This is why you'll be over at my place at six tomorrow. We will drink scotch and play video games and swear blood brotherhood. Booyah!

Antinous

Clever little punk used her own work against her. How could she argue with his reasoning when it was based on hers? Joan had to give him that. It looked like she was busy tomorrow.

Sheila had hinted around regarding brunch, but as Joan had been noncommittal, there were no plans. Therefore, there was no reason to explain what she was up to that evening to Sheila, or even face her, when she would easily get the truth from Joan. Let this be something she didn't think about too much in advance, for once. The timing was good, giving her little time to over-think it. She'd replied with Laconian grace, simply accepting the invitation and his address.

There was plenty of time to regret it on the way there and Joan did. She'd dressed, without thinking about it, in her uniform, black and white like a priest or referee or waiter. This was ridiculous.

But the light shown amber in the front windows of the address she'd been given, the porch steps were shallow and easy to climb, the door swung inward smoothly, and then the boy was there, no baseball cap this time, the blond hair sticking up in all directions with a carelessness that might just be carelessness, not art, wide eyes and wide grin and wide welcome, his hand out, clasping hers.

His arm landed around her shoulders, briefly, guiding her into the living room. Joan had feared frat house, at the worst. This was simple, but clean and orderly. The couch might be generations old, but it was sturdily built and held up stubbornly against time. The coffee table was wood and glass, low and rectangular, holding the gaming system and the controllers. Alien looking things, swollen, like butterflies on steroids. Beside the controllers was a bottle of twelve-year-old single malt and two heavy-cut glass tumblers.

"So you made it, Hadrian. Sit down. Let me pour for you, we'll go old school."

Joan accepted the tumbler. "I'm curious, why scotch and video games? Seems incongruous. Beer and video games makes more sense."

"Ah, but you don't drink beer."

"How did you know that?"

"Asked Sheila. Besides, I thought that scotch would evoke the right emotion."

"For what?"

"For ruthlessly slaying zombies." Billy tilted his glass toward Joan's and they clinked the rims.

Joan took a sip. The scotch was slow on the heat, but lasting. It reminded Joan of her father, the sense memory coming on without warning and she was ten again, watching her father in the evening having his glass of scotch in his recliner, facing both the television set and the open front door, looking out on the porch and the street. He looked out the door, and beyond, ignoring the entertainment, though the fiction was dad wasn't to be disturbed during his unwinding time after work while he watched the news. Joan knew he didn't watch the news. He looked away into nothing, compressed down into a silence that took him hours to thaw, until he could put them to bed, her and her brother. Joan felt the helplessness again, unable to understand her father's silence, or his need, but yearning to do so, to bridge the gap between them. Even at ten, she'd known that wasn't possible. In watching her father she'd absorbed his practice of long silence and burying pain. The scotch came flavored with memory.

Billy handed her one of the swollen butterflies, and Joan had to put the glass down and hold it clumsily. There were buttons, knobs, commands, involvement. Complexity.

"I've never been much of a game player," Joan said, turning the controller over in her hand.

"Gamer. And that was obvious. This is why we are starting you out on the most basic and satisfying of all video game genres, zombie destruction." Billy flopped down next to her on the couch, parallel, thigh touching hers, and took up his own controller.

"I'm not sure I have much of a taste for killing."

Billy grinned sideways at her. "Come on."

"Well, how could I know if I haven't done it?"

"You won't be able to stop once you try. It is addictive on the most primal, bloody, cathartic level. All lizard brain, no thought. It's like meditation, but with payout."

He ran through a quick and dirty series of commands that would allow her to shoot, hit and run. That, he asserted, was all you needed. The rest was flourish.

The second round of scotch was poured as Billy fired up the system. Joan felt her nervous system arrested mid-firing, felt her adrenaline response kidnapped and turbocharged. It was glorious. Time went away. There was only stimulus, response, heightened sensitivity to noise, color, and motion, action and reaction. Billy and she, both represented by pixilated men in dark suits wearing sunglasses indoors to express their cool, fired guns that rarely needed ammunition. He knew the game like the back of his hand, the ruined house, the complex beneath filled with science experiments done by evil corporations, or the military, or the government, or all of them. At first she followed his lead, charging through debris-filled corridors, blasting away at dark shapes as they sprang out from everywhere. Zombies, when blasted, exploded with such satisfying completeness, such an addictive noise.

By the third round she was leading the way, teaching Billy new angles of fire, the value of generalship, strategically initiating attacks, fighting back to back with him, guns blazing away, heart light, laughing at death. It was glorious in a way she hadn't felt since, well, long ago. Joan felt lifted out of herself, free, pure and happy. Pouring the scotch, he'd been true to the Ganymede role all night. This was four? The game was on pause; Joan leaned back and was suddenly aware of how stiff she was, how long she'd been in the same position. Time came back. They'd been slaying zombies for hours, and she'd had no idea. She took her glass and walked out on the porch. He followed. The sun was gone; the streetlights were on. The time, in the summer, when her mother would insist she run home. Be home by the time the streetlights come on. Here it was, past that border, into the wilderness.

He sat on the rail, back against the corner pillar. She leaned on the rail, hands spread. She was afraid briefly that he would ruin that fragile peaceful moment, puncture it with a word. Like the end of a movie, when you are still in that world and don't want to come back down just yet. Billy sipped at his scotch and looked out in silence. She'd had too much scotch to drive home. No great matter, she could walk; it was a clear night and it wasn't that far. Just down Elmwood. She drained the tumbler, and set it decisively on the rail. She stood up, posture returning after hours of being someone else. Billy caught her eye. Not yet. Joan nodded to him, briefly, sketching thanks. He inclined his head, briefer still, and she walked away, down the porch steps and into the warm night.

The e-mail came two respectable days later, so Joan would admit if pressed to it, though she spent most of the preceding days pacing. She was a dyke, a butch dyke. The last person anyone would suspect of dating a boy. Transmen, Joan thought, could date other transmen, gay men, straight girls, femme lesbians, bisexual women, but not butch lesbians. That was just too odd, strange, askance, oblique, queer, weird in the old strange magic way.

Joan tried looking at it not as a fixed form, but liquid within a fixed form. Billy was a boy. That she had no trouble acknowledging; she'd been in the community long enough to have some exposure to trans issues, and tried to be open-minded. She just didn't have any trans friends before. It wasn't her issue, so she paid it respect out of solidarity of sexual minorities, but didn't cast much thought to it otherwise.

It helped that Billy was pretty; Joan could admit that. You could look at him and still read him as a particularly andro dyke, or a fey boy, the outside, but his presence read male to her. Sheila had said that he ID'd as queer. What in the world did that mean? He was clearly on testosterone; he had that voice.

His beard was coming in like a blond fifteen-year-old boy's, but still coming in. His body had changed, muscle rose and swelled, fat distribution changed, his hips were unshielded, naked, allowing his jeans to sag where a girl's might cling to her curves. Yet he knew dyke courtship. He'd lingered in the community; he must have female socialization. So then, was this just romancing a pretty dyke boi? No stranger than butch on butch, or butch on boi, no stranger than that great strangeness, female masculinity attracted to itself, or its kin, or brother, or reflection.

But Billy's masculinity, while languid and playful, while sunny and boyish, wasn't female. Her masculinity was far grimmer, somber, experienced, filled with sad knowledge of the world. It was a masculinity of control and discipline, not free and unaggressive and unconcerned with status as his. What was it that separated them—personality, experience, self perception? Surely he'd been butch when he was a girl, Joan thought. No, seen as butch. Billy hadn't been a girl. She had. How could she separate his individual case from the gender? What was Billy and what was boy, and why not boi? If he'd been a girl, even with their age difference, Joan had no doubt that they'd be lovers. No question. So what was the hesitation now? His companionship was unprecedented. She felt more herself with him. He was young, and that was a concern. How serious could he be? Any age difference in a relationship was a potential conflict. So great an age difference made them strangers to one another's world. Queer? Hadn't that gone out in the nineties? What did he mean by it? Not male, not female? Still lesbian identified? Boydyke? Trannyfag? He desired her; she could feel it. He desired her masculinity. Did that make him gay? Make them gay men? Of what century or epoch?

Joan had to decide whether she was going to contact Billy... or not. If not, was she waiting for him to contact her? Or another option entirely involving renunciation? If not, what tone to take? The e-mail, blissfully, set the tone at neutral and established the names, who they were, in standing to one another.

Hadrian,

There's nothing quite like the lingering satisfaction of mass slaughter of zombies. We couldn't have felt more full of life after hunting lions in Egypt. "Barbarian Legion" is showing on the Antique Stuff channel on Thursday, and you're not yet cool enough to have seen it, yet it will stir your martial heart. You were a fine soldier, Hadrian, a fine commander of the legions. Come see what happened to your army in the fourth century.

Aim high and squeeze gently,

Antinous

No sooner had she read it, than the phone rang. Joan started rather sideways as a rabbit might jump from a fox or a wolf.

"Hello?"

"Joan!" It was Carol's voice, no mistaking the particular enthusiasm and energy.

"Carol."

"Am I catching you at a bad time?"

"I honestly have no idea," Joan said before quite thinking about it.

"Is it one of your research fugues?"

"I'm sorry, my what?" Joan asked, shocked into the conversation at last.

"Sheila confided in me about them. Well, I worry when you don't come to the planning meetings, so I guess I was talking about it one night and Sheila took me aside and told me. About how you get so caught up in your work, you forget the outside world for days at a time. I would hate to interrupt anything important like that. You get so passionate about your work."

"Do I? No, no, I wasn't working, just reading e-mail."

"Oh, is there anything good?"

"Hard to say yet."

"Well, one woman's spam is another woman's treasure."

"What can I do for you, Carol?" Joan asked, trying now to sound polite and focused.

"We said at the meeting we'd talk another time about my idea."

"Oh, well, now?" Joan asked, wondering if there was a way she could dodge this. Her mind wasn't in Michigan right now, or at a potluck.

"No, silly! I wouldn't ambush you. Thursday night."

"Thursday, oh, well, sorry, Thursday isn't good for me."

"But I checked with Sheila, just to see if it would conflict for you. I hate to waste your time if I can know ahead of time, and Sheila said you were free as far as she knew, and who would know if Sheila wouldn't, right?"

"I haven't told Sheila about this. It's a meeting I just set up."

"What sort of meeting? I thought your classes were done for the summer. Sheila mentioned how much you were looking forward to being free. No students to supervise, no classes, nothing."

"A private meeting."

"Private, oh, a date! I'm sorry, Joan; I didn't mean to press you on it. You can be so noble about things, play them so close to the vest. I won't say another word about it."

Until she got off the phone and dialed again, Joan thought. She'd just intimated to the entire Feminist Film Festival phone tree that she was dating. Now everyone would pop blood vessels to find out whom. It was the beauty of the community. Nothing remained unknown for long. Denial would be taken as confirmation, as would no comment and direct confirmation. The key was to maintain a dignified silence and plausible deniability.

Remarkably, it took Sheila fifteen minutes after she and Carol had hung up to call Joan in a frenzy.

"Tell me you are lying. Lying like a dog to get out of a pseudodate with Carol. There is no other explanation for her knowing something that I don't, not something crucial, like you dating again. Hello, entire best friend vetting rights abrogated here!"

"I wasn't lying, but Carol took it a particular way I hadn't meant."

"That's a load of hedging. She grilled the hell out of me about your schedule, so I have it very clearly in mind. You are free on Thursday."

"No, I'm not."

"Are you going to make me ask?"

"I'm watching a documentary with a friend."

"Who? And what?"

"It's about the use of barbarians in the army of the late Roman Empire. Who would be Billy."

Sheila sounded disappointed. "Oh. A documentary with Billy doesn't equal a date. Carol made that part up. Wait, I thought it was scotch and video games."

"That was Sunday."

"So you are hitting it off."

"You could say." Joan felt her throat thicken. She didn't want to talk about Billy just yet, no matter Sheila's best-friend rights. But she would if she were asked.

"You've needed some male bonding. Particularly with someone who gets you. Roman army documentary indeed."

She'd already told the rest of the city, so Joan e-mailed Billy back.

Antinous,

The fighting has stirred my martial blood. We must go to war again, back to back, soon. I ask myself, are the undead my enemies? Then I think, anything trying to eat my brains is my enemy and worthy of destruction. Thursday it is.

Hadrian

"Why is it always the way, the bogeymen of our grandfather's day are the neighbors of ours?" Joan asked.

"You mean the Germans?" Billy asked, watching the screen.

"Not just them. The very barbarians the legions had fought against in the early Empire formed the core of her legions in the twilight."

Billy glanced at her. "The lesson we keep missing seems clear enough. When the barbarians come to the gate, let them in and make them welcome."

"Easy enough for you to say, you are a barbarian."

"I am not!"

"With that corn-silk mop? Celtic. Gaulish at best, half barbarian."

"Yeah, well, I'm not a Viking or anything."

"Shame. Least the Vikings were great warriors."

"What are you implying about my ancestors?"

"Gauls."

"You're calling me French! Take that back."

"I cannot be made to retreat from the truth."

"Fine, we'll duel about it later." Billy handed her a glass— wine this time, red, fitting for the theme of the night. He was still in his role as Ganymede, as Antinous to her Hadrian. After the documentary, they diagrammed and refought the battle of Alesia, with the Gauls coming out no better. That, Joan maintained, proved her point about Billy's heritage.

"I object. I was born in Bithynia, and my ancestors are all Greeks."

"Fine, you're my Antinous? Pour me more wine."

"I live to serve you, Hadrian."

"Shall we duel?"

"The zombies await."

It became a highlight to get an e-mail from Billy, something that brought her a lift. Nothing heavy, no approaching of the border they had almost crossed that first night on the porch. It seemed easy, and fast, and affectionate. Billy never approached her without Joan's feeling better in some fashion—wiser, smarter, kinder, and braver, than she had before. She couldn't say why exactly, but it was his gift. They became friends. It happened rather formally, as the best friendships often do, with cognizance of the potential importance, nobility and sacrifice that might be called upon.

They were watching *Captain Swashbuckler*, Billy's concession to Joan's movie choice, after a series of gladiator films he'd picked. In the beginning, he scoffed at it—the old fashioned special effects, the bombastic dialogue—but somewhere around the great sea battle, he started to watch in rapt silence. There was one particular scene that was burned into Joan's memory from first seeing the movie at twelve with her male friends, acid etched there by the first explosion of young romantic bonding ardor. The freebooter's ship the *Golden Fox* was sinking, her decks awash with blood. Captain Swashbuckler stood, cutlass in one hand, pistol in the other, holding the deck against the Queen's soldiers so his men might retreat. The First Mate protested, but Captain Swashbuckler pushed him into the lifeboat, calling out, "Let my death have meaning! My friend, let me die for you!"

Billy, in profile, said "I'd do that for you."

Joan swallowed, hard. "Me too."

They clinked their wine glasses together. After the first night they hung out, there had been no more scotch. The fire was a little too deep for the summer nights just yet. The friendship was formally recognized.

It was shortly after this they started talking to one another. The formal level of intimacy had been acknowledged—the potential, the desire for intimacy, if you will. Nothing heavy to start with, and usually while absorbed in other activities, they started to talk. Joan began it, talking, while blasting the head of a zombie boss into green goo.

"Scotch reminds me of my father."

Billy dove to the right, taking out a pair of lurking undead behind the crates. He rolled, came up spitting fire, and took off running back to her side. "That good or bad?"

"Both, I guess." They paused in a way station to get their body armor repaired and their guns reloaded. Joan told the story of her father sitting in the evenings, watching out the door.

"What does it taste like?" Billy asked, chambering his shotgun.

"Sadness or regret," Joan said and shrugged.

"We'll make a new memory for it."

"When?"

"When the time is right."

Billy, equally casually, started talking about his father, a man gone from his immediate life since grade school. His parents divorced, his father remarried, Billy grew up with his mom.

"Dad's all right, just like millions of other divorced and remarried dads…distant."

"How is he with you?"

"He's come around. Mom's totally cool."

And just like that, the door was opened to a new topic, one that led to many others; levels added to their intimacy. When Wednesday night came, they'd been hanging out all day, nothing special, when a real conversation sprang up. They often did, sparking naturally, then lightly and fearfully tended by both participants, hesitating to put any great weight on words just yet. Billy started talking, and Joan was afraid to rupture that intimacy. The conversation lasted hours, and only later did they realize that Billy had missed Sheila's seminar.

Joan got a call about it while she was walking in the door. She snapped her cell open and tried not to sound like she was just coming in.

"Hello?"

"You're hanging up your coat, I can hear it. So he was with you!"

"I have no idea what you are talking about."

"Billy missed class tonight."

"Oh, shit. Sorry, that was my fault. I got him to talking, and we lost track of time."

"This is my own fault, I know, in a twisted way. I knew you guys would hit it off. Now I find myself missing you because you have a new friend to play with. I'm a horrible human being."

"You are the most wonderful woman who ever lived."

"You're effusive. I have no idea what that means. You've never been effusive before."

"I'm just happy."

"Damn. Can it be that simple?"

"Only if you work real hard to let it be."

Her answer was off the cuff, but got Joan to wondering. Could it be that simple? Could, at forty-two, she simply meet and simply like, with the lighting blink of affection confirmation, a twenty-four year old boy? A queer boy, a transboy. That boy. Billy. Could she let herself feel with such ease and directness? Heedlessly.

Time meant less these days. It was summer magic again, the endlessness of pleasure. That was part of it—the boundaryless nature of their affection, their bond. It existed and had been acknowledged; now there was only action in the sharing of it. Happy, simple, and animal. Boyish. Billy called her up and said they should go for a bike ride, so Joan bought a bike and they did. All over the city, lingering by the water, by the lake, along the banks of the river, where they threw stones and broke glass bottles in a branch of a ruined mill. Billy threw hard at the last bottle and missed spectacularly, ricocheting it back towards his head. He had to duck, flinging up his arms, from his own missile. Joan stepped up and neatly sidearm shattered the bottle at the neck.

"Nice. You free tonight? There's a free concert on the steps of the art gallery."

"Can't. I have to meet with Carol the treasurer, whom I've been putting off to play with you."

"This is the first time you've said no to me."

"What, now you're going to pout?"

"Worse. Whine. Like an abandoned puppy beneath your window, with heartrending howls I will disrupt your meeting with Carol the treasurer."

"We'll be meeting at her place."

"Oh." Billy tossed away his last stone. "Guess I can't disrupt that. Have fun."

They'd biked back into the city in silence. Billy waved and rode off without a word. It shouldn't have mattered to Joan the way that it did.

Carol lived out in the suburbs, with a large fenced lot that included a swimming pool and a generous lawn. It made sense to have a large gathering there. Carol argued against it from the moment Joan showed up.

"Oh, no, I can't have the Michigan Memories potluck here."

"Why not? The space seems perfect." Joan looked at the emerald expanse ringed with chain link fence and free of flowers. A well-controlled green space. They were in Carol's kitchen while Carol boiled water for tea.

"I'll be having the sprinkler system pulled out and rerouted. The entire lawn will be trenches and pipes. Can't have anyone here," Carol said, closing the blinds.

"That's too bad. What about Barb?"

"She's going to be out of town."

"Marta?"

"Having in-laws stay."

"Oh. Where does that leave?" Joan asked foolishly.

"We could do it at your place, in the city."

"Whoa, I'm not sure I have enough room."

"Sheila said it would be perfect."

That stopped Joan in her tracks. Sheila had said her house was perfect? Suggesting it? Why in the world had her friend sold her out?

"I suppose, if Sheila said it."

Carol's ill-concealed smile of triumph told Joan that she'd given away too much. The potluck was now at her house. They hashed out some of the details, but Joan had already given ground, and wasn't listening much. Billy had ridden off without a word. That wasn't entirely unusual, but they'd only known one another for a short time, so getting to know what was usual and what wasn't for him was still in progress. Joan's upbringing and experience made her shy of conflict, and she sought to avoid it at almost all costs. Great energy was spent in handling conflicts before they came up, with maintaining a frozen dignity that kept many lesser problems at bay. Trouble was, problems were a side effect of dealing with people. Chaos and uncertainty came hard on the heels of opening up. Heels. We're back to Achilles, Joan thought.

Joan recalled how terrified she'd been when she and Sheila had disagreed for the first time. It was over something stupid, the placement of a standing lamp in their dorm room. Joan read herself to sleep every night, and used a short bedside lamp for ease. Sheila, trying to provide a better environment for both, ended up making Joan retreat into a furious silence, feeling like her habits were being questioned and set up for adjustment without her approval. Getting used to living with someone else was jarring, even combative, for the space-conscious loner. Sheila, raised in a much larger and closer family, found Joan's retreat incomprehensible, and went ahead and set up the lamp. When they finally fought about it, when Joan finally exploded and spoke her mind, she started shaking like a runner after a marathon. Adrenaline coursed through her, made her angry and large and swift, ready to punch and destroy. Her relationship with Sheila was done, damaged forever now that they'd fought, so Joan started packing right in front of an incredulous Sheila. It took some time for Sheila to convince Joan that their relationship wasn't irreparably ruptured, it was a minor disagreement. Joan had to learn to fight, and more difficult still, to get over it, to learn anger and put it in her toolbox of emotions. Sheila was fluent in it, and never cruel. She led Joan along slowly.

Joan and Billy hadn't disagreed on anything. When they fought, it was about things— events, historical figures, and proper execution of a double automatic flying shot or a testudo formation—not about emotions. Fighting was then sparring, playful, enjoyable. Dominance was demonstrated, awesomeness acknowledged, and the matter at hand gotten back to, whether zombies or Romans. There had been none of that. He asked her to hang out that evening; she'd said she was busy, simple exchange between friends. He'd ridden off. No drama, no scene, just simple and done.

That was part of the relief of hanging with Billy, the simplicity of it. Ask, answer, and move on. No drama. His sunny nature never seemed to falter. At first, Joan had been waiting for the conversation, the big talk about their first night spent together, the scotch and video games. The analysis, the questioning: who are we and what are we doing? She didn't want that. When Billy didn't broach the subject, she felt herself relax in stages, until she took what he offered with both hands. There was simple acceptance and action, without having to explain herself. Since meeting Sheila, Joan hadn't felt so purely liked as a person without having to be anyone else. She could, for the first time in decades, come at friendship with her own nature.

We think we've achieved standing, that age and experience give us perspective, distance, even wisdom. Sometimes. What Joan hadn't factored in was the emotion of it. You can be the best educated person in the world, have the finest incisive mind, a preternatural facility for organizing and shifting information, making new connections, analyzing facts, and still be dumber than a box of hammers about emotion. No matter how well we know, we still have to feel. The homo sapiens paradox, apes with yearning toward Heaven.

Joan surfaced from this reverie to find Carol still talking.

"So we'll have the planning meeting on Thursday and get the phone tree working. That gives a few weeks until the event, but we can pull it off."

"Right," Joan said, nodding at whatever Carol had said, hoping she hadn't just signed away her immortal soul.

"I can get the tables and chairs ordered, but I'll have to look at the space. Is tomorrow afternoon all right with you?"

Carol was looking at her intently, expectantly.

"Sure." It was after Joan had agreed, only when she saw the look of surprise and pleasure on Carol's face, that she realized what had happened. Carol hadn't been expecting it to work. She'd just invited herself over to Joan's house tomorrow. Oh, piss. This was what came of not focusing, not keeping her guard up.

"How was your date?" Carol asked, looking down at her agenda.

"Everything I hoped it would be."

Joan got home at nine, not late, but the sun was inching away over the backyard fence. Most of the time, Joan adored the view from the second floor of her sprawling Victorian. Joan loved the long narrow yard facing west, a sunset court, meant for sitting in the unruly garden in the dusk hours as the sunlight bled off, lighting candles and talking while the wine poured. Pity she'd never done that here. Oh, Cody and she had had a few dinner parties, but Joan was remanded to the kitchen for most of those. She hadn't entertained here on her own, though she'd owned the house before Cody came along, and after she left. She'd need to be more of an extrovert to host.

Now Billy would throw a great party, Joan thought. It would be pleasant, even fun, to be working the kitchen if she knew he was greeting the guests, making the best use of his golden retriever personality to make everyone feel at home. They would balance one another. Joan liked that he was so unlike her in personality, that he kept his pain hidden under both artful and natural optimism. She'd watched him, questioning the ability of any person to be so happy, but he never cracked, never offered her bitterness or regret. He kept his comments on other people to the positive or neutral, a sign of character not learned but inborn. Naturally, this made Joan fascinated with the edges of his cheerfulness, where it might start to fray, where she'd be able to glimpse the other emotions well concealed around this one.

Joan wandered out into the backyard with her laptop. She opened it, idly, while trying to picture fifty people in her backyard. Would the tables even work? Maybe round tables, not the long rectangular ones. They could get five of them in here; as long as they stayed out of the garden it would be doable. Not a lot of space, but perhaps. Joan wasn't expecting an e-mail, but was hoping for one. Electricity ran through her hands, up her arms. He had written.

Hadrian,

We need a brooding urban vigilante night. Midnight Avenger in 3-D. You have to see the fight scenes in 3-D or it isn't Midnight Avenger. As you turned down my last request, this isn't a request. Midnight Avenger shows at, what else, midnight at the Regal. I'll see you there.

Antinous

Nothing about this afternoon other than the confidence he'd see her later. Joan knew she'd go as soon as she read the e-mail. A midnight superhero movie? Who else would she do this with? Who else would know enough to ask her to go?

She drove up from the back parking lot, partly from habit, partly to see if he were waiting outside the theater. He wasn't. It was ten minutes to midnight, and the front of the theater was crawling with people Billy's age, eighty to ninety percent male, the film's target audience. She would have to wade through them to see if he were in the lobby. If on her own, she'd turn the car around right now.

Joan strode determinedly through the crowd, refusing to be intimidated away from the film, even though every male eye that bothered to follow her did so with a faint puzzlement as if she was entirely out of her environment. This was their realm, their hour, their subject, their entertainment. What was a middle-aged woman doing here? For that is what she was.

He was in the lobby, standing under the *Midnight Avengers'* six-foot-high scowl in a banner ad. Joan hadn't paid any attention to his height before. He was one of those people always slouching, leaning, perching, draping, and never standing up straight. She was five eight; he was maybe five foot five. Yet, he was one of those people remembered as taller. Looking at him now, leaning casually, not scanning the crowd with anxiety but looking around, meeting eyes when they cast his way; he looked fearless. He turned and smiled right at her.

"Here's your stub and your 3-D glasses. Popcorn?"

"No, thanks. You were pretty sure I'd show, buying me a ticket?"

"I'm pretty sure in general."

They took seats in the back, slouching in the chairs. Billy had his canvas sneakers on again, and they were unlaced. It bothered Joan less now. She put her 3-D glasses on.

"How was the meeting with Carol the treasurer?" Billy asked, scooping a handful of popcorn from the tub.

"Disaster. I was suckered into having the Michigan Memories event at my place."

"Michigan," Billy said evenly, looking at the screen.

"Sheila and I go every year, so I got handed the curator duties on the local section of the Film Festival installation. The theme is Michigan Memories. I'm supposed to gather video and photos. We'll talk about it later, the movie's starting."

There were heroism, and darkness, monstrous villains to be defeated only by a lone vigilante with courage, will, and blind determination in the force of justice. Thrilled, Joan let it wash over her. The fighting was epic, crashing into their personal space, debris shattered in explosive showers, car chases that ended in rolling, blazing glory. After, they sat and let the crowd push its way out of the theater, then they walked slowly toward Joan's car. Billy kept his 3-D glasses on.

"Do you need a ride?" Joan asked, realizing that Billy didn't have a car.

He opened the door and sat down, glasses red and blue like insect's eyes slipping down around his neck. "You're not tired."

"It's two o'clock in the morning, Billy."

There was amusement in his grin. "Tell me you can come down after that. It'll take me hours. What do you have planned for tomorrow?"

"Carol the treasurer is coming over in the afternoon to measure my backyard, or something like that."

He nodded, pleased. "Then we have plenty of time. Stop at my place, I'll grab what we need. We're going to your place."

This surprised Joan, as they never had spent any time at her house. "Why?"

"My roommate has finally come back from her road trip, and I suspect you'd rather hang out without more company."

"I didn't know you had a roommate."

"Isn't it fun to find out new things?"

At his house, he sprinted up the shallow steps. He was gone for five minutes to gather supplies and, presumably, converse with his roommate. Billy came back with a worn Army satchel well stuffed from the weight hanging on the strap.

"Okay, we're good."

They hadn't spent time at her house, but Billy romped into the living room by instinct, turned on a few lamps but ignored the overhead light. He sat down on the floor in front of the fireplace, cross-legged, and upended the satchel. Comic books spilled out en masse.

"Would you like something to drink?" Joan asked, more aware of who she was supposed to be in her own space. Billy, not looking up from his pile of comic books, seized her hand.

"Sit down. Relax. This is me."

"I'm well aware of that," Joan said tartly, but sat down on the upholstered footstool. Billy let her hand go. He held up a comic book with a lurid cover: a woman in a chain mail halter and thong stood poised atop a heap of enemy dead, braced on a massive two handed sword, a look of wildness in her flashing eyes and floating hair. "Sword Queen."

"Oh, we're on to the ogling girls stage of bonding?"

"Did we ever leave? You don't know Sword Queen? This is good shit. Female protagonist, good stories, brilliant warrior queen of her barbarian people, trying to resist the might of Rome and defend her homeland and her people's way of life against the invaders."

"Historical mishegoss."

"But fun! How do you expect people to love history if they don't get to hear the stories? Sword Queen and her loyal companion Carthax, fighting back to back, making their last stand against the fading light of the Empire."

"I'm not a comic-book reader."

"Yet. You're a snob. That's fixable. Hadrian didn't disdain any field of knowledge. One issue. If you don't like it, after that, I'll relent," Billy said.

Joan took it, reluctantly. Billy fished in the satchel again. "And, the second ingredient in coming down." He held up a joint. "Smoke?"

Joan took it without comment and lit it up, pulled deeply, then handed it to the boy.

"I see you are familiar with the ritual." Billy took a drag, then held his hand out to her.

Joan took the joint back and inhaled with enviable lung power. "You don't have to introduce me to everything, Billy. I've been here longer than you have."

"I'm well aware of it, Hadrian, why do you think I sought you out?"

"Antinous caught the Emperor's eye, not the other way around."

"Modern life is complicated."

Joan stood up and left the living room. She came back with a cigar box and a great scientific mass of glass, and set it down on the floor in front of her, sitting cross-legged opposite Billy. "You smoke shake. I have something more selective." She took out a film canister, a seven layer metal grinder, and a tiny Chinese ceramic cup, blue and white. After grinding and sifting, she poured the leaf into the cup and held it out to Billy. He inhaled deeply, closing his eyes. The bong was glass, multi-chambered, German, practically a work of art. Joan dropped an ice cube down the neck, to the pinches, loaded the bowl and handed it to Billy. She picked up the remote to the CD player and turned it on. Dusty in Memphis.

"Modern life has its pleasure."

Sometime later, Joan tossed aside a Sword Queen comic and reached for the next issue. Billy, lying on the couch with his feet up, was reading the next issue. Incense sticks glowed cherry and candles, melted into protean state, licked up the last tongue of flame, adding to the haze. Joan commanded the other end of the couch, her back against the arm, so their legs fell parallel in the middle.

"Hurry up. I want to see what she's going to do now that her army has mutinied, the Gauls are surrounding the camp, and her lover has betrayed her."

Billy closed the comic halfway, keeping his place with his left hand. "Knew I'd get you hooked."

"Yeah, well. So I'm human."

"You've never admitted that before, we are making progress. You deserve a reward." Billy handed her the Sword Queen issue, leaning forward. Joan heard a strange noise and looked up, unable to place it, until she saw the quality of light in the sky. It was birds, chirping at the coming sunrise. She leaned back against the arm of the couch.

"Why do I feel so at ease with you?" Joan asked aloud at the same moment she thought it. Smoking took away her inner filter. She felt the pulse kick up in her throat, a fear reaction, until he looked at her solemnly, unusual for him. The novelty of it arrested Joan. His face was designed, she thought, for smiling, for laughing, for warmth. He would have wrinkles around his eyes, his mouth—all well earned and honored in the pursuit of friendliness—to mark every smile he'd ever shared. One day, when his face was more lived in, his character would be more evident. For now, his beauty did get in the way. Skin like a snow peach, absurdly pink and white and prone to redness in the sun to match red lips, bludgeoningly blue eyes, an excess of color and size that belonged in one of his comic books. Hair pale to colorless, chilled blond, brows all but invisible, and rough tender growth of change on his cheek. No baseball cap tonight. He looked at her, and his mouth was solemn, his brows down.

"Because you are Hadrian and I am Antinous. The Emperor and the favorite."

Joan smiled slowly in answer, enjoying it more than needing to correct it.

"See, I would never tell you that you should smile more, because you should do whatever you are feeling. But I will say I have never seen anything quite as beautiful as you when you smile for real."

There was the border; they were back on the porch on the first night, and this time he'd walked right up to it. Then he pushed the border back, by crawling up to her side of the couch and settling himself in next to her. Joan held very still.

"Billy, you're going to get me singing some Dusty Springfield here in a minute if you don't move away."

"By the time you get past my name you'll be kissing me."

Joan took the dare and tried it, but Billy was right. By the time she got to his name she was kissing him, really kissing him. Then Joan pulled back.

"Billy."

"Antinous."

"Antinous," she granted him, for he was. In the first shreds of dawn light, he was golden, languid, and as full of mystery as Hadrian's beloved.

"You're not going to make a speech, are you?"

"Probably."

"Let me. I'll respect your cock, and expect you'll respect mine. Enough speech." Billy went back to kissing her. Joan slid her arms around him on the couch, pulling him in. His arms were rounded with muscle, new muscle, but there was still a softness of youth to him. There was also impatience, when he finally betrayed his nervousness in the way he kissed her, a little too hungry, as if he couldn't believe it were happening. That, too, spoke of youth. Joan felt both lust and tenderness, sifted together so finely they were indistinguishable. She pulled back from him in smaller kisses, until she closed his lips and was apart from him. The scruff on his upper lip was still soft, but coming in more coarse.

"What?" he asked, his lips moving back toward hers.

"Not just yet."

"Never?"

"Not never, but not just yet. Lie with me for a while."

They lay facing one another, thigh to thigh, bodies meeting, arms around waists, heads close. The difference between talking and kissing was slight.

"You've got some shoulders there."

"Made them myself."

"Nice."

"If you like those, you should feel this." Billy took her hand and put it on his flank.

"You have been working out."

"And this. Squeeze. Pure muscle." He guided her hand around the bend.

"You should be very proud."

"If you are pleased, my lord, I am happy."

"How could I be anything else, Antinous? The most beautiful boy in the world, my favorite, shares my couch with me." Joan stroked his side, from shoulder to hip, in a long, circular caress. Certain areas of his body she could touch, those areas he'd led her to. The rest was conflicted territory.

"Then why do you look haunted again?"

"Not haunted, honey. Thinking."

Joan felt Billy's hand rest against the side of her face. "Can I make you stop?"

"Yes, I'm afraid you could." Joan shifted her gaze, and hooked a finger in his collar. "Why two t-shirts?"

"Protective covering. Haven't had top surgery yet."

Joan nodded, her hand resting along his collarbone. "Do you have it planned?"

Billy's smile was blinding. "August."

"You sound happy."

"I am."

"Is it okay if I touch your chest? I mean, I'm not sure how you feel about—"

"How do you see me?"

"Pardon?"

"Am I your boy?"

"Yes."

"Then go ahead."

Joan did. Billy's lips moved close to her ear. "Share with me many kisses, upon your couch, as we meet with the holy union of our thighs."

"You paraphrase lost Aeschylus beautifully."

"I bet you say that to all the boys."

There was exploration and retreat, regrouping and sallying forth again, Joan hesitating and Billy pulling her onwards. There was a tangle of limbs, still clothed but well entwined. The light went from dawn to day, exhaustion coupled with momentary peace, caresses slowing to soothing, to stillness. They fell asleep, her arm around him.

This is how Sheila found them four hours later, when her crutch knocked over the fancy German art glass bong. Sheila hopped back on her good leg, let the door bang closed, and then looked at the couch, where her oldest friend's dark eyes were looking at her, startled, over the very comfortable-looking, passed-out Billy boy.

"Oh, for the love of fuck," was all Sheila could manage before she crashed down in the recliner.

"Shh," Joan said.

Billy stirred, smiled, and opened his eyes. "Hey. Sheila?"

"Dr. Cross," Joan corrected, feeling very foolish.

"I think the boy can call me Sheila now, Joan."

"What's going on? What time is it?" Billy asked, sitting up. He looked like he didn't let go of sleep easily.

"Billy, would you mind going in the kitchen for a bit? Joan and I need to talk."

Billy looked to Joan first, who nodded. He raised his eyebrows; she pointed down the hall.

"Kitchen. Coffee top shelf, cabinet left of the fridge. French press, kettle on the stove. Cups in the side cabinet. Would you?"

"It's my calling." He wandered away down the hall, loose limbed, scruffy, unfazed by the night.

Sheila watched Joan watch Billy walk away. When Joan looked back at her, Sheila dramatically swept the room with her eyes, from the knocked over German bong, to the puddled candles, spider's leg remnants of incense sticks, the guilty cigar box, to the sea of comic books, tossed around the room. She then looked at Joan, sitting up now, staring back at her with sleep-deprived eyes like a disturbed owl.

"Good morning. Evidently we haven't met. I'm Sheila. What's your excuse?"

Joan ran a hand through her hair. "I don't know that I have one."

"Dogs and cats living together, I tell you. When I said you'd hit it off, I wasn't thinking of that kind of hit it off. What are you up to?"

"I'm not sure."

"You could have told me," Sheila said more pointedly.

"I don't know what I'd tell you."

"That you are knocking boots with Billy boy?"

"That's not what this is."

"I'm glad I got here before Carol did."

"What?" Joan looked at her blankly.

"She called me, something about coming over to see the backyard for the party. I said I'd drop by...to keep you from being alone with her. Now that I'm here, I don't think that was a problem."

There was a waiting stillness, an indrawing of breath. Joan got up, and started cleaning up the room, whisking the German glass and cigar box away, piling the comic books back into the satchel. Sheila, hopping, helped her out.

Billy wandered into the room like a lost god, Hermes searching for the route back to Olympus. "Is it safe to tell you the coffee is ready?"

"Safe, no, but welcome. You, old friend, need coffee stat." Sheila waved Joan toward the kitchen. Joan followed Billy down the hall to the kitchen, trying to understand why she was so lightheaded. Lack of sleep? Lack of sense? An urge, formerly undiscovered, to dive off ideological cliffs headfirst? To question a few things that would, if questioned too far, shake her to her roots?

"How do you take it?" Billy asked, not making it sound at all like a double entendre, no matter how Joan heard it.

"Strong and sweet," Joan said, looking at the halo the sun slipping in the open back door made of his pale hair, bristling with light tongues of flame.

"Hope you don't mind about the door, I want to let the air in," Billy said, following her look.

"That's fine." The coffee was ready. She had to get close to him to take the cup. That was a problem, as she seemed to exert gravity over his terrestrial body, pulling him in before she knew she was extending the invitation. But his arms felt good around her back, one eventually sliding up to drape around her neck as he settled in against her. She cupped his chin, conscious of their pose belonging on an Athenian wine krater showing the courtship of men and youths. She need not importune him, unlike that pictured erastes, as he melted to her as soon as he had the chance.

"Hey," he said, rubbing his head against her cheek in broad, cheerful affection.

"What are you, a cat?" Joan pulled her head back, but she laughed.

"Least you didn't go the low route and call me a pussy."

"The next time we are doing anything violent, I am so going to hand you your ass for your insolence."

"I'm glad we can still be friends the morning after," Billy said, laughing.

"We are."

"So we're friends. Am I still your boy?"

"You are."

"Awesome."

They kissed, hands entwined.

"I expect that you are drinking lots and lots of coffee in there," Sheila yelled from down the hall.

Joan tried to smother a laugh against Billy's lips, then his throat, when the laugh fought back and won. "Do you realize how very queer all this is?"

"You are Hadrian to my Antinous. You are my fine, dark Abelard and I your Heloise. We're so damn queer we're right around the circle almost to straight again." Billy looked fully pleased with himself.

"This bravery, it can't be learned, you were born fearless." Joan looked at him, for the first time, with everything she was feeling open in her face.

"It's selective. I'm not all Hulk smash all the time. I know what is mine and who I belong to."

"Who?"

"You owl."

"Are you always this impossible in the morning?" Joan asked, knowing the answer already. His eyes were bright, dancing, not at all fazed by the night, holding the endless capacity of youth for rebounding. She was in for a world of trouble.

"I don't know. I'll check in with you in a few days."

"Pre...sumptuous."

"Fully sumptuous, thanks."

Joan kissed him. There wasn't anything else to do with what she was feeling. She went right on kissing him, forgetting the day and the open door. She pushed him back against the counter and kissed him with abandon, one arm around his lower back, the other hand on his hip. It took a strangled, gasping yawp, halfway between a cat regurgitating and a mouse getting stepped on, to push them apart.

Carol stood in the backyard, some ten feet from the wide open kitchen door, watching with a look of shock. Oh, piss. Joan took her hands away from Billy where they'd lingered.

"Carol."

Carol, hand in front of her mouth, started to recover from the shock and babbled apology. "I am so sorry, I didn't know, I was just checking the garden out, the gate was open, and we'd made plans, and Sheila is here, I saw her car. Oh my."

"Carol, this is Billy," Joan said, deadpan. She would have to start locking doors now that she had a reason.

"Billy?" Carol hadn't been looking at whom Joan had been kissing, and her assumption was obvious. Carol's eye went from Billy's face to his shoulders, down his body, back to Joan. "Oh. My."

301

"Hey, how's it going?"

"Billy is one of Sheila's students," Joan said, then wished she hadn't tried to explain as Billy's hand was still resting proprietarily on her hip, curving around suggestively toward her ass. There was plenty of explanation there already. Billy glanced at her for a fraction of a second, and Joan added, unable to not honor the relationship, "And my friend."

"You certainly seem very friendly."

"Carol, why don't you and I take a look at the space?" Joan looked at Billy, knowing he waited for her signal. He nodded nigh imperceptibly and went back to pouring coffee, ignoring them. Joan walked out the door, closing it behind her with slow deliberation. Joan and Carol walked the perimeter of the yard—Joan a step ahead, Carol with arms folded and eyes evasive, Joan wide open and brazen about it, having already stepped into the tar pit. Why swim now?

"I was thinking five tables, three along the fence there, one at each end of the garden."

"Was that your date the other night?"

"Yes. So, we could put the food table on the deck. It should be fine for buffet style. Drinks coolers underneath. I have a grill, but it is older than time itself."

"I'm sure that's fine."

"Great. Do you need me to order the chairs?" Joan asked, knowing Carol already offered, but needing something to say. Carol wasn't much looking at her, more looking back at the closed kitchen door with thin little glances, like slices of sashimi, pink and hot and translucent.

"That'd be fine."

Okay, Joan thought, Carol was disengaged from the conversation. Joan could hardly blame her, as they had the same source of distraction who was now waiting in the kitchen with coffee, and not out here in the unforgiving noon sun with a disgruntled lesbian potluck planner.

"Great! Thanks for coming by, Carol. I appreciate your help." This, Joan thought, was a mighty funny way to shape the events for memory.

Joan wasn't back in the kitchen moments before Sheila came clacking down the hallway urgently. "Carol just came storming out the front in high dudgeon. She didn't even stop when I spoke to her. What is going on today?"

"Hello, Sheila. Carol came by early. Around back where the kitchen door was open. While I was pushing Billy back against the counter and ravishing him." Joan tossed up her hands, the world having tipped over into absurdity for her some hours ago. Billy perked up at this description, puffing up a bit.

"What? What did you do?" Sheila looked from Billy to Joan and back again.

"Introduced them. Walked Carol around the backyard. I let the gods know I was happy and called down fate on my head."

"You've sucked me into a Greek tragedy? Joan, really. Autumn is much more important a season for those. Can we all go sit down and drink coffee, please, if we are going to keep having ridiculous conversations?"

They sat on the couch, Joan between Sheila and Billy.

"So you are knocking boots?"

"Not yet," Joan said.

"We're going to be knocking boots?" Billy asked, hopefully, leaning in to her.

"You'll be the second to know."

"But you are keeping company, and now Carol will let the FFF phone tree know you are dating a young man."

"I'll roll that rock up a hill once I get there." Joan looked to her left, then to her right. "Sweet friends, I am exhausted. I'm for bed."

"Care for company?" Billy asked, his tone light enough to be a jest, but none of them took it to be.

"Not just now. I need some time on my own," Joan said gently. It was enough for Joan; she needed the people she dearly cared for to go away.

Billy shrugged.

"You'll get used to it. She does this hermit thing every so often," Sheila said, across her, to Billy. Sheila read her impatience immediately, and knew enough not to take it personally after all this time. Joan walked Sheila to the door. Sheila tilted her head back toward the couch and the couch's occupant.

"You okay?"

"I'll let you know when I do."

"Call me later."

It took Joan longer to ease Billy out. He lingered, transparently wanting to stay. He seemed a little baffled, and deflated, when she kissed him lightly and led him to the door. You don't have the right to declare that you're staying, not just yet, Joan thought. Though he seemed to sense his power, that he might be able to do it if he wanted and get away with it, he hesitated, and left.

For Joan, thoughts had to be encountered, developed, examined, conversed with, then flipped over and reworked from all angles. Occasionally they had to be seized and hauled down for the death roll. It took time. Joan was one of those people who rarely felt anything without stepping back and thinking through it. The habit was strong and deep; as if, to reach her heart, emotion—born from her mind like Athena from the head of Zeus—had to filter down slowly, drip by drip. Like bile.

Joan felt like she needed more time, this time, than she'd ever needed. Last night had changed things. But in what way and with what fallout? She and Billy were involved? Well, yes, they were involved, but in doing what she wasn't sure. What Joan was sure about was that, in the same fragile moment it began, she and Billy's companionship went public in a big way.

There hadn't been time to plan or stage or spin or shape, just the primal reaction of emotion pulling the flesh together. Admiration and desire got tangled up and the border was crossed into no-man's land. One man. Was she ready for this? Coming out again to her entire community?

Erastes and *eromenos*, lover and beloved, Hadrian and Antinous. Queer enough to be almost straight again. Could she get used to saying "boyfriend"? As far from extroverted as she was, Joan still loved her community, her people. Coming out had been one of the great defining moments of her life, so caught up in lust and terror and raw joy at the potential, the possibility that there might be love in the world for her, sex and passion in her way, in the way that would touch her neglected heart. That was the moment when she decided to accept herself for who she was and build the future on that, not on the false. It had been her most courageous moment, aside from standing by and up for Sheila when she had come out the second time as bisexual.

Then Joan slowed down, and did what she had avoided for more than twelve years. She looked back at her own behavior during that time, without the comfort of self congratulation after the reconciliation of the friendship. She looked dispassionately, from the outside. Joan had, after the initial shock, said the right words in public to defend her friend's defection from the community. When confronted on Sheila's behalf, she staunchly asserted that Sheila had devoted years and energy to the community, that her own actions should be her defense. Her decades of activism on women's and lesbian issues, the organizing, and the shifts at the battered women's shelter, the LGBT student alliance, the Sexuality Education Center, the Feminist Film Festival committee. Sheila was involved in the health, safety, justice, and artistic expression of the community, and dating men wouldn't ruin that.

Fine, staunch words Joan spoke, but she hadn't believed them, had she? She'd held on to the form of friendship, the public form, but retreated from the intimacy. How was that honorable? She stood up for Sheila's name and reputation, and stopped asking how she felt. Joan hadn't been a real friend to Sheila, not in the years she wandered away, hurt. Joan had gone off into her solitude to think things over for years. Where had that left Sheila?

Joan called Sheila that evening, after a few hours sleep, a few hours of thinking, a light haze of brooding now burned off.

"Hey."

"Why, hello! Are you calling me from the horizontal, and are you alone on that plane?"

"I'm vertical and alone," Joan affirmed.

"That always was your problem. How's puppy boy?"

"Sweet William is home, I'd assume. I haven't contacted him yet. I wanted to talk to you first."

"Am I being asked for my blessing?"

"I'd like to ask you for your forgiveness."

"Oh, sweetie, I'm not that mad you didn't tell me about Billy."

Joan drew in a large breath and clenched it behind her teeth for a moment before exhaling.

"I owe you an apology. As not just your friend, but your best friend, or so I thought. So I congratulated myself on, these past couple of decades."

"You are and always have been my best friend."

"Let me get through this. I let you down, Sheila. You trusted me enough to come out to me, after I came out to you twelve years before. You had every right to expect compassion and support, after what you had shown me, after our years together, and in consideration of who we were to one another. You got lip service. I said the right things, but inside, I felt betrayed. You left me. I felt that. I felt that you left the community too, and that it would never be the same between us. Your loyalty was shifted. I couldn't deal with that, with losing you, so I held on, and said the right things, acted the part of your friend. But I pulled away, and I didn't talk to you. I didn't trust you, or love you enough to tell you any of this, and it cost us years of friendship. You are the finest woman I have ever met. You teach me daily about action, not just words, about compassion, about devotion to the community. You should love who you love, and all I should say is congratulations. You never left me, I left you. I'm so sorry I was a coward."

Joan could hear that Sheila was crying.

"I never thought I'd hear you say that. I thought we got back together, that was the best possible outcome. We'd just skip over the pain and never talk about it again. Thank you, Joan. For all your bombast, for all your retreat and brooding, you hold yourself accountable to your own standards and don't forgive behavior in yourself you find shameful elsewhere."

Joan e-mailed Billy shortly after hanging up with Sheila. She felt better than she had in years. Her friendship with Sheila was more grounded and real than it had been in years. There was something in that to look at. Friendship was more than the high gallantry of romantic words and gestures; it was full of places to screw the hell up, places to ruin what was essential to happiness. There was responsibility, follow-through. If she, Joan, were serious about taking on a new relationship at that level, possibly a lover at the level of friendship for the first time, she had to keep her eyes open going in. She and Billy would have to talk.

Antinous,

I have a bottle of single malt, twenty-five years old. A year older than you are. Would you drink some with me, and talk for a bit? It is time to make a new memory for scotch.

Hadrian

There, Joan thought, that seemed to be the right tone. Warm, requesting, allowing for possibilities. Allowing, she thought, for the possibility that he would say no. She didn't have his sunny certainty, but it was best to be upfront about that. It was the difference in experiences. He might not know yet, but she did, that most relationships end. Most end sooner rather than later. Going into a romantic relationship, allowing herself to fall, for Joan, involved the cold-eyed look toward the end of the day, the division of spoils after the final fight. Infatuation was sweet, passion was wonderful, but eventually somebody will hit a deer at three a.m. two states over and call you, hysterical, and you come running. That relationship, the deer guts sacrificed on the chrome altar, was the one Joan yearned for most deeply. She had sense enough to realize it might not exist at all, or perhaps it was so rare that the flesh rarely intersected at the same time. It might be asking for too much from the Universe to have both.

Joan checked her e-mail after an hour. He'd responded in five minutes of when she'd first sent hers.

Joan,
Come get me.
Billy

Joan sat in her car in front of his house for two minutes after killing the engine. She knew he was listening for her to come to the door, knew that it would be open, and it was. He had his hands in his pockets, and he smiled at her with just his lips. Billy, she recognized, was sad in degrees of that smile. If it opened fully and made grooves in his cheek, he was delighted. If it came on slowly and peaked at half-mast, he was pleased. A quicksilver grin was a bark of laughter, combined with the left raised brow it was a snort. A smile with mostly the lips, but a hint of teeth—veiled, unveiled, turning away—was shyness but still happiness. The feral canine fest of his killing smile, replaced by the side flash of congratulations on a kill well made. These she had seen, savored, cataloged. This, the small, sad smile, lips closed, hands hidden, was new. Billy thought that she was breaking up with him, that her spending time alone, or wanting to, was an automatic sign of disaster. As social as a puppy, it would never occur to him to be alone in pain. He might not want to speak about or examine or even acknowledge it, but he would ease it through company. That would be important to know.

"Hi."

"Hi."

"I'm glad you decided to come over." Joan started the car.

"Yeah, well, you never asked before, so I thought I should say yes."

It was hard to get a proper shrug executed sitting down, constricted by the shoulder belt, but Joan admired his try.

"It won't be the last time I ask."

"For real?"

"Yes."

They were quiet the rest of the way. It was a companionable quiet now, not a fearful one. Anticipation, rather than dread, filled the background.

Joan lit a few candles and set them on the mantle. Billy sat on the couch, watching her, alert, but slouching. The bottle of scotch, squat, brown and unlovely, sat on the end table next to a pair of Dixie cups adorned with a red and blue superhero. Joan thought that cast the right mood. Billy reached for them, but Joan stopped him.

"Let me. We're going to talk a little, and then we'll see if you want to do any more pouring."

"Is it time for speeches?"

"I think so, yes."

Joan poured out two fingers into the waxed-paper cups and handed Billy his. The stopper was ancient, carved into the shape of a stag and lion, parallel, facing opposite directions. Joan tapped it back into the bottle.

"My father left me this when he died. I'm not sure how he got it, but he had it for ten years when he passed. That was fifteen years ago. When we first hung out, you said that we would make a new memory for scotch." Joan looked at Billy and sipped at the Dixie cup. The superhero flexed his chest on the cup, bullets bounding off like grains of rice off a bride. "I'd like that, Billy. I'd like more too."

Billy held his cup tightly, making the edges concave, starting to smile his pleased smile.

"Hear me out before you start grinning, honey. I've thought this through and come to the conclusion that you can't think everything through, you have to feel and experience as well. I care for you, Billy. I think you know that. I'm attracted to you too, you handsome imp. This makes things all kinds of complicated, but I'm not convinced we couldn't work through those complications. You are also, and this isn't negligible, twenty-four. That makes us strangers of a kind. Yet what we do have in common is deep, and ancient, and rare. We have to acknowledge that most relationships between people with our age and other differences end eventually. This may end sooner or later. I think we can agree to make the absolute most of it, for as long as it lasts. It is worth more to me than all the rest to keep you as my friend. If you like, I'll be your lover as well."

Billy's eyes got very round above the Dixie cup. "I'd like that."

Joan smiled. "Good. No more speeches."

Billy held out his cup, and they touched waxed rims with a kitten's delicacy. "No more speeches! It gets too Buffy Season Seven." He drained his cup and then slid over next to Joan on the couch. She set hers on the floor.

"I can give another speech about how you don't have to spend the night, or if you'd like to, I can make up the couch for you. It's a good speech, runs about forty-five minutes."

"If it will make you feel better, but I'm sleeping in your bed."

"So it's that sort of memory we're making. More scotch?"

Billy took the bottle from her, deftly plucked the stopper, and poured for her. He grinned at her when he handed her the cup, daring her to respond.

"Thank you, Antinous."

He smiled his face nearly horizontal, his cheeks bunching with delight, muscling back his lips, thrilled to the bone. "Anytime, Hadrian."

It wasn't like being in bed with a girl. Billy and she laughed and wrestled the way up to her bedroom, and didn't stop just because the kissing had started. He was stronger, but she had leverage and experience and knew enough not to put all her weight on her back leg, so she hooked his knee and dropped him on the bed. From there they met in the center, kneeling, dare sparking in her eyes. He met it without hesitation, and tore off the first of his t-shirts. She matched him, removing hers. Then they lost the thread, and started removing one another's clothing, or trying to help in a way that didn't help at all.

They were at the border again, on the wall looking east into the great primeval forest, hoping that the Gauls wouldn't come. Joan halfway expected Billy to charge over, leap like a stag across a brook in the dappled sunlight, with no more effort or hesitation. He did not. The pace changed; Joan felt it, attuned to this music. Billy was looking at her, with eyelids heavy, slowly lowering them like a pleased cat. Light caught the absurd blue, shielded now, taking on the mystery of another sullen, beautiful boy. She knew. He was her sidekick, her beloved, her partner, her warrior, her favorite. She, his lover, his partner, his warrior, his emperor. So she took the gift from him as soon as he offered it, knowing the emotion of this moment from a thousand summer imaginings, long ago, when *honor* was still a word she believed in, and *friend* was the most beautiful word she ever knew. With the stillness of perfect conviction, she stripped him bare, so he lay beneath her, her boy. Joan felt something crack open in her that could be heard, she was sure, in the living room. On the street. Crack like bone, crack like ice. She swallowed to try and get around the emotion, but there was no way around it, it was everywhere. He guided her and she was inside him, he bucked up under her, her colt with springtime in his legs, prancing, tossing his proud head, unbroken but open to her. She held to his hips with the muscular effort of rising and falling with him. She took his cock in her fingers, reaching around, and he groaned, sensitive, larger with the testosterone. Caught between her hands, he was writhing, pinned, fixed, wings beating and limbs thrashing not to get away but to get closer, in agony to push away. She was baptized in his sweat. There was a groan that became a shout—here, here I am in the flesh and here I make my stand, exalted beyond and finally collapsed back into my own mortality.

Billy's head turned in profile on the pillow, mouth slack with pleasure, struggling to get enough control to smile. She shifted her weight, just a hint of movement of her hips that allowed a kiss of air in to his heated skin. She went to remove herself from his back, but he took her hand and kept her there.

"Are people supposed to be happy? Is that what this is? Shit, why do we keep killing one another?"

"Are you going to suffer for the pains of the world every time we fuck?"

"I'm happy, you heartless bastard. Let me be flowery."

"While I am nailed to your body like a slave to a cross?"

"No, my Emperor. I can think of better things to do with the night."

Joan woke up slightly baffled, soaking wet, and underneath Billy. All in all, it was not a bad morning. Billy was facedown, sprawled on her, arms and legs akimbo. Joan slid carefully out from under him. Once she was free, he groaned, frowned with his eyes closed, and flopped onto his side. A mortar attack wouldn't rouse him.

Joan sat at the kitchen table, waiting for the coffee to be ready. What a night. What a week. They'd gotten out of bed to slay zombies, to cook, to walk in the garden barefoot, to watch gladiator movies, to go back. They'd also spent time talking. Somehow Joan had planned a potluck during that time without a great deal of help, understandably, from Carol. The potluck was tonight. Joan had noticed that Billy, though he tried to conceal it, got very quiet when she mentioned the potluck or the event or Michigan. He'd never commented, in fact. That silence was teeth closing on hard words. She resolved to ask him what was going on before the potluck.

It was easiest to put the coffee on a tray, slice some strawberries, and pull out some croissants and head back upstairs. She set the tray on the nightstand and crawled back into bed. Billy, she'd learned, was best woken by giving him a more pleasurable alternative to sleep. Joan crawled up behind him, still passed out on his side, and started biting at the nape of his neck. This woke him up rapidly. The coffee was cool long before they got to it.

Billy sat with the sheets draped across his knees, back against the headboard. "I've never had breakfast in bed before."

"That is a crime and a shame. Perhaps you never earned it before?" Joan handed him a coffee mug.

A smile of triumph lit his face. "So I earned it. I knew it."

His torso twisted as he reached to the side and picked up one of his t-shirts and pulled it on. He usually did this immediately upon waking, if they'd slept without clothing. It was one layer in bed, two out. Joan had noticed that, while she was allowed to touch his chest, it was more for her benefit than his. Billy was, in effect, being accommodating to her. From smaller conversations they'd had, she knew he was looking forward to his top surgery, to chest contouring, to being able to go without a shirt. He didn't communicate hatred for his body, but there was a level of discomfort she'd noticed. He loved having his musculature commented on, loved being praised, loved fucking, loved being fucked. He was, in all respects, her boy, beloved to her lover, as unconcerned with status in bed as out, willing her to take control, to be his Emperor. What was most marvelous to Joan was how they were with one another outside of bed. The camaraderie had continued, the companionship, but now, after slaying a zombie horde or arguing over Star Wars versus Star Trek, they would fall into bed laughing and fuck like teenagers, all energy and enthusiasm. They saved the high-flown romantic language for their out-of-bed time and only used it in context. The finest thing they called one another was friend.

Billy tore into the croissants. "These are good. Where did you get them?"

"I made them."

"You can cook? Really?"

"Hush. Just because we've eaten a lot of take out the last week means nothing. I believe I was distracted and kept falling into bed. I've also had to plan a potluck, thank you. Speaking of which, the tables and chairs are getting delivered today. Are you sticking around for the party?"

Billy nodded while taking a swallow of coffee.

"Good." Joan lay on her left side, propped up on her elbow, not unlike a man reclining on a supper couch in an Etruscan tomb painting. "May I ask you something?"

"Sure."

"This may be my perception. When I mention the potluck, or the Michigan Memories event, you always clam up. You don't say anything. Even odder, you don't smile. Is there something there?"

Billy put down the coffee cup. He rubbed a hand through his hair, scratched at the back of his neck. In a moment he reached for his other t-shirt and put it on as well. He'd never done this while still in bed. "Not everybody has the same memories of Michigan."

"Have you been?"

"Inside? No."

"Would you like to go? Sheila and I go every year."

"You know I'm having my surgery in August," Billy said, looking away.

"But if you weren't? If I asked you to go, would you?"

"No, I wouldn't go," Billy said simply.

"But you could go in. I see guys like you all the time," Joan said, feeling increasingly at sea. Billy wasn't making eye contact.

They'd never departed so entirely from one another and been in the same conversation.

"The policy. Womyn born womyn only." Billy looked back at her.

The festival's official policy: you had to be born a woman and lived your entire life as a woman to get in. Transwomen were officially barred. Joan hadn't thought about it in years. There had been some flap about it in the nineties; there was that place across the way, Camp Trans? Some sort of protest.

"They want space apart from men. I respect that, even if I think they are wrong about the policy. I think all women should be allowed in. But if my trans sisters aren't women enough, then I'm too much man."

"I've never heard you call yourself a man."

"I usually don't. Boy, sure. I usually feel more queer. This is a matter of honor."

The doorbell rang. Joan, being the one dressed, sprinted down to find the rental company there with the delivery. She had to open the back gate, show them in, shoo them out of the garden, then sign for it all, the piles of chairs and the large round tables. By then Billy was dressed and breakfast in bed a distant memory. The conversation stayed lost, subsumed in the preparation for the event. Billy helped her set up the chairs and tables, then pleaded a need for a shower and fresh clothing. He assured her that he would be back in time for the potluck, and he walked away.

There was plenty to keep Joan occupied: her own cooking, the setup, Sheila coming customarily at the friend-assistance stage, other guests coming later at the early-guest phase. Soon it was late afternoon and her backyard was filling up. Parking along the street got thick and competitive. The table groaned beneath dishes, summer cornucopia. Women's voices were heard in the garden exchanging greetings. Sheila took up a post at the table closest to the back deck and commandeered a space for Joan as well, when the time came. For now, Joan directed traffic from the deck, organizing the food, letting the people choose their own organization. Sheila watched her from under the railing.

"Where's Billy?" Sheila looked to Joan's side as if the boy might be expected to pop out like a horror movie monster.

"Not here."

"Did you fight? You sound odd."

Joan abandoned her post and went and sat next to Sheila. Two other women were sitting across from them. "Not a fight, he pointed something out to me I wasn't looking for. Do you ever think about the trans policy?"

"Michigan? Sure."

"What about it? Isn't the whole womyn born womyn thing only in place to exclude transwomen?"

Sheila tilted her head, appearing to consider this. Joan knew that her friend's sense of justice was more finely tuned than her own and much better leavened with compassion. "No, I don't think it was at first, even if it is being used for that."

"What do you think? Is it right to keep transwomen out?"

"It is exclusionary," Sheila admitted.

One of the other women at the table, Belinda, cut in. "I don't think it's about exclusion. Womyn born womyn want a chance to get away and be in one another's company. Transwomen don't have the same life experience as women who were born female, grew up with a female body."

"It's about safety. How can you be safe when men are walking around the land?" Her partner Rachel added.

"Whoa. How did we get to men and safety? We're talking about women." Joan put up her hands.

Joan noticed, for the first time, that a crowd was starting to gather around the table. The chairs were pulled out, and people sat. Other women stood in a circle around them, listening closely and calling out.

"I know a woman who saw one of them walking around naked, saw his penis and everything. That's triggering for survivors! How can we be safe with that invasion?"

"Can we please call transwomen 'she'? Using male pronouns is an insult and not a clever one," Sheila said.

"They are still male."

"Don't Janice Raymond me."

"How do you know what I'm talking about?"

"Janice Raymond, *The Transsexual Empire*. I've read it. Have you? It says all transsexuals rape women's bodies. Raymond means MTF transsexuals, who she repeatedly and wrongly calls men."

Joan cut in. "If the idea is all women born and having grown up female feel the same, have the same experiences, then I don't fit. I felt more like a boy as a child."

"You say so. You were a girl. You looked like a girl, you were raised as a girl, and the world treated you like a girl."

"Which is exactly why I turned out to be such a good woman, right? We always grow up exactly as we are treated. You're straight, right? Like your parents."

"You're afraid to be a lesbian, that's why you want to be a man."

Sheila's hand gripping her arm like an eagle's claw kept Joan from responding physically, though she was an inch off her chair when her friend stayed her, as Athena stayed Achilles by seizing his hair. Joan sat back down with a forced smile.

"I don't want to be a man. But I can understand people who are men, despite what their body looks like. Or who don't feel like men or women. I've come to see that as different from my experience, but allied. We're in the same community."

Joan looked up and saw Carol, now in the crowd, move forward to catch the exchange.

"Where is this sudden personal interest coming from, Joan?" Carol asked, sweetness cracking all along the surface of her voice. She would have informed everyone already that Joan was dating a boy. With this quip, she invoked that and disarmed Joan. So Joan faced the circle empty-handed. It was the moment before the Gauls charged, before the zombies poured forth from every door, the moment she wanted to be back to back with Billy, facing down everything that came at them. But that is a luxury; we are more often called on to answer for ourselves without warning or armor.

"You are right, Carol. It is a personal interest, something that a friend of mine pointed out to me. But it is worth looking at, no matter where the inspiration came from. Transwomen are women. Michigan is all about gathering together to heal, create, and recharge with only other women. That doesn't happen out in the world. It should be respected."

This calmed the circle some; Joan could see it. Good, the pause of breath before the jump.

"As curator of the Michigan Memories installation this year, I will be opening the submission to all women's memories."

The murmuring started again and kicked up fast as paper on a fire. It wasn't an angry sound, but there was complexity to it, fear at the base. It might all backfire on her; it might be the last she worked with this committee. Why not go out in a blaze of glory?

"Look, I know this is a difficult conversation, but we only benefit from adding more women's voices. Transwomen will be encouraged to submit their Michigan memories." Joan sat back down, satisfied to let the circle debate as it would. The first eye she sought was Sheila's.

"You throw a hell of a party."

"I learned something about courage recently. My oldest friend taught me. How long has he been standing there?" Joan looked through the rail to the deck where Billy, just inside the gate, was watching.

"For most of your speech."

Billy smiled at her, glowing with pride, surprised, elated. Joan smiled back at him.

"Sheila, I want to talk to you about something."

"You're not going to Michigan this year?"

"Only with your blessing. My boyfriend is having some surgery. I'd like to stick around and look after him."

"Times change, we change, or we get kicked off the merry-go-round. There's your blessing and words of wisdom all at once. Go tell Billy."

Joan squeezed Sheila's hand before pushing away from the table. The path was complicated between where she was and where Billy was; some women stood in small groups in the way, but Joan slipped around them and went up to where Billy was waiting for her.

The End

Books By These Authors

Lynn Ames

Heartsong
The Flip Side of Desire
The Value of Valor
The Cost of Commitment
The Price of Fame

Georgia Beers

Finding Home
Mine
Fresh Tracks
Too Close to Touch
Thy Neighbor's Wife
Turning the Page

JD Glass

Punk Like Me
Punk and Zen
Red Light
American Goth
X
Yuri Monogatari 6 (Sakura Gun [London])

Books By These Authors

Susan X Meagher

Arbor Vitae
All That Matters
Cherry Grove
Girl Meets Girl
The Lies That Bind
The Legacy

Contributing Author to:
Undercover Tales

I Found My Heart In San Francisco series
Awakenings
Beginnings:
Coalescence
Disclosures
Entwined
Fidelity
Getaway
Honesty
Intentions

Susan Smith

Burning Dreams
Of Drag Kings and the Wheel of Fate
Put Away Wet